The Curiosity

The Curiosity

Stephen Kiernan

W F HOWES LTD

This large print edition published in 2013 by
W F Howes Ltd
Unit 4, Rearsby Business Park, Gaddesby Lane,
Rearsby, Leicester LE7 4YH

1 3 5 7 9 10 8 6 4 2

First published in the United Kingdom in 2013
by John Murray

Grateful acknowledgement is given to Ice Nine
Publishing Company for permission to reprint four
lines from the Grateful Dead song 'Ripple', lyrics by
Robert Hunter © Ice Nine Publishing.

A CIP catalogue record for this book is available
from the British Library

ISBN 978 1 47124 427 8

Typeset by Palimpsest Book Production Limited,
Falkirk, Stirlingshire
Printed and bound by
www.printondemand-worldwide.com of Peterborough, England

Mixed Sources
from well-managed forests and other controlled sources
Cert no. TT-COC-002641
Forest Stewardship Council
FSC

PEFC Certified
This product is from sustainably managed forests and controlled sources
PEFC
PEFC/16-33-415
www.pefc.org

This book is made entirely of chain-of-custody materials

To Chris, my endlessly generous friend

PART I

RECLAMATION

CHAPTER 1

CANDIDATE BERG

(KATE PHILO)

I was already wide awake when they came for me. I lay on a metal bunk, in a gray walled room with a whitewashed ceiling, while Billings and an ensign hurried toward me through the bulkheads.

Later, after everything had happened and people were seeking explanations, the talk went around that I possessed foreknowledge of what was to come. Honestly. My sister, the ever-snarky Chloe, had plenty of wisecracks about that one. Since apparently I could see the future, she teased, I ought to be able to predict what her husband was buying for their anniversary that year. My impulse was to reply, 'what you deserve: nothing,' but I corked it. Put me at the front of a biology lecture hall, I'm as collected as a game show host. But Chloe's over-confidence makes me stifle myself, the classic younger sister's self-censorship. A catty comeback would have been as unlikely as me having premonitions about things which no one could have predicted.

The people who spread those rumors forget that I am a scientist down to my toes. High-school honors back in Ohio, bachelor's degree from the University of Virginia, PhD from Yale in molecular biology, a year each in cell research at Johns Hopkins and the Salk Institute. Hardly the crystal ball type.

The conspiracy theorists were worse. Everything I did apparently revealed my circuitous strategy to mislead the entire world. They had web pages for floating their possibilities, they had blogs, they dug through my trash. The plot was supposed to enrich me in some way, though exactly how was something no one ever explained.

These people need to find some healthier hobbies. If they spent half an hour in my presence, they would realize that the conspiracy idea was nonsense. Anyone who knew me before the inexplicable occurred would have said I felt happiest in a lab, could become infatuated with data, remained committed to the slow, incremental progress of sound research. I completely lacked the guile to con the world into filling my pockets.

Now that the media has decamped from my doorstep, now that the zealots are busy condemning someone else, now that the president no longer uses my name with contempt, I hope to reclaim those quiet habits that served me before the world went wild. Maybe they can preserve my wobbly sanity. Maybe they can mend my shattered heart.

Because love, honestly, was what motivated me.

Love was both curiosity and its fulfillment. Love was the miracle everyone overlooked while fixating on an accident of science. Love, it pains me to say, love was a beautiful man rowing a little boat, alone, away from me, into the infinite.

But first there was adventure. The reason I was already awake that night in my cabin, quite logically, is that the ship was turbulent. I was a passenger on a research vessel, a converted ice-breaker, 19 scientists, a crew of 12. Also one journalist, annoying everyone a little but me most severely. That night there were high seas as we beat a course north, though admittedly once we'd put 800 miles between us and the Arctic Circle, there was not much further north one could go, up on the frigid crown of the planet. It is an interesting sensation, feeling all the world beneath you. Like you are on the edge of things, away from the center, forgotten.

No wonder we were the ones to find something. No one else was looking.

Rough water that night meant the engines were laboring. They strained to climb a wave as the vessel tilted to stern, then whined as the ship pitched forward and raced down the pinnacle's other side. The tossing threw a pen off my desk; it rolled up and down the floor while I attempted to read in my bunk. The paper in my lap, a Norwegian study of iceberg migration, suffered from either shoddy data or sloppy translating. Also I was exhausted. In August that far north the sun only sets for a few hours, so opportunities to sleep are precious. If not for that night's washing-machine weather I would have been happily snoring. Sometimes the ship's speed did not match a wave's shape, so the vessel would belly-flop in a trough, shuddering the length of its 181 feet.

In the small hours I managed to doze. I dreamed I was swaying in a hammock, in my Ohio childhood backyard. Chloe yelled at me from a tree overhead, something about trying harder. But we'd never had a hammock. All at once the ship stilled, the decks no longer heaving, the engines making a steadier thrum below decks. I awakened.

There it is. A perfectly obvious explanation. Also, because I woke with a chill, I decided to dress warmly right away. Later, the media made much of the fact that I had put on my under-diving layer, snug navy blue insulation instead of regular clothes, as if I'd known we'd soon be in the water. The simple truth is that I was cold and it was all I had clean. I did not even have fresh underwear.

The timing is curious to consider: Billings scrambling on his way while I search for a belt, his haste the opposite of my leisure. I am slender to a fault, almost no hips at all, breasts so small Chloe says I never really developed. The only way I have a shape is if I wear something around my waist. I could not find the belt for my diving suit, though. Finally I spotted it, coiled under my bunk. I threaded it through the suit loops while digging my feet into deck shoes. One glance at the mirror, I decided to throw a yellow T-shirt over the whole thing. The fact that the ensign and Billings entered the forward cabins just as I opened my door is not even coincidence. It is a foreseeable circumstance; they were coming to tell me precisely the news I was about to seek for myself.

No magic. No conspiracy. If we are ever to comprehend the subsequent chain of events, we must begin by shedding speculative nonsense. The facts are incredible enough. What we now know is that life does not end quite as permanently as we have always thought. We can keep a 'dead' body alive indefinitely, breathing, its blood mechanically circulating, until the organs are procured for transplant. We can restart the heart of a person who has been 'dead' from cardiac arrest for up to six minutes. Now, as a result of that night in the Arctic, we also know that temporary reanimation of a 'dead' mammal is possible. Above all, we know that this achievement redefines human existence as radically as harnessing the power of the atom did in the 1940s.

May I say that it was amazing? That we uncovered solid truth in a vast empire of unknown? That we found something so arresting, it captured the attention of the world?

But that is not all. We also learned that these discoveries will affect the lives of scientists who venture with insufficient caution into such turbulent waters. There is no potential for salvaging a ruined professional reputation, but maybe the possibility exists for the restoration of personal dignity. There is no way to bring back what has been lost, but maybe telling a tale of beauty is a form of mourning. Thus do I, as one member of the small society overwhelmed by these events, seek to set the record straight.

On that night – it was 2:12 a.m. Greenwich Mean Time, and we were above 83 degrees latitude – I pulled open my cabin door just as Graham Billings had raised his hand to knock on it. I nearly walked into his knuckles. A uniformed sailor hovering at his elbow, Billings grinned that crooked grin of his.

'Uncanny,' he said. 'We were just coming to wake you. Brilliant.'

Graham Billings: respected plant biologist, chaired researcher at Oxford, happiest with a freshly poured pint but also author of numerous papers involving incredibly painstaking work on plankton's role in the global food chain. His findings were reliable, his patience flabbergasting, his documentation unparalleled.

Billings was also my sole ally in the hostile work environment of that expedition. While I was technically his shipboard boss, he completely outranked me in publications, field experience, scientific prestige. I relied on his advice daily: which bays to try next, which bergs to investigate, which divers to assign to each crew. In the small hours we sat in the galley before spread-out maps, debating where to sail next. All through that journey Billings showed a bemused deference to my authority, which I repaid with unmasked respect. Best of all, he provided about half of us with a foolproof cure for seasickness: soggy rice washed down with mint tea. It proved so dependable, we were all in his debt.

'Good morning Dr Billings. Ensign.' I nodded at them. 'Why are we stopped?'

'A candidate berg, Dr Philo. How did you know we were coming to fetch you?'

'I didn't.' I brushed past him, tucking the T-shirt under the belt. 'How large a sample?'

'Well Doctor . . .' He hurried after me into the tiny officers' galley. 'You know how hard it is to estimate before probing how much of the berg contains hard-ice—'

'How big, Billings?' I poured a mug of coffee. 'Tell me.'

He drew up short, the ensign nearly stumbling into him from behind. 'Well. The thing of it is.' He paused, opening his fingers wide, that grin turned up to one hundred watts. 'If it's the real stuff, Kate, this would be one bloody whale. Easily 300 meters per side.'

'The largest candidate berg ever found,' the ensign blurted.

During grad school my roommate was a junior city editor of the local paper, and she said her role in a crisis was to be its opposite. The bigger the story – plane crash or car pile-up or political scandal – the more important it was for her to remain calm. Then reporters and photographers could be marshaled into an instant team, get the story's immediate angles, still start the press on time. I always valued that approach in my work, so much that it has become a kind of professional reflex: when someone blurts like that ensign did, I feel my inner magnetic field swing to the opposite pole.

'Probably just a big ice cube,' I said, shrugging.

Inside, of course, I fluttered. *This is exactly why we have come all this way.* We had bounced between the ports of Thule in Greenland and Alert in Canada, around the stark and lovely Queen Elizabeth Islands, then set a course due north, the last land left far behind, all in high iceberg season, week upon week despite the obvious hazards. A find like this was precisely why Carthage, the egotistical bastard, had hired me. I was too young for the job, inexperienced in field work, utterly green in positions of command. But he had assays to attempt, grants to win, and if I may be so blunt, asses to kiss. Oh, he could commit the loftiest snobberies imaginable, but whenever it promised to enrich funding for the Carthage Institute of Cellular Seeking, the genius scientist had that particular pucker perfected.

At least I have my dignity. I have my button, too. These days I live in a small corner of the country, my name a national synonym for deceit. But every night I go down to the docks, regardless of weather, to stand in silence, to think about a man I loved, a price I paid, while on a chain around my neck hangs a plain brown jacket button – my one memento from the whole escapade. Just a button, I know, a small souvenir, a nothing. Yet it is enough to remind me that I did right, that at his most vulnerable time I saved a man from the wolves of our society, so I make no apology. There on the dock I reach up, I touch my fingers to that button, I am proud.

When Carthage offered me a job with his Institute, I told myself that early astronauts probably felt much as I did: whatever their achievements in other fields, they had no credentials for walking on the moon. Who could? When you are that far ahead of anything anyone has done before, the idea of relevant experience is laughable. Besides, what person with a professionally inquisitive mind would turn down so rare an opportunity? It was a chance to work with one of the most celebrated minds on earth, investigating the most vexing biological and ethical questions. That's why people like me were willing to decline tenure-track offers from major universities in order to work with a man whose narcissism was as famous as his discoveries.

Curiosity, I should add, made me available personally as well as professionally. I had hugged my wonderful college sweetheart Dana goodbye a dozen years before, as he went off to medical school in Seattle and I began doctoral studies in New Haven.

It might as well have been love itself I bid farewell to, the work was so demanding. When friends announced engagements, I researched my dissertation. While they nursed babies at 2 a.m., I pulled all-nighters with a microscope. The gropings of grad school lacked depth and duration because the work was so relentless, everyone's future so uncertain. The few shallow occasions at professional conferences invariably collapsed from their own pointlessness before we even reached a hotel room.

My last real relationship had been with Wyatt, a law professor so newly divorced you could smell it on him like fresh paint. The more he insisted he was fine, over her, honestly, the more I saw how much healing time he still needed. When he called me by her name one morning, I knew I had to go. At least he had not done it in bed.

Since then I found that urban single life in your thirties resembled a seventh-grade dance: wringing your hands hoping the good ones will ask you, saying yes to the others because it beats being a wallflower. There were creeps, hurriers toward the bed, promisers who eventually demonstrated the art of instant disappearance. Sometimes there would be a nice guy, a few sweet months before he reconnected with his college sweetie, met someone younger, or grew tired of competing with the lab for my attentions.

I used to think of myself as a woman with a fiery libido. My boyfriends would have agreed. Yet somehow I landed in a celibate life. Carthage could not have scripted a better preparation for his team. I accepted the job. Three weeks later I was dragging suitcases aboard this ship. Nine weeks after that, I woke in the night when the decks stopped heaving.

Now I took a good gulp of coffee, but it was bitter from sitting too long on the burner. Worse, it was too cool to warm my hands. I poured it down the sink, gave Billings's elbow a squeeze.

'Let's see what we've found.' I strode off with the men a few strides behind.

Oh, I was purposeful; for about fifty steps. When I entered the stateroom below the bridge, the entire tech team was there. I pulled up short, but no one said anything. A third of them should have been at their monitors, the rest asleep till their shifts, but now they lined the walls. One technician, a dependable guy named Andrew, grinned like a kid at Christmas.

'Hello everyone,' I called. A few men nodded but still none of them spoke. A shiver of curiosity went through me. *What was I going to see up there?* I paused at the bottom of the stairs, Billings close behind. 'Let's hope today is a good day,' I said, feeling inadequate to the moment, then turning to ascend.

The bridge was like the backstage of a theater: professionals bent to their controls in dim light, headphones on, brows furrowed in concentration, while the captain faced forward, giving hushed orders like a stage manager. In front of him, outside thick windows with frost fringing their corners, searchlights made daylight on the decks. Directly under our feet, the research lab hummed with esoteric equipment that most laymen would struggle to so much as turn on, yet the bridge's tools were intimidating to me. As usual, I was the only woman present. I compensated by frowning at everything.

The captain, Trevor Kulak, wore a similar expression. He stood in a wide stance, made a curt nod. 'Dr Philo. You might take a look at the short range.'

'Over here, Doctor,' said a boy at a radar monitor. He may have been a sailor in the reaches of the North Atlantic but he was a boy nonetheless. I crossed to him, peering down at his monitor. Open waters remained dark green, but when the radar arm scanned in an arc, a mass of light green filled the screen.

'What is the scale here?' I said.

'A thousand meters, Doctor.' The radar swept from bottom to top again, revealing a solid object shaped somewhat like Australia. It looked nearly as large, too.

'We're approaching leeside,' the captain announced. 'We'll moor in the calm.'

I bent back to the monitor. 'So the long dimension on this berg is what?'

'Four hundred twenty-two meters on the side facing us. Preliminary scan indicates three intrusions of hard-ice.'

'Excuse me, is that a lot?'

I turned and sure enough, the question had come from Daniel Dixon, reporter with *Intrepid* magazine. I swallowed my irritation. It was part of Carthage's plan, having a media man along. 'Think of the ink,' he'd said. 'Press equals money.'

Dixon was a tolerable guy, to a point. He tended to stay out of the way, asked open-ended questions. On the long haul north from Woods Hole he helped pass countless tedious hours by telling stories from his days on a newspaper's crime beat: the city's largest mansion built entirely upon embezzlement, price-fixing by funeral homes, a woman held against the wall by her hair while her madman husband stabbed her sixty-six times. Dixon was heavy-set, which normally is no problem for me, but he seemed to take up an undue amount of room. I mean, my father was as round as an apple, yet I could never get enough of hugging him. So it wasn't Dixon's size, it was his way of infringing on personal space, little as there is on a ship anyway. Besides, no one likes being leered at.

Also Dixon's inquisitiveness could be tiresome. He refused to let anything go unsaid, but sometimes you just didn't feel like explaining. Like now. 'You tell him,' I said.

The radar operator shrugged. 'For a candidate

berg, this would be about five times larger than any prior find. If it turns out to be the real stuff.'

Dixon pulled out his ever-handy notepad. 'How can you tell before you even touch the thing?'

'Size. Weight.'

'Don't listen to him,' said the technician one seat down. 'It's about buoyancy.'

Dixon moved closer. 'Tell me about it.'

'It's basic.' The technician kept his eyes on his screen. 'Ice has a mass density of 0.917 grams, so 91.7 percent of the berg should be underwater. But if it formed rapidly, in a polar typhoon for example, then salinity and density will be higher. As much as 92.5 percent of the formation could be submerged, which is why we call it a candidate berg. A higher level of density indicates heavy veins of hard-ice.'

Dixon scribbled away. 'How much of this one is underwater?'

The first radar operator ran a scan, then a calculation on his keyboard. 'I'm getting . . . 93.1 percent?'

'Impossible,' said the second technician. 'That would be the highest ever recorded.' He slapped the keys at his device. When the number came up he was silent, so I spied over his shoulder: 93.151.

'Huh,' said Dixon, writing the number down. 'And why is that important?'

'Just look.' The radar boy changed the scale on his scanner. As it swept upward, the green arm left behind clear veins of white. They resembled tree roots, capillaries, chambers in a lung. 'See?' he continued. 'This candidate berg presents an opportunity to find larger specimens for the Carthage Project's next steps.'

Dixon jotted on his pad. 'You really believe all this bring-it-back-to-life stuff?'

'Are you serious?' scoffed the second technician. Then he glanced my way, saw I was watching, shrugged. 'Who knows?'

'And you?' he asked the boy.

The crewman smiled. 'I'm just a radar operator, sir.'

I'd had enough, so I moved to stand beside Captain Kulak. He observed in silence as men below scampered across the deck. Much of the ship was rimed in white, cables and rails wearing a thick coat of frost. The crewmen, clipped to guy wires, were zipped inside insulated suits that shed water like the skin of a seal. They shouted vowels to each other because consonants were lost in that scathing wind.

'Or, I,' hollered a goggled form at the bow. A port side crewman standing at a harpoon gun waved his acknowledgment, bent to aim, fired. A twelve-foot steel dart plunged like a giant flying fish into a wave, out the other side, and deep into dark beyond.

'Ar-ar, I,' the man in goggles bellowed. A starboard man fired next, his steel shaft also zipping out of sight. Then he made a little jump, giving two mittened thumbs up, at which the goggled man turned to wave his arms in an X and Y up at the bridge.

There was a flash behind me. I turned to see that Dixon had his camera out.

'Not now,' Kulak growled, shaking his head. 'Pete's sake.'

I remember the next part so well. It was the littlest harbinger. But there I go, falling prey to superstition, when the facts indicate that it was merely operator error.

Captain Kulak nodded to a helmsman on his right, who toggled a throttle. A cable on the deck drew taut. Suddenly the ship yawed steeply to starboard.

'Whoa,' Dixon yelled. I seized the nearest chair, Billings grabbing my arm.

The men on deck scrambled to keep their feet. One who was unsecured fell sideways. The other crewmen watched helplessly as he slid across the deck. At he last he caught a railing, wrapped both arms around it.

'Steady,' Kulak cleared his throat. 'Even hands, sailor.'

'Aye sir,' answered the helmsman, tugging another handle. Winches drew up the slack in the cable on the other side, their motors complaining, as the vessel righted. Then the winches cranked both cables slowly in, evenly, ice cracking away as the wire coiled on its reel. Kulak frowned but the harpoons held. By inches, the ship snuggled close to the berg, like a tug docking with an aircraft carrier.

I could feel Dixon standing near me, Billings on his other side.

'Hold at 10 meters,' Kulak called. The winches paused; the ship's engine idled. Then he turned to his left. 'Raise the lights.'

A crewman pressed several buttons. Bright beams revealed a wall of bluish white that extended beyond the lights' range. It felt like we were tethered to a skyscraper.

'Dear God, Kate,' Billings whispered. 'Look where you've brought us. What if this one is full of hard-ice?'

I only pursed my lips, too tense to answer.

'Can those units run any higher?' the captain asked.

'Aye sir,' said the crewman. The beams opened their focus, tilting upward, spreading light. Still they could not reach either outer edge, nor did the top of the berg come into view. The only sound in the room was Dixon's pen scratching.

'This thing has to be five stories high,' Captain Kulak said to no one in particular. 'Can you give me any more?'

'One moment sir.' The crewman punched buttons on his console. The starboard light drew back and aimed upward. Finally the top of the berg emerged like some frozen Matterhorn, a painfully bright reflection against the blackness above.

Billings let out a low whistle. 'God in heaven.'

Kulak crossed his arms. 'Ladies and gentlemen, we have the largest candidate berg ever discovered.'

For some reason, everyone looked at me. Dixon stilled his pen, Kulak raised his eyebrows, Billings grinned like a kid. I considered, then gave a scientist's assessment.

'Maybe,' I said. 'Ten million tons of maybe.'

CHAPTER 2

ICE CREAM

(DANIEL DIXON)

The thing of it is, Kate Philo was like a porch light left on all night. Sure, she was as smart as a calculator, a quicker study than that lady propulsion engineer at NASA – no tortoise herself. Kind as well, Dr Kate was, and not in the sugary beauty contest way, but genuinely friendly to everyone from chilly Captain Kulak to the lowest ship-rat deckhand. And if I'm going to be honest here, I can't help mentioning: she had an ass on her like to break your heart. Not a man alive could help noticing.

But in the world of serious microbiology, where socially awkward cell savants claw one another for ever-dwindling research dollars, where half the field is not on speaking terms with the other half, Dr Kate was like an innocent: asking people's opinions, actually listening, sometimes doing the unthinkable and taking their advice. I suspect every man on that ship was fantasizing about her. I sure was, no shame in that, and it provided one of the few positives for that whole sorry expedition.

I mean, can you imagine a worse gig? Four months in the Arctic Ocean? For a longtime science writer like me, it's not exactly covering a shuttle launch, or profiling the savior of lowland gorillas, or forecasting when Florida runs out of fresh water – all stories I've filed for *Intrepid* over the years. All the other staff writers were on assignment, my editor insisted, and there was nothing else promising in my inbox, so I figured, what the hell. Nobody told me that once you pass the Arctic Circle, life is as dull as the middle of a desert.

Plus, all they're looking for is ice. Yes, they want a 'candidate berg' full of 'hard-ice,' but that's just a classic case of new science: create a new terminology and overnight it's all serious and objective, integrity just leaking out the sides. It's just ice, dammit, which is about as rare in this godforsaken place as oxygen. Look out any porthole in any direction. Meanwhile we're missing the real sights. We could have stopped at Prince Patrick Island, with its stunning escarpments and snaky river oxbows, but no, ice it is, as if there were something special about that particular chilly form of H2O beyond what you can find back home in your ordinary freezer and float in a nice highball of scotch. And all the way up here, with every pebble of the world's landmass to your back and nothing in front till you come around the other side? Ice is daylight, ice is breakfast. Stand on deck two minutes and watch what forms on the parka hood from your breath. Ice here is as plentiful as pennies in heaven, gills on fish, Carter's little pills. Still, every third day this ship comes across some whoop-de-doo find. Except that after we tether up and they spend half a day scanning the damn thing, it turns out to be not the kind of ice they're looking for, and off we go again.

I am not fooled. Not for one second. This trip is nothing but a giant head-fake. It's all part of the colossal monument to himself Erastus Carthage has built. Obviously the guy has already cleared a place on the mantle to put his Nobel. Plus, with the way he never stops rattling his tin cup for grants, I suspect he might be feathering his personal nest a bit too.

In the humble opinion of yours truly, Professor Carthage is running the greatest snow-job money-grab this country has seen since P.T. Barnum. Look, I pulled my parents out of a burning house when I was fourteen – poster-people, by the way, for the stupidity of smoking in bed. Here is what I discovered when I stopped coughing my lungs out and looked at them there on the lawn, mom curled into herself like a fifty-year-old fetus, dad's teeth wide like he's biting the air for a decent breath. The lesson: there is nothing deader than dead.

I don't care if Carthage can jolt some shrimp into jumping around for half a minute. You can do the same thing with certain rocks, if they contain enough tin. I aim to blow this fraud's cover, plain and simple.

That is the only reason I came along – to tear that arrogant prick down. And may I just say, the trip has had precious few compensating amenities. Dull food. No booze. About two people on board capable of telling a decent joke. The only perk, come to think of it, is the perfectly shaped, wonderfully toned and tragically unattainable derriere of one Kate Philo, PhD.

This one night on the ship I can't sleep. Blame the usual stew of loneliness and lust, I'm all but sucking my thumb. Then they find another candidate berg. I do my usual lurk and scribble, but no one talks much because the ocean's heaving like a roller coaster. When we motor into sight of the iceberg, it's a stunner. Bigger than an aircraft carrier, and brilliantly white. Funny when you grow up knowing the Titanic story, how seeing these things is about as comfortable as strolling up to a rattlesnake. There's a weight in your gullet. The crew goes mute, which does not exactly make for scintillating copy. Eventually they call Dr Kate to the bridge, and I'm figuring the least it will do is improve the scenery.

She arrives in a yellow T-shirt and one of those blue poly-propylene outfits, the super tight kind they wear under the wetsuit for diving in frigid water. The crewmen, most of them as young as daffodils, take a good long gawk. One catches my eye and shakes his head, like *can you believe it*?

Now it's two hours later. Dawn coming but no one's going to bed. They're poring over this latest find, in the research room downstairs of the bridge. Basically they perform a sonar scan of the entire iceberg, a process as exciting as the discovery of vanilla. But David Gerber is seated at the console, which means there may be some laughs yet.

'Come into my palace,' he says, waving to me and Dr Kate without taking his eyes from the screen. He has crazy curly long gray hair like some drug-addled jazz pianist, held back by a communications headset at an odd angle, and a three-day beard. 'Come see what free association has done for our bold expedition this fine day.'

Gerber is not a water guy, nor even a biologist. He's all theoretical math, Princeton-trained with Stanford computer science thrown in, a legitimate maniac and I've met him before. He led the repair team when the Mars Rover broke down with a few thousand miles left on NASA's warranty. A massive problem to solve, with programming, by radio, from 55 million miles away. He did it though, the Rover restarted, and that is a pretty neat trick. I covered that story for three weeks and never once saw evidence that Gerber had troubled himself to sleep. Getting a guy with that horsepower away onto a time-wasting cruise like this one? I cannot imagine what it cost.

The challenge with Gerber is that he is also a heavy toker. Day and night, dinner and breakfast. Used to be, I could never tell when he was straight and when he was high. Then I decided just to assume he was always high, and it worked fine.

Also he streams music constantly, obsessing on one thing only: the Grateful Dead. No other music, no other band. He has albums, bootlegs, a fetish about recordings with guest artists. Gerber once boasted that he'd collected twenty thousand songs by the Dead. He's memorized more obscure facts than a tour guide at the Baseball Hall of Fame.

I like it. The optimism of the songs, the lightness of attitude, it's a break from the usual grind. Sometimes Gerber gets lost in one of the band's long improvisations, staring into space during the endless musical self-indulgence, but otherwise his obsession is harmless. One time, because I cranked my share of rock in my day, I made the mistake of pretending. I recognized 'Sugar Magnolia' on his computer speakers, and declared that the live *Europe '72* version was superior to the studio original on *American Beauty*.

Gerber laughed. 'The Dead performed that song 594 times and recorded it 49 times. My personal favorite was October of '73, which came out in 2001 on volume nineteen of Dick's Picks. Yes, it was "Sunshine daydream" in Oklahoma City.'

Then he cackled, scratched his mangy hair and went back to his computer.

Good thing Gerber's a genius because anyone else wasting that many brain cells wouldn't have half a dozen left. Tonight he beckons us closer, 'Come my children, come.'

I stand to his left, Dr Kate the other side. Five displays arc around his desk. Three show screen-savers of fractals branching to infinity. Of the remaining two, the upper one plays a video feed from the ship's bow. It shows a trio of men in expedition wear, plus thick flotation vests, working the sonar scanner over the surface of the ice. Like rock climbers they're linked by ropes, which are anchored to the top of the berg somewhere up out of sight. Everyone moves slowly, as if they're on the moon. It's cold enough out there, a body could die of exposure in minutes. An accidental dip in the brink? Don't even want to imagine it.

The scanner weighs 200 pounds, and moving it around is complicated by all the clothes. I did one stint with the device, so I could write about it, and 10 minutes was all the experience I needed. The cold froze my nostrils, then crept down my throat, and I swear it was headed for the bottom of my lungs. The temperature felt malevolent, like creepy fog in a horror movie. Don't let anyone feed you that bunk about nature being beautiful and kind. Watching these men struggle on the video feed, I was forever convinced that nature would have been more than happy to see them frozen solid dead.

'Forget the movie, campers,' Gerber says. 'Here's the real story.' He taps a pen on the lower screen, which shows what looks like a simple 3-D grid. 'This new little trick should save days of scanning.'

Dr Kate leans for a closer look. 'What have you got here?'

'A matrix of the iceberg's interior. I was tinkering online and stole two ideas I found – a parking garage CAD system, and a layout scheme for archeological digs. Now we'll know more exactly where we find hard-ice, and where there are deposits of our tiny carbon formerly-alives, so we can fetch them easier and with fewer samples damaged.'

'So what does it show us?' she says, still bent forward.

Gerber punches keys and clicks his mouse, and the screen changes dramatically enough that the good doctor straightens. 'Holy cow,' she says.

He pulls his ponytail forward, checking the split ends. 'Yeah, not half bad.'

He's displaying an outline of the entire berg, with green lines in a perfect grid throughout, and white veins where hard-ice runs through the ordinary kind. It looks like ore in a mine. Here and there, red stripes ribbon the hard-ice. 'That's your potential reanimation material,' Gerber explains. 'Carbon. Presto.'

'This is fantastic,' Dr Kate says. 'It will sharpen documentation too.'

'Amazing what some guys can accomplish with the right tunes playing. Hey people' – he's speaking into his headset now '– hold there a second. Hold, team.'

The men on the iceberg stand still, while Gerber taps at his keyboard. 'We got garbage data on that last core, fellas. Walk it back and re-sound, would you?'

We can't hear the reply, it's in his headphones only. Gerber watches the men retracing their steps, and smirks. 'Billings, you have my deepest sympathy, but it was junk data. Try it again.' He grins at us. 'All right: please. Pretty please.'

The men wrestle the scanner backward, and Gerber taps keys. 'Same deal, dammit. Let's re-run again.' There's an edge in his voice. He listens a moment. 'Don't blame me, dude, I don't know. Has one of you goons got your thumb over the lens?'

He listens, then frowns. 'What I am receiving is solid carbon for that section. Every bit of it. Ditto the 4 above it and 5 of the surrounding 12.'

Dr Kate taps Gerber's shoulder. 'What's going on?'

He waves dismissively at the screen, where amid the green grid there is now a block of solid red. 'The reading here is that the entire cubic foot is full of carbon. Which is as likely as throwing a shovel at a coal mine and finding a flawless diamond.'

'May I?' Dr Kate holds out her hands and Gerber places the headset in them. She fits them over her head, keeping her fingertips on the earpieces. 'Billings, instead of the usual pattern, could you guys please run one cube north?'

I watch the monitor as they hoist the scanner onto a new spot. Despite the moon suits, their body language reveals reluctance and annoyance.

'See?' Gerber points at his screen. There's red again, a solid block. 'That one is full of carbon too. Dammit, I debugged this stuff all the way through yesterday. Maybe the sonogram is down. What's the wind chill out there tonight anyway?'

'One more to the north, would you please?'

She's listening now, concentrating on what they say.

'Shit, there's a third row,' Gerber says. He throws a pen against the table. 'I hate what the cold does to my equipment.'

She holds up one finger to silence him. 'How deep are we scanning now?' She listens again. 'Really? The underside?' She smiles. 'Excellent work, gentlemen. I am going to suit up, and I'd like Squad Three on this one. Let's say full gear in 40 minutes, on my mark of 4:18, GMT. That's all for now. Way to go, guys.'

Gerber is looking up at her like a baby bird waiting to be fed. She hands the headphones back to him.

'I need you to be my shipboard brains, Gerber. Save the scan data real-time, and back it up on two hard drives, OK? In the water we'll go full video, with snapshot captures on my marks. I want this recovery sequence unimpeachable.'

'You don't think it's the equipment?'

She laughs, one high note. 'Gerber, don't you get it? I don't know if it's a seal, or immature beluga, or shark. But something big is frozen in there. Really big.'

'It's so exciting,' Gerber deadpans. He tilts his head at me. 'I'll alert the media.'

Dr Kate has closed her eyes and I can imagine the wheels turning. Then she turns to a technician across the room. 'Please inform the captain that we are harvesting from this berg immediately. Someone call Carthage to keep him posted.'

Gerber snorts. 'Always we must feed the beast.'

But if she hears, it does not show when she pauses at the door. It's a thing you can observe, how Dr Kate calms herself. Like soothing a baby, maybe, or comforting a dog in a thunderstorm, she pulls herself together. But this time it doesn't work. The excitement is heightened by her restraint. And it is nothing but lovely.

'One more thing. Tell the galley to start feeding everyone ice cream. We are going to need a ton of freezer space.'

She hurries out, I can hear her footsteps on the steel floor, and I'm left wondering: how did she know to come to the bridge right when the ice turned up? How did she know to wear diving clothes before the scans had begun? Usually Billings supervises the scans from the control room. Why did she send him out tonight instead?

Gerber plays his cursor back and forth over the red blocks. 'Come out, come out, whatever you are.'

I move next to him. 'Any guesses?'

'None.' He scratches his head. 'Hell of a big shrimp?'

'I'm going to make coffee,' I say, and stroll off toward the galley – only half because I want to keep alert. Truth be told, it also means I'll pass the suiting room, maybe glimpse the good doctor wrestling her sweet bones into a nice, snug dive outfit.

I mean, it's not like she's given me anything else to think about.

CHAPTER 3

NOT BAD

(ERASTUS CARTHAGE)

You stand at the railing knowing that they do not believe you: scientists, researchers, lab rats from across the country. Funders, bless their wallets. Underlings too, those pre-doctoral peons who serve well as exploitable implements but get underfoot like so many neglected cats. And the media, any demonstration would be wasted without at least a few reporters to gawk and scrawl.

'Are we ready?' you call in the direction of the speakerphone.

'Just one moment more, Dr Carthage,' replies the chief post-doctoral fellow, a red-haired Yalie whose future depends on situations like this. If there is any benefit to life in the academy, it is the subservience of young men and women who know that a single letter of concern in their file, one rumor of falsified lab results, so much as a whisper of faint praise by you at the major conventions, and their career at this scientific altitude is over. Instead of working with leading minds in splendid labs, they'll be teaching freshman biology at some dead-end college in nowhere America.

The team works behind glass that runs the width of the room. It was costly, that window, but you designed this lab as much for display as for research. You imagined a day like this, you dreamed of it. Yet now that it has arrived, it feels not like a granted wish but like an inevitability. Reason and inquiry prevail once again.

Some tasks take place under lab hoods, because one can never be certain which germs might also enjoy re-entering the living world. Team members wear white coats, per your instructions, but since they labor in jeans on ordinary days the coats are purely for show. But then, the whole exercise serves that same purpose – this morning's demonstration, the conference this afternoon with you delivering the keynote. Until your ideas take firmer hold in the public mind, and funding becomes reliably perpetual, everything is for effect. After all, once the discovery occurs, science is mostly theater.

You are not remotely nervous. The lab has replicated this process nine times in front of an audience. Plus twenty-two assays before the first paper appeared, with a long list of co-authors and your name at the top.

Thomas – your untitled and unpaid assistant, butler, secretary, shadow and man Friday – has performed the day's introductions, provided coffee, stroked the egos to the perfect heat. For the moment your role is figurehead. Master of ceremonies.

'Are we ready?' you repeat.

'We're on the last parameters, sir,' comes the reply.

You consult your watch. Six minutes past the hour, the precise interval after the scheduled start that sharpens an audience's curiosity. So your patter begins.

'Gentlemen – and lady,' you nod at the *Post* reporter, 'thank you for coming today. We are pleased to demonstrate recent accomplishments by the Carthage Institute for Cellular Seeking. Today we will reanimate . . . which is it doctor, copapod or krill?'

'Krill,' replies the speakerphone. The technicians wear masks, again purely for appearances, but making it impossible to tell who is speaking.

You knew the answer anyway, of course. There is no piece of this demonstration that lacks for preparation.

'The *euphausia superba*,' you inform the audience, 'an excellent creature. Low in the food chain, the biomass of this Antarctic species exceeds 500 million tons, roughly double the biomass of all human beings.'

'We're ready now, sir,' the speaker declares.

'Permit me to provide a context,' you begin. The next four minutes contain the view-from-space version of everything you have learned over the past thirty-six years.

'Let us begin with the familiar: plants. They make these.' From a side table you pick up a sunflower seed, and display it for all. 'Appears dead. Contains life. We are so accustomed to these little dormant packages, we scarcely register that they possess all the materials necessary to become alive.'

You replace the seed and show them a pine cone. 'This comes from a lodge-pole pine, a Western evergreen that can grow to 160 feet. Yet this cone will open to release seeds only upon experiencing a temperature of 140 degrees Fahrenheit. After a volcano or forest fire, this is the species that restores a scorched countryside with a carpet of green. Certain extreme conditions are necessary to reveal its inner life power.'

You place the cone exactly where it was, ready for the next presentation. A glance at Thomas shows him focused entirely on you, though he has heard this speech on countless prior occasions.

You continue: 'In addition to plants, there are four other forms of life on this planet. Four, and each one has a phase of apparent death which is disproven by life that eventually results. Let us first consider the bacterium, which works similarly to seeds. It awaits favorable conditions – especially moisture, temperature, and a host – and then experiences a rebirth. Next are fungi such as mushrooms, whose latency we recognize every time we add hot water to seemingly lifeless yeast. The third kind, protists such as amoebas, reproduce identically, such that it is impossible to tell which is offspring and which is the original, confounding the concept of any particular entity dying.'

You have wandered along the great window, hands holding your lapels, appearing to pace absently though you have timed your arrival to the word. At the far end, you halt.

'This shallow perception of mortality also extends to the remaining life form, the animals. You think you know when they live and die. But today we shall change your minds, as we reanimate *euphausia* by finding the seed-like mechanisms within.'

They shift in their seats. You can tell it is not a matter of getting comfortable, but of growing anxiety, which is how you like it.

'One caveat,' you say, raising a hand. 'Today contains merely one portion of a five-phase process.' You count on your fingers. 'First, reclamation, which includes finding and identifying a viable sample. Second, reanimation, which you will witness momentarily. Third, recovery, in which the specimen gains function. Fourth, plateau, in which it achieves equilibrium. Fifth, frenzy, which, as you observe, will speak for itself.'

You wave your arm. 'Commence the exercise.'

As the lights dim and the overhead comes on, the eyes of every person present go to the screen. It is that simple. The Yalie is explaining hard-ice now, how it forms under stupendous pressure, coupled with the most bitter weather this planet's climate can conjure. This was the first of your discoveries, nature's cryogenics. No need to ponder why species would develop this survival mechanism, turning their corpses into seeds for a future time. No need to become all Darwinian about it. Already the audience members begin to believe; their fixed stares at the overhead screen prove it.

'Excuse me.' The heir to a defunct newspaper fortune has raised his hand. His last check ran nicely into six figures; you remember the exact feel of him placing it, folded discreetly in half, into your palm. 'How old is the sample we are seeing today?'

'About seventy years,' the post-doc answers. He places a sliver of ice into the animating vessel. 'This specimen was dead, in the traditional sense, before anyone in this room was born.'

Thomas, schooled by you in seizing opportunity, steps forward. 'This hard-ice discovery occurred in a calving of Antarctic shelf three years ago. Funding for that mission came from a benefactor here today. The specimen has been stored at 120 degrees below zero. This particular find has proven among the more reliable for reanimation.'

Well done Thomas, you think. In truth, all hard-ice samples perform equally regardless of age or origin. But none of the ants in this audience could understand the professional publications, so there is no harm in encouraging a funder to believe his ice is special.

'When hard-ice forms,' the post-doc continues, 'any creatures in the water undergo extremely rapid freezing – so fast that the usual crystals of ice do not form. That speed leaves cells intact, and with unique chemical properties, namely abundant oxygen and glucose. Everything is preserved as it was when alive. Our challenge is to guide it back. Observe.'

The screen displays a microscope zooming in, a blur of gray-white ice and then, with arresting clarity, dozens of tiny frozen sea creatures.

'Is that an electron microscope?' asks the woman from the *Post.*

'Naw,' a technician says. 'You could find one like it in any high-school lab.'

You make a mental note to have Thomas scold that imbecile. If it's a second offense, he will be fired. Nothing about this process should appear easy or offhand.

'You can see that these formerly living objects are perfectly preserved,' the post-doc continues. 'Like seeds waiting to find the right soil. Now we perform two tasks simultaneously: providing the thawing bath, and galvanizing the samples with electricity and magnetic forces. Think primordial ooze, but instead of millions of years of randomization we have precise chemistry, and instead of a lightning strike we provide highly calibrated amperage.'

Technicians scurry to and fro. Thomas answers another question from the newspaper brat. A congressman's staffer wants to know what all of this costs.

'It varies from sample to sample,' Thomas replies, 'because the expense of procuring hard-ice fluctuates widely. Extraction involves sea voyages lasting months, sonar-scanning hundreds of bergs to find a vein, then mining specimens out of submerged ice, all without compromising the material. That's the expensive part. Reanimating creatures back here, comparatively, is about as costly as turning on the lights.'

'Today's krill, for example,' the congressman's pet persists. 'How much did it cost to find the material, bring it here, store it, and now reanimate it?'

'This Institute,' you interject, doing your best at that moment not to look at Thomas, 'has the luxury of receiving private funding, which grants us the liberty of keeping our financial information also private. The point is not to avoid accountability, but to cultivate flexibility and responsiveness to findings, in stark contrast with today's typically rigid governmental funding of the sciences. We are following the model Peter Marshall used in Great Britain seventy years ago. Operating a private lab enabled him to identify the electron transport mechanism in mitochondria when no one else was able.'

'Didn't he win the Nobel for that?' asks the newspaper heir.

You hold your hands out, give a little bow.

'We're ready,' calls the post-doc. That is your cue. You reach into your pocket for a stopwatch and hold it at arm's length. They all glance, but return their eyes to the projection screen. They do not want to miss the mystery. They want to shed their skepticism. They want, in some inexplicable way, for you to become the hand of God.

'Please watch closely,' the post-doc says. He lowers a skim of ice, thin as a piece of paper, into the warm bath. It dissolves immediately. The screen overhead divides, one side showing the bath, the other displaying a technician's hand on a black dial. He turns it clockwise. 'We are now adding a weak electric current and a powerful magnetic field.'

You start the stopwatch. And barely suppress the joy in your throat.

The water shows an agitation so small it could be a trick, the eye manufacturing what it wants to see. An expectant silence possesses the room. You love this moment, the anticipation. Then, ever so slowly, one krill unbends from its cold prison.

'Recovery,' you explain, and at that the hand on the dial cranks hard to the right. Instantly the water is full of activity, krill opening and closing like inchworms stretching to reach the next leaf. Several seem to move, in a straight line that indicates a purpose or destination. Two bump one another, then veer away. Another jumps clear out of the microscope's field of vision.

'Plateau,' you tell them.

The woman from the *Post* puts one hand on her chest. 'Oh my God.'

It never fails to thrill you. These tiny beings that appeared to be dead, there is no other way to phrase it but that you are bringing them back to life. The krills' motion rises in tempo. It looks like play. As their activity continues, you cannot resist projecting all sorts of emotions onto them: exuberance at being alive again, comfort at being warm, delight at encountering others of their species. One day might it be possible to mate two reanimated krill?

Now the energy shifts. Their motions grow frantic, violence on a microscopic scale. You announce: 'Frenzy.'

Perhaps they are living the krill's version of the most fulfilling life they can, because they know at any moment it will end. Or perhaps they are panicking, for the same reason. If only they had consciousness, if only they could communicate.

Eventually the energy decays on the screen. The creatures slow in their motion. Finally they stop, save one whose extremities twitch like a just-dead beetle. Then it too goes still. You click the stop-watch loudly, and with a flourish so that everyone notices.

'Whew,' says the newspaper scion. 'Amazing.'

'Now then.' You squint at the watch's dial. 'Two hundred and fifty point seven seven seconds.'

Flabbergasting. The longest yet for a krill, by 40 seconds. Your modifications to the chemical bath have proven groundbreaking. The staff knows better than to show it. They are all business. You make eye contact with Thomas. He is smiling behind his hand.

'Yes,' you continue, 'and since this particular species of krill lives for an average of four days, that means we restored vitality to these creatures for the equivalent of 1.21 percent of its lifespan.'

Thomas forces down his grin. 'If we did that with a human of an average life expectancy, we would be bringing him back from the dead for 21 days.'

'Of course,' you place the stopwatch on a shelf, 'no one is talking about doing anything with humans. We have many smaller life forms with which to experiment first.'

'Can you do it again?' asks the *Post* reporter. 'Can you reanimate these same krill a second time?'

Thomas shakes his head. 'Once is all.'

She looks about herself. 'So now they're really dead?'

'Still.' Thomas smirks. 'Two hundred and fifty point seven seven. Not bad.'

Like apostles they precede you into the conference center, the select group who witnessed the demonstration this morning. Now they will proselytize on your behalf. Thus do the disciples of reanimation grow in number and fervor.

Outside the hall there is the usual crush: admirers, self-promoters and media. Thomas does his part, pulling you forward no matter who has your ear. Or sleeve, this woman is actually holding your sleeve. Does she have any idea for how long your project just reanimated a krill? No, she just tugs away like a mongrel with a rag.

'Sarah Bartlett, UCLA,' she brays. '*Cell* just accepted my paper questioning the ethics of your work, for the next issue. I want you to know there's nothing personal—'

You circle your wrist to twist her hand away. 'Of course not. Likewise if I called your work immoral, you wouldn't be offended either.'

Bartlett persists like a gnat. 'If I were attempting to redefine mortality, I would expect at least a little criticism. Questioning is what gives science its energy—'

'Discovery is what gives science its energy,' Thomas interrupts, 'and Dr Carthage has somewhere to be.' He draws you on and the woman falls back into the general clamor. An amusing idea enters your mind: should you travel with a fly swatter?

Finally you reach the conference room, a windowless rectangle. Appalling to note how the architecture of functionality has created such featureless caves. Hundreds of chairs stand arrayed in rows. Urns of coffee and trays of bland danish line the back wall.

At the podium, Bergdahl notices you and accelerates his presentation.

'In flash freezing, the rapidity of temperature reduction prevents large water crystals from forming, thus preventing cell membrane damage.' He shows a slide of two cells, one cold but intact, the other irreparably ruptured.

What he has not said, this tenured Columbia University bio-savant, is that no one has been able to freeze tissues rapidly enough in the lab. They all burst. Only nature, with the intensity of cold, winds and iceberg collisions, can form hard-ice. That is why you bear the bankrupting expense of polar searching.

'In some species,' Bergdahl continues, glancing your way, then back to his notes, 'cryobiologists observe that dying creatures produce glycols instantaneously, as certain frogs do during hibernation, lowering their tissues' freezing point.'

Thomas inspects your suit, brushing away invisible lint. Bergdahl finishes, applause applause. Stepping offstage he veers toward you, but something in your demeanor detours him toward the coffee.

Thomas hands your bio to the man who will introduce you, then scurries off to load your presentation into the projector's computer. The introduction begins, you have three minutes to clear your thoughts. Believers are easy. Doubters require work. For them you have data, stories, and a film. It shows an immature shrimp, for nine seconds, tossing in a laboratory dish. But this is no ordinary shrimp, nor any typical nine seconds. This film captured the first successful reanimation. Now – attacked by scientists, criticized by zealots, hailed by drug companies, seized upon by the families of the thousands of people who are cryogenically frozen, alternately praised and feared by politicians – this video darling is changing the world. On the Internet its hits number in the millions. If only you could have charged a dime for each one . . .

Thomas returns, his brow furrowed. He knows better than to interrupt you at this moment. But he is holding a chirping cell phone. You nod and he lifts it beside your ear.

'This is Carthage.' The voice on the other end is singsong amid the static. 'Slower,' you say. The voice describes a candidate berg, the largest ever, ribboned with hard-ice, scans showing block upon block of carbon. The biggest, the richest, etc., etc.

Your introduction is nearly finished. The man at the podium is listing your publications, next will be your awards, and then you're on. If the find is even half the size described, then the revolution has begun. You will need more labs, more researchers, more funding. A seal or immature whale? How can the Swedish academy ignore that? A trickle of sweat runs down your ribs.

The voice on the phone requests instructions.

'Why are you asking me?' you reply. 'What about that woman I put on board to supervise? Philo. Tell her to harvest the primary find and ignore the rest. Send regular updates to my people at the center.'

You turn from the phone. 'Thomas, take care of this, will you?'

He closes the phone, bowing in wordless apology.

'Ladies and gentlemen,' says your introducer, 'please welcome Dr Erastus Carthage.'

A third of the crowd gives you a standing ovation, another third claps politely, and the remainder sits with faces of stone. It's amusing how they segregate, as when the president addresses Congress. Onstage the microphone is set for the height of your introducer, about four inches too low. Probably no one in human history has ever sanitized the mike stand. The count of sweaty hands palming it over the years must number in the thousands, but there is no alternative. You cannot bend at a moment like this. You raise it so you can stand at full height. You resist the urge to wipe your hand on your pants.

Still, what you have on your side is reason, impeccable techniques, dozens of successful reanimations, the whole grand payoff of the scientific method. Who needs confidence when you are backed by all human thought since the Enlightenment?

'Good afternoon,' you say, arms wide as though you held a beach ball. This is your signature move, practiced before a mirror, your gesture for the multitudes. 'I am so glad to be here. I am so glad to see you.'

You bow toward the group that did not applaud. 'All of you.'

CHAPTER 4

PREPARING TO PLUNGE

(KATE PHILO)

The singular thing that everyone failed to tell me about was beauty. Work? Oh, they crowed about that: so many hours in basement labs you lose track of whether it's morning or night, much less the day of the week. The loneliness of a new idea, when all pre-existing thought is allied against you. The bitter politics of academics, where generosity is fatal, forgiveness impossible. The potential for good work to be plagiarized and great work dismissed. The reality that you will never experience anything remotely approaching wealth. When I sought early career advice, no one left out those ingredients.

My father used to say, I love him for this, 'Kate, aren't you too smart for science?'

Once during the last fall of his life, he surprised me with an unexpected visit at grad school. I was lecturing, deep in the thylakoid membrane's role in photosynthesis, thrilled as always to be in front of a classroom, even a large hall like that, when I glanced up to spot him standing at the back. A small round man with a foot-wide grin, my dad. To have him see me in that light, well, I am grateful that it happened before he died.

That night we did New Haven, touring its modest graces amid perpetual hard times, ate a fine meal he insisted on buying me, then kissed goodbye at his hotel. But it wasn't enough, because the next day my father stopped by the lab on his way to the airport. I was working at a hood with safety glasses on. He hugged me hello, then lifted the plastic shields from my face. 'My daughter is way too pretty for this nonsense.'

Was some of it nonsense? Of course. Orals, comps, mandatory reading lists, they were all created to scare away the uncommitted, even if some of those people had the best minds. Much of it was lonely, too, your nearest confidantes nonetheless your competitors for jobs and grants, your dissertation topic a multi-year gamble over your future. Persistence, that was the paramount virtue. Also knowing your place.

Beauty though, beauty they forgot to mention. Yet in science, I see it all the time. Some days it is all I see. Ever since I thumbed my first slide onto a microscope in fifth grade, a rectangle of hard glass I'd dipped into pond water that looked lifeless and smelled of decay. Yet under magnification it displayed a realm so varied and energetic I felt dwarfed. They were busy, those little beings, whatever they were. Paramecium I suppose, algae and a few larvae. Because they revealed whole worlds of life I'd known nothing about, they sparked my earliest curiosity. They were miracles.

So, in subsequent years, were the students. Most doctoral candidates pay their way by teaching underclassmen. My peers moaned constantly about the time consumed by preparing lectures, grading papers, holding office hours. All that effort would be better spent in the lab, they said. I was the opposite: energized by the young minds, compelled by their interest, excited to show them not what I knew but how I felt about wanting to find something out.

Had it not meant throwing away the years I'd already invested, had it not meant a victory for Chloe's claim that I was neither smart nor committed enough to complete a PhD, I would have been more than happy to stay right there, teaching undergraduates. Seeing a young mind grab hold of a difficult idea, wrestle with it, then eventually brighten with understanding, that was the only nostalgia I felt as my career advanced. Even at Hopkins, where the brains around me were as honed by exertion as the biceps of weightlifters, still I sometimes yearned to stand before a bunch of kids and explain why oxygen was brilliant.

My recompense was learning the many facets of beauty, how it occurs in patterns from tiny to giant. Pull the plug on a bath tub drain, there's an elegance to how the liquid runs out, a tidy efficiency worked out between gravity and water molecules and the shape of the pipes – but that's not all. The spiraling water looks just like a weather satellite's image of a hurricane, bearing down on the Gulf Coast some rain-drenched September day. What's more, they both replicate the spiral of galaxies, the same shape responding to similar forces, identical laws, although one is a draining of soap bubbles and the other a cascade of stars.

It's true with ice, too. A century ago a man in Vermont named Bentley invented a method of photographing snowflakes and enlarging the images. That's where the no-two-alike idea originated. I've seen his photos, in a book my high-school physics teacher lent me years ago. There is beauty beyond doubt, one amazing hexagon after another. But that's just one kind of interesting ice. There's the groan of slabs grinding one another in springtime river melts. There are filigrees like ferns on the bathroom window on frosty evenings after your shower. There are icicles, glaciers, jinglers in your cocktail. There is hard-ice, the secret ace of water's countless forms.

Of course it's important to know what H2O is, what its uses may be, how it sustains life, what pollution or neglect can cause. There is a whole lexicon on the physics of ocean waves, the potential to generate electricity using tides, the nutrient depletion of soil erosion, the natural irrigation of rain. But my science, if I ran the world, would never lose sight of the other part of the equation. The beauty.

Squad Three is ready to dive. I stand with them on deck. Dawn came hours ago, as it does this far north in August. I'm in my black scuba suit, insulation layers beneath, I've poured warm water down the neck opening to make my body heat last longer. The dive team is all work, underwater saws and drills strapped to the rusty red platform, lights and regulators, checking their masks to make certain no bit of skin, however small, is exposed. They are as fidgety as horses before a race.

Billings paces on deck in his parka. Normally after an all-nighter he'd sleep through extraction, but not this time.

'Don't play any games with calving,' he shouts over the wind. 'You do not want to deal with fragments.'

Communicating this way reminds me of college parties, bellowing over the stereo. I nod in answer. 'Don't worry about me.'

'Are you taking small samples too?'

Half-listening as I review the crew's preparations, I shake my head.

'Won't Carthage shit himself though?' Billings leans in. 'He could do decades of work with the other veins in this berg.'

My regulator hisses, I tap the mouthpiece silent. 'I can't risk losing a unique find just to collect trinkets.'

'There are a good fifty studies in this iceberg, all priceless. If not for this seal or whatever, you'd be ecstatic over those trinkets.'

I tug my gloves on snug, snapping the fabric at my wrists. 'Are you saying we let this go so we can collect the little stuff?'

'Bloody hell Kate, listen to me.'

I turn to him then, unaware that he was growing angry. 'Go ahead.'

'You know perfectly well how much I have carried that twit over the years, how many times I dove in freezing water to extract samples he took credit for, how many bloody papers I'm listed as third author even though I did all the work.'

'We all know Carthage. What's your point?'

'The seal will be his. He'll hog it all. But that could leave the other work for me. If Carthage wakes a large animal, he won't care about shrimp anymore. Maybe I could claim my own bit of terrain.'

It is the longest speech I have ever heard on deck. I look down into my face mask for an answer. In any lab on land, Billings would be in charge instead of me. I am in his debt, too, for helping me throughout this voyage. Even this reach of ocean was his idea, when I was inclined to chart a course west. But if I screw up the primary extraction, Carthage will destroy not just me but the career of every person on the dive team.

'Hey campers,' Gerber squawks in my earpiece: 'what's the hold-up out there?'

'Nothing,' I say. 'We're fine.' Then I face the squad to yell over the wind. 'OK crew, let's cut this thing with a nice margin so we don't lose anything important. Squad Two should prep for seventy minutes from now, to mine for small samples.'

Diving masks nod up and down the row. Billings makes a dignified bow; he leads Squad Two. I pull the mask over my face, climb on the platform. The team follows in the awkward walk of flippers, like so many penguins about to plunge off their floe.

As everyone grips the chain-link railing for balance, I turn back for a look. I remember that moment now, with all that has happened, as a traveler a century ago might have recalled her steamship pulling away from the pier: here comes an unfamiliar culture, a different language, a new world. Gerber stands at the tech room window, his hair a crazy halo, flashing us a peace sign. On the bridge above, the captain speaks from one side of his mouth. A winch groans and the deck crane hoists our platform off the deck, dangles it in the windy air between ship and iceberg, then eases us into the water.

The ocean presses on my calves, then my hips, upward. This close to the berg, there are no waves to topple me. Only the water, taking my shape. *Can there be anything more intimate?* The shock of the cold doesn't hit till we're up to our necks. I start my watch's chrono function – time, after oxygen, being the most valuable commodity here.

'Mark,' I call to Gerber, which he repeats in my earpiece, so I know he'll have snapped a photo of the team being lowered into the sea.

Then the water is over my mask, I'm immersed completely. So I do what I always do in that first moment: tilt my head back and let out a long exhale. It leaves the regulator in one fat bubble, which hurries upward like a helium balloon released by a child on a summer's day. Beauty.

CHAPTER 5

BASEBALL MITT

(DANIEL DIXON)

'Mark,' Dr Kate calls over the radio, and Gerber presses a button beside his monitor. The image on an upper screen freezes for half a minute – a hand axe striking at the ice – while the video feed continues on the TV below. It's fascinating, if I linger on the still shot, how easy it is to spot hard-ice: when the axe hits, regular ice falls away and leaves something like white concrete. How had scientists before Carthage failed to discover this stuff? It's like peeling off wax drippings without noticing the main candle.

I jot that simile in my notebook for later, because there's nothing else for me to write at the moment. I'm just watching while they work. But I can tell this iceberg is different, if only by everyone's seriousness. Gerber has not made a joke in hours. He even turned down the Grateful Dead bootleg of the day; it's barely white noise from his speakers. The way his chair is positioned, he can't see the 'mark' images overhead. He's bent toward the live feed playing before him. The tech crew concentrates on screens in front of them too: sonar scans, temperature gauges, water content monitors.

The first team works their full shift, then the second squad digs into a side vein. They call it harvesting, Billings removing cores the size and shape of fence posts. They must be sweet with specimens, because by the end of that shift Billings is singing in his headset. I've heard beagles with better voices.

They must be freezing out there, bone-aching cold that takes days to recover from. Every so often a piece breaks loose, and everybody scurries. They can't help approaching an iceberg with fear. It's like handling snakes, there are too many stories of something going wrong. Plus, both crews have been underwater nearly three hours each. During breaks they skip breakfast and napping, despite having pulled an all-nighter. When Billings's team made its second dive Dr Kate stood beside Gerber wrapped in a chocolate brown blanket, calling 'mark' every minute or so. It feels as focused as an operating room.

As soon as his dive ends, Billings returns to the control room. Dr Kate gives him a hug, the lucky dog. Instead of a fresh crew, she orders her group to suit up again.

During the transition I visit the bridge. Captain Kulak has stayed at his post longer than any time since we set sail. The daylight view outside stuns me. Peaks of white and blue float in a black metallic soup, a sanctuary for whales, or Martians maybe, but no place a human being should linger. Soon the crane hoists Dr Kate's team overboard, easing them down like miners lowered into a coal shaft. Aside from Kulak's commands to the crane operator, no one speaks. Neither is anyone going anywhere.

Then there's not much to see, except cables into the sea with ice forming at the waterline, so that's my cue to head downstairs again. Gerber, Billings, the techs, they're so absorbed they don't react when I enter the room. For once I am not asking questions. I am just observing, making notes. If Dr Kate is willing to endure a third shift in that frigid gloom, they're getting close, is what it is.

'Mark,' she calls, and the screen shows a flipper, extended down and away from the seal's main body. It is a slender animal, I'd say. Almost 6 feet long, maybe 2 feet wide, though it's hard to tell exactly through the blur of ice. Then the video feed shows an underwater circular saw, biting into the hard-ice 2 feet from the flipper.

Gerber reaches for the cup of coffee I gave him an hour ago, definitely cold by now, but Dr Kate calls 'mark' and he brings his hand back without taking a sip.

Either these people are incredible actors, every one of them, or they are captivated by Carthage's crazy fantasy, or, possibly, they genuinely believe they can harvest this animal in the ice and bring it back to life. The implications, which I have denied relentlessly until this day, are boggling. There are something like 40,000 people around the world who are cryogenically preserved, waiting for a day that technology enables them to reawaken. There are another 60,000 people at any given moment lying in hospital ICUs with incurable illnesses. Imagine if they could be frozen in hard-ice till a cure is found, or some anti-aging medicine developed, and then reanimated. There are almost 100,000 people awaiting organ transplants. Imagine if you could freeze the bodies of recently dead people, then thaw what you need for parts later. It would make transplanting like going to the fridge for a beer.

I can't believe I am starting to think like this. Most of the researchers are rookies, so I understand why they might get starry-eyed. But Gerber?

'Hey mad scientist,' I call. 'Want me to freshen that coffee for you?'

He does not take his eyes from the screen. 'What'd you say?'

'Coffee. You want some more?'

He doesn't answer. Dr Kate says 'mark' and he snaps the image, then turns to me. 'I'm sorry. What?'

I hoist my mug at him. 'Coffee?'

He turns back to the monitors. 'Help yourself.' Then he checks his watch. 'Hey Dr Philo, I'm looking at our clock here.'

There's silence in the radio, then she squawks on. 'And?'

'You know you have 4 minutes till ascent?'

'Three minutes forty-four seconds,' she answers.

'Not that you're counting.'

'Nope. Mark.'

He presses his button. The image freezes on the overhead screen, long chisels working a cleft in the hard-ice. It's like defrosting an old-style freezer with a kitchen knife, only underwater, and you're inside the freezer.

Her radio squawks again. 'Can you tell from there how close we are?'

'Definitely.' Gerber nods. 'I'm worried about that flipper getting too thin a boundary. Exposure would compromise—'

'I only want to know what species we have, then I'll let it be.'

'You and your curiosity. Just be careful. That berg is starting to destabilize. And the fragment—'

As if to prove Gerber's point, a slab of white the size of a minivan breaks free. There's a groan through the monitor, like a whale giving birth. The slab spirals lazily onto its side, then grinds along the underwater face of the berg. Divers rush away in all directions, kicking their flippers furiously. One scrape from a beast like that and your suit is torn, immediate frostbite, or it brushes your air hose and you're dead.

Kate hasn't moved though, she's fixed on her carving like a jeweler cutting diamonds. The woman can concentrate, I'll give her that. Gerber snaps a photo of the ice block as it rises, silently, trailed by offspring the size of steamer trunks. The other divers gradually swim near again.

'Call it a shift, lovely,' Billings says into his headset across the room. 'I'll be in after you, straightaway.'

Dr Kate does not answer. Now only inches of ice lie between the specimen and open water. I see how the flipper fans open at the end. It looks like the wingtip of a hawk, the way feathers spread when a big bird glides.

'That fragment did us a favor,' Kate says, 'but this is one awfully skinny seal.'

Gerber shuts his music off completely, rolls his chair forward till his nose is inches from the monitor. 'What the hell is that thing?'

I'm standing beside him now. 'Fuck if I know.'

'Should I tell her it's 40 seconds till ascent?'

No one answers. We can see the crew working beside the animal, wedging it toward freedom. It is almost ready to come away.

'Wait, team,' Dr Kate calls. 'Hold there.' The video feed shows her swimming deeper, under the very bottom of the iceberg. 'Shine a light back this way,' she says. A diver leans in her direction to reveal the specimen in silhouette. The ice is cloudy, full of air, so the seal looks suspended like a work of modern art.

Next Dr Kate positions herself further below. She's set aside all her tools but a brush, and she's using it on the last bit of ice along the flipper.

'Hey Kate,' Gerber says, 'you OK there? We're

at major risk for breaking the hard-ice seal. You know how we mothers worry.'

Instead of answering, she beckons to the camera man. The feed blurs as he flippers his way down, then settles near her hip, pointing the lens upward.

Billings leaves his computer and crosses the room to see what's happening. The other technicians have all gone silent. A beeper announces the time for ascent, but Gerber slaps it off. Everyone's watching the monitor now.

'Mark,' she calls, and Gerber presses the button. The screen shows a shadow, reaching, a dark something.

Dr Kate maneuvers beneath the animal, then releases a huge breath. Fat bubbles rise into the pocket around the flipper, trapped in the ice's shape for a moment, then escaping to one side. It's like an underwater caress.

'God in heaven,' Billings says. 'She's melting it with her breath.'

'Mark,' she says, as a layer of ice separates, falling away. With the back-lighting so bright, the flipper is taking a clearer shape. Silly as it sounds, I can't help asking, 'Does that look to any of you like a baseball mitt?'

Gerber squints at the screen. 'It *does*, kinda. Only smaller.'

As the next breath bubbles upward, Dr Kate reaches high and hooks her gloved fingers into a tiny crevice. She tugs, twice.

Billings whispers, 'Careful.'

All at once the ice falls away, a big plate. Someone gives a yell. Divers rush in, blocking the camera. 'No way,' someone shouts. 'Impossible,' says someone else.

'Mark,' Dr Kate yells. 'For God's sake Gerber, Mark. Mark.'

Billings stands in my view, until I elbow forward so I can see. By then the divers have collected themselves. The video shows Dr Kate restraining them in the black water.

'Gerber,' she says, her voice stern like a cop's. 'Clear the control room.'

'Say again?' He looks around himself. At some point he has stood up.

'Clear the control room at once. Also secure this video and the back-ups as proprietary and classified.'

'All right everybody,' Gerber raises his voice, 'you heard her.'

Billings steps away and the technicians all rise from their chairs, two of them poised to escort me from the room, but I remain concentrated on the screen overhead.

'Tell her it's too late,' I say to Gerber. 'Tell her I already saw.'

'Saw what?' he says, leaning back to squint at the screen. And there it is, blurred by ice and bubbles, but undeniable. 'What *is* that?'

'Just what it looks like,' I tell him. 'A human hand.'

CHAPTER 6

SUBJECT ONE

(ERASTUS CARTHAGE)

'The heavyweights are assembled, sir.'

Thomas stands at attention, good soldier. You hold up one finger, while with your other hand you finish writing your thought. Oxygen, it is all about oxygen. Muscle function relies on salt, yes, and the brain requires a steady electric current. But ultimately life is oxygen. Without it, human existence withers faster than a leaf in the fall. Thus oxygen saturation may be a pivotal ingredient for this latest reanimation. Latest, and obviously greatest.

'Thomas,' you say, putting the pen aside, 'here we are. Seven months since we brought our incredible find back to civilization. Seven months for the world to realize the potential of our work, should it succeed with this frozen gentleman. Is this our finest hour?'

He ponders while you stand and don your blazer.

'Our finest hour has not yet occurred,' Thomas answers.

'Right you are. The meeting today is merely our

due. The time has come for the nation's finest minds to assemble as advisors, and thus acknowledge our achievement. But this moment is like Darwin's presentation to the Royal Society prior to publishing the *Origin of Species*. Our triumph Thomas, the actual victory, remains ahead.'

You tug your sleeves snug, then squirt a gob of hand sanitizer from a bottle on the credenza. You give both hands a vigorous rub. 'Who has accepted our invitation?'

Thomas lifts his clipboard and begins reciting the names of the physicians and researchers gathered that morning, as you stroll toward the lecture hall. Each one triggers an association for you – Rosenberg of Harvard (smells of cigars), Cooley of Jonas Salk (a first-class sycophant but a Nobel finalist four years back), Borden of St Aram's (never heard of him, and an MD not a PhD, but he came highly recommended).

Another staffer joins you in the corridor, he is dark-skinned, a new hire, and hands you a cup of tea.

You nod in return, take the tea and blow on the surface. Thomas is still reading. You raise a hand. 'Enough. Let them introduce themselves as they speak. Let us begin.'

As you sweep forward the new staffer reaches to open the door and the edge of it catches you squarely in the mouth. It is like a blow. You stagger backward, tea spilling, hand to your face. 'Jesus God, you oaf.'

'I am sorry sir, I am so sorry.'

You draw yourself to full height. 'Name.'

'Sanjit Prakore, sir,' answers Thomas. 'From the University of Auckland.'

Well Mr Prakore—'

'Dr Prakore, I'll thank you.' He bows.

'Oh I beg your pardon,' you say. You touch your lips, then inspect your fingertips. 'In that case, *Dr* Prakore, you are fired.' You wave two fingers like a little broom. 'Get thee gone.'

'Sir.' Thomas is at your elbow. 'Dr Prakore is the world expert on the use of magnetic fields to direct oxygen streams at the cellular level. *The* expert, sir.'

'Then let him expert somewhere else.' You face Thomas. 'Is my lip bleeding?'

'No sir.'

'It was an accident, Dr Carthage,' Prakore says, 'and I wish to apologize.'

'Not accepted. Thomas, are my lips swollen?'

'You can barely tell, sir.'

'Dr Carthage, I left a tenured position to come here. I moved my family.'

'With any luck you are still partially packed. Begone.' You hand Thomas the tea cup. 'Step aside. I can open my own damn door.'

A projector throws images on a screen at the front, snapshots from the seven months of thawing: a hand emerging, the bottom of a boot. Here is a belt buckle, there the lapel of a coat. The final shot shows the specimen's face, whiskered like a bobcat, blurry beneath a glaze of remaining ice. As that photo appears, the world's first glimpse of the frozen man's face, no one needs to call the meeting to order, nor ask for quiet.

'Your idea?' you whisper to Thomas. He tilts his head and you nod approval.

Eminences fill the lecture hall. A stenographer taps her keys to record all that is said, while a videographer trolls along the walls. Sixty-eight, you count them, all leaders in their fields and thinkers of the first order. Sixty-eight tributes to reason, to you, and to this beguiling creature you have named Subject One.

The first hour proceeds predictably. Gilhooly monopolizes the microphone, ever infatuated with the sound of his own voice. Then again, he does know his electrons.

Next comes Petrie, moustached, chief anatomist at U.C. Berkeley, the slender stalk of him in a wrinkled gray suit. 'When the item to be reanimated is minuscule, questions of temperature gradients are inconsequential. But with the mass of a human being, many challenges arise. We could thaw and reanimate his feet, for example, while his skull remained frozen solid. This organism is infinitely more complex, with interdependent parts, each required for the whole to function, each with unique densities and viscosity – and thus different rates of thawing. We must therefore devise a means for warming Subject One uniformly. At present I cannot provide an answer, only the question.'

Petrie pets his moustache and sits without an extra word. The next fifteen minutes provide exactly what you had hoped for: lively discussion of warming methods. Here is the beauty of the scientific method, the dialectic, the contest of opposing ideas leading to a third and better way. Your lips hurt, but when you brush them with your fingertips it is not to assess the pain. You are monitoring any swelling, lest your appearance at this singular event be in any way marred. The last word on thawing goes to a strapping kidney transplant specialist from St Louis, who offers something he learned in younger days as a high altitude climber: the best antidote for hypothermia was administering warmed oxygen from within. Raising the lungs' temperature proved the fastest way to warm the blood. Perhaps Subject One could be thawed in the same manner, from the inside out. Well, well. An innovation you had not considered.

The tape rolls, a dozen post-docs take notes, Dr Billings stands against a side wall with a droopy face. Can anyone express boredom more articulately than the British? Dr Philo, by contrast, stands alert, as if her entire body were an ear.

An unfamiliar man comes to the mike. 'May I add to the discussion?'

He identifies himself as Orson, of Linda Loma Hospital in San Diego, a medical ethicist. 'This marvel we are contemplating is stretching our minds in wonderful ways. But I would encourage all of us here to pause, and consider that Subject One is also a human being. He inhabited a set of circumstances at the time of his death – family, a job, a faith. Our potential to awaken him raises many issues. Would he want us to do it? Does he have descendents who ought to be consulted? Will he suffer from our actions?'

You write on an index card and display it to Thomas: 'Who invited him?'

'I propose that we keep Subject One on ice,' Orson continues. 'Let us convene ethicists, theologians and thought leaders, to weigh what we are doing before we do it. Otherwise our scientific triumph could prove to be a deed of unprecedented cruelty.'

There is a smattering of applause. Can they be serious?

Then Gilhooly is shouting, something about impeding the progress of science. Likewise Petrie is on his feet. 'Who do you think you are?'

Orson holds his ground. 'I am an appeal to your conscience. If you have one.'

Pandemonium. In an instant, everyone is standing, voices raised. Is the energy useful? Quickly you deduce that it is not. This is a contest of egos, the central question forgotten. You sit at the front, watching your masterpiece disintegrate. The videographer stalks the room with the camera on his shoulder. Thomas looks to you for direction. You wish you had thought to bring a gavel.

A diminutive man steps forward, looking like a

child at a bullfight. He has a black beard, groomed almost to a point, and somehow it makes him seem shorter. He lowers the mike stand, then clasps hands behind his back. 'Excuse me.'

The others continue shouting, pointing at the ceiling. One fellow throws his necktie from side to side, perhaps to punctuate his outcry.

'Excuse me,' the little man persists. Something about his shortness has an effect, and the people nearest him begin to quiet. He appears unmoved, waiting without a single gesture of annoyance or haste, not so much as adjusting his glasses. You take an immediate liking to him.

'Excuse me,' he says a third time, and inexplicably, it is enough. The shouters sit, grumbling a final word or two. Once the room quiets, he waits a moment more. It is a commanding move. You tuck this lesson away for another day.

'I am Christopher Borden, of St Aram's in Kansas City,' he begins. He has a nasal voice, elfin, yet he speaks with authority. 'I am a transplant surgeon. To answer Dr Orson, and all the discussion here, permit me to describe something I have witnessed hundreds of times which, to judge by the credentials of today's conferees, I believe none of you has seen once. I refer to the restarting of a human heart.'

He turns to address the full room. 'In a transplant, we remove the heart from a donor already pronounced dead, place it in a bucket of cold brine, bring it to the recipient, and connect it vessel by vessel. A lot of sewing, nothing fancy. Fifteen minutes.'

He smiles a little. 'All that time, the donor heart is warming up. We have all kinds of equipment ready to restart it: shock paddles, adrenaline needles. But they're rarely needed. Once the heart is warm and attached, usually it starts up again all by itself.

'Think of it.' Now he is speaking to you, no one but you. 'It may not matter what we want for science, or what we think is ethical. All we must do is provide the right environment, and let the heart do what it desires. The heart wants to beat.'

He tugs on the pointed tip of his beard, and waddles back to his seat.

There are others, but their concerns are technical. Borden has silenced the ethical debate. Scientists stand in line at the microphone, willing to offer ideas for successful reanimation. Late in the third hour Thomas comes to your side and whispers.

'Sir I hate to interrupt you—'

'Then don't.'

'There's something you need to see.'

You frown at him.

'Sir, you know I wouldn't bother you if I didn't think it was merited.'

He knows just how to put it, doesn't he? Thomas is really coming along. The current speaker is an endocrinologist from Chicago, who wonders if Subject One's sperm can be extracted by syringe and reanimated separately. When you start for the door the endocrinologist stops talking, pulling back his head as though slapped.

'Excuse me,' you say. 'An urgent matter has arisen that requires my immediate attention. Please continue,' you gesture at the endocrinologist, then the video camera, 'for the record of course, and I will return momentarily.'

As Thomas leads down the hallway you clear your mind, readying it for whatever comes next. He arrives at a smaller meeting room, with windows along one wall, and steps aside for you to enter.

You stride to the glass, cast your gaze six flights down, and observe. A dozen people stand on a patch of lawn across the street. They carry hand-painted signs: *Don't Toy With Life*, *Respect the Dead* and one, *Stop Playing God*, shaped like a stop sign.

'Clever,' you say. 'How long have they been here?'

'A noon news program reported that your conference was happening. They arrived an hour later.'

You nod, then notice a familiar bulk, thick as an aging linebacker, working the group's perimeter with his notebook. It's that reporter from the ship, his name momentarily escapes you. Utter fool, but he has proven reliably sympathetic, which is to say possibly useful. You rub your hands together. 'Splendid.'

'Sir?'

'Do they have a name, these people?'

'A guard downstairs said they call themselves "One Resurrection," sir. They believe Jesus should be the only one to rise from the dead.'

'Do these idiots not understand? We are not raising anyone. We are bringing forth the reanimation potential that has always been there.'

'Nonetheless, sir, our work is blasphemy, apparently.'

'But wait.' You tap a finger on your pursed lips. They are still tender. 'Wasn't there someone else?'

'Excuse me?'

'Some other person was raised from a tomb. In the New Testament. What was his name?'

Thomas steps back. 'I'm sorry, sir. I wasn't raised in any religion. But I'll find out.'

You raise one hand to stay his departure. Below they appear to be chanting something. Through the glass, you cannot make out what it is. Those not holding signs clap along with the chant.

'Is there something more, sir?'

'Dismiss the good doctors. Give them each $5,000 and my thanks for their time.'

'Yes sir.' Thomas scribbles on his clipboard. 'Anything else?'

'Bring me that Midwestern physician, the heart transplant man.'

'Dr Borden?'

'Exactly. Bring me Christopher Borden. And then we must rename the Institute.'

'Really, sir?'

'We are no longer seeking. We have found.'

'Pardon the question sir, but isn't the Carthage name enough?'

'We need a name that is an irritant, Thomas.

Like the grain of sand in an oyster.' You point out the window. 'Do you know what I see down there?'

'Malcontents, sir?'

'No,' you sigh. 'Money.'

CHAPTER 7

THE LAZARUS PROJECT

(KATE PHILO)

Where did I come from? I don't know. Why was I put on this earth? I don't know. Where will I go when I die? I don't know. What an intrepid woman scientist I am. Everything that really matters is something I don't know.

As I walked through the city that morning, the tang of spring sharpening the air, multitudes on their way to work, I could not shake the feeling that marching beside me was one beast of a don't-know. What were we going to do that day? What were we daring to attempt? Sometimes I couldn't decide if I wanted us to succeed or fail.

By then I lived in Cambridge, in a tiny side-street apartment. Though I strolled past Harvard every day, my only affiliation was with Carthage, who had become more freelance than ever. Tolliver at the National Academy emailed me, told me to be careful not to ally too much with one enterprise. He was probably right, but there were so many directions this research could go, I felt like I had lots of options.

So did my commute. The T could get me to the lab in minutes. I preferred to walk: crossing the Charles River, wending through Back Bay. Work was intense enough, I needed the decompression of the walk home too. It takes time to regain a relaxed attitude about all the don't-knows.

We put our eye to a microscope and there's a universe we never knew existed. We do the same thing with a telescope, same realization. There are ideas too, from Darwin and Gauss, from Pasteur and Newton, that reveal universes as clearly as any instrument.

That morning, an otherwise ordinary day in April, I was marching to the main lab, now known as The Lazarus Project, for possibly the biggest day of my life. Ever since I'd aligned my fate with Carthage's, there had been a steady sequence of biggest days.

The morning of the find, back in August, that had been huge. Within hours Dixon had called the story in from the ship to his magazine, which immediately sold it to the international press. By the next morning the whole saga was in print, from the midnight wake-up to everyone eating ice cream. My name made papers worldwide before we'd reached landfall. Strangers found my online address. Three offered me jobs. One decided I was Satan. My sister Chloe sent a snarky email about me falling for another cold guy and urging me to make sure no one stole my limelight – presuming I had done something significant. *Thanks, Chloe.*

When we docked in Halifax, TV cameras waited on the wharf. They pounced before the engines were off. We had our gear to haul, not to mention moving our frozen friend, but they insisted on a statement from me. I nearly asked them: *What do you want me to say?* Forty score and seven years ago some unknown guy got iced? No? Did you know Dixon has already named him 'Frank', as in 'Frankenstein'? Too dehumanizing? Then how about this: We have a frozen body. We have a technique. It works on creatures an inch long, for about two minutes. Beyond that, we'll get back to you.

Besides, with all those cameras pointed at me, I looked about as put-together as any woman would after ten weeks at sea. Skin like leather, hair like a hurricane. My fifteen minutes.

But Carthage was there, Carthage took charge. He made sure we received royal treatment: a nice hotel, warm meals, a hot shower so long my skin pruned like a baby's. His insistence that Billings and I accompany the body by train, that was showy for my taste. There were trawlers right there in port equipped to haul tons of frozen fish. There were refrigerated air freight carriers at an airport just miles away. Carthage maintained his method would guarantee temperature consistency, but we knew he had another motive.

That meant twenty hours with Billings on the trip south. On the overnight we did the proper, correct, appropriate thing: we got smashed.

'Don't worry, lovely, I'm not going to attempt some tawdry seduction on you,' he said, wobbling in the aisle against the sway of the train. 'Socially spastic, few deep allegiances, suspected of border-line Asperger's.' He flopped into the seat beside me. 'My brother aside, you're the closest thing I have to a friend.'

'Excuse me?'

'We've nine hundred miles to cover.' He held up a large bottle. 'This seems like the best way.'

'Bourbon?'

'Yes, I drink like a Yank now.' He flashed his crooked-toothed grin at me. 'But it does the trick.'

I was won over. 'At the risk of being too formal, could I go get us a couple of glasses?'

'Brilliant.'

We sipped and supped, we told old tales, we laughed ourselves weak.

The following noon we chugged into customs to learn that Carthage's slow train had been a masterstroke of media manipulation. Just over the border, American cameras stood in a line, reporters shouting questions. Anticipation had brought them to a froth.

That meant my face appeared on a national magazine cover three days later, looking not scien-tific but hung over. Billings was pale as a frog's belly. He even asked one reporter if he knew where a poor soul could get some tea.

That welcome marked the beginning of a media

avalanche. By the time we'd stowed the frozen man at Carthage's Boston lab, we were non-stop with talk shows, radio interviews, meetings with reporters over breakfast, lunch and dinner. It was more exhausting than fun, to tell the truth. More spectacle than substance. I felt like a magician, wiggling my hand over here so no one notices my deception over there.

A week along, I was in a hotel pulling off a blouse before bed when I encountered an unfamiliar odor. I put the shirt to my face and discovered the scent of stress about what we were doing, about doing it in front of the whole world. Imagine declaring on TV with certainty things you harbor huge doubts about. I stuffed the blouse into the lower suitcase with my shoes. I had enough to contemplate besides the smell of my own fear.

The science, to begin with. We ought to have been in the lab, not the TV studio. We were delaying all the potential discoveries, while proclaiming about the extremely little that we knew.

Something else also made me nervous. This was not some mute creature we'd found, some oddity like an oversized lobster or a giant squid. This was a human being. The research imperatives had to be ethically different. We saw signs of it everywhere.

The boot, for example. Soon after settling in the Boston lab, we'd done a preliminary scan through the shell of hard-ice, and the frozen man was wearing boots with the maker's faded imprint on the heel. This wasn't just any guy, I realized. It was a particular guy, with a particular life he'd died out of. He had a shoe size, there had been a place where he bought boots. Carthage saw only the media potential, or the possibility of funding from the boot company if it still existed. Thus it became my job to find out everything I could about our frozen man. Even with two inches of ice encasing his body, there were many indicators: the clothes, mutton chop sideburns, height, and yes, boots. I remembered a friend's cadaver dissection in medical school, how she was fine with all of it until she got to the hands. Then she encountered fingernails, ring marks, a thumb whose callus came from some unknown lifetime friction. The humanity of her assigned body was no longer deniable. That is what the frozen man's boot did to me.

I discussed it with Billings. We'd begun having lunch together every Monday to review findings and generally gossip. 'My advice is to be careful,' he said. 'We serve at the king's pleasure, and all he sees in that block of ice is Subject One.'

'That's my whole point. We're dealing with a person in that ice.'

'There are about three thousand assays we might conduct with materials at hand, none of them possible without Carthage's good will. And I needn't tell you that our man is more intent on fame and glory than on ethical particulars.'

‘That’s why I think my job is to raise these questions.’

‘Thus do I repeat: careful.’

Good advice that I was unable to follow. Instead I found myself daydreaming in the control room, imagining the frozen man’s former life when I ought to be watching the monitors. During my tasks in the sterile, chilly observation chamber, I found myself pausing to study his whiskered face through the blur of ice. Hello in there.

Later, Carthage told the press he thought in those weeks that I’d gone soft, lost sight of the goal, that sort of thing. Actually, after the boots, I felt the goals becoming clearer. They just weren’t the same as his.

Carthage treated the frozen man like a diamond. He had the doors at the Lazarus Project’s Boston office, now our headquarters, changed to bullet-proof glass. Guards stood at both entries, and it took the swipe of a security badge to get into the control room, into the elevators, even into the bathrooms. It made me nervous. I often checked my bag multiple times on the way to work to make sure I hadn’t left my badge at home.

The walk to work crossed the park where sometimes as many as twenty people gathered daily to condemn us. Carthage won a court order to keep them from the front door, but truthfully the security goons scared me more than any protestors. One Friday, back in March, it was chilly and raining so I brought down an urn of coffee. The guards turned away, didn't even take their shades off. The chanters thanked me, however. One even God-blessed me. An old man offered me cookies. I took one too. Why not?

Not all were so pleasant. One tired-looking woman was there with her kids every day, a permanent sneer on her face. Was this vigil some kind of home-schooling? If so, it was hard to say what they were learning. She was the one who snarled at me the day before Halloween, when I brought over some candy corn.

'Keep your poisons, you sick monster.'

Trick or treat to you too, sister.

That was six months ago. Yesterday the protestors lost their final court challenge, which sought to prevent us from attempting to reanimate the frozen man. I was relieved, but the ruling had troubling aspects. The judge agreed to let the Project continue, fine. But his decision called the frozen man 'salvage goods,' meaning that he was our property, and no protestor could determine how we treated our property. Not so fine.

Though I knew we'd have a crowd later, that morning only the woman with her kids was there. She looked haggard, like a photo of a dust-bowl victim. As I approached, her kids seemed happy enough. The boy drove a toy truck along the side-walk's edge, making engine noises. The girl sat on the bench reading, her feet swinging.

Still I was anxious walking past the mom. The girl didn't look up but the boy noisily reversed his truck so I could pass without stepping over him. I gave them all a smile. The mother caught my eye and it was like being slapped. No words were necessary. Her look was pure cold hate.

I hurried over the crosswalk to the front doors. A guard looked at me with as much expression as a mannequin. He wore a flak vest and rested his right hand on a gun.

'Good morning,' I chirped, lifting my I.D. into his line of sight despite passing him every morning for nearly eight months now. He nodded without speaking.

I noticed something new in the atrium, a digital counter of some kind. The numbers were 2 feet tall, so anyone outside could see. At the moment they read 00:00:00:00.

A media crowd loitered in the normally empty foyer, though it was only 8.30 and we were not initiating till 10. Still, I was part of the 9:30 briefing, so I signed in at the security desk, hustled to the elevators, swiped my badge and grabbed the next one. The reporters spotted me, rushing over to shout questions as the doors closed.

Like that, the morning's calm evaporated. So the future of the day took shape: my main task would come before the reanimation attempt, turning my collected observations of the frozen man into a profile. My job was to tell everyone who this Subject One was. I'd gathered a few clues, researched several more, believed I had a fair idea of the man and where he came from.

Time would reveal that I had only the barest inkling.

CHAPTER 8

PROCEDURE FORTY-SEVEN

(DANIEL DIXON)

Why Carthage chose me, I have no idea. There are nine TV crews here, plus the AP and Reuters, and an even dozen newspapers. Wilson Steele from the *New York Times*, author of two books on cryogenics, flew up from D.C. So did an associate editor from *National Geographic*, a woman who has stood on both of the planet's poles, brought there by her own two feet. I am not being modest when I say this is out of my league. These are the heavyweights in my biz, the ones whose employers buy paper by the ton.

So you should have heard my editor at *Intrepid* gasp in disbelief when I told him Carthage was going to use a press pool for the reanimation, and that he had chosen yours truly to report for it. All the other media will work from the story I file. No tape recorder allowed, just old-fashioned handwritten notes. A global byline for me, no less. I love it, but I don't get it.

The briefing is moving as slowly as a coal train.

Granted, we ought to know the science at least superficially. An intro by the techies makes sense. But after all these months of waiting, I can't keep still.

Then who should present next but Dr Kate, who I haven't more than glimpsed since our shipboard days. She looks as delectable as ever, wearing a forest-green dress, looking slender and strong. Amazing what happens when a woman gets months of ocean salt out of her hair.

'Here is what we know about the frozen man so far,' Dr Kate says, settling in at the podium like a teacher comfortable with her class. 'Some of this is evidence, some is deduction. The curious among you may find it interesting.'

The projector throws a photo on the screen behind her: that famous outstretched hand, an image now seen round the world. 'The partial thaw enabled us to learn a few things,' she continues. 'He is male. He has no wounds nor, according to a CT scan, any internal bleeding. He was dressed not like a sailor but like a professional, possibly a ship-owning merchant.'

Dr Kate steps away from the podium. 'Already these findings raise questions: why was he on a ship? Where was he going? If he drowned rather than freezing, will that mean a lack of remnant oxygen in his cells, thus no hope of reanimation? Still,' she takes a deep breath, 'here's what intrigued me most.'

The projector shows a rough gray surface, with

a vague shape in the middle. 'This is the bottom of his right boot. If we look closer, with side lighting for contrast—'

The next slide shows a big C, with wheat sheaves on either side like you see on the back of old pennies. Dr Kate is smiling now.

'This image is the trademark of a bootmaker. With a little digging, I determined that it belonged to Cronin Fine Footwear. That company, before being destroyed by fire in 1910, was located in Lynn, Massachusetts.'

'Wait a second,' calls out Toby Shea, a reporter from *The Boston Globe*. 'Are you saying the frozen guy was from around here?'

She nods. 'His boots were, at least.'

'Could we please desist from referring to Subject One as "the frozen guy"?' Carthage has stood, hand on his belly like a portrait of Henry VIII. 'There is anthropological value in Subject One's history, but the central concern here is one of science. To wit, thank you Dr Philo and allow me, ladies and gentlemen, to describe what happens now.'

As Toby Shea hurries to the back of the room, dialing his cell phone on the way, Carthage launches into an explanation of the reanimation process: how the immersion solution will control melting, how pumping warm oxygen into the man's lungs will thaw the body's interior, and lastly, how a strong magnetic field will lift the electrons of his body to a higher valence.

'If we are correct,' he says, rubbing his hands together, 'if this reanimation works, then we may have also identified the missing ingredient for the origins of life. What caused the primordial ooze to organize itself, all those billions of years ago, into separate objects, with internal coherence, purposes like survival, and a means of reproduction? What started the incredible machine? What was the spark? The great Albert Szent Gyorgi once said, "What drives life is a little electric current kept going by the sun." If Subject One awakens, however, we might venture that the primary catalyst for the creation of life may not have been electric, but magnetic.'

His eyes are bright. Erastus Carthage may be one of the world's most disagreeable human beings, but everything he has 'ventured' – all the way back to his college thesis about soy's impact on soil nitrogen – every one of his theories has proved correct.

I hate that my skepticism is weakening. I still can't stand him, but Carthage is giving me a killer byline, a global exclusive, on the story of a career. Also, let's be honest; it's still wide open whether this concept can work. Will we end up with some century-old guy who sits up, asking for a cigar and directions to a place where he can take the world's biggest leak? Or could we find ourselves with a charred carcass that experienced nothing more than post-mortem defilement?

'Dr Carthage?' It's Steele from the *Times*. 'There

is growing dissent over your work, from religious conservatives to cell scientists of some standing – notably Sanjit Prakore from the University of Auckland, who was briefly part of your institute. They say you're being hasty, perhaps even immoral. How would you respond?'

Carthage shrugs. 'They have questions. You have questions. Everyone has questions. Today we will find some answers. The time for unknowns has ended.'

He claps his hands twice. Techies, grad students and post-docs all leap into action. Until this moment he has not acknowledged my presence. Now, with the slightest lift of his chin in my direction, he signals that yours truly should follow him into the control room.

Gerber is already in there, Grateful Dead riffing away at top volume. 'Not Fade Away.' He spots Carthage and lowers the music, but his grin is mischievous and he's humming to himself. Could he be high? Not possible, this business is far too serious. But he jiggles his eyeballs side to side at me, and I have to wonder.

The room is packed with equipment: monitors, gauges and enough medical gear to crowd an ICU. There's also some kind of counting device, with red numbers set at 00:00:00:00. Because of the haste with which things came together, all the wires run straight up into the drop ceiling, so looking across the room requires ignoring the cables and power cords running vertically from every desk.

The staff physician struts past, a short bearded guy by the name of Borden. I haven't had a sit-down with him yet, so I toss him a question as he passes. 'Hey doc, what are you expecting today?'

He halts like a soldier, turns slowly to me. 'I expect us to replace God.'

Not what I was prepared for, is what it was. 'Excuse me?'

'What we do today will render the creation myth obsolete. We are as gods ourselves now.' Off he struts like a rooster ruling the barnyard.

'Dr Humility strikes again,' Gerber calls loudly. To everyone else it's a typical Gerber non-sequitur, but I know what he means.

I turn the other way, toward the far wall, which is all window. On the other side of the glass – in the now famous temperature-controlled chamber – lies a body with a veneer of ice like the plastic of a convertible's rear window. I can make out his ratty sideburns, the cut of his clothes. The room is sealed, equipment sterilized, and air filtered down to the microns to minimize the infection risk. One modern germ in this guy's antique immune system, and we could kill him as we wake him.

Billings is in there too, wearing surgical scrubs and a mask. He's checking the bedside gear, marking something on a clipboard. His brow is furrowed.

The corpse – is that the right word for this thing? – is suspended by straps under its head, torso and legs, hanging over a vat of salt water. They call it the animating vessel, I call it a tub. A bank of gauges on the wall show the water's temperature, salinity, pH, conductivity, viscosity and a few other things. This modern-day Frankenstein is going to take a great big bath.

Thomas is running the reanimation. Nobody ever briefed me on his degrees or credentials. Most days he's a glorified secretary, but today Carthage put him in charge. What's that all about?

Before I can consider this any further, Carthage gives one of those signaling chin lifts. Immediately Thomas pulls a clipboard from his briefcase and calls the room to order. 'Subject One reanimation commences now, mark time and date.'

Technicians along the side wall all slap counters atop their computer screens. Gerber switches off his tunes.

I feel the room's tension, but I do not believe. My parents were beyond saving. Death is final. This is theater, nothing more.

'Let's try not to screw this up now, shall we, people?'

That little motivational speech comes courtesy of Borden, our own lab Napoleon, who makes a little circle with the point of his beard as if to stretch his neck. I read annoyance on faces all over the control room.

Thomas takes a pen and checks the first item on his clipboard. 'Procedure one: begin oxygen pump.'

Gerber pulls his crazy hair back from his face, sucks a hissing in-breath through his teeth, then presses a button. A compressor begins moving beside the body, an old-fashioned ventilator with visible bellows. From the machine, a tube runs into a black box that contains a heating coil. From there it snakes into Frank's mouth, taped into place, and I don't know how far in it goes. The bellows contract, the dead guy's ribs rise. The bellows expand, his chest falls. It's all machine, but still it's spooky to see his body move. Through the audio feed we can hear flakes of ice dropping to the floor. Billings hovers over the body. Any skin newly exposed, he swipes dry and attaches electrodes.

'Procedure two: 50 percent immersion.'

Dr Kate works two handles by the side wall, and the straps lower the frozen man's body into the salty bath. She stops when the water is even with his ears. Again Billings places sensors, on one of the screens I see him reaching inside the dead guy's shirt. A gauge says the water temperature is 104 degrees. Hot tub time.

Thomas continues with procedures, item after item. I pay partial attention as he drones on, procedures nineteen through forty-four. They take maybe two minutes each, a few run longer. Mostly I'm concentrating on the cameras. One shows the frozen man's hands, another his face, still another his torso. If anything happens with this body, if anything changes, we will see it and the videos will capture it. A notion occurs to me then, the difference between a Frank and a Subject One: the first kind is a person who deserves some privacy. The second kind is a lab object that is not going to receive it. This is definitely not private. The guy could wake up and shit himself, and we'd all be right there watching, his every grunt and grimace immortalized on video.

'Procedure forty-five.' Thomas is grinning like a jack o' lantern. 'Commence magnetic field.'

A technician near Gerber turns a large black dial. 'Done,' he tells Thomas.

Gerber turns to me. 'Remember magnets when you were a kid?'

'Excuse me?' I say. For nearly two hours, no one has been speaking but Thomas.

'Remember?' Gerber says. 'How you'd try to force the ends that didn't like each other to touch anyway? My family had these colorful letters of the alphabet, for the fridge, right? Those little suckers had surprisingly strong aversion to one end of the other letters. That's what we're doing now with the electrons in this guy's body. Pushing the magnetic dislike.' He sniffs. 'I know it's complicated science, but I keep thinking about those fridge letters.'

'Gerber,' I reply, 'sometimes you are one spacey dude.'

He laughs, then sings quietly. '*Friend of the devil is a friend of mine.*'

'Procedures forty-six and seven,' Thomas continues as if he hasn't heard us. 'Commence electric signal and initiate reanimation clock.'

And there, far down the aisle of desks with their climbing wires, Dr Christopher Borden flips a light switch on the board in front of him, then another, then another, down a long row of them. He stops with four switches left.

There's a low hum, and a meter jumps on the gauge before us. Carthage is staring at the floor. Dr Kate covers her mouth with both hands. We wait.

I watch those video screens. Zilch. The only change is that the last of the ice has melted, and we see his face at last. It's thin, hungry-looking, and blue as if it were bruised. His lips are pursed, like he died in the middle of an argument. It strikes me again: this is a dead man. I know the look, believe me. He is just as gone as mom and dad on the lawn that night with the house in flames behind them, and me on my knees sucking air like a sprinter. You could fill the room with flowers and play sugar-sweet organ music, it won't change a thing: this experiment is on a dead guy.

The electronics hum, the ventilator wheezes, the clock counts. Nada.

Thomas casts his eye up and down the procedure list. Carthage reads the gauges one by one. Gerber sits back in his chair, hands behind his head. We wait. Nothing.

Thomas coughs, kicks weakly at the air. 'Hell.'

'Patience,' Carthage says. 'We've waited decades. We can withstand a few minutes more.'

Abruptly he turns to Borden, who tilts his head back as if he's been asked a difficult question. Carthage clears his throat. 'Doctor?'

Borden blinks slowly, like an owl. 'You should know, we're nearing the ceiling.' He flips another switch, then one more. 'Anything above that, you're not going to want what wakes up anyway.'

Which makes me wonder why he designed a system with those two remaining switches in the first place.

Carthage turns back to the gauges. We wait.

And there it is, the faintest thing: a beep.

No one needs to tell me what it means. Another fifteen seconds pass, and we hear it again. One beep. Carthage nods at Thomas, who uses a remote to start the red counting device. One second passes, two, five, while the numbers to the left stay at 00:00 and the ones to the right blur through tenths and hundredths of a second. A device beside the clock reads 4 bpm. The EKG oscilloscope shows one set of the peaks and valleys of a heartbeat. Now there are two beeps and a silence, and the reading is 6 bpm.

Carthage has his eyes closed, one fist against his chest, like a conductor in a moment of orchestral bliss. A flurry of beeps, the reading is 12 bpm, then silence. I'm watching the clock, jotting in my notebook when each beep occurs. But there are no more. Dr Kate goes to the window, peering in on the motionless body. The silence stretches: half a minute, 45 seconds, a minute.

Carthage opens his eyes. 'Dr Borden?'

'There is a risk.'

'Which is?'

He clasps his hands like he's making here's-the-church. 'We could . . . possibly . . . set him on fire.'

'I am listening,' Billings calls into the audio feed. 'Good morning gents, the man in the oxygen-saturated room is paying attention here.'

Carthage ignores him. 'How high would we be going?'

Borden runs his eyes down the row of switches. 'This would be, I'm approximating here, about the voltage of an electric chair execution.'

Dr Kate spins with her mouth open, but Carthage speaks before she can: 'Proceed.'

'Are you sure?'

Thomas speaks up: 'Dr Carthage is always sure.' And Carthage gives the slightest revelation of a smile.

'Really would hate to get roasted alive, you know.' Billings backs away from the tub, edging toward the door. 'This is safe, right lads?'

'You bet,' Gerber mutters. 'If you like toasted marshmallows.'

And Borden throws the next switch.

The electric hum grows louder. The video feed shows water around the frozen man jiggling as though it were about to boil. A little steam rises.

Dr Kate shakes her head. 'This cannot be right—'

But the beeping starts again. It's stronger, the oscilloscope shows regular peaks and valleys, the counter reads 31 bpm.

'We're getting blood pressure,' calls a post-doc whose desk faces the wall. The lights of his screen are reflected in his glasses. 'Fifty over thirty-two.'

'Amazing,' whispers Dr Kate, and I watch her return to the window beside Frank's body. She touches two fingers to the glass. 'This is a miracle.'

Carthage frowns at her. The beeps gain steadiness: 44, 54, 61 bpm.

'Dr Carthage, we're at 90 over 66. And steady.'

'Ladies and gentlemen,' Carthage declares, 'we have reanimation.'

Everyone roars. There is loud cheering, clapping of hands. Gerber yells 'woo-hoo' and spins himself careening on his chair. Borden lets out a whoop: 'We did it!' Billings puts two fingers in his mouth and whistles. Thomas pumps Carthage's hand like he's a politician who just won an election. 'Congratulations, sir. Congratulations.'

I stand there mute, feeling about as smart as a cow. Damned if I know what to do with my skepticism now.

Carthage waits till the noise subsides, then turns to Gerber. 'Start weaning.'

'Whoa.' Gerber's eyebrows rise. 'Already?'

'Start.'

Gerber starts to speak, then catches himself.

'You're the boss. Your funeral.' And he turns down the pressure in the ventilator.

Immediately the beeping dips, the post-doc calls lower blood-pressure numbers, everyone looks to Carthage. He holds one finger up and waits. Sure enough, a moment later Frank's heartbeat recovers, gains ground, rises in tempo. And then Carthage, that egotistical genius, that bastard, smiles.

'What's funny?' Gerber asks.

'We are playing him,' Carthage says, 'like a violin.'

'This man is not a toy,' says Dr Kate, though Carthage keeps smiling like a politician on inauguration day.

With that I discover something incredibly basic that I have been missing the entire time. These people hate Carthage. All of them. Yet they are here anyway. They are that hungry to be part of a discovery. How I will ever put that in an article I have no idea, but it is as clear as the beeping every time our Frankenstein's heart beats.

Carthage lifts his chin at Gerber. 'What portion is vent and what portion is him?'

Gerber scans his instruments. 'We're 20 percent. The rest is our icy sailor.'

'Cut him off.'

Dr Kate turns. 'It's too soon—'

'Cut him off.'

'Easy now,' Gerber stands, moves away from his desk. 'This is a lot all at once, here. Let's catch our breath for a second.' His back to us, he shakes his hands as if to dry them. 'You'll kill him, you know.'

'Obviously I disagree.'

'It is annoying how almighty smart you think you are.'

'Do it now.'

Gerber turns to face us. 'Just chill for one minute, would you?'

Carthage snorts. 'And establish his dependency on life support?'

'How about we let him take fifty consecutive breaths?'

'Right. Now.'

I am writing all of this down, every word. And realizing that Gerber, in his domain, possibly has stature greater than Carthage in his. No wonder he's standing firm.

'Everyone is expendable,' Carthage says through clenched teeth. 'Even the illustrious David Gerber.'

Gerber laughs. 'Then so are you, dude. And if this experiment tanks, which of us do you think it will hurt more?'

'Everyone please,' says Thomas, sliding into Gerber's seat. 'There's no need—'

'Thomas, no,' calls Dr Kate. And Gerber comes rushing.

But even a layman like me can see that it is done. The control is all the way down. In the chamber, the ventilator bellows have stopped. The beeps continue nonetheless. Thomas escorts his clipboard back beside the boss. 'There.'

Carthage nods at him, a little silent attaboy. Creepy.

Gerber stands with shoulders drooped. 'He's breathing on his own.'

Dr Kate moves near to him. 'Yes.'

'Whoa,' Gerber whispers. He returns to his desk and flops in the chair. 'Way to go, Mr Frank. You just broke all the rules.'

Suddenly the breathing stops, the beeps cease, the EKG flat-lines. The room goes as quiet as a cemetery.

'Well there it is,' Gerber says to Carthage. 'Now do you want the vent back up?'

Carthage holds a hand out. 'Wait.'

But the machines are silent. There is no heart beat.

'Blood pressure's cratering,' a tech says.

'We're losing him.'

'Body temp is 92,' Billings calls. 'Nearly thawed. Our window is closing.'

The room responds with silence. Carthage nods at Gerber. He presses buttons, the bellows recommence. The frozen man's chest rises and falls as before. But the beeps do not restart.

'Give me more magnetics,' Carthage orders.

'Right away,' a technician replies. He spins the dial on his desk all the way to the right. 'That's everything we have, sir.'

Still no beeps. 'We're in trouble,' Dr Kate says.

I'm scanning the room, ready to scribble whatever happens next, but there's no action, no words. That little freeze goes on a long time. I cannot believe my story is going to be about how Carthage's arrogance brought the whole thing down.

Finally he takes a deep breath. 'Dr Borden? More charge please.'

'Seriously?'

Carthage does not answer. Borden considers his row of switches. 'Erastus, each of these circuits carries ten times the power of the one before. If Subject One were alive, the present amperage would kill him. If we increase, there's just no telling.'

'Excuse me gents,' Billings says, waving one gloved hand. 'Permission to leave the chamber, Dr Carthage?'

'Erastus,' Borden says. 'He may explode.'

'Unseal the chamber, please,' Billings says. 'Right now.'

Carthage claps his hands once. 'Senior team, quickly, I want your opinions.'

Thomas lowers his clipboard. 'You do?'

'Dr Philo, do we risk explosion or cease our experiment?'

She looks him in the face. 'We say we are seeking answers. Nature is giving us one, unequivocally clear and direct. People are not krill. Let him go.'

Carthage barely blinks. 'Dr Gerber?'

He runs fingertips over his keyboard. 'We're boiling him like a lobster. Stop it.'

'Dr Billings?'

'You would risk my life for the chance to restore his? End the reanimation.'

'Dr Borden?'

The little doc ponders. ‘I told you before that the heart wants to beat. Maybe this one has been stopped too long. Or maybe we should have kept him frozen till we’d tried more species between shrimp and something this huge. But today we cannot change what we do not know.’ He stares at his switches. ‘Shut it down.’

‘That leaves you, Thomas.’

‘Oh sir.’ He turns to him. ‘What do you want me to say?’

‘Ha.’ Carthage claps a hand on Thomas’ shoulder. ‘You should be a diplomat.’

Thomas blushes, of all things. Now I’m dying to know the back story. Did he grow up fatherless or something?

Meanwhile Carthage pulls out a bottle of hand sanitizer. He squirts a blot into one palm, then puts the bottle away. Casually, without hurry, he wipes his hands one on the other, between the fingers, wringing the thumbs. You’d never guess what we’re in the middle of. At last he faces us.

‘We are to stop then? It is unanimous? Subject One cannot be reanimated? Let us be cold for a moment, and calculate. What would be harmed if we try and fail?’

‘Our consciences,’ Dr Kate says instantly. ‘Our decency.’

Carthage sniffs in her direction. ‘Dr Philo, always in earnest. And never shy about questioning the ethics of her boss. I remind you that Subject One is as full of potential as a fetus, if he receives our successful intervention. If we fail, the worst that can come of our efforts is that he will remain as the rest of the world sees him: dead. Meanwhile we have the slim but scientifically sound possibility that we might be right about cells' latent life-force. And that being right could save humanity from untold future suffering. Perhaps your mighty ethics could soften somewhat, given that opportunity?'

'Well,' Gerber leans back, 'there is such a thing as desecration of the dead.'

'We're guilty of that already,' adds Dr Kate.

Carthage waves them aside. 'Superstition. Also, beside the point.' He faces the full staff, arms wide. 'People. Aren't you curious?' He laughs, it sounds like a bark. 'This is the only thing that matters: don't you want to know what is possible? Aren't you dying to find out?'

He gives them a moment to digest his argument. Then he turns, and if the man had worn a cape he would have flourished it. 'Borden.'

'Yes sir?'

'Now.'

Borden raises his hand, presses one finger against the switch, hesitates.

'Now,' Carthage repeats. And the little doctor flips the thing up.

At once every gauge tips all the way to the right, overrun by voltage. There are sparks among the wires overhead. Several computer monitors turn off. The lights flicker, then the room goes black. And there we all are, dumb as a box of rocks, standing in the dark. There is not even the sound of ceiling fans.

A few seconds later the lights blink back on, the fans start, computers reboot. Gerber pulls back his wild hair and faces Carthage. 'Backup generator?'

Carthage nods. 'Always have a plan B.'

And the beeping starts again. There is no hesitating this time. It is steady, climbing, and sure. When it reaches 20 bpm Borden turns off that highest switch. The beeping continues. Now the progress is linear. One by one he lowers the switches, and Frank's heart holds its pace, settling at 90 beats per minute.

'That's it,' Borden says, throwing the last switch down. 'He's on his own.'

Billings slumps against the chamber door. 'God in heaven.'

The counting clock shows 15:47 has elapsed since that frozen heart first started beating. At 20 minutes Gerber begins ventilator weaning, minuscule steps this time but reaching full withdrawal in half an hour. The other techs report steady blood pressure. Billings returns to the body and records his observations: finger twitches, eye motion.

No one is celebrating this time. It is a solemn business. I ask Thomas for a copy of the procedure list and he hands me the original – can he have no idea what this thing will be worth? – and tosses the bare clipboard on a desk. Then I slump in a corner and wonder what has just become of my world-view.

'Rock solid.' Gerber sits back. 'Sixteen respirations per minute, 92 beats give or take, zero life support.' He clasps hands behind his head. 'Baby's all grown up.'

'Well.' Carthage tugs his collar like his tie is too tight. 'I suppose I don't need to tell you all how disappointed I am.'

'*What?*' It's Borden this time. 'What are you *talking* about? What better result could you possibly expect? What do you want?'

Carthage rubs his forehead with one hand. Then he stares through the glass at the living, breathing, silent creature. 'I want consciousness.'

CHAPTER 9

THE ANCIENT DICTIONARY

(KATE PHILO)

Within hours of reanimation Gerber had designed a way to stream the frozen man online live. It was a massive invasion of privacy, but after I'd committed the apparently unforgivable offense of questioning Carthage's ethics in front of the whole staff, I remained too far in the doghouse to make an effective objection.

In fact he put me on the night shift. It was a clear comedown from supervising all the researchers on the ship, but truthfully I didn't mind. I liked the quiet control room, the hum of machines, the silent body breathing away in his chamber. Whatever misgivings I felt about the Project and my role, the frozen man had a reassuring presence.

Often Billings was there, toiling with his small specimens. Sometimes I'd convince him to take a break from cataloguing, the drudgery of organizing chaos before experimenting on it. He'd been right about that giant berg. It contained a trove of small species, including hundreds of flash-frozen sardines.

Dixon now had a desk in the lab offices, where

he sat most nights pounding the keys of his laptop. While he was working, the man had impressive focus: scowling, impervious to distraction, pausing to dig through his notes before plunging back in. When he took breaks I would engage him in conversation, hear war stories about his newspaper days. But the moment he sensed me beginning to feel sympathy or connection with him, he would utter something coarse or sexist, driving me away from him, back to my work.

Gerber was present most nights too, as unsleeping as an owl, though I didn't understand why. What more systems design work could there be? I supposed he was doing basic science, which is to say he was being paid to think.

I can't say that I had many tasks myself. The electrodes remained securely in place, barnacles on the man's chest and back. Computers monitored everything day after day without a single crash. I felt like a nightwatchman, everything but the flashlight.

Meanwhile the red digital clock counted up the frozen man's new existence, 9 days, 9 hours, plus change. Gerber's tracking program changed camera angles every 30 seconds. Simultaneously, vital signs, plus brain and heart activity readings scrolled continuously across the bottom of the screen. Anyone wanting this data could download it for free. In the first 24 hours, our web site had 14 million hits. They stayed an average of 26 minutes, which Gerber declared exceptional for the Internet.

'Most people don't even have sex for that long,' he said. Across the room, Dixon snickered into his coffee cup.

Gerber spent his nights trolling the blogs. Not surprisingly, the frozen man made the web buzz like a hive. Each morning Gerber emailed the wildest finds to all Project staff, until people complained of the inbox clutter. After that he hung a little bulletin board on the control room wall, with a scroll above: *Perv Du Jour.* Periodically he thumb-tacked his latest discovery there, which most staffers read each day the minute they arrived at work.

One night, for instance, Gerber hung screen captures from frozenmantwin.com: photos of our guy with imaginary siblings he might have had. One person posted an actor who'd played the grizzled sheriff in a 1960s TV western, someone else suggested an Olympic swimmer with sharp cheekbones. Others were more inventive: a skinny monkey with wide facial hair vaguely like the frozen man's sideburns, even the flared front grillwork of a tiny, fuel-efficient car.

Not all responses to the reanimation were odd. Both of Massachusetts's senators called with congratulations. The president of M.I.T. sent flowers. I was meeting with Carthage when they arrived. While Thomas centered the arrangement on the credenza, I suggested that we invite sociologists to study who was following the reanimation online most fervently. Carthage glared at me, barked, 'Focus.'

A cardiologist in Milwaukee said the frozen man's EKG matched that of a person in deep rest. 'It's like the day after a marathon and his body is recovering,' he said. Dr Borden, Carthage's pet physician, calculated the frozen man's appetite and wastes and said he had the metabolic rate of a hibernating reptile. I thought: how humanizing.

A Chicago epilepsy researcher downloaded encephalograms and declared that 'Subject One is using as close to one hundred percent of his brain as had ever been measured for a human.' I wondered how she could draw such a broad conclusion with only three days' data. But once she had told CNN it was 'like he was shining a light in every corner of his mind,' the phrase replayed worldwide every thirty minutes for a day and a half. She may have rushed to judgment, but it made her a household name.

The popular culture backlash was close on her heels. Tabloids speculated on whether the frozen man was an alien. Religious conservatives held public prayer vigils, between calls on Congress to shut us down. 'Lazarus was raised by the Son of God,' one congressman said, pointing at the sky. He had white hair and a fantastic speaking voice, nearly operatic. 'Who do these Boston blasphemers think they are?'

My sister Chloe sent emails, her tone evolving based on the news coverage: 'how did you land a job with people so smart?' became 'what are you doing up there anyway?' and then 'what is wrong with you parasites?' *Gee, Chloe, aren't you special?*

The cryogenics companies, whose freezers were stuffed with bodies, watched their stocks soar. A national news magazine ran a cover story, 'Rebirth of the Biotech Age?' Our front desk fielded over 600 requests for interviews, all declined. For reasons known only to himself, Carthage continued giving Dixon exclusive coverage of the Project, putting his byline on newspapers around the world. Thus the reporter never gave anyone a moment's peace. Twice I felt his humid breath as he leaned over my shoulder to watch me work. It took a long cold glare to get him to back off.

Then a security guard spoke to the TV cameras clustered outside the front door like a pack of neglected dogs: 'These people are secretive,' he said, taking his sunglasses off for once. 'We don't even work for the building's owners. The project hired us so no one could snoop on whatever they're doing in there. Who knows what they're up to? Who knows what their plans are?'

Carthage watched the news, raised an eyebrow, made a call. The security company replaced the guard while we began occasionally using the loading door in back to get in and out of the building. But the damage was done.

Still, the postal service had to deliver our mail in a separate truck. It sat in the basement in wheeled canvas bins, envelopes to the brim till someone had time to open them. Gerber pulled one letter at random. It said the staff of the Lazarus Project was the spawn of Satan. He laughed till his crazy hair shook. Billings tried another, from a Texas billionaire wanting the Lazarus Project to revive his dead stud thoroughbred.

Meanwhile late night TV comedians joked away: perhaps vice president Gerald T. Walker should come to Boston, to see if the Lazarus Project could bring *him* back from the dead too.

Yet by noon of the fifth day, the web comments primarily complained about how boring the video stream was. Don't you love the world's attention span? Bring a man back from a place beyond human conception, and people will be amazed for approximately one hundred hours. I sat down to read the postings, but after about ten I had to stop. Here was a ravenous beast with an insatiable appetite. I wondered how these people would have responded to the painfully slow work of Pasteur, who developed germ theory only after the deaths of three of his children. Or Fleming, inspired by the horrific rate of World War I infection deaths to work ten years seeking an antibacterial agent, only to discover penicillin by accident. Or Salk, chasing polio for eight years while tens of thousands of children were afflicted, their lives saved only by the prison of an iron lung. *Ho hum, very nice, now how about curing malaria by Monday?*

Gerber started a new protocol: editing each day's tapes into ten-minute summaries. Carthage asked Dixon what time would be ideal for publicity, so the tape releases occurred to suit the noon and 6 p.m. TV news cycles. The media appreciated the editing, and most led their newscasts with our tapes. But just after the third release a madman shot up a mall in the Midwest. We became yesterday's story.

Carthage was disappointed but it was fine with me. We needed more time for science. Chloe, despite her digs, had a point. We did need to understand what we were doing. What was the goal? Also what would we do if the frozen man actually woke, spoke, became fully alive in this new time?

No one wanted to discuss these things. No one even contacted the research vessel, hunting hard-ice off southern Argentina, to say we had restarted a dead man's heart. The crew was slaving out there in a frigidity I knew too well, as solitary as a satellite in space.

One night I walked to work with an equally isolated feeling, like I was adrift in a vast sea. Maybe my mood was caused by the rain, a spring downpour that left puddles in the streets. Also the sidewalk protestors had become more numerous, thirty or so. One snarled at me as I hurried past. Then it didn't help that Gerber and Billings were both so intent on their work when I arrived, they had not even paused to say hello.

The all-night shift stretched ahead like a straight, flat highway. In minutes I had confirmed that the monitors were working fine, no adjustments needed. The video tracking changed angles on schedule. The counting clock marched onward. Various devices had begun their daily automatic backup.

I surveyed the control room. Headphoned, Gerber

stared at his screen while typing ridiculously fast, waiting for an answer to appear from the ether, then bursting his next reply. Billings was inventorying samples, inking labels, thumbing them on test tubes.

His obsession had created a distance between us. Days earlier I'd approached Billings in the lab for the lunch we shared every week since the bourbon-soaked train ride. 'Hey Graham, it's almost one. Do you want Chinese or Italian?'

'Is today Monday?' He kept his eyes to the microscope.

'All day and part of the night.'

'Truly sorry, lovely,' he said, turning his head while remaining bent toward the table, 'but I'm right out flat. This little bloke on the slide won't live but another hour.'

'No problem,' I said. 'Next week.'

He didn't answer, eyes already back to the lenses. Wandering back to my desk, I realized something: after the power failure during the frozen man's reanimation, in which Borden had risked an explosion, Billings hadn't returned to the main chamber once. Maybe he was avoiding lab politics. Or maybe he was excited by those small creature specimens. Billings had performed so many reanimations on tiny creatures, he was sharpening predictions of which organisms would wake and which wouldn't, how to increase survival times, how to use less electricity. I'd read the notes, his typical staggeringly good documentation. Still, he'd moved his computer to a corner, dodged most monitoring shifts, skipped staff meetings unless Carthage himself called them.

I considered Billings again from across the room. He slid a tray of newly marked specimens back into the portable freezing rack, then pulled out a fresh one: two hundred test tubes without labels. He coughed mildly, settling in his seat for the new batch.

Finally I allowed my eyes to wander in the one direction where there might be something engaging. The chamber. The frozen man lay in there breathing as slowly and steadily as waves hitting a beach. Two days before he had wiggled a pinkie. The next morning the staff consensus was that it had twitched, the distinction being that it revealed only nervous activity, not intentional motion. I disagreed, but the final documentation called his move a reflex. Otherwise the man was as still as a statue of the Buddha.

I went to the glass. The frozen man's clothes were ragged but tailored. He still wore those signature boots. His sideburns looked almost comical, Spanish moss on his cheeks. Borden had proposed washing him, shaving him, dressing him in fresh garments. Carthage said not yet, no point in disturbing the body until it reached stability. Until then, no one was to enter the chamber without specific tasks or explicit permission.

Yet there I was. Standing at the intersection of science and magic, fact and speculation, cold research and warm curiosity. Then the frozen man breathed – not the usual deep slow bellows, but a gulp, as though he had said the word 'hoop' on an in-breath. I spied my colleagues, both absorbed, neither aware of my existence much less my temptations.

Oh, temptations. Sometimes we give in after a long tussle with our consciences. Other times we surrender with a kind of glee. I hurried to the security panel, punched in the access code, waited for the door to hiss aside, tiptoed into the chamber.

The cameras panned mechanically to face me, so I felt like a fool. Of course the monitoring system would record my every motion. The damage was done. Still, what misdeed was I committing? Breaking an arbitrary rule? I could argue that I was responding to a change in the patient's respiration. The video would confirm it.

I approached the padded table on which he lay. His chest rose and fell. There was no other activity, no further 'hoop.' Just a body in the deepest imaginable sleep. Leaning over, I studied the frozen man's face. Deep lines crow-footed out from his eyes, as though he had spent a century not waiting in ice but staring at the sun. His jaw was straight and angular. Sideburns puffed from his cheeks like the tufts of a lynx. His expression was perfectly, inscrutably blank.

I leaned down, who can say what possessed me? Call it curiosity, call it wonder. I brought my face closer to his neck, nearly to his chest, felt his presence. This man was not an abstraction but an actuality. Never in my life did I feel clearer about wanting to know about something. I took a good deep sniff. He smelled like leather, old leather.

Suddenly I remembered finding my father's briefcase in the back of a downstairs closet. I was thirty, it was ten days after he died, Chloe was preparing our childhood home for sale. The briefcase held no papers, it was as retired as my father had been. But when I lifted it to my face, the leathery scent contained the memory of him: a lovable round man who over the decades encouraged me in every enterprise that captured my attention: dolls, dentistry, design, then dissection and doctoral studies.

The frozen man's smell was similar, but dustier, richer. Like an ancient dictionary. I should have brought a clipboard, to record my observations. But what value is there in documenting something as subjective as scent? I straightened with a sigh. In the morning, Carthage would demand explanations.

At once I realized. Inadvertently – I will maintain that view till my final days – accidentally, I had placed my hand on his wrist. We were skin to skin. I jerked back as if stung. Or as if I had done the stinging. Had I washed my hands when I arrived at work? No, not since eating supper hours earlier. Then I'd walked through Boston, held stair railings, used my keyboard, swiped my security badge. My hand could have carried all manner of potential infections. I backpedaled from the table, then spun for the door and the quiet sanctuary of the control room.

Billings had gone somewhere, the tube tray half-filled. Gerber hunched forward, contemplating the floor between his feet while his forehead pressed the keyboard, one letter repeating endlessly on the screen: VVVVVVVVVVVVVV.

I sat at my desk and willed myself calm. I made a show of checking email, not registering what was on the screen. My infraction might prove minuscule. Probably I had not done the frozen man any harm. Maybe where I'd stood made it impossible for the cameras to see.

His skin was warm, like any man's.

I noticed something then, a grittiness on my hand. I rubbed my thumb and pinkie against each other, there were granules like sand. I brought my forefinger to my mouth. I tasted.

Sure enough: salt.

CHAPTER 10

CONTAMINATION

(ERASTUS CARTHAGE)

You are never the person who cannot sleep. Your life is so hectic, your hours so full, the end of the day has for decades provided a reliable routine, dull as it is effective: washing up, drawing drapes, elasticing an eye shield into place, and sleeping like a child. No nightmares, no waking till morning. Pity those whose sleep is a lesser experience.

Yet here you are. You've stirred in your bed, watched the clock drip away a tedious hour, mashed your pillows and tugged your sheets and still your mind can't stop a cycle of thought that spirals only to the end of this project, straight to ruin. Unproductive, but rest draws no nearer. In capitulation you've dressed, left the hotel, taken an appallingly filthy cab, and arrived at the Lazarus Project to find the place all but asleep.

The control room is unmanned. Totally unacceptable. What if Subject One experienced distress? The monitors are off, breaking the video feed. What if Subject One began to move with intention? It would not be captured for posterity, nor for proving success, nor for persuading future benefactors. The only mildly reassuring discovery is that Gerber is away from his desk. You wondered if that oddball ever slept.

The reanimation clock marches onward, now reading 11:14:46:22. Eleven and a half days gone already. Time is the enemy and you know it. If Subject One follows the pattern of every other creature revived by your lab, more than half of the opportunity with him has passed. Twenty-one days, that is the outermost lifespan projection, based on the patterns of revived krill. Three weeks, and the man shall be once again dead.

Moreover, you know well that sound research does not occur quickly. The scientific method is a taskmaster sterner even than you. Yet the Project has mere days remaining, after which this costly reawakened flesh will frenzy itself back into uselessness. The media is already gone, except for Dixon. The extra animation staff returned to their regular lab jobs. You have even received offers from nursing homes – nursing homes! – as though Subject One were some weak-bladdered geriatric, rather than one of science's greatest achievements.

Time may occur in seconds but you feel its weight by the ton. Nonetheless, grains of sand are cascading through the neck of the research hourglass, while the creature lies inert, there in the dimly lit chamber, his heart beating on like the world's most expensive watch. Thus have matters at the Lazarus Project stood for eleven and a half days.

You cross to the schedule chart, and observe that it is Dr Philo's shift. She has abandoned her post. Were she present, you would fire her immediately. But wait: there is an instructive power in dismissing someone in the presence of others. Tomorrow morning, with an attentive audience, heads will roll.

Till then, the boss is on duty. A superstitious person would say you couldn't sleep because you intuited that Subject One was unwatched. Superstitious people are fools.

You turn the video monitors on, screens crackling as they warm up, and wonder how things could have slipped so far. Has frustration distracted you? The science was unimpeachable. The methods, if inelegant, were defensible. And the findings were revolutionary. Your discovery that cells whose function ceased through rapid freezing were not dead but rather possessed a residue of latent energy, and your application of this revelation to raw material provided by the laws of chance and opportunity – these achievements ought to stand on a par with Einstein, Darwin and Freud. Then why has Subject One not awakened? Why hasn't this damned slab of meat opened his eyes?

No danger of that happening anytime soon, either. A yawn insists itself on you. The clock shows there are hours till morning. Which is better, then: for the next shift to come to work and see you covering the lapse, or for them to arrive and find no one here? In the former case, the implication would be that people can shirk their duties and expect a superior to compensate. You can't have that. You will leave a note on the control desk, so that whoever has the next shift feels the fear of imminent consequences, and conveys that concern to others in the Project. There's a pad and pen on the back table.

'Tonight upon inspection the control room was empty and video feed turned off. Worst, the subject was unattended, risking his life and the future of this project. Tomorrow will bring a return to utmost discipline.'

There. Three sentences. You tuck the paper between rows of letters in the master control keyboard, and start for the door. But at the last minute, some movement at the periphery of your vision turns you back.

You hadn't looked since the screens warmed up but now it's there on all the monitors. Dr Philo is not absent, she is inside the chamber. She brought a metal stool, on which she perches like a bird. She's wearing a white surgical mask, but otherwise has ignored sterility protocols and dressed in jeans and a blue T-shirt. She's looking the subject directly in the face. The motion that caught your attention was her arms, coming up to hug her knees.

And then, from the video feed, you see her commit the unthinkable. She reaches forward and places her hand on the subject's forearm. She has touched him, skin to skin. She has contaminated everything.

You reach down for the switch that opens

communication with the chamber. Someone has moved it. Impossible. You search the desk and cannot find it. There it is, under a sheaf of papers, Gerber's clutter where there should be cleanliness and order.

You press the button marked SPEAK. 'Dr Philo. *Dr Philo.*'

She does not turn or even blink. The chamber's audio must be turned off somehow. How could you have missed the Project's weakening discipline? How has Thomas failed to keep you informed? Her hand remains unrepentant on his arm.

You feel an impulse to rush in there and – what? shout? assault her? – but any further intrusion would worsen the biological impact. Does this imbecile not understand about bacteria, immune systems, germs?

She has risked everything you have accomplished, your entire life, for some meaningless sentimental gesture. How can she not see this? She sighs, you can tell even through her mask. You thought you had hired a genius, that's the word Tolliver from the Academy had used about her, genius. Instead Dr Philo proves herself no more than a schoolgirl, fretting away over this inanimate subject like some strange reversal of sleeping beauty. It occurs to you: if she kisses him, you might kill her.

But there is another motion, caught in the overhead camera on the ceiling. You grab the switch panel that controls the video feed and zoom in on his face. Yes, there is no doubt of it: his expression is changing. His facial muscles work. They twitch, they frown. Praise the fates that you restarted the video equipment when you did. Here is history, witnessed by you and logged, real time, on a tape that belongs to you alone. The images could be hawked online at prices that might subsidize months of hard-ice collection.

The subject still moves. His throat muscles clench and release, clench and release. His jaw lanterns side to side. You zoom the camera lens even closer, not wanting to miss the slightest detail. Nothing surpasses reason and the scientific method. And then he does the most astonishing thing: he coughs. It comes through the monitor, the audio must be working in that direction at least, and you stand amazed. More than one hundred years after his life appeared to have ended, Subject One has coughed. Never before has a simple human throat-clearing had such profound implications.

He coughs again, harder, his face showing sharp displeasure. His wrists tug at the restraints. Then his mouth opens wide and he takes a huge breath, a great gulp of air. Yes, you say to him in your mind. Life. Breathe it in.

And then the miracle, if such things existed: his eyelids flutter. They pull. They strain. The subject opens his eyes. They are wide, hazel-colored, struggling to focus. Finally something clicks into working order. With rapidity those eyes take in the room, the lights, the machinery, and lastly Dr Philo with her hand on his arm.

The expression on his face is utter terror.

‘Are you—’ he croaks, then swallows, then attempts again in a whisper: ‘Are you an angel?’

Dr Philo hooks her surgical mask down with one finger and you can see that she is smiling. It is a grin for the ages.

‘No,’ her voice chimes through the audio feed. ‘I’m Kate.’

PART II

REANIMATION

CHAPTER 11

THE BUTTON

My name is Jeremiah Rice and I begin to remember.

There was a girl, she had fiery hair and ran toward me. I feel her fervent breath on my neck. She liked to dig in my pockets. I would put things there for her to find: a stone, a candle stub, a penny. She had the littlest hands and her name was . . . her name was . . . It will come to me.

I was born Christmas Day, 1868, which makes me, well, how does one count? Thirty-eight Christmases passed before I went to sea, and one more whilst abroad. How many since then? I cannot say. They have not yet told me the year. Till this moment I had not thought to ask. I am too busy reorganizing. Remembering.

They arrive in pieces, my recollections. Fragments as though I gathered broken glass. I flinch, and wince, and inhale in gulps. When the flood grows overwhelming, I sleep, deeply like the ocean that took me. And wake once again to amazement.

My father went to war, they tell me, and came home changed. My sisters were years older than I, born before he went soldiering. My mother made a habit of prayer for his safe return, and when that was answered, of thanksgiving. My sisters said that after the conflict he rarely conversed, worked twice as hard, and often stared at things in the distance. Delivered into this life nine months after his return, I knew him no other way.

It was a war about skin. Cotton too, the price of shoes, and whether a nation ought to accept the severing of its bonds over internal strifes. I learned these things in school, which now is vague like a group of desks in a field of fog, blurred voices and a chalkboard just at the edge of sight. The war about skin I remember, because of the day of my mother's burial. It was 1880; I was twelve. For some reason she'd chosen to butcher uncooked pork with a paring knife, punctured her thumb, and the infection climbed her arm like black string under the skin. It progressed so rapidly, even amputation would not have saved her. On the walk home from the graveyard my father began to speak.

'Never do a job with a too-small knife,' he began, in his usual epigrammatic manner. But then he continued, remarking on the war, its causes and his experience. I had never heard him utter so many consecutive sentences. Although we'd just left a burial, grief like a yoke on my shoulders, still I felt giddy with the intimacy of his revelations. Antietam, Vicksburg, Gettysburg. The sound a ball made as it rifled past your ear. The way a body resisted when you thrust a bayonet, and then gave under the blade. The sight, calming and frightening both, of enemy fires across a meadow at night.

It was, he explained, all he had known until then about death. Useless though, he concluded, because it failed to prepare him to lose a wife.

On that single occasion he spoke of it, never after. But once was enough for me to recall all this time. Oh time, now there is a marvel. Here on the other side of my mortality, I would like to see Mr Darwin explain this one. I would like to hear Mr Edison's theory. I would love to hear Wilbur and Orville make a flight of these fancies.

Thus far the people here explain little. They feed me gruel and attach things to me. There are numbers and noises, measurings and masks. They speak curtly and fear the dark. Still I am in restraints. Canvas holds my wrists and ankles as though I were a convict. Hm. Life's ironies are never subtle.

Cold in childhood, I remember that too. Frigid mornings when the bucket by the stove wore a skin of ice. Dawns in January when my turn came to light the stove, and I blew hard on the reluctant embers. Dressing whilst still in bed was another way to warm, I discovered one morning when the rafters bore layers of rime from my breath rising through the night. I walked to school under clear cerulean skies, and learned that cold is a particular beauty, its own brilliance for those who are hardy – and wearing wool, ha.

Perhaps that is what brought me to adventures, the appreciation of cold. I presumed that because I loved nature, nature loved me. Now I know better. Nature does not know I exist. Nature goes about its affairs, and if I stray from a path in the woods, a bear may eat me. If I dive from a cliff, the rocks will tell untroubled truth upon my flesh. And if I go a-sailing, seeking unnamed species in the northern seas . . .

Not yet. I am not ready to remember that particular cold quite yet. But what was her name? Her fingers when stretched wide reached smaller than my palm. Her voice was high like a cricket, melodic like a wren.

The only one I trust here is the first one, present at my waking. She comes when the others are gone. She turns down the lights, a pleasure in a room with neither night nor day. She releases my wrists and tells me to unbind my ankles myself, so that I may be the agent of my own eventual freedom. I do not comprehend her meaning but her tone is one I trust. Merely I bend my knees, enjoy my legs' motion, and hold my own counsel. She insists I am not a prisoner, they want to protect me from illness.

The one who seems the boss would not last five minutes in the shoe mills of Lynn. *Lynn, Lynn, city of sin, never come out the way you went in.* Someone would arrive at work one morning to find a hogtied foreman's hand in a gear, mangled to uselessness. Or his necktie noosed on a rafter, the fellow tiptoe all night for his life's sake. Or, on one occasion, his carcass in a vat of tanning chemicals, nose down.

Then they would bring the suspect to me, he would confess, and there would be my Solomonic duty – measuring his conduct against its provocation. Law versus justice. I am a servant of the former who hoped to achieve the latter. I remember the courtroom but not the building that held it. What, though, what was her name?

My wife – goodness, I had a wife – was Joan. It comes back to me directly now, a marvel from some cobwebbed bin of the mind. I hear her voice from a moment of irritation. Distracted by the courts, I have forgotten some chore. The horses need fresh feed. The farrier did not come as scheduled. We are low on coal. But that is not all. There was another side to Joan which only a husband would know: any time I reached for her, slid an arm around her waist after supper, or woke in deep night to find our bodies spooned in their bedclothes and my wrist between her breasts, or blinked in the light of a new dawn having awakened with desire, always her reply was the same: I am willing. Always that, she never once refused me. I am willing. I can hear that whispered generosity even now. What a thing, how she gave herself to me, and how ardent her body was with mine, till we shined, her understanding and her compassion and possibly even her pity, all in that quiet phrase: I am willing.

It was a decent home, not grand. Gaslights, good chairs in the parlor, a front hall with wide stairs. We sought an honorable life at no one's expense, and that ambition brought us to the threshold of greatness but not its inner rooms.

Perhaps that was what led me to exploration. Vanity, and the desire to make a name for posterity. After all no one remembers a magistrate, however just. No one but drunkards and wife-slappers and horse thieves, and the unfortunate victims of their deeds. Yet I submit that it was not weakness which widened my horizons. It was the power of curiosity, of wanting to know. So many great minds in that time were enlarging our sense of the world. Who would not wish to dine at the tables of discovery?

Here they make the same claim. Hm. I listen to them all day, puttering around me as though I have no ears. They say I am a first. Not a miracle, because there are scientific explanations, but nonetheless. Thus they measure my body weight and heart speed and arm strength. They draw my blood, I watch it pulse from my body into their glass tubes. They snip my hair into a clear bag. One afternoon a man went finger to finger, toe to toe, trimming my nails into a little white tin. Meanwhile I must eat particular foods, void in containers they remove as though sacred, and remain in this tiled room with the long window that looks upon their desks and nothing beyond.

They say my name will be known forever. I say, not yet. Not until I tell it to them. I have saved that secret for her, the one I trust, since it fell back into my memory during the afternoon as if dropping from the sky. Until I say it aloud, my name is a fist of coal, warming me silently while one remembrance after another tiptoes forward from its chilly hiding place. Yesterday she promised to tell me where I am, what year it is, and how I came to be alive. I relate to her that these questions, in my time, could only be answered by God. She laughs, and tells me no such luck, she is just a thirty-five year old biologist from Ohio. Still, as the day drones along I cannot wait for the others to leave, and her to come.

Say what you will about the human spirit. I am but four days awakened in this new world. Yet already I have preferences, already I have hopes.

I wonder what has become of precious Lynn now. Wait. It was not precious to me. I preferred Boston. Lynn was Joan's home. When she consented to marry me, it was with the understanding that we remain near her mother and brothers. A chilly crew they were, every one, but her father had died in the war between the states. Thus Lynn was her sanctuary. Hm. Now I recollect that she was older than me, my Joan. By six years, and whilst my sisters snickered and implied, I felt it no compromise. Joan had dignity, and a generous way before I knew about her willingness. Age explained why we only had the one child. The girl's name, though, her name . . .

People work oddly in this time. They claim to stand on a frontier of humanity, yet strike me as uniformly joyless. Instead of performing tasks together, they sit each apart, staring at a square of light, speaking into a flat cone, and rarely addressing each other at all. The rather, they bicker like chickens.

At day's end in the courthouse there was a hush, as in a library, and a feeling that something important had happened in which we all took part. People came to us with their conflicts, enmities and betrayals, and we sought by inches to make sense of it all. It was solemn, and often I walked home under the weight of responsibility.

Here at a fixed hour they darken their squares of light. They push chairs in against their desks or leave them indifferently askew. They grunt goodbyes. Clearly I am missing something, for they seem exhausted by their labors though mostly what they did was sit.

And then she comes. The only one to tell me her name. The one who neither complains of her tasks, nor troubles her fellows. She carries a board with a spring to hold the papers. She has shown me the words she writes there, a neat and minuscule script. I have learned much from her already: there is a thing called blood pressure, it measures the energy with which the heart pumps vital fluid through the body. Edison's inventions, which transformed the humble shoemakers of Lynn into factories of mass production, also led to the lights that hum overhead. Apparently the workers here tolerate their insufferable boss because he alone had the capacity to bring this enterprise together, and thereby to coax me back into wakefulness. They are all in his debt. So, I suppose, am I.

Tonight she is late, but I do not worry. I know she waits till others have gone. She says a machine in the other room records all that we say and do, just as court clerks of my time would mark down every syllable of testimony as though it were scripture. People all around the globe see those recordings, through squares of light like those in this office. She has explained these concepts several times and I still do not comprehend. When I am strong enough to withstand the germs that outside people carry, she has promised to bring me into the other room and show me. I do not understand this concern about the germs. Is the world that drastically unhealthier than when I was first alive? Is the air so different?

At last she arrives. One remaining scientist comes and goes, busy with tasks. She tosses things on a desk, then hurries to start various machineries. She moves with feline grace. No one notices. Oh, I misspeak. One person has noticed, the heavyset man who writes down everything that everyone says. I know his kind. I was a judge for eight years, then participant in a celebrated Arctic voyage. I recognize a reporter when I see one.

Midway through her tasks, she hangs her jacket on the back of a chair. I spy a glistening on the shoulders. Ha. It is winter. There are still seasons. Longing swells in my chest. There is a world outside in which snow falls in the evening. I cannot wait to see it, smell it, feel the cold on my face like the touch of familiar fingertips.

A memory appears then, complete, like a jewel. An evening when I returned home late from court, hoping that the little girl would still be awake. I am striding up the last hill toward home, scent of supper in the chilly air. It is December, a few flakes falling, the fat ones that melt upon landing. All the way home I have been preoccupied with the case before me, a procedural knot I must somehow untie. When I see the gas lights out front, I realize I have forgotten to put something in my pocket. I feel a minor panic.

There are four buttons on my vest. I never use the bottom one. I clasp it firmly, knowing that if Joan discovers this deed I am certain to hear her disapproval, and yet yank that button free. The fabric does not tear. I pick the remaining threads away, the vest appears as new.

Tucking the button in my pocket as I march up the walk, and lo – the little one is not inside readying for bed. She is outside, waiting for me in her red wool coat, and runs to greet me as though out of a dim corner of the mind. Her shoes slap on the stones. I remember my delight as if it were just this moment. I squat down to embrace her, she burrows against me like some wonderful animal. Her tiny hand digs in my pocket, and her chilly little nose pokes right in the middle of my cheek.

Agnes. Her name was Agnes. My daughter Agnes.

The woman from now rushes into my chamber before I can hide my tears.

CHAPTER 12
THE SMELL OF MEMORY

(KATE PHILO)

On my walk to work that night, a bluster of unseasonably late snow caught me unprepared. All I'd worn was a light fleece jacket, not nearly enough for the wind and wet. I hunched into myself, hurrying to stay warm, thinking about the night of work ahead. Suddenly a protestor stood in my path.

'You, woman, are going to burn in hell,' she snarled as I jumped in surprise. She pointed at our building. 'Just like all the rest of them in there.'

I stepped back, taking in the full gang on the sidewalk. The group had definitely grown, up to maybe forty. Half stood under umbrellas, the rest clustered in raincoats or ponchos. There was no one else on the street, it being Friday night and the weather nasty. The front door guard was inside by the security desk. I was on my own. So I brought myself to a calm place.

'Every one of you,' the woman cried. 'Life is sacred and you are demeaning it.'

'Life is sacred, I agree,' I said, using an intentionally quieter voice. 'But what we are doing—'

'Stop.' She clapped her hands over her ears. 'Don't you dare try persuading me, seducing me with false science. What you are doing is morally wrong, and you know it.'

'I know no such thing,' I replied. 'I was simply trying to tell you—'

'Don't,' she said, backing away as if I held a gun. 'Don't you dare.'

Another protestor, an older man, guided the woman away by her elbow. She stared back at me with venom. I escorted my rattled self across the street.

Minutes later in the control room, I could think of plenty of snappy replies I might have made, but none was the equal of her passion and certainty. Where did it come from, this twisting of faith into judgments of others that bore no doubts?

Meanwhile the red digital clock reminded me that 14 days had passed since the frozen man's reanimation, 2 weeks in which life was being redefined. Or, to be accurate, the old definition destroyed but the new one not yet written. Carthage made regulations about the rare circumstances under which entering the observation chamber was permitted. Essentially, male technicians helped the frozen man upright to go to the bathroom, or performed rudimentary occupational therapy to restore his atrophied muscles. That was all.

Watching them manipulate his legs like so many parts of machinery, I complained; Carthage ignored me. It felt like the rules were designed to prevent my efforts, or anyone's, to humanize the poor lab creature we'd awakened.

If not for the frozen man trusting only me, speaking clearly only to me, I probably would have been unemployed. Carthage had sat at his desk a few days earlier and made that clear, Thomas nodding along with him. My ability to remain calm in dramatic circumstances served me well in that particular chewing-out.

So did the frozen man's behavior. When Carthage entered the chamber, the person in the hospital bed conspicuously looked the other way. Perhaps he'd heard himself referred to as Subject One a few times too many. How I longed to know his true name. But he was occupied with trying to understand what had happened to him, his reaction alternating between panic and lethargy. So I spent my nearly idle nights at his bedside, easing him into the now. He'd ask questions in a frightened voice. I would answer almost in a whisper. Around everyone else, the frozen man was silent. Without me, there was no link. It was not an ironclad means of job protection, but someone had to establish rapport across the centuries.

My father would have told me to resign. Dust off my resume, renew contacts, maybe sublet the apartment. Tolliver would always take my call. In hindsight, that advice would have been sound. But at the time, no one knew where we were headed. So I decided to indulge Carthage, for the privilege of witnessing history.

Moreover, this scientific marvel was not a special bacterium, nor a cloned sheep. We were now responsible for a living human being, which carried moral obligations whose depth we had not even begun to fathom.

My remaining tasks, however, barely reached the clerical level. PhD notwithstanding, I took every overnight shift without complaint. Arriving at work that snowy evening my job was to check monitors, reset recording devices, perform other administrivia. Billings was busy downstairs, experimenting on sardines. Gerber was M.I.A., but would likely surface before dawn. The last tech grunted 'have a good shift' to me and escorted his backpack out into the weather.

I slipped off my coat, hanging it on a chair, and scanned the gauges. The frozen man's blood pressure had dipped, all in the last 15 seconds. Then I heard him through the audio monitor, snuffling.

Of course I dashed in. Respiratory stability had been an ongoing concern. I raised my hand to slap the red button on the wall, hesitated, then punched the password into the numeric keypad instead. No point calling the cavalry till I'd investigated.

It was not his breathing. It was his heart. The man was crying.

What I did – sure to bring a fresh round of recriminations the next day – is what I believe any human being ought to do for a fellow traveler on this planet who is overcome by sadness. I rushed over, I hugged him.

The frozen man curled into me, sobbing. I wrapped my arms around his shoulders. He tried to lift his hands but the straps prevented him. He fell back then, clenching his jaw to regain self-control, so I made my next mistake. Or no, others later called my actions mistakes. I call them caring. I undid his wrist straps. Covering his face, he spoke through his fingers. 'I am ashamed.'

'Don't be,' I reassured him. 'Please. There is no shame in sadness. Besides, being restrained like this would depress anyone.'

I knew Carthage would not hesitate to put the frozen man's weeping on the web, if he thought it would generate donations. I felt the impending invasion of privacy with dread. *This was not science, it was voyeurism.* Here was a moment for me to retreat, cover my ass and stay out of trouble, yet my impulse was the opposite. Only a monster can see a person weep and not take action because of something as lowly as a boss. So I leaned down, opened the ankle straps, lifted his legs so he could know he had liberty.

From the hallway I fetched the wheelchair set aside for a moment that everyone thought was months away, but which had now arrived. By the time I rolled it to the bedside, the frozen man had composed himself. He was sitting up, stretching his ankles this way and that. 'I need to tell you something.'

'And I need to show you something,' I replied. 'You first.'

'My name.'

'Your name? Fantastic. I've been dying to know. Please.'

He put a fist on each thigh. He straightened his back. He looked me in the eye. I cannot express how riveting it is to make eye contact with a man from another time. Because it was thrilling, I went calm: folding my hands. Waiting.

'My name is Jeremiah Rice.'

'How do you do, Jeremiah Rice?' I laughed, clasping his hand, giving it a vigorous shake. 'Kate Philo, at your service. It is a pleasure to meet you.' I hesitated. 'May I ask how old you are?'

'The last birthday I recall was my thirty-eighth. Today I deduced with fair certainty that my last clear memory comes from nineteen hundred aught six.'

'Well, you have a mighty gap between your thirty-eighth and thirty-ninth years.'

'A paradox that warrants considerable explanation on your part.' He tugged on one whisker. 'Is there anything from my time that remains in the here and now?'

'Good question.' I scanned the chamber, looking for something reminiscent of a world so far in the past. But it was all new, everything: fluorescent lights, digital clocks, the security keypad instead of an old-fashioned key. 'I'll have to get back to you on that,' I said. 'But Jeremiah, that's a Biblical name.'

'I came from a mother of faith.'

'Were you in the clergy?'

He shook his head. 'I was a judge.'

A judge. How lucky was the Project, to have reanimated a public figure? I stifled an urge to run to the computer, ferret out the history of the man with that name and profession. There would be ample time for digging later. Instead I pointed at the main camera, his eyes following my finger. 'World, this is His Honor Judge Jeremiah Rice.'

'Good evening.' He smiled wanly, not at the camera but at me.

'You are remembering things now?'

'All day.' His smile vanished. Then he turned his face sideways, as if listening to something in another room. 'It has been a flood.'

'Do you think you could handle some new memories? Created right now?'

After a moment, he returned from wherever he'd gone. 'That would be welcome.'

'Excellent.' I knelt by the bed, drawing slippers onto Judge Rice's feet. 'Remember I said I had something to show you? Well here we go.'

One summer in college, when I was still debating whether to pursue medicine or bio research, I worked in a nursing home in Atlanta. One afternoon Nurse Emma pulled me aside. She was an enormous woman with a small head, an almost comical appearance, but she possessed the confidence that comes with rock solid competence.

'I seen how you hoisted that big fella earlier on today, and you listen honey. There's only one way to lift a fat old man without you hurting yourself,' she said. 'You watch me now. Like this.' She squatted, bending her legs like a longshoreman, keeping her back as stiff as wood. 'All the hoist is in the knees.'

Emma was right. Over that summer many workers injured their backs, but I used her lifting technique without coming to harm. I also fell in love with colorful, patient, frail old people, watching nine of them die before I went back to school. I cried openly over each one, Emma shaking her head. 'I took you for a weeper, sure, but criminey what a faucet you got.'

The grief from those nine put an end to my career indecision. Laboratory creatures were never going to break my heart. Or so I thought.

Remembering Emma's instructions now, I squatted beside the bed and extended my head. Judge Rice hesitated, so I lifted his arms and wrapped them around my neck. He pulled back. 'Forgive me, Dr Philo. I am not accustomed to being so familiar.'

I faced him. 'Did you ever have to surrender some of your reserve to a physician, or give up your privacy?'

‘Of course. Once on the voyage when I lacerated my thigh, the ship’s physician cut away my trousers before the whole crew.’

‘Well, I am a kind of doctor.’

‘You are? What kind?’

‘Cells, actually. Cell biology.’

‘What are cells?’

‘Ah. A long story. Let’s just say they’re a very tiny part of the body, of which I am a doctor.’

‘I surmised that you were a student. From observing the way they treat you.’

‘That’s a long story too. For now I just want you to think of me in a medical way, all right? My supporting you when you stand, that’s therapeutic.’

‘Therapeutic.’ He raised his arms again, lamely, but I ducked under them and locked his hands behind my neck. Next I straightened, lifting him from the bed. Judge Rice’s legs touched my legs, his torso draped against me like in some high-school slow dance, we stood in an almost embrace. I felt myself flush. So much time had passed since I’d last been that close to a man, experiencing the solidness, the weight of him. I looked past Judge Rice’s shoulder to see the time on the control room clock, 8:52, fixing it in memory to put in my notes later as the moment he first stood.

‘You smell good,’ Judge Rice said.

‘Thank you,’ I said, stepping sideways like a half waltz, bending my knees, depositing him gently in the chair. I hurried around behind so he would not see me blush. 'It's lavender.'

'Where are we going now?' His voice sounded small, almost young, vulnerable.

'That is my question precisely.' Billings stood in the doorway with his arms crossed. 'Kate, dear, may I ask what you think you are doing?'

'Freeing the prisoner.'

'As your friend I urge you to reconsider. Merely entering the chamber could be grounds for dismissal.'

'Pardon my manners,' I said, easing the chair forward. 'Dr Graham Billings, allow me to introduce Judge Jeremiah Rice.'

'How do you do?' The judge held out his hand.

'A judge? It is an honor, sir.' Billings shook hands, recrossed his arms, glared at me. 'You will do this man no good if you are fired.'

'He has been strapped down for 14 days. How long do you think is acceptable?'

'Lovely, you have to maintain a long view of these things. Patience now makes possible all sorts of actions later.'

'Is 15 days OK? 16?'

'You know the politics here. Give an inch to gain a mile.'

'Or to lose another inch,' I said.

'I don't understand,' Judge Rice said to Billings. 'Have I put this woman in some sort of employment danger?'

'Yes,' Billings answered.

'No,' I said. 'I am making my own choices here.'

Billings shook his head. 'Don't do it.'

'Please step away from the door.'

'What about potential infection?'

'Judge Rice has an immune system just like us.'

'But it's utterly unschooled in the hazards of this era.'

'Are you kidding? He was born in 1868, half a century before antibiotics. His immune system could probably kick our immune system's butt.'

Billings staggered. '1868? How do you know this?'

'He told me, Graham.'

'We brought back a man born in 1868?' Billings leaned back against the wall, his mind grappling with this new fact. I rolled the wheelchair past him. The security door hissed closed behind us with Billings still in the chamber.

'I did not understand any of that conversation.'

'Don't worry, Judge Rice.' We cruised through the control room into the corridor. 'Everything is going to be fine.'

'Could you tell me please where we are going?'

I grabbed both handles so we could roll faster. 'To see the world.'

When the elevator reached the top floor, I wheeled Judge Rice into the hallway.

'How did you do that?' he asked.

'Do what?'

'The door closed on one room, but opened on a different one.'

'Oh,' I laughed, 'that's an elevator. We're on a different floor of the building now.'

'Brilliant,' he said. 'How does it work?'

'Well, I don't know exactly. There's a motor on the roof, and cables down to the room we were riding in. It runs up and down a column through the center of the building.'

'Ha ha.' Judge Rice wagged his head side to side. 'A great invention.'

I started wheeling him again. 'I suppose it is.'

When we found the roof access, I discovered it was up a flight of stairs. This was a new experience, to reach the end of where we could roll yet see the destination in plain sight.

Judge Rice tilted his face, considering the stairway as if it were a mountain whose altitude needed assessing. 'What is up there, Dr Philo?'

'The rooftop,' I said. 'Outside, there's a pretty good view of the city.'

'Which city might that be?'

So no one had told him where he was. I shook my head. 'It's Boston.'

'Ha ha.' His eyes brightened. 'I *love* Boston.'

'I thought you might have been here before, since you're wearing boots from Lynn. You'll find the city considerably changed.'

Again Judge Rice cast an eye up the stairs. 'I've

observed how strong you are, Dr Philo. Nonetheless, I don't imagine you could carry me.'

I locked the brakes. 'How about a team effort? The old college try?'

'Excuse me?'

I laughed. 'It means to do your best. Or something like that.'

'*A man's reach should exceed his grasp, or what's a heaven for.*'

'Did you just make that up?'

'Hardly.' He raised his arms toward me. 'Browning.'

I used Nurse Emma's lifting technique, brought Judge Rice beside the railing, slid under his arm, pulled his hip against mine. 'You were well-read, in your old life?'

He took a hesitant step. 'Not especially. I was weak on Homer, for example. Although I loved Shakespeare and Swift, I had no use for Milton whatsoever.'

I smiled. 'I feel the same way. Milton and I have never gotten along.'

'You're teasing me.' He was smiling too.

'More like laughing at myself. Ready?'

Judge Rice took a deep breath. He brought his hand down on my shoulder, gripped the railing, stared straight ahead. 'Ready.'

I moved forward, he lifted his right foot, I hoisted, we rose one step. In that fashion we inched our way up, toward the rooftop and revelation.

* * *

The fire door was metal, heavy, and jammed shut. I leaned Judge Rice against the wall and banged the door with my shoulder. It moved about an eighth of an inch. 'I did not expect this,' I said, banging it again.

'It's fine,' he panted. 'Fine.'

I looked at the sheen of perspiration on his face, his lips white at the corners, and worried that I had made a terrible mistake. What his heart rate must have been, that poor muscle that had only been beating again for 14 days. 'Should we go back down?'

'Not when we've come this far. Assiduity always prevails.' He gestured with his chin. 'You're hitting too high, Dr Philo. Kick it like a mule, right near the handle.'

I stepped to the side and followed his advice. After two kicks the door swung wide. A gust of wind banged it hard against the outside wall. 'Good advice, Judge Rice,' I said, turning in jubilation.

He was on the ground, clutching his throat. I bent beside him, my mind already halfway down the stairs to slap that red panic button. 'Are you all right? Is it your lungs? What is it?'

He swallowed hard, as if he had a stone in his throat. 'You can't smell it?'

I looked around. It was just a concrete stairwell, metal stairs. 'Smell what?'

'The ocean.'

'Oh yes, the salt air. The wind must be from the east tonight.'

'*Poison*,' he gasped. 'It's like poison.'

I searched his face. 'How could it be? I don't understand you.'

He tapped the end of his nose. 'It wasn't just water I breathed in, Dr Philo. It was *salt* water. Salt water that killed me. It feels like someone is scouring my sinuses.'

The wind banged the fire door again. It was early April, but a late winter storm was heaving itself against the city. A gust swirled in on us, part snow, part dust.

'Come on, Judge Rice.' I hooked him under one arm. 'We did this too soon. I'm taking you back down.'

'No,' he said, his face gone hard. I had a feeling the judge was in charge now, the authority from the bench. 'If I am to experience a second life, mystery though it remains how such a thing could be possible, I must live it. I must see the here and now that is my new home.'

'Are you sure?'

He set his jaw, raised his arms toward me.

'Well, then,' I said, 'only a few more steps.'

As I lifted him that time, he leaned heavier into me. I could feel the heat of his body, his exertions. We turned the corner, reached the threshold. Then he took his hand from my shoulder, shuffling the last few steps on his own. I let him go, hovering in case he stumbled, as he moved himself forward into the dark.

I am not a praying person. But I had a moment then, when I wished very hard for him. That he would not be overwhelmed, that he would not get sick, that he would not go crazy. I wished on his behalf, then followed to where he stood.

Judge Rice covered his mouth with both hands, staring with eyes wide. Below lay the streets of Boston, its edges softened by an inch of fresh snow. Streetlamps cast amber down the avenues. Smoke rose from chimneys and pipes near and far. Cars followed the paths of their headlights. A taxi honked twice. Pedestrians crowded the nighttime sidewalks, headed to friends' apartments perhaps or home from a movie. The protestors had departed the green across from our building, leaving a small snowy park. To the right rose the spire of the North Church, to the left stood the sixty-story John Hancock building, its glass skin reflecting the surrounding lights. A jet came roaring into view and Judge Rice startled at that, bending his knees as if to bolt, then followed the aircraft with his gaze as it banked east and out to sea. A police car brought his attention back, blurting its siren just long enough to cut through an intersection.

I stood beside the frozen man, seeing the city with new eyes. It was complex, it was beautiful, I felt a compassion for its people almost like pity. He lowered his hands, any pain from the salt air now anesthetized by the luminous spectacle at his feet.

'Well your honor,' I said to him. 'What do you think?'

Judge Rice shook his head. 'Humanity,' he said, 'you've been busy.'

CHAPTER 13

ON THE RECORD

(DANIEL DIXON)

'That's what he said? We've been *busy*?'

'I told you that already,' Dr Kate said.

I dutifully wrote it down. 'And again, the reason you took him up there?'

'He was grieving. Look at the tape. He'd been crying. Being restrained had depressed him.' Unconsciously, she pulled her hair back. 'After fourteen days, it would depress anyone.'

She wore snug jeans, a white top that looked like it would be soft to the touch. She had a tired look, from working all night and then having to stay for this meeting. Dr Kate slipped off her shoes, turned in the chair and tucked her feet under her butt. I had to scan my notes for a second, just to collect myself.

'What else?' she asked, sounding bored.

We were sitting outside Carthage's office, summoned by Thomas that morning. Billings was there too, sitting apart and keeping his nose in his notes. The door was closed, a murmuring from within. Who would Carthage be meeting with, that early in the day? I was always first, to review the previous day and discuss the highlights tape Gerber pulled together for morning release. Today Carthage had put me off twice, and now this. The security guys downstairs called Thomas away, which gave me a private reportorial interlude. 'How did you plan to get him back down the stairs without assistance?'

'I do not think that calling a couple of techs in for fifteen minutes constitutes a capital offense. Besides, what about Judge Rice? Now we know his name, his profession. The doors of his history are just beginning to open.'

'Look, Dr Kate.' I chewed a second on the heel of my pen. 'How do I say this without making it a leading question?'

She did a slow blink. 'Lead away.'

'Well, this Project is Carthage's baby, is what it is. No Carthage, no ice ship, no Jeremiah being woken up. And Carthage could not have been clearer about what he sees the purpose of this project to be. Research, so that many more people can be reanimated down the road. I've heard him on this till my ears had blisters. Yet you blew all of that off. Took the guy out of the chamber, risked infection, exposed him to the dirty Boston air without so much as a surgical mask.'

'What's your question?'

'Well, I guess it would be this: what were you thinking?'

'There is a balance to be struck here, Mr Dixon.

I would think you'd get that already.' She scooted forward in her chair. 'I am a scientist by profession and inclination, which means I care deeply about what we learn here. But I am also a human being, mindful that Judge Rice is a human being, so I also care about *how* we learn.' She rubbed her forehead. 'When I was in grad school, we injected mice with cancer so we could try possible cures on them. We bred rabbits just so we could take their blood for testing new drugs. If you are really generous, and keep in mind the lofty larger goals we were after, still you could say we were in a morally gray area. Now that we have a person, this . . . this *guy*, in my view we have moved totally out of the gray. I no longer work for Erastus Carthage. I work for the Lazarus Project, which includes taking the best care I can of Judge Rice.'

Billings made a faint cough. I looked sidewise. He was definitely eavesdropping. It had been a long time since he turned a page. Oh well, no skin off me.

'What about the hug though? Not quite so scientific, Dr Kate. Did you forget the cameras were on?'

She pursed her lips. 'The right thing to do is also the right thing to do in front of a camera.'

'Even if it gets you fired?'

'I have only been thinking about that all night long.'

'You can't do old Frank much good if you get canned.'

'Judge Rice, you mean.' She smiled. 'Actually he helped me prepare for this meeting. He offered excellent advice for keeping my job. The judge's legal mind remains quite sharp.'

'Even so, your termination may be what is happening next, right?'

'Well.' Dr Kate sat back in the chair, crossed her legs, folded her arms over her breasts. The body language equivalent of a turtle in its shell. 'Isn't that what we're both here to find out?'

I had to admit it. Yours truly could not figure her out. She was hot, she was young, yet I'd never seen a guy within two miles of her. No ladies calling either. She works for maybe the world's most controlling boss, yet she refuses to kiss his pompous ass like everyone else. An idiot would know that the hug, unstrapping, leaving the range of the cameras, any of that would make Carthage pop his clogs with rage. Dr Kate did it all anyway.

She's not stupid, though. I'd tracked down her grad school advisor, now a geek beyond salvation at the National Academy in D.C., and he said she was a bona fide genius, smarter than Carthage and Gerber combined.

Sure. Perhaps a slight overstatement, Herr Professor? But his praise did lead me to track down her dissertation, on monoclonal antibodies and T-cell lymphocytes, and I curled up with it for a nice evening's education. I have digested my share of opaque research documents over the years at *Intrepid*: bending light, gravitational fields, evolutionary shortcuts in worms, but Dr Kate's? Not a chance. It might as well have been written in Cyrllic.

'I notice you're not answering me,' she said.

I came back to the present. 'I don't know anything. I'm just the scribbler.'

There was a bark of laughter from inside Carthage's office. Who could possibly be in there? My job is to know, yet here I was in the dark. Pissed me off. But I got my answer about three seconds later.

'Great then, Dr Carthage, terrific.' Out stepped Wilson Steele, senior science reporter at the *New York Times*, all six foot four of him. He'd authored two books on cryogenics too: a scientific treatise titled *Margin of Possibility* and a popular one called *On Ice*, which I'd read – and loved – years back. In other words, there goes my exclusive access, my global bylines. I guess the moment was bound to arrive eventually. But damn.

'You have my direct line,' Carthage was saying, while Steele worked his hand up and down. 'Don't be a stranger.'

'No sir,' Steele said. He turned to go, spotted me, and made his giant hand into an imaginary pistol so he could shoot me as he passed. 'Nice work you're doing, Dixon.'

Bastard.

Carthage had already retreated into his lair. 'Come in, come in,' he called after. Of course I stepped back so Dr Kate could go first. Billings stood and snapped his notebook shut, when all along I'd figured he was the meeting after us. I hung back half a second, and Wilson Steele leaned toward me with a whisper.

'You're not really buying any of this crap, are you?'

'What are you talking about?'

'Don't be coy, man. You hanging in till you can expose the whole fraud?'

I chuckled. 'I used to think that way. But this place is legit.'

'Sure it is, Dixon.' He winked on his way to the corridor. 'Sure it is.'

'Daniel?' Carthage called from inside his office. 'Any time now.'

I hustled right along. What was Steele up to?

Carthage sat at his desk, squirting some of that cleaning goop onto his hands. Apparently even a *New York Times* reporter counts among the unwashed. He waved us toward three chairs. 'Be seated please.'

Dr Kate did so, quick and quiet. Billings sat as down as slowly as an undertaker meeting with the bereaved family. I'd never given him much thought, because I pegged him early on as a lousy interview, but right then he gave me a creepy feeling. I shook it away. Time to cast for bigger fish.

'Dr C,' I said, all brass tacks, 'I thought I had the exclusive for the press pool on this story.'

'Excuse me?' Carthage jerked his head back as though I'd spat on the rug. 'What are you talking about?'

'We had a deal. I give you glory ink, you give me sole access. So why is Wilson Steele coming out of your office? I'd like to know if we're in a new game now.'

Carthage shook his head. 'Daniel, Daniel, Daniel. You need to have confidence. I called you to this meeting precisely because I trust you, and wanted you to witness something. Likewise you need to trust me. The Lazarus Project is your story, no one else's.'

'Then what about Steele?'

Carthage dropped his shoulders. '*The New York Times*, Daniel. Even the president of the United States gives them special treatment. Am I to consider myself superior to the president of the United States?'

You already do, I thought. Dr Kate was studying her feet. Billings was reading diplomas on the far wall. 'Of course not,' I said.

'You have enjoyed weeks of stories, published in newspapers around the world. What more could you want?'

I looked at Dr Kate again, then back at him. Carthage smiled. 'Oh, don't you concern yourself about her any more, not one molecule.'

I studied my notebook a second. What the hell, I'd already had a good ride out of this story. What did I have to lose?

'I want the book.'

'The book?'

'Eventually there has to be a book about this

project. The whole chronicle, from hard-ice to wherever the rainbow ends. And it ought to be written by someone who was present for the whole shebang.' I spread my hands wide. 'This book will document work that makes history. It will give a layman's view of how amazing the Project is. And I would guess, given the web traffic, that it would be hugely popular.'

'Making the author both famous and wealthy?'

'Every writer wants to be read. If someone's going to tell this story, why not me?'

Carthage stood. 'Why not indeed?' He paced a moment, then retreated behind his desk. 'Once again you are two steps ahead of me, Daniel,' he sniffed. 'You are perfectly correct about the need for a book. It could serve many useful purposes, for this project and the people it employs.'

'What about the person it reanimates?' Dr Kate interrupted.

Carthage ignored her. He nodded at me. 'I hope you will commence work on this book immediately, Daniel, and write it simultaneously with your news reports.'

'Thank you, Dr Carthage.' I slouched in relief.

Carthage sat again. 'Now.' He rubbed his hands together like a gambler about to roll hot dice. 'Daniel, I wanted you to be present, so you might convey to the public the standards of professionalism the Lazarus Project strives to maintain.'

I waved my notebook, not really following him. 'Ready when you are.'

He turned his full attention on Dr Kate. And then I understood. He wanted me to watch him fire her. She was not quite as indifferent to his power as she pretended, either. Her face had gone white, her eyes narrowed like she was facing into a strong wind, but she remained calm.

'Dr Philo, why do we have cameras in the animation chamber?'

She considered a moment. 'Science, publicity, voyeurism.'

'You are mistaken. I could not care less about the pecadillos and peculiarities of Subject One. It is all about documentation.'

'All?'

'Likewise, your job is science, not social work. When Subject One cries, you do not hug. You take notes, you interrogate.'

'Interrogate? Judge Rice is not some talking maze mouse.'

'We may provide Subject One with counselors at a later date. Psychology is neither your background nor your responsibility. Your task is to gather data. We need to know, to measure, and to record.'

'As a result of my involvement we now know a great deal more about the person we reanimated. I have not done anything wrong.'

With two fingertips, Carthage straightened a paper on his desk. 'Dr Philo, surely the degree of skepticism this project faces does not escape you. If we are ever to be believed, I need an unassailable record of everything we do. Therefore,' he cleared his throat, 'therefore any misconduct captured on camera, and any activity which occurs beyond the monitors' watchful eye, not only undermines my credibility, it jeopardizes the future of this entire effort to save humanity and alter something as massive as our definition of mortality.'

'If you check Gerber's records of our site traffic, you would see the numbers are always higher when Judge Rice is active. Which is to say when he is interacting with me. People are hungry to see him live and move.'

'Saturday morning cartoons are popular too, Dr Philo.'

'Do you consider the revelation that Jeremiah Rice was a Massachusetts District Court judge to be cartoonish?'

'Irrelevant,' Carthage shouted, rising to his feet. He took a deep breath to collect himself. 'I am weary of your recklessness and insubordination. You have been warned repeatedly. You have violated the rules repeatedly.'

'I told her not to do it.'

It was Billings. I'd forgotten he was even there.

'Thanks, Graham,' Dr Kate said. 'Way to throw me overboard.'

'Pardon me, Dr Billings?' Carthage said.

'I'm telling you I stood in the way, at the chamber door, and reminded her what your rules are, and told her not to do it.'

I have always hated people like that, brown-nosers who will knife anyone just to save their own asses.

Carthage approached Dr Kate. 'Is this true?'

'Almost verbatim, and completely beside the point. If you measure my conduct by the outcomes, they indicate not that you should reprimand me, but that you should revise the rules. Maybe give me a raise.'

'Don't speak nonsense.'

'If I had followed your regulations,' she continued, 'this walking, talking man would still be unconscious. Meanwhile precious days would be going by. Or if you somehow woke him, he would still be unspeaking. Or if you somehow got him to talk, no one would understand him. Without me, all you'd have in that chamber right now is an expensive piece of muttering meat.'

Nice turn of phrase, I thought, though I was writing so fast I could not take the time to register Carthage's expression. When I looked up, he was over by the window, gazing down on the protestors. I swear he liked them.

'Allow me to spare us both the turmoil of further bickering,' he told the window. 'You are fired. Immediately and forever. Clean out your desk and surrender your security badge within the hour. Good riddance and good bye.'

Dr Kate studied the digital clock on the wall – it was synchronized to the one in the control room counting how long old Frank had been alive again, just like the one in the hall and a huge one down in the atrium. Only 41 minutes till it hit 15 days. But I could tell by how long she stared at the clock that she was using a ploy every bit as phony as Carthage's pose by the window. After a moment, she said, again with that uncommon calm, 'I refuse to go.'

'What?'

'I will continue to come here, doctor, no matter what you say. If you order the security guards to stop me, I will alert the media so they can film you keeping me out. Who knows? I might even cry.' She folded her hands in her lap. 'I will also invite Judge Rice, who is not the property of Erastus Carthage but rather is a free citizen of this nation, to come to live in my home. I have already retained an attorney who only awaits my instruction to seek injunctive relief against you imprisoning the man you call "Subject One" for one more day. If you oppose me, I will sue you immediately for sexual discrimination in the workplace. While you spend a fortune defending yourself, funding will wither under the deluge of bad PR.'

She stared him dead in the eye. 'Dr Carthage, I am helping this project and this person. I am not your enemy. But if you fire me, you will make me one.'

I'd worked for female city editors with less backbone, interviewed female homicide detectives with less pluck. Carthage was on his way to becoming the most famous scientist in the world – a Stephen Hawking, a Carl Sagan – and Dr Kate Philo was facing him down. Her firing would make the papers, sure as Sunday. But this scene, this very moment I would save for the book.

Carthage scowled. He cleared his throat. 'Do you understand the legal consequences of blackmail?'

'Of course.'

'And it is not lost on you that this conversation has witnesses?'

'No more than it is lost on you Dr Carthage, I'm sure, what a jury would make of security and video records confirming that the one and only woman employed by The Lazarus Project is also the one and only person assigned to work nights, every night in fact, with no time off for three straight weeks.'

The phone rang. 'Thomas, get that please,' Carthage barked. She had him cornered. And here yours truly thought this was going to be just another goddam work day. I flipped my notebook to a fresh page, ready for round two.

Instead Carthage regained himself, and chuckled. 'Following your syllogism, perhaps my error was in hiring a woman, no?' He crossed to the desk, casual as a car salesman. 'I am well accustomed to people wanting to keep their jobs with me. Typically they beg. Or plead, or promise to do better. It's appalling. There's no dignity. But this is the first time I've experienced professional fisticuffs. I must admit, I'm rather enjoying it.'

'I wish I could say the same,' Dr Kate replied.

'Daniel, take note.'

'Sir?'

'Observe.' Carthage squirted sanitizer on his palms, then rubbed them together. 'Often in science we must remember Ockham's Razor, the philosophy which holds that the simplest explanation is also the likeliest. Thus I will keep my actions extremely simple.' He sat against the front of his desk and looked down at her. 'Dr Philo, your employment here is terminated.'

'Sir, it's the vice president.'

It was Thomas at the door. Carthage blinked. 'What are you doing interrupting me?'

'Of the United States, sir. Gerald T. Walker. He called to say he's a great fan of the project, and watches every video update on our site.' Thomas wrung his hands. I had an image flash in my head of a kid who needs to pee. 'He'd like to speak with you, sir. He wants to meet Subject One.'

'Truly?' Carthage was glowing, I swear, face like a coal. He circled behind the desk, his attention redirected, his pique evaporated. 'Put him through, put him through.'

'Right away. Oh and sir?'

'What is it Thomas?'

'He wants to meet Dr Philo as well. Insists upon it. Apparently this morning he saw the hug.'

'Gerber posted new video already? Without my authorization?'

'It's 12:15 sir. You've been in back-to-back

meetings, and you did instruct him to release on schedule on days when you were unavailable.'

'Jesus God.' Carthage pointed at Dr Kate. 'The vice president of the United States, that grinning fool, saw her infernal hug?'

'He said he loved it, sir. Made him cry.'

I laughed, I couldn't help it. Carthage flashed me an annoyed look, then stood by his phone. 'I am waiting for you to put him through.'

Thomas vanished and a moment later Carthage's phone rang. But he did not answer it on the first ring. 'Dismissed,' he said, waving us all toward the door. 'To be continued.' The phone rang again and he lifted the receiver to his ear slowly. 'Erastus Carthage.'

We crowded into the waiting area, Thomas behind his desk pretending to do something on his computer. I still had my notebook out.

'Listen, lovely,' Billings said, 'I'll make it up to you.'

Dr Kate snorted. 'If it hadn't been for that lucky phone call, you would be making it up to an unemployed woman.' And she stared him down.

'You'll see,' he mumbled. 'I'll think of something.'

Billings shuffled off, tail between his legs. Dr Kate put her hands on her hips and gave me the high beams next. 'Is there something more that you want?'

'Are you OK?'

'Fine,' she said, rubbing her forehead. 'Just suddenly feeling very alone.'

Up close, her face overwhelmed me. I had to stare past, and there was Gerber in the control room, headphones on, eyes closed, dancing slowly, probably as high as a seagull. What a place.

'Well, I think that was incredible,' I said. 'Totally amazing. Was that all from the judge's advice? Do you really have a lawyer already lined up?'

'On the record?'

'Or off, whichever you want.'

She narrowed her eyes at me, calculating. 'No comment.'

I laughed. 'You were bluffing.'

'No comment, I said.'

Dr Kate turned on her heel and continued on to the control room. And you can bet I stood there and watched her go.

CHAPTER 14

THE CHAPERONE

(ERASTUS CARTHAGE)

Ten million, that's all you need. Not a nickel more.

Ten million dollars and you could recruit a stronger staff, hire a web developer, employ a real scribe instead of playing ventriloquist with a hack whose ambitions outstrip his abilities. Who knows what you could accomplish with a full-time publicist? Exposure, credibility, fame. There is a prize they give out in Sweden for people like you.

And the lab? Of course you'd launch a second research vessel, to conduct hard-ice searches at both poles simultaneously. The flood of material they would find would predicate a second reanimation chamber. With ten million, you'd avoid any need to partner with those unseemly cryogenics people. You'd alleviate the concern of your existing income source as well. Oh, and then. *Then* you'd offer an intensive fellowship for top PhDs, to share your discoveries and advance reanimation around the world. Yes, you are a generous man. Let them come and learn. The Erastus Carthage Academy for the Advancement of Humanity. Nice ring to it. Dignified. Perhaps Harvard would offer your academy a home. Or M.I.T. Which reminds you, did Thomas write the president of the university a thank-you note for those flowers? You can't recall signing it.

Are they looking tired now, days later, on your credenza, these roses of praise? Later today they'll go in the trash. For this morning, though, you need them to make an impression, to lubricate the request for ten million dollars. In good federal coin, no less.

Why shouldn't you ask? Isn't your project in every newspaper in the world? The *Times* put Subject One on the front page, byline Wilson Steele. The *Post* ran his face, in close-up, under a giant headline: 'Here Comes the Judge.' Aren't the pundits crowing about the return of American supremacy in the sciences? Hasn't China, like some lumbering elephant outwitted by a clever mouse, hastily opened a lab to chase your theories? What riches they must be throwing at lesser scientists, to recruit them to a copycat project. For the director, of all people, they hired the nobody you fired last month, the one who soiled your suit with tea. That lackey a research director? Thank you for the laugh. See if you catch Erastus Carthage in this lifetime.

China has done you a favor, nonetheless, by launching a new space race, the Sputnik of mortality.

All you seek, in order to keep America ahead, is a mere ten million. In the bloated federal budget, it's a fraction of a fraction of a percent. In today's dollars, it's barely anything.

And who better to carry your request to Washington, who more ideally equipped to state your case, than Gerald T. Walker, a man mocked for excessive smiling, but nonetheless one heart-beat away from being leader of the free world? In less than an hour, this fan of the Project and the videos, even that absurd hug, will be here. The mountain is coming to Mohammed.

The timing is ideal. Subject One is upright, speaking clearly. No one can predict how long that may continue. This is the now of all nows.

Walker's advance security has scoured the building. All morning you heard the protestors chanting below your window, TV cameras bestowing precisely the attention these souls so desperately seek. Who cares that they despise your work? Their passion is still a kind of worship. You cannot resist spying on them.

There is a soft knock at the door. You hurry from the window. It is the physician, and you greet him with a nod. 'Dr Borden, I hope you bring good news.'

'I bring the potential for good news.'

You sit at your desk, gesture him to a chair. 'Tell me.'

Borden bustles to the chair, then does not so much sit on it as perch. 'Here's what we know, Day 16.'

The man always comes gratifyingly to the point. You nod. 'Proceed.'

'It has something to do with salt. We're seeing all the expected signs of accelerating metabolism: heart rate, blood pressure, respiration, the gamut. If we did not intervene, he'd be lucky to make 21 days.'

'Based on body mass and the krill projections?'

'Yes. But our nutritional mix has brought mitigating effects. I'd say it's 40/60 that it will work. Frankly though, even if this succeeds I can't predict for how long.'

'Forty percent odds are better than none. And all because of salt? It's that simple?'

'Perhaps slow mitosis while frozen in ocean water alters cell chemistry in some permanent way. You'd need a mitochondria expert to tell you. But the implications are clear. For reanimated creatures, no salt means longer life.'

'How much longer?'

Borden places the fingertips of one hand against those of the other, as if he were holding an invisible sphere. 'How speculative would you like me to be?'

'Best and worst cases.'

'Best case is that we've broken the code, and Subject One lives indefinitely. Subject to the usual diseases, ex-wives, gun shots, et cetera.'

'And worst?'

Borden tugs on his beard. 'Five mornings from now, he doesn't wake up.'

In the moment you allow yourself to digest this

news, the intercom on your desk buzzes once briefly. 'Yes Thomas?'

'Dixon time, sir.'

You'd instructed Thomas to keep him waiting in the outer office a neat twenty minutes. By now he will have reached the perfect simmer.

You rise. 'Dr Borden, you are doing an excellent job.'

'It's an honor to be part of this enterprise.' He stands, then bows, actually bows, before turning for the door.

Dixon, ever the awkward one, enters the doorway first, and they do a little hint and feint to get past each other. The reporter finally makes his way in, the bulk of him somehow an unpleasant surprise, as if you'd forgotten, the soiled trousers, the sports coat with those crude leather patches on the elbows, a half-crumpled notebook in his hefty mitt. You wonder if he has ever lived one intellectually rigorous moment in his life.

'I am glad to see you, Daniel.' You force a smile.

He collapses into the chair Borden just occupied, then poises his pen over a legal pad. 'You going to make a statement on the veep's visit?'

'No no, Daniel.' You wave the idea away. 'I didn't ask you here in your capacity as a journalist. You'll be present for the Walker meeting anyway. No, I just wanted us to have a little talk.'

'About?'

The man is incapable of recognizing a dramatic

pause. His mind is not weak, you consider, merely hasty. Also sloppy, very sloppy.

'About the future, Daniel. For you, for our valuable if impertinent Dr Philo, and for our precious Subject One. No need to take notes just now.'

Dutifully he sets the pad aside, interlacing fingers across the middle of his girth. 'I am all ears.'

'Yes. Well.' You fold your hands as well. 'You see Daniel, the result of our encounter with Dr Philo yesterday is a fortuitous one.'

'How so?'

'Progress in one direction can sometimes cause a researcher to overlook opportunities in an altogether different avenue. And so it is with Subject One. His immense worth as an object of study had dominated my thinking, at the expense of recognizing his value in winning supporters to our cause.'

'You mean fund-raising?'

'I mean friend-raising, Daniel. To contradict the protestors, to avoid soiling ourselves with politics, and yes, to develop a population of interested parties who might enable this project's work to reach its fullest potential. That is where you come in.'

'I don't follow.'

Simply incapable of a pause. 'Bear with me a moment, then.' You sigh, then press on. 'My design is this: let us give Subject One his liberty, so to speak. Let him experience America as it is today, a place transformed from what he once knew. As a tour guide, let us assign the feisty Dr Philo. Let her show him around. Let them be seen. Let the public share in the story, and amplify the spectacle.

'And here is the genius of it.' You lean against the desk and bend toward him. 'To chronicle their every adventure, let us dispatch Daniel Patrick Dixon.'

It is a professorial delight you experience at that moment, watching the idea dawn on him. While he warms his mental hands before the fire of your proposal, you continue. 'If they see marvels, you will tell us. If they are dismayed, you shall render it. If a private bond develops between them' – you pause and deduce by his nodding that he understands your implication – 'you will inform the world. Who will not hunger for every new detail in their explorations?'

Dixon keeps nodding, eyes down now. He drums a pen on his thigh. 'So I'm supposed to follow them around?'

'Sometimes overtly, sometimes less so. Thomas has cameras for you, still and video. Also recording devices.'

He lifts his gaze. 'I am not going to be anyone's spy.'

'Of course not, Daniel. Remember, you are not in my employ. What you are is a reporter, doing his job, getting the scoop.' You swing a little gung-ho fist for him.

'Dr Carthage, let me tell you something.' Dixon places his notebook on the rug beside the chair.

You steel yourself for a confession, please may it not be sordid or embarrassing. 'When I was a kid, just fourteen, my family's house caught on fire. Both my parents died. I pulled them out but the smoke had already gotten them. So I started out with zilch. Literally, no clothes, no family, not even a toothbrush. I'm not saying life owes me anything, everyone has their share of misery. But if I have a shot at getting a little bit back, you know, enjoying just a bit of comfort and cushion, well, only an idiot would say no.'

So there it is. The orphan boy, starved for glory. But you nod slowly. 'Possibly your whole life has been preparation for this moment,' you say solemnly.

'Maybe so. Who knows?'

Thomas knocks at the door, right on cue. 'Final checklist time, sir.'

'Yes, of course. Excuse us, please.'

Dixon stands, starts for the door.

'Daniel, you've forgotten something.'

He turns, spots his notebook, and hustles his big frame to fetch it.

'Be my eyes, Daniel. Be the eyes of everyone who wants to know about this incredible feat. Watch Subject One. Watch Dr Philo. And tell the world what it desperately wants to know.'

Dixon pauses at the door. Is he choked up? 'With all my heart, sir.'

Then he is gone, out on your mission. And you don't even have to pay his wage.

Thomas comes to your desk with a checklist for review. It's all precaution, every i was dotted hours ago. As you scan the list your buzzer sounds again. 'What is it?'

'Front-desk security, sir. Vice President Walker has arrived.'

'Thomas, come with me to the conference room. I'd like you to see this.'

'I'd be honored sir.'

Admit it, you feel a flutter. Now the Lazarus Project goes public. Even if Borden's lifespan prediction is wrong, there will be time to make a valuable impression. If all goes well with Walker, you will begin a national publicity campaign first thing tomorrow. If the past sixteen days have stoked the people's fervor, now it is time for the bonfire.

You lean over the intercom. 'Send him up.'

PART III

RECOVERY

CHAPTER 15

PRESS CONFERENCE

(DANIEL DIXON)

Carthage offered me the first question, a definite courtesy, but I asked to go last instead. That way I would get to watch all the others file in, take their seats, the usual murmur of the ink-stained readying to do their first-draft-of-history business, all the while knowing that I was going to get the punch line.

The chilliness with which the reporters greeted each other, curt nods and low banter, reminded me of watching a jazz group set up. Damn if you would see so much as a smile between them. Nor was there a single howdy-do in my direction.

Well, let them act so frosty. Yours truly already knew my closing question. Six words, and short ones at that. But I could guarantee that old Frank's answer would lead every news report worldwide.

A few correspondents pulled out the day's papers to brush up on the story, but everyone knew the real news was the photo, shot by me, placed above the fold in every rag I'd seen that morning: Vice President Gerald T. Walker shaking the judge's hand, his famous toothy smile so damn wide you would have thought he was meeting the pope. The veep, former governor of a cotton state, had never even been to Boston before. Now he had made the editorial page, a caricature that turned his whole face into an idiot grin. Columnists were speculating that yesterday's photo-op signaled his interest in the top job: Oval Office and Air Force One and my-fellow-Americans. Even if half the pundits were twits, a generous estimate given the ones I've known personally, there was old Frank figuring in presidential politics before he'd done much more than wake up and scratch his belly.

Maybe the protestors helped, since they were increasingly headline-ready. There were more of them now, fifty or so, agitating around the building. Their energy was higher too, which I attributed to Walker becoming our newest friend. Nobody gets powerful without making enemies. The protest group had a boss now, an organizer who made sure the signs were legible and who lined people up behind TV interviewers so the crowd looked as big as possible. He was movie-star handsome, with a Kirk Douglas kind of chin, and was forever toting a clipboard and bullhorn. I made a mental note to find out his story.

Carthage set the news conference up in the first floor atrium. Through the tall windows spilled pale May sunlight. A blue curtain hung behind two podiums, framing a sign that read 'The Lazarus

Project,' with yellow rays in all directions like a kid's drawing of the sun. Not the sharpest logo you ever saw.

Meanwhile I watched the TV crews set up. Pretty-face on-air talent gals stood beside the riser, holding white cards for cameramen to fix a brightness level. Funny thing about TV women: they all have skinny faces, cheekbones you could crack an egg on, but they carry big butts. Maybe all those hours in the anchor chair?

The red digital clock said we were an hour into Day 17 for old Frank. But my watch said five after one, and the press conference was supposed to start at one sharp. Not like Carthage to be tardy. The only explanation would have to be the surprise he had planned. I jiggled my leg in my chair till the guy next to me asked if I could please stop.

But I was excited. This was one hell of a story, is what it was. I'd covered the space shuttle explosion, back in my cub days at the paper in Florida. I'd followed a seedy governor right into the arms of his mistress, so close on his heels I could see firsthand why he'd been tempted. Then I'd found research papers that fudged the side-effects of a blood pressure drug, killing four women with clots and placing me forever after on the science-writing path. After that I'd interviewed iguana-taggers in the Galapagos, particle accelerator geeks in France, climate change gurus at the edge of the Gobi Desert, trajectory physicists in mildewed bars at Cape Canaveral, nanotechnologists in California clean rooms, tectonic savants at the lip of volcanoes, metallurgists in roasting foundries, AIDS researchers in giant, silent labs, sky listeners at the foot of their array of massive creepy radio wave tracking dishes, and none of them, not one, came close to the magnitude of this bit of news. What if we truly have found a way to cheat death, to make it temporary? Jeremiah is good for a week of hot copy maybe, but what he represents is much greater. What if we did it?

Worthless musings deserve a hard interruption, and that's just what I received when the last reporter hurried in, excuse me here and pardon me there and in general calling as much attention to himself as if he'd used a foghorn. Wilson Steele, dammit, settling cozy in his seat like a duck on an egg.

No matter. *New York Times* or not, his opening paragraph tomorrow would still come from my six-word question.

The room went quiet like the hush in a concert hall before the curtain lifts, when the crowd somehow knows. I checked my watch. It was exactly six minutes after the scheduled starting time. Dr Borden entered first, walking stiff-legged like a marionette. Carthage came next, followed by a couple of techs tagging along for ballast, plus Thomas with a sheaf of papers. Gerber waddled into the doorway but moved no closer, rubbing a knuckle in one red eye. He couldn't possibly be stoned now of all times, could he?

'Let's begin,' Carthage said. He folded his hands

chest high. It looked effeminate, plain and simple. But then I remembered his germ phobia. Maybe this was his way of not touching the podium. A few techs began moving through the aisles, handing out papers. The second podium stood empty, a hint of what lay ahead.

'My staff is distributing time-lines,' Carthage said, 'for any of you joining this story today. Also a summary of findings, biographies of myself and our staff, and a complete list of my publications. We've also updated our web site this noon with current videos and data. With me today is Dr Christopher Borden, and other staff as needed.'

Carthage adjusted his stance. He stood in the spotlight, cameras pointing at him, reporters alternating between glancing his way and writing down every word he said. Carthage scratched his chin and shutters clicked by the dozen. He smiled. It wasn't pretty.

'I'd like to make a brief statement first.' He cleared his throat. 'Five years ago a predecessor organization to the Lazarus Project found that cells which ceased metabolizing due to rapid freezing – a layman would say they had died – nonetheless contained energy supplies to live longer.' On he went, reliving history no one cared about. They would wait him out though, indulging him so they could hear what they came for. Eventually he veered back into their sights.

'The human being we have reanimated proves to be a man of intellect and judgment. He participates in our research with as much enthusiasm as his limited energy permits. We understand that some people question our motives. Our goal is not to generate controversy, of course, but to offer the promise of greater lifespan for all of humanity. Now.' He opened his arms like a priest at the altar. 'Your questions?'

Hands shot up all over the room. Carthage pointed. 'Yes?'

'What kind of shape is the awakened man in?'

'Dr Borden, if you please?' Carthage stepped aside and the short doc moved to the podium, pulling the mike down to his level. Carthage frowned.

'Overall his physical condition is remarkably good. All organs and muscle systems are functioning normally, or what would be normal for someone his age who hadn't been frozen for over a century.' Borden tugged on the tip of his beard. 'The primary unusual thing is that his metabolism is spectacularly slow. Like a hibernating bear. He consumes fewer than 800 calories per day, and sleeps 20 hours out of 24. After only mild exertions, his fatigue is enormous.'

'So he's not some sort of super-human people need to be afraid of?'

Borden chuckled. 'Judge Rice is as dangerous as a teenager who sleeps till noon.'

The group laughed along, more hands rose. Carthage chose a woman in the front. 'Just how much is all of this costing? Is this judge a good use of research funds?'

'It's far too soon to know what our studies will yield,' Carthage said. He used the sleeve of his jacket to raise the mike again. 'As for the price tag, this facility cost a fortune to equip, and the polar research vessel is spectacularly costly to operate. Thus far,' and he leaned toward Thomas, who stood against the wall, 'thus far all of our financing has been private, with no federal help. Though we did have an encouraging conversation with Vice President Walker. The better question, if I may, is what price you are willing to put on a recovered human life? Moreover, we hope and expect our initial investments to be spread out over many reanimations and many avenues of research. It's not as though we built all of this for Subject – for a single person.'

'A follow, please: how much have you spent so far?'

He considered her a moment, weighing something, then reaching a conclusion. 'To date our expenditures have neared twenty-five million dollars.'

A murmur passed through the room. Gerber in the doorway whistled, earning him a glare from Carthage. He just smiled.

The reporter had her hand up again. 'One more, please. Can you tell us who your funding sources are?'

Carthage narrowed his eyes. The cameras clicked at that image, and I saw him draw back, then force that sideways smile. 'We are fortunate to have supporters who enable us to pursue our work unfettered by external interference. Should the government choose to assist our project, we intend to make our methods open-sourced, so scientists the world over can build on our findings for the betterment of all mankind.'

'What do you make of the controversy around this project?' asked another reporter. 'You know, people who say you are playing God?'

'I would say that any endeavor of this significance and potential is bound to upset people who are afraid of change. But controversy is not without merit. Healthy dialogue is necessary and even welcome. Remember, though, our caution is not like the secrecy around the Manhattan Project, for example, where the goal was to kill hundreds of thousands of people. Our work is for life, is all about life.'

'May I also say,' Borden stood on tiptoe, holding the podium for balance, 'to the people who say we are playing God, that we are not playing anything. We do not play. This work is far too complex, the stakes far too high. These people who criticize us simply do not understand. They are ignorant.'

Oops, I thought. Sure enough, the room went quiet while every single reporter wrote those sentences down, or tapped them into a laptop, so many heads bent like school kids to their lessons.

'I think,' said Carthage, clapping his hands. Normally that brings a room to attention, but this time they were all still scribing. He clapped again. 'I think the best way to express what is going on here, yes, is with a visual aid. Thomas?' he turned stiffly. Thomas hurried from the room like a puppy sent for slippers. Borden returned to his place, and Carthage rubbed his hands together. While the reporters remained silent I counted, waiting to see how long Carthage had told his team to let the anticipation build. There was no question he would have thought about that, calculating the ideal level of suspense. I reached forty-eight-Mississippi, an eternity for a crowd to wait, when the atrium side door opened.

Thomas came first, all efficiency, a little robot. Dr Kate followed in a calm stroll. She wore a navy blue dress, fitted like a hug of cotton from her collar bone to her knee. Half a step behind, holding her upper arm for support, shuffled none other than His Honour, the man who lived twice, the face known 'round the world, Judge Jeremiah Rice. He was dressed in surgical scrubs, of all things, and had bare tootsies. Carthage must have overlooked that detail somehow, because the guy's feet looked bony, pale, and cold. Meanwhile Dr Kate scanned the crowd like a Secret Service agent at the president's elbow.

It took them a moment to realize what had happened. Then the photographers leapt forward, the reporters all standing and shouting at once.

'Judge Rice?'

'Jeremiah.'

'Mr Rice, one question?'

Jeremiah winced at the noise and Dr Kate stepped between him and the crowd. 'Easy does it,' she called. 'Easy now. Come on.'

In that instant, that very second, the future came clear. I could predict exactly what they'd do, what they always do in cases like this. Today they'll lift him up, the higher the better, a god among men and, friend, can I buy you a beer? Tomorrow though, tomorrow they'll bring him down as hard and fast and brutally as they can. And when they're finished, there'll be so little left on the highway, even the crows won't be bothered to come down and pick at it.

The judge stood at that second podium and the ritual began. Where and when were you born? (Lynn, 1868.) Where did you go to school? (Lynn elementary and high school, Tufts University, Harvard Law.) Who appointed you judge? (The governor, I can't recall his name, my memory is still incomplete.) Wasn't thirty-eight a young age for a judge? (Most people back then did not live past fifty, so advancement came early for promising men.) What do you think about the Lazarus Project and being reawakened? (I feel gratitude. Life is the ultimate gift.) What things are you most interested in doing? (Regaining my energy and learning about the world as it is today.) What do you miss most?

He paused at that, our old Frank. He looked at his feet, white and pathetic. We all looked too. He nodded, then raised his glistening eyes. 'My family.' He swallowed audibly. 'My wife and daughter.'

I'm pretty sure Dr Kate acted by reflex. After all, how could you not feel sorry for the guy? But when she reached over and gave his hand a squeeze, every camera shutter in the room made its little happy sound.

'That's enough for today,' Carthage said. 'As you see, Judge Rice is very much present and alive. We will provide ample opportunity for further interviews as his recuperation progresses. Let's have one last question, then.'

I raised my hand. So did many others. So did Wilson Steele. He had a large hand. Carthage scanned the room as if trying to choose, conducting some kind of evaluation based on the length of our arms or something, then lifted his chin in my direction. 'Yes?'

'My question is for Judge Rice.'

Our old Frank smiled at me. 'Yes? How may I help you?'

Oh I was ready. And no one had thought of this angle but me. It takes someone whose parents died right in front of him, to know what six words pack the most wallop:

'What was it like to die?'

There was a collective intake of breath. Jeremiah didn't flinch though. Instead, he took a step forward.

'Like being squeezed, to be honest with you. Like being pressed flat.'

He came around in front of the podium. Dr Kate watched him, ready to pounce, her head tilted to one side like a teenager in love. The judge dropped one hand to his side, the fingers as relaxed as a man on vacation, and placed the other on his belly like Napoleon addressing the troops. At once I knew he had prepared for this moment. He'd been thinking about it, about when he would have to tell his story. Now the time had come. In a way, it might have been a relief to him. And I had made it possible.

'We were approximately at the latitude of Ellesmere Island,' he began. 'The voyage's goal was to replicate in northern waters, if possible, Charles Darwin's findings from a southern clime. My role was to serve as impartial witness, an auditor of the science. Five months we'd been at sea, and the research progressed splendidly. Natural selection revealed itself everywhere we looked – in nature's variety, in the brutality of the food chain, in the fecundity of species. Think of a shoreline pool that fills or empties based on tides. Sometimes it is dry land, sometimes ocean, and yet even in a region that is frozen for eight months of the year, this pool is crowded with creatures happily adapted to that inhospitable existence. Evolution is the planet's animating machinery, we came to believe. Evolution is life's striving toward God.'

An earful, is what the judge gave us. He placed one hand on the podium and I pictured him in black robes, sentencing a criminal or resolving some civil dispute, and delivering a speech a lot like this one.

'Our inexperience as sailors, however, became the more apparent as winter began to close upon us. One morning we awoke to find ourselves in a bay whose throat had all but frozen. We'd nearly imprisoned ourselves for the winter. Sure starvation. Several hard sailing hours and not a few jarring hull-scrapes later, we regained open sea. That afternoon on deck we deliberated whether to return to Boston. Ironically, I was opposed. The call of home was melodious indeed, but not yet so loud that I did not hear the siren song of further exploration. However, despite total deference to the captain on matters nautical, the vessel was a democracy on expedition issues. We voted, I was heavily outweighed, and we pointed the bow south.'

As he continued the room remained silent, wonderfully poetically silent. The scribblers and skeptics could not have been more entranced if he'd drugged them. Here was a man from way back of beyond, speaking to them as plain as paper. They wrote and they listened and they swallowed every word.

The judge shook his head. 'I digress. Our ninth night homeward, we sailed straight into the teeth of a storm. For severity of the gale, it surpassed all experience. At no time was any portion of the ship level, nor reliable underfoot. The cold made it infinitely worse. Imagine your hands . . .' He held his forward like they belonged to someone else. 'Imagine them soaked by Arctic brine, chilled as if to be ice, trying to pull a rough rope around a winch. There was no joyous exploration any longer. The rather, it was cold bones, suffering morale, and hearts warmed only by fear. The heavens delivered one furious gust, and our mast broke. Splintered. We began to founder, even with foresails raised. The captain ordered all hands out to master the broken rigging, which swung wildly in the rage. I was among those bent to that task.'

Our Frank hesitated. 'Might we pause, gentlemen and ladies, to remember my crew mates? They were decent men all, dedicated to expanding human knowledge, and I cannot imagine that they survived the night.' The judge raised his gaze toward the ceiling. 'Might we offer them a moment of prayer?'

And he closed his eyes.

I scanned the atrium. It's not every day someone interrupts a press conference to pray. The reporters were obviously uncomfortable. Some reread their notes, a few studied the room's corners, I saw a cameraman pick his nose. Wilson Steele though, lowered his head. I could just imagine what that bastard was praying for. Too bad he didn't know about my book deal.

'I thank you,' Jeremiah said. 'To continue: I was woefully inexperienced in storm conditions. In my haste to secure the sheets I neglected to bind myself to the rails. A massive wave crashed over the bow, pouring its foaming tonnage across the deck, and yanking my feet from under me. A salty river bore me headlong toward the stern, another bit of jetsam and wrack. I grabbed at everything, ropes and cleats, to no avail. The rush of water took possession of me, and in one indifferent gush it swept me over the side.'

Again he paused. Still the room was silent. Amazing, I thought. He was working them over with an old-fashioned sea tale, and they were falling for it with all their might.

'Oh, that water.' He wagged his head. 'My final experience on this earth was of a cold so intense it inspired my awe. In roundabout answer to your question sir,' he gestured at me, 'it did not feel like pain, oddly enough, but like pressure. From all directions at once, as though I were being squeezed in some great thermal vise. I took one breath of salt water and coughed it out. It was agony, like scraping a wire bottle-brush on your softest interior places. I foundered, rising and falling with the waves as the ship surged away. Then I felt my body stiffening, my fingers swelling as the water within them turned to ice. It was as though nature was racing itself to see which would finish me first, drowning or freezing. Greater than the physical pain was the terror, my body's dread of ceasing to exist. Against the weight of sodden garments I struggled to the surface, glimpsed the stars, gasped a magnificent breath of clear air, and knew no more.'

Our old Frank sniffed. His eyes took a walk over everyone in the room. I admired his poise. He was no fool, this judge of ours. He had a destination in mind with his story.

'What is it like to be dead? Here is all I can say. There was a moment of thrashing, there in the Atlantic, and then a moment of calm. There was dismay that I was dying, then there was acceptance. I went either into black or into white, my mind keeps changing about that detail. Then? Nothing, neither heaven nor hell, not that I recall at any rate. If indeed I entered some divine provenance, the loss of its recollection was the price I paid to return to this world. No, what I remember is coughing, thorns of pain in my chest whilst I was coughing. Someone put a warm hand on my arm, and it was comfort enough to cause me to open my eyes. I found myself looking at your world, your time, this place you people have made.'

He held his arms wide. 'Now I am among you. The newspapers call me a miracle. My conclusion is the rather. I am the mere embodiment of your collective will, a sign of our species' desire to continue, a manifestation of your determination over the span of a century. Jeremiah Rice is the accidental, unwitting, and immeasurably grateful beneficiary of all that humanity endeavors to be.'

God, it was perfect. Freaking perfect. Our species' desire to continue? Old Frank smacked it out of the park. Carthage announced no further questions. The reporters chattered while gathering their things. Gerber held the side door open, saluting as the staff trooped out. Dr Kate sashayed along, delectable as ever. Jeremiah hesitated at the doorway, glancing back at the crowd. In that moment, one last reporter saw his shot.

'Are there surviving family members?'

That stopped the judge like a bullet. He turned toward a room instantly quiet. 'Excuse me?'

It was Wilson Steele, standing handsome. 'Are there surviving family members?'

Well. It was plain on the judge's face that in the days since being reawakened, his foggy mind had not yet traveled to that particular place. His expression changed from curiosity to pain, to wonder, then to pain again. 'I have no idea.'

Then he sagged like a flat tire. 'Forgive me,' he said, bringing a hand to his brow. 'I am suddenly so tired.'

If Dr Kate had not caught him, I believe he would have hit the floor. She rushed him from the room, which began buzzing like a band saw. The reporter next to me was already on his cell phone, shouting to the newsroom I imagined on the other end. 'Genealogy,' he said. 'Find out pronto if this fucker has any family.'

The crowd so cool at one o'clock now clambered over itself in a rush for the door, worse than a grade school fire drill. The race to find a descendant was now underway, my question totally overwhelmed.

Carthage stood aside, observing the mayhem with cold eyes. Then he swept out after them all.

Time for me to get hustling too. First, though, I counted Steele's question back to myself. The bastard did it with just five words.

CHAPTER 16

THE HISTORY OF AVIATION

(KATE PHILO)

The first blood call came soon after the six o'clock news. I'd just arrived for my shift, hadn't even removed my coat. The reception phone was ringing so I hit the transfer code to grab it at my desk. The man was speaking before I'd said hello.

'Hi my name is Henry Ray and I'm Jeremiah Rice's grandson. I live in Chatham and I can drive up tomorrow if he wants to meet and we can talk about our family and say hey. Or could I maybe talk to him right now?'

'His grandson?' I said. 'Wow. Hang on one moment, OK?'

I put him on hold, then looked for help. Gerber sat at his terminal with music leaking from his headphones. He was straight-backed, concentrating on the screen as if planning his next move in chess. To me it looked like a simple graph, three parallel lines, but clearly Gerber saw something more. Both hands floated by his chin in the OK pose, wiggling side to side. Is it possible, when a person is relentlessly odd, to be annoyed by him yet feel affection at the same time? I scanned the control room but everyone else had gone for the night.

'David?' I said. 'Gerber?'

'Aaahhh.' He continued shaking his hands, but now the fingers were fanned wide. 'No no no no.'

'Look, I'm sorry—'

'What?' He slumped in his chair, pulled the headphones down to his neck. His crazy hair swelled out like a released sponge. 'What is it? What?'

'I am completely sorry to interrupt you, but there's a caller—'

'They were making the segue from "Not Fade Away" into "Going Down the Road Feelin" Bad'. And I was right, *right* on the verge of figuring out what these freakishly similar numbers mean.' He poked the screen, I saw that his fingernails badly needed clipping. 'What can it possibly be? Is the building on fire? Are we under attack?'

'Sorry, it's not so dramatic.' I smiled at him. 'There's a man on the phone who says he's Jeremiah Rice's grandson.'

'Oh goodie, a blood call.' Gerber swiveled his chair left and right. 'That didn't take long.'

'Blood call?'

He grinned. 'Just talk with him for a minute. You'll see.'

'What do I say?'

'You're smart, Kate.' Gerber leaned back. 'Sound him out.'

I hung my coat on a chair, lifted the phone. 'Thanks for holding. My name is—'

'Oh you bet no problem. Look, the thing is, I have plans to be in Boston tomorrow morning anyhow, so I could come by the lab no problem, you know, and meet him and stuff. Jeremiah Rice, I mean.'

'I see. Well, that's certainly convenient, sir. It's exciting to hear from you. However, we're still trying to be careful with Judge Rice's time. I'm sure he'll be eager to meet you. But his energy is still so limited.'

'Oh. OK, sure. Makes sense. Except, um, yes except that I was already going to be in town. And it's like an hour and a half drive each way, you know?'

'Well sir, we'll have to consider how best to arrange this. I'll need to consult our executive director.'

Gerber, hearing only my side of the conversation, nonetheless swirled one finger around his ear. I covered the mouthpiece. 'You are not funny.'

'Blood, I tell you.' He put his running shoes up on my desk. Filthy.

'Pardon me sir, I'm sorry I didn't get your name.'

'Henry Ray. Grandson of Jeremiah Rice. Direct descendant. Yes, direct.'

'Mr Ray,' I grabbed a pad, jotting his name. 'We haven't really prepared ourselves for visitors, to tell you the truth. Or prepared Judge Rice, for that matter. Is there a number where I could call you back?'

'Oh sure, no problem. Only like I say, I'm going to be there tomorrow and everything. So why don't I just come right on by? And meet him, you know?'

Then I understood. I looked at Gerber, his face wearing the smug expression of a person two steps ahead of me but three ahead of the caller. 'Mr Ray, please excuse the question, but how are you related to Judge Rice?'

'How? You're asking me how?'

'Yes sir.' Gerber was nodding emphatically at me now.

'Well, everybody around here has known it from the second his picture was in the papers. He looks just like me. I mean just, just like me. Same chin, same nose, same chin. Everyone who's seen the picture says so. Also my grandfather was a fisherman, lost out of Gloucester in 1906, in that famous fall storm.'

'How are you related, please? You said it was direct.'

'Well that's the thing of it. Because Jeremiah's son was my father. Timothy. Has to be. His Timmy was my old man.'

'I see.' I gave Gerber a look. He pretended he was jerking an invisible penis, I turned in the other direction. 'Mr Ray, I think there's been some confusion here today.'

'What do you mean? Like I ought to come another day? Because really, an hour and a half is not so bad, no problem, if we ought to do it some other time.'

At last I realized how naïve I'd been. 'What I mean to say, sir . . .'

Why did I hesitate? Gerber obviously had no qualms. Why did I have the impulse to undo the caller's self-delusion gently? I suppose I'll never know. But it is worth noting, given what came later. There was an inclination, in that early time, to be kind to the people who would prey on Judge Rice. An innocence on my part. My attitude would change soon enough, but not yet.

'I mean to say, sir, that Judge Rice's ship did not sail from Gloucester. He set out from Nauset.'

'I'm not following you.'

'Also he did not have any sons. I'm sorry, but—'

'Are you calling me a fake? Are you saying that I'm a fake?'

'While I am not denying there might be a strong physical resemblance—'

'Listen you bitch. Listen to me. Don't give me that crap. I'm the guy's grandson, you hear me? I got the chin and everything.'

'Sir, I really don't think there's any call for that sort of language.'

'Oh fuck you. You fucking people are all alike. You just want to cash in on him, and keep away the man's own family. You people are sick, I swear to Christ. His own grandson. You are just fucking sick.'

He hung up on me. I set the phone in its cradle. 'Wow.'

Gerber's grin could not have been wider. 'Is everyone all right?'

'That was an experience. I understand you now, anyway. You mean it's a blood call because he was claiming to be Jeremiah's blood relation.'

'Nope.' Gerber took his shoes off my desk, leaned forward like he was delivering bad news. 'I mean it's a blood call because the world is full of vampires.'

Across the lab, at the reception desk, the phone rang again.

By 2 a.m., one hundred and fourteen people had claimed to be Jeremiah's kin. I set the phones to go directly to voice mail, so I could get some work done. Eventually though, the switchboard started pinging – which means the general voice mailbox is full, and which came over the intercom too loudly to ignore.

Just returned from one of his contemplative midnight walks, Gerber scampered past me to his desk. 'I'd say there's a phone call for you.'

He flounced into his chair, clapping the headphones into place and squinting at the screen. The imp.

I surrendered, plunking myself down at the reception desk, playing back messages, writing names and phone numbers on a legal pad while more calls came in. The voices were young and old, male and female, alike only in their needy tone. Some did not even leave contact information. Those who did, I diligently wrote down, leaving it for others to assess the callers' merit or sanity.

Let Carthage sort them out. They all believed Judge Rice was their father, grandfather, long lost uncle. Could there really be so many missing ancestors? Or that many people desperate for a connection to this reawakened man?

I began to worry that we might fall into the cesspool of celebrity, which I consider the opposite of science: haste instead of caution, surface over substance, the bright flash of a camera instead of the droning overheads of the lab. Something triggered the anger of that first caller, some desire or expectation, something he thought he deserved. It was the first piece of a puzzle I would need months to solve.

When the mailbox was finally empty I took a break, strolling over to see Gerber's latest *Perv Du Jour*. So far some had been hilarious, some too weird to believe. That night's installment was obscene.

The site Gerber had found was sexyfrozenman.com. People had taken still shots of Jeremiah from our site and doctored them entirely in a sexual fashion. One showed his head pressed between two enormous breasts. In another, someone had tattooed a red mermaid on his cheek, again with ballooning breasts. A third attached his face to a bodybuilder's torso, gave it the penis of a giant, and pasted a twig-thin man kneeling before him. Still another showed a woman's naked bottom, with Judge Rice's head tilted beneath as if he were performing oral sex on her. What a world. The one Gerber placed highest was a digital alteration of the judge's face, his sideburns lengthened to give him more of an animal look, his smile drawn backward into an expression of ecstasy.

That was the moment I felt my first flutter. I'd been so busy protecting Judge Rice, I had forgotten the experience of lifting him into the wheelchair that night. I checked on Gerber, who wagged his crown along with whatever music was playing in his headset, then looked again at that top photo.

I confess it: I found myself wondering things I would never have contemplated a few weeks earlier. What had sexuality been like one hundred years ago? Was desire shown so openly? We are different now, surely. We know more, are exposed to more. I remember Dana, my track star boyfriend for two years of college, what a sexual laboratory we were for each another. I became so adept with a diaphragm he called it my Frisbee. Did Judge Rice have a similar familiarity with his wife? Of course he did, though it must have been different, must have. Then there was the anesthesiologist I dated during grad school, who found nothing more erotic than the two of us showering together till the hot water ran out. Did the judge's house even have running water? Now there is the Internet too, where every predilection has an address, easy access, total anonymity. How would a man from modest times fare in this modern world?

Gerber appeared at my elbow. 'They're getting weirder, aren't they?'

'This is all so completely wrong.'

He laughed. 'And normal.'

'Can you imagine how appalled Judge Rice would be if he saw this?'

'People were probably just as dirty-minded in the old days.'

'I guess now I know why you call it *Perv Du Jour*.'

'This is just one form of perversity. But there will be lots of others, you'll see. The multitudes have made our judge the meat of the moment. Some buy the magazines, some watch the news. But right now lots of them are going online and perving on our handsome hero. Tonight it's plain horniness. But I promise, whatever sites I find weeks from now, whatever way people find to indulge their fantasies about this man and make their projections on to him, I guarantee the content will be perverse.'

The reception phone rang but I let it go. 'Personally, I'm hoping people move on with their lives, so we can prioritize research again and begin to help Judge Rice integrate into modern society.'

Gerber chuckled. 'Personally, I wish that woman there had a nicer butt.'

'Excuse me, what do those lines mean?'

It was Judge Rice. He'd woken somehow, stood pointing at Gerber's terminal, where those parallel lines were displayed again. He was still wearing scrubs.

In a flash I tore down the *Perv* posting. 'Judge Rice, what a surprise.' I crushed the papers into a ball. The digital counter read 16 hours into Day 17, but the regular clock said 3:19. 'To see you up at this hour. Good morning. Everything all right?'

'I had too much energy to sleep,' he said. 'Good morning, Dr Philo.'

'They're you,' Gerber answered, strolling over to the judge. 'Over the past 6 days. This one is your heart rate, that one's your respiration rate, and the top line is your blood pressure.'

He nodded. 'They are parallel, sir.'

'And rising a little bit each day.'

'What does this tell you, sir?'

'Your body systems are still waking up, I guess.' Gerber rubbed his nose. 'The weird thing is, they're all doing it at the same rate. It's a metabolic mystery. But I am not "sir".' He held out his hand. 'I'm Gerber.'

They regarded each other. I hurried the balled-up papers to the furthest trash can, my relief at shielding Judge Rice from the *Perv Du Jour* becoming a charge of amusement at the characters now shaking hands. Talk about spanning the century: a deliberative lawyer from the past, an oddball savant of the present, considering each other like two forest apes who have unexpectedly encountered a being of a similar species.

'A pleasure to meet you, Mr Gerber. My name is—'

'Oh-ho, I know who you are, Judge Rice. I've been here the whole time. I was even on the ship when they found you. And not to be sticky about it, but it's actually *Dr* Gerber.'

'I see. Thank you Doctor.' He pointed at Gerber's headphones. 'May I inquire what those ear covers are? I've noticed you wearing them often.'

'Well, they're for listening. These days we can capture music played in one time and place, and replay it anywhere else, over and over. And for me personally . . .' Gerber held them up and laughed. 'I guess what they do is help my wacky mind focus. Keep my thinking from going to places too wild for me to handle.'

'Might I try them?'

Suddenly I felt like an anthropologist. I observed from across the control room while Gerber wheeled another chair to his desk, placed the headphones over Judge Rice's ears with unexpected care, adjusted the fit, tapped a few keys to begin a piece of music. Here was the judge's first true taste of modernism.

I was close enough to hear vaguely that a song had begun.

Judge Rice's eyes went wide. 'Ha ha. My goodness.' He spoke loudly, as if we were wearing headphones too.

'That's "Lady with a Fan",' Gerber said. 'One of my favorites. From the album *Terrapin Station*. That's what 1977 sounds like. Pretty sweet, huh?'

'So much is happening at once,' he bellowed.

Then, for the first time I had ever witnessed, Judge Rice smiled.

Gerber of all people. I had always imagined it would be me to introduce Judge Rice to the modern world. I thought I would be his teacher. I know I began the process, that night on the roof. Yet as that song played, I did not feel possessive. In an odd way, who better than Gerber? Brilliant for all his eccentricity, a man without guile.

'What is this light-throwing device, anyway?' Judge Rice said, lowering the headphones, tapping the computer screen. 'You people sit here for hours, though it looks incomparably dull. What can possibly be so compelling about it?'

'Well, you're right that it's dull.' Gerber scratched his wooly scalp. 'But that's only half the story. It's called a computer. Think of it as a telephone you can use to call anyone in the world.'

'Telephone?'

Gerber turned to me for help. I held up open palms. 'Oh no, this is all you.'

'Thanks a million.' He made a face, then turned back to Judge Rice. 'OK, you know what a telegraph is, right?'

'I've sent and received telegrams, yes.'

'Well, today instead of dots and dashes going down the wires, we send a person's voice. What this machine does is connect nearly all the wires on earth, which therefore connects all those voices. Also it stores the words we write, the pictures we take,' he tapped the headphones, 'even the songs we sing.'

'When my friend here' – Judge Rice pointed at me – 'says you people are recording everything I do, is this what she means?'

'Here, watch this.' Gerber's hands flew over the keyboard, and a video began playing on his screen. Judge Rice rested one hand on the podium. *For severity of the gale, it surpassed all experience. At no time was any portion of the ship level, nor reliable underfoot . . .*

'Ha.' Judge Rice tapped a forefinger on his chin. *'What a piece of work is a man, how noble in reason, how infinite in faculties.'*

'Right. What you said.'

'From *Hamlet.*'

Gerber grinned. 'I suppose if I throw the Grateful Dead at you, it's only fair that you lay Shakespeare on me.'

'Do you realize how this invention could transform judicial proceedings? If all of the world could act as eyewitness?'

'Wait a second. You've been a judge long enough to doubt evidence, right? Check this out.' Gerber slapped some keys, slid his mouse around to edit the footage. 'Aw, you made it easy by standing so still.' Gerber hit enter, the machine spent ten seconds filling a status bar, then an equally smooth clip began to play on his screen. *The ship was level, reliable underfoot. It surpassed all experience.*

Judge Rice burst out laughing. 'But of course,

of course. If humanity can find a means to new truths, it can also produce new lies.'

'You learn fast, brother.' He touched the screen. 'If you watch your left hand here, you'll see it jumps slightly, which gives away my editing. If you look closely.'

'Nonetheless it is an impressive tool. Does it contain maps?'

'Of pretty much everything, yes. You can see the whole world, or your own street.'

'How useful that would have been on our expedition,' Judge Rice said, bouncing a fist on his thigh.

'Well now,' Gerber tilted his chair back. 'We've heard about the bad part, but there must have been *some* good. What was your favorite thing about that trip, anyway?'

'So many things.' He considered for a moment. 'An example, if I may.'

'Please.'

I held my tongue, enjoying the moment in front of me.

'We had been nine days asail from Thule, Greenland, halfway between the Arctic Circle and the pole. Our panorama was gray water, gray sky, white foam at the waterline and little else. When we reached the coastline it revealed no human presence, only a landscape grim and austere. Then we spied an outpost as desolate as despair, a cluster of shacks populated by souls with hardy skins and rough language. Yet they welcomed us as kin, fed us like royalty, with fish and other foods of which we were entirely ignorant, and with their coarse humor we passed the night laughing like children at a clown. Upon hoisting anchor the next dawn, pink skies and a pearl sea, we saw it all as if with new eyes.'

'Saw what, your honor?'

'The beauty of it all. Exploration became incidental to the experience of beauty.'

'Yes,' I whispered. 'Exactly.'

We were silent, even Gerber, as though the world had paused. The drawing forward I felt in that moment was like how the moon pulls on tides. I did not admit to myself what I was feeling. Still, I must have been staring.

'What is it?' asked Judge Rice, touching his cheek. 'Do I have something on my face?'

'Just whiskers,' I said, jerking away. 'Only whiskers.'

'Danger, danger, danger,' Gerber said in a robotic voice.

'What is your meaning?'

'Whiskers.' Gerber spun in his chair like a top. 'Whiskers whiskers.'

'You shut up.' I smacked him on the arm.

'*Dangerous* whiskers.'

'I don't understand,' said Judge Rice.

'Our friend here is an odd duck,' I explained. 'Pay no attention.'

'A duck with whiskers,' Gerber exclaimed, still spinning.

The judge studied him a moment, then raised one finger. 'About these machines,' he said. 'If I may persist.'

Gerber stopped abruptly, one foot hooked on the leg of his desk. 'By all means.'

'Why would you want to be able to talk to anyone in the world? Also why would they want to talk to you?'

'A million reasons.' Gerber faced his computer, clicking through several windows. 'To learn, to share knowledge, to gossip. People even fall in love through these machines. And look,' he scrolled through screens of emails. 'These are letters, from all over the earth, people who are curious about you. More than anything, though, these boxes contain the greatest library ever imagined.'

'How is that possible? They look entirely too small.'

'It's easier to show than to explain. Tell me a subject you'd like to know about. Something you were interested in, way back when.'

'Quite simple,' Judge Rice said. 'Aviation.'

Gerber turned back from his screen. 'Beg pardon, your honor?'

'In 1903 two brothers flew an aircraft on the dunes of South Carolina. Ever since it has been a fascination of mine. Mankind behaving like a bird, what could be more inventive? *"To strive, to seek, to find and not to yield."* Oh, and I recollect from that night,' he faced me, 'when you took me to the rooftop. I witnessed a huge flying machine, possibly the loudest thing I have ever heard. There. I would be interested to see what progress the world has made in aviation.'

'Perfect choice,' Gerber said, rubbing his hands together. 'A history of aviation. But I have to warn you . . .'

'Yes, Dr Gerber?'

'You will be amazed at how creatures as smart as human beings could also be relentlessly stupid.'

'Now Gerber,' I said, 'I know where you're headed. There are two sides—'

'No kibbitzing,' he interrupted. 'You said this was all on me, remember?'

'Just don't leave out the beauty.'

'Not at all.' He patted Judge Rice on the knee. 'That's exactly where I intend to start. And on the year you went to sea.'

Gerber, when it came to online searches, ran as quick as a weasel. In seconds he had information about 1906. That year the Germans invented zeppelins and the French created seaplanes. On the Fourth of July an American flew an airplane nearly a mile. He also set a new speed record, 47 miles an hour.

'Incredible,' Judge Rice said, shaking his head. 'Like lightning.'

Gerber searched year after year: when airmail began, the pilot held letter bags between his knees, dropping them overboard as he flew over their destination. Orville Wright crashed but survived, his passenger the first person to die in a powered airplane accident. The first cross-country flight took three and a half days. Engineers moved the propellers from behind the wings to the front.

'Well sunshine daydream, here's a find,' Gerber said, 'from 1912.' He clicked on a video that streamed historic footage, grainy and gray. A floating biplane set off amid blocks of ice in a cloudy harbor. Next a camera mounted on the plane revealed glimpses of an industrial shoreline and several blurry islands. Then in sharp relief, a giant copper symbol flickered into view.

'Oh my heaven,' Judge Rice exclaimed. 'The Statue of Liberty.'

'Bingo.'

'I'd forgotten.'

'She's still there,' Gerber said. 'But now we reach the summer of 1914, and flying becomes a different business. Stupid takes over.' He showed clips of dogfights, photos of the first bombers, portraits of flying aces with white scarves thrown over their shoulders. 'These are from World War I.'

'Truly the whole world at war?'

'Probably felt that way. But look, they were even dumb enough to be optimistic about that. They called it "the war to end all wars".'

'Did it?'

Gerber clucked, tapping his keys. 'What do you think?'

'Excuse me,' I said. I'd begun to think ahead, aviation in the next thirty years, and what Judge

Rice was about to learn. The former teacher in me could not keep mum. 'I think we ought to put some balance in here, you know Gerber?'

'Balance the stupidity of human nature? Against what?'

'Some of the good things, perhaps?'

'Not a fair fight, stupid wins by a mile. But hey.' He pointed at the next desk. 'That computer's still on, Kate. Knock yourself out.'

I leaned toward Judge Rice. 'There's a whole century of things for you to learn. Some of them may be tough to take.'

'I appreciate your protective spirit, Dr Philo.' He took a deep breath, released it slowly. 'Permit us, though, to complete one line of thought.' He turned to Gerber. 'How many people died in this war that failed to end all wars?'

'Not sure.' Gerber slurped his coffee. 'Twenty, twenty-five million?'

Judge Rice blinked. 'That can't be right. Twenty-five million human beings?'

'Give or take. Hang on.' Gerber tapped away. 'Just pilots, since that's our theme for the moment, let's see.' He tried one search, then a second gave the answer. 'Here we are. Twenty thousand pilots died.'

I felt as stunned as Judge Rice looked. 'It does not speak well of our kind,' he said. 'We invented this machine, devised ideally for adventure, discovery and economic utility, yet applied it to the opposite purposes.'

'Well, the war ended eventually,' Gerber said. 'Innovation didn't. Look here: the first commercial flight, 1919, eleven paying passengers, Paris to London. No guns, no bombs, very nice. And in 1921 the first African-American pilot.'

'African-American?'

'That means he is a black man. A Negro.'

'A colored?'

'Yes,' I said. 'But today we use respectful words. We don't want to offend anyone. You would probably do best to refer to black people as African-Americans.'

'We do not want to offend black people?' Judge Rice rubbed his chin. 'Hm. Excellent.'

'You think so?' Gerber said.

He nodded. 'My father fought in the War between the States. And in my time, any fool could see the unfairness in work and wages. It also appeared in my courtroom of course, almost daily.'

'Huh,' Gerber scratched his head. 'Well, people feel even more strongly about it today. Let's keep playing history though. Here's the first parachute, so people can jump out of planes and not get squished like a bug . . . aaaand here's an early crop-duster.'

'What is that aircraft dropping?'

'Chemicals to kill weevils on plants, mosquitos and things like that.'

'I much prefer hearing these peaceable uses for flying. But I imagine you could drop poison on your enemies in much the same way.'

‘You have no idea how inventive we are in that department,’ Gerber said. ‘Us stupid humans? We drop things on enemies like nobody’s business.’

‘But that’s not the whole story,’ I said.

Gerber sniffed. ‘You bringing up that silly balance thing again?’

‘Half a second.’ I flounced into the desk beside him, performing a search of my own. ‘Judge Rice, do you see this picture? That’s Robert Goddard, standing beside the first liquid-fueled rocket. Goes straight up into the sky, for miles.’ I hit some more keys. ‘That was in 1926, the same year a new flying speed record was set of more than 250 miles an hour.’

‘Two hundred and fifty?’

‘From here to the Statue of Liberty in under an hour.’

‘I marvel.’ Judge Rice grinned. ‘In my time, that journey took a good week on horseback.’

‘Well,’ I tapped in another search, ‘two years later somebody broke three hundred. Meanwhile a man flew solo across the Atlantic.’

‘In one flight?’

Gerber chuckled. ‘Not exactly a lot of refueling stops along the way.’

‘But such a distance . . .’

‘Yes,’ I said. ‘Since we’d achieved faster and farther, somebody had to go higher. Here’s a man in 1930, a balloonist, he reached forty-three thousand feet up. The next year, another man reached fifty-one thousand. Oh and here you go, this is a good one. Right at the height of the Depression – let's see . . . that was a period of economic calamity, banks failed, stocks plunged, dust-storms destroyed farms, millions of people were out of work—'

'You're doing a great job of making this uplifting,' Gerber said.

'All right,' I conceded. 'Perhaps Judge Rice would be glad he missed that era. But in the middle of all of those problems Wiley Post did a ton to lift people's spirits, and he did it with flying. He was a colorful man, see him here with the patch over one eye? Anyway in 1933 he was the first person to fly solo all the way around the world. Fifteen thousand, five hundred and ninety miles.'

'In 1933, you say.' Judge Rice lowered his eyelids, doing mental math. 'If not for the expedition, I might still have been alive.'

'Well huh,' said Gerber. 'Still, you wouldn't have always been pleased by what you saw. We haven't even touched World War II.'

'There was another war?'

'There have been wars damn near all of the time that you were gone.'

'But couldn't these inventions unite us? Create a common ground?'

'They did,' I interjected. 'Millions of people are connected all over the world now. We continually grow in our knowledge and appreciation of people who live differently.'

'Either that,' Gerber laughed, 'or we kill them.'

Judge Rice sighed. 'I am fatigued. Before I rest, however, and set my mind to work on understanding all of this, I'd like to see the limit, if I may. The outer edge of what humanity has done with aviation thus far.'

Gerber looked at me. 'Is that OK?'

'You're asking my opinion?' I said. 'Then no, I would rather you didn't.'

'Is history as terrible as all that?' Judge Rice asked.

'He's going to find out eventually anyway,' Gerber said.

I had no answer, which Gerber interpreted as assent. 'OK judge, I'll show you. But it ain't pretty.' He typed away on his keyboard. 'I think I'll skip the Hindenberg, and start with this.' He cut to a clip from Vietnam, the streak of a jet, a douse of napalm, the jungle bursting into flame. 'Not exactly slapping mosquitos, are we? Now for your viewing pleasure we have the drone, a flying bomb controlled by someone far away.' A missile streaked low and loud across the sky of a desert village. On the ground, men in turbans cowered, pointing and shouting.

'Next we have a jet itself used as a weapon.' I knew what Gerber would show then, and sure enough, the silver bird swept in on that cloudless September morning and impaled itself on a tower of steel and glass. I have seen that image a thousand times; it still stabs me.

'Oh my heaven,' Judge Rice said. 'Oh My Lord.'

'That used to be the tallest building in the world,' Gerber continued, as the first tower collapsed on itself. He kept typing, calling up information without mercy.

'Here's the real deal, your honor, the outer limit. Armageddon in a can.' He played a compilation of nuclear explosions: instant suns in the desert and on the ocean, cars tossed and buildings shredded, one mushroom cloud after another. 'The good news is that you're just seeing tests here. Only two of these bad boys have been used as weapons. But then again, each one leveled an entire city.'

I pulled my eyes from the screen to see Judge Rice with both hands over his mouth. I put a hand on his shoulder. 'Are you all right?'

'The violence of it,' he said. 'Such laudable ambition, such courage and invention, all perverted into methods of killing.'

'It's not that easy.' Gerber picked up his coffee mug but paused before drinking. 'Think of the war your father fought in. Would you send him into battle with an inferior rifle? Or was the weapon somehow justified by what he hoped victory would bring?'

'But an entire city, with one bomb? And that building, using the aircraft like a giant bullet? It boggles the mind.'

'Time to step in here,' I said. 'We need to give some perspective.'

'Come on, Kate,' Gerber said. 'Don't go sugar-coating—'

'Judge Rice, I'm not saying anything you've seen tonight is false. But there are balancing things. There is another side.'

'In truth,' he said in a low voice, 'I hope so.'

'I may not be as quick online as my friend here, but take a look at this.' I typed in a search, then streamed a video of wooden crates floating down from the sky under white parachutes. 'This is a food drop. For a city on the ocean that was flooded by an earthquake out to sea. The roads are destroyed, the people are cut off. Using planes, we are giving them food, medicine, materials for shelter.'

'Aw, shall I break out the violins?' Gerber said.

I scowled until I saw that he was smiling. He widened his eyes, rolling them side to side, the kook. I smiled back.

'Then there's beauty. Some people have turned flying into art.'

I found a video of a man with a hang glider. He stepped off the side of a steep and snowy mountain, sailing into the thermals. He was skilled with his giant kite, tipping up on one wing, then plunging near the ground only to loft away again, hover, finally glide off into the scenic distance. A dance in the air.

'We're not just killers,' I said, tapping in the next search. 'We have our redeeming qualities.'

Judge Rice did not answer. The next clip showed a stunt pilot, smoke trailing from the tip of each wing as he soared straight up, tilted upside down, tumbled wing over wing as he plummeted earthward, then caught on the wind to spiral upward again.

'Oh my goodness.'

'Finally, let me show you what can happen when we're not being "stupid" but instead work on a loftier purpose.'

Gerber sat back, hands behind his head. 'I hope this is what I think it is.'

The footage was easy to find. A man in a bulky white suit with a square backpack descended a ladder, planted his boot in gray and shallow dust. 'That's one small step for a man,' his voice declared through radio static. 'One giant leap for mankind.'

The video cut to two men erecting an American flag, bright sunlight behind them. One of them hopped leg to leg, eventually bouncing clear out of the frame.

'Where is that person located, please?'

'That's Neil Armstrong, Judge,' Gerber said. 'Totally dumb human if ever there was one. And the completely stupid place where he is standing?' Gerber nodded at me with a big grin. 'It's the moon.'

'The moon.' Judge Rice slumped in his chair, all the wind out of his sails. He rubbed both eyes with his fingers. 'Dr Philo?'

'Right here.'

'Hm. Would you kindly help me to my room now? I am exhausted.'

I remember when Chloe had teeth pulled before

getting braces, how her eyes looked hooded by the dopey anesthesia. Judge Rice's lids had a similar heaviness, which had come on in an instant. I lifted him nursing home-style, his arms around my neck. We stood a moment together, his body's fatigue resting against my body's alertness. Gerber watched but I did not care. We maneuvered away through the desks.

'The moon,' Judge Rice said. 'They were standing on the moon.'

'Yes your honor.'

As I led him into the chamber, the man from the past held me close against his side, as if I was the only thing to keep him from falling off the face of the earth.

CHAPTER 17
ONE WHO LINGERED

(ERASTUS CARTHAGE)

'It is simple,' you say to him. 'Either you contribute to the discoveries here, or the Project cannot afford you.'

Billings nods ponderously. You peer at him over your glasses. He looks terrible, pale and fatigued. But then, he is a Brit, and in your experience that entire nation could use a few days of hot meals and naps in the sun.

When he speaks, though, Billings's tone is unexpectedly firm. 'Dr Carthage, it would be my pleasure to describe for you, at whatever level of detail you desire, the relentless scope of discovery I have accomplished while every other person in this organization has been distracted by Jeremiah Rice.'

'If you dismiss Subject One as a distraction, you fail to understand the import of this entire Project.'

'So sayeth the man who knows not half of what goes on in his lab.'

Touché. After all, you were surprised by negligence in the control room. Likewise you were unaware that Dr Philo had been violating protocol and visiting Subject One, with the video monitors off no less.

Yet you smile. Is there anything on this earth more amusing, really, than an Englishman? Ever since the days of colonies in India and Hong Kong, they have possessed this odd sense of superiority, which they believe to be chivalric honor but you recognize as foolishness. Nobility to them, vanity to you. Why did a Norwegian beat a Brit to the South Pole? Because Scott, the Englishman, refused to use sled dogs. It wasn't fitting for a gentleman to rely upon animals in such a quest, he wrote in his journal, as if he were pulling up a chair at the Round Table. Thus Amundsen not only reached the pole first, returning in one piece, but thus, also, was Scott's journal recovered from a corpse.

Smile erased, you lay a palm flat on your desk. 'I am delighted that you are finding your time well spent, Dr Billings. Would you do me the honor of acquainting me with your progress?'

Billings marks your tone with a good British sniff. But he does not parry, only demonstrates the proverbial stiff upper lip and opens his notes. 'The giant iceberg which provided us with Judge Rice also yielded nine hundred and fourteen lesser samples. They fall into eleven species. We have conducted assays on ten percent of each one. Within ninety-two samples therefore tested, across all species the results are consistent.'

'Thrilling,' you say, because you cannot resist. 'Who doesn't thrive on consistency?'

Billings closes the notebook in his lap. 'Shall I stop here? There must be someone else you can condescend to.'

'Unless you intend to leave that notebook here as project property, and abandon all of your assays underway, I'd advise you to humor me.'

'Humor you, doctor? Have I not already done so, well beyond the call of duty? Who tried to keep Dr Philo from removing Judge Rice from the chamber? And who informed you first thing the next day about what had happened?'

'What I deduce from that incident is that you failed to persuade your colleague. And while I grant that Dr Philo is one of the more annoying human beings on this earth, nonetheless I admire her pluck. Whereas for reasons that go back literally to my own parentage, I have always hated a tattletale.'

That scotches him. Billings has no reply. You continue.

'Dr Billings, you assume I have not read your weekly reports. You assume wrongly. In reality I have been indulging you for all these months since the expedition returned from the north, waiting in vain for you to provide a single idea worthy of publication. Meanwhile the rest of the project is "distracted" by redefining human mortality. If I am mistaken, now is the time for you to change my mind.'

'Metabolic rates,' he says. 'All that motion in the

later reanimation period? It's not frenzy; it's not fear. The creatures all start at an incredibly slow metabolism. Remember when Dr Bolton compared Judge Rice to a sleeping bear? Hibernating is a fair analogy for the early reanimation period. But then, and this is the fascinating part,' he hitches forward in his seat, 'the creatures increase energy and motion at the same rate, because their metabolisms are increasing at that rate too. Shrimp or lobster, krill or cod, they all start slowly and then accelerate.'

You straighten a paper on your desk. 'The implications would be?'

'Breathtaking, were there not a human subject involved. We would be publishing papers by the dozen. Their shared thesis would be that the rate of acceleration is predictable. It varies only depending on the species' size – bigger means slower. But the fundamental challenge for post-animation survival is metabolic.'

He has confirmed Borden's findings, even enlarging upon them. And because it's Billings, his documentation will be superior. But has he found anything more substantive than withholding salt? The digital clock says Subject One's eighteenth day will commence soon. 'Have you solved the problem of extending Subject One's lifespan?'

'Not yet. I have two hypotheses. Minimizing his salt intake may work temporarily. But I suspect we would receive a lasting result by saturating his chamber with oxygen—'

A knock at the door prevents Billings from

continuing. Thomas enters two steps. 'Sorry to interrupt—'

'Apparently that seems to be your primary activity these days, Thomas.'

'With apologies, Dr Carthage.' He points at the window. 'But I thought you would be interested to see what's going on outside.'

You sigh. 'I'm too busy for protestors right now, thank you. I know they've found an organizer—'

'Better than that, sir.'

'One moment.' Holding a finger up at him, you turn to Billings. 'Your little creatures. Have you found at least a way to keep them alive longer?'

Billings sags like an airless balloon. 'Not yet.'

'Sir,' Thomas persists, a hand stretched toward the window. 'I urge you to take just one minute.'

You slide back your chair, rise without hurry, and stroll to the wall of glass. 'What can possibly be so urgent?'

Instantly you have your answer. Below, there is a spectacle: hundreds of people stand around the front door. The crowd spills down the sidewalk in both directions, with more people clustered in the street. The usual protestors have drawn back – intimidated, you'd wager. The group at the door looks unruly, possibly mob-like.

One woman stands apart from both clusters. She wears a white beret, and there is something arresting about her. Some focus, some patience. But your attention returns to the rabble, where people shove and angle their way forward.

'Jesus God. Who are all these people, Thomas?'

He hastens to stand at your elbow. 'Offspring, sir.'

'Excuse me?'

'That is what they allege, at least. Grandsons, granddaughters, cousins and nieces and nephews. They all say they are relatives of Jeremiah Rice.'

'Bloody nonsense.' It is Billings, looking down from your other side. 'There are nearly a thousand people down there. Judge Rice would have to be the most prolific man since Methuselah.'

You sigh audibly. Is every person you hired for this project secretly a dolt? 'None of those people is a descendant of Subject One. Not one. Yet neither are they con men or fools. They believe something deeply, even if it is a fiction. What they express is the public's yearning to connect with Subject One, and with the work of this Project. Don't you see? I don't mean to dismiss your metabolic findings, Billings. In another time I might have found them compelling, especially if you had longevity results. But today something of a different order is underway. We see evidence of it everywhere. This is clear empirical data, right here on our doorstep. Do you understand?'

'Three more months,' he replies. 'Ninety days and I'll provide you with long-term survival answers. I am incredibly close.'

'I'll compromise,' you say. 'But desist with the reports. They clutter the mind, and my desk. Thomas, schedule Dr Billings on my calendar for ten weeks hence.'

'Yes sir.'

'Ten weeks? Well . . . well. I'll do what I can. Thank you, Dr Carthage.' Billings backs away. 'Thank you.'

Why do people who fawn make you wish for a breath mint? After all, you have given him seventy days to produce what any realistic scientist knows could take years. Billings collects his notes and hurries off. But his very haste, when the human display at your feet is infinitely more interesting, undermines your confidence that he will find much of anything. After so many years with an eye pressed to a microscope, the man simply does not know where to look.

'Thomas, call the police and have these people removed.'

'Yes sir.'

'Alert the media as well. I want this crowd on the evening news. We must inform the world that the Lazarus Project is not some sort of popular club, which any member of the proletariat is invited to join.'

'No sir.'

And thus you stand there until the police arrive, the TV cameras only minutes later. A hundred or so people meander away; you imagine they do not want their folly broadcast to the world. The rest insist on being heard, meeting Jeremiah, being allowed inside. A policeman in charge climbs on a bench and reads something loudly enough that you can discern his tone through the glass. It is neither friendly nor patient.

The crowd begins to disperse, first at the edges and then along the sidewalk. A few people who had worked their way nearest to the entry appear reluctant to surrender that advantage, even when it becomes clear that no one will be entering the building. One man shoves a police officer, but finds himself immediately on the pavement, face down while handcuffs are applied. A cameraman leans so close he could have locked the cuffs himself. His footage will certainly be on television that night.

The rest of the crowd needs no more incentive to depart. You take a call, you dictate a fund raising letter, you return to your perch. It has, so it seems, a gravitational pull. The rabble has left, the police and media are gone, the protestors remain quiet for the day. You give yourself a good glop of sanitizer, rubbing your hands one on the other as if warming them.

Only then do you notice that the woman in the white beret has remained in place all this time, standing on the green across the road. She has not moved. Now she takes off her hat, loosening a cascade of corkscrew curls. She casts her eyes over the façade of the building, as if looking for something in one of the windows. Her scrutiny continues a long time, whole minutes. Eventually she tucks her curls behind her ears, sets her hat snugly in place. She gives the building one more scan, her expression unquestionably in a minor key, then shuffles away with her head down.

And you wonder.

'Thomas?'

He pokes back in the doorway. 'Sir?'

'Please tell Dr Philo that in addition to her current duties, she is now to research the legacy of Subject One. Children, real estate, investments, the works.'

'Yes sir.' He hesitates. 'By the way, I notice we are now well into Day 18.'

'Your point being?'

'Just three more days till we see Dr Borden's methods confirmed. We are almost out of the woods.'

'That, or ruined.'

'Yes sir. Is there anything in particular you'd like Dr Philo to seek?'

'All of it,' you say. 'She deciphered his boot, and that was before we knew the man's name or job. Now I want her to find out everything.'

CHAPTER 18

SEVEN KINDS OF APPLES

My name is Jeremiah Rice and I begin to remember.

They did not expect to succeed. That remains the only plausible explanation for their failure to anticipate the awakening of a human being, with a personality, with attitudes and attributes, with desires. They made no accommodation because they were entirely unready for such a thing. They had no plan beyond ambition.

Perhaps a monkey accepts imprisonment in the zoo as the lot of the ignorant beast, but a man knows in his soul when he is not free. The passage of a century eclipses none of my perception of present realities: I am under constant observation. I have neither proper clothing nor cash. I pass my days and sleep my nights in a chamber more laboratory than boudoir. There is an electronic combination to enter or exit my quarters, and I have not been entrusted with the number. The people of here and now mean me no ill, I believe, but neither does the mule-driver to his mule. Free man that I am by law and Constitution, I have no liberty to speak of. Until my overwhelming aviation experience with Drs Gerber and Philo, no one had bothered much to acquaint me with the brilliant and violent nature of the time in which I again live.

The exception, quite clearly, is Dr Philo. She attends kindly to my care at all times. She it was who told me where I am, and in which month and year. In rare moments she reminds me of my eldest sister, whose years of teaching school gave her a patient and instructive way. Dr Philo's efforts to ease my transition, to gentle my introduction to here and now, are compassionate. Whilst she answers to many in this enterprise, however, I surmise by observation that none answers to her. Normally I would need no ambassador, but these times are far from normal. I might advocate more effectively on my own behalf, had I the energy. Instead I frequently endure fatigue as severe as it is sudden. I remain optimistic, however; each day exhaustion afflicts me less.

I recall when Joan was confined with the swelling and fatigue that became Agnes. Mornings I would bring Joan's tea to our chamber with a bit of bread and cheese. Whilst wholly contradictory to Joan's prior habit of leaping into the day with guns ablaze, cats scampering under the furniture and myself taking orders in longhand, she found that eating before rising proved an effective prophylactic against nausea. Moreover I discovered a pleasure in providing for her in this way, before I hastened off to court and my day of disputes small and large.

Joan complained that I was spoiling her. Today, at this remove in time, I sincerely hope so. Who leaves this world having known too much love? Who departs this life having received an excess of kindness?

Besides, she was perpetually tired in those months. If I returned home for the midday meal, I might discover Joan upstairs napping. Evenings she retired early, such that I frequently savored my dram of port by the fire alone, wondering whether solitude might become the primary atmosphere of my parental life. Hm. I think now on those quiet hours, and better appreciate the inexpressible richness they contained: a true and loyal wife creating our child within herself.

Joan recovered from her exhaustion within minutes of bearing Agnes into the world, which I recall optimistically each time I now experience an episode of lapsed vigor. So too, by degrees, did an intimacy return between us of surpassing tenderness, with Agnes beside us nursing, or murmuring in her bedside cradle. When I pause in my exertions to understand the here and now, and contemplate the severing of that kindness, that mercy, the ache is so acute I half-expect to see some place on myself that is bleeding.

The magnitude of what I have lost eclipses my amazement at being alive again. I have been parted from Joan more than one hundred years, yet my confused heart feels only the passage of weeks since our ship sailed for the north. This is why, much as I desire to visit Lynn, I feel reluctance as well: it would be as though returning from our great voyage, but the additional reality of her absence would incapacitate me. Whenever my mind turns in that direction, my body literally shudders.

Yet also I wonder, as I battle with heartache and fatigue, and as my eagerness for freedom recovers, with what odd idea am I now pregnant? What new prospect does my existence birth upon the world?

The answer thus far seems the rather, to lie in the opposite direction. That is to say, the world apparently wishes to birth itself upon me. I have received interview and introduction invitations by the thousand. Dr Philo diligently screens the requests, prioritizing them, assessing their value to me and to the Project. Thusly did we select an unusual first foray into public life, my novitiate experience with the world of today. Remembering the social pleasures of market days in Lynn, I had professed an interest in witnessing a place of common trade. After some conversation, we settled on a location Dr Philo said offered the likelihood of anonymity, whilst providing ample opportunity to participate in contemporary commerce. She said this place was called a supermarket.

Ha ha, the experience proved as overstimulating as a carnival. It began the moment we stepped out of the laboratory building. A crowd of people stood gathered, waving signs in a half-circle around some strange devices on waist-high stilts.

'Damn,' Dr Philo said. 'Wouldn't you know we'd step into the middle of one of their news conferences?'

'What is happening here?' I said.

'They're doing a little show for the TV cameras,' she said. 'Let's get out of here, before someone—'

'There he is,' a man shouted from the crowd. They all turned, fifty strong, as one. The cameras followed suit. A comic memory came to mind from a pond of my boyhood in Lynn, throwing a bread-end in the shallows at one mallard, only to see dozens of ducks suddenly swimming in my direction.

'It's him. Wait.'

'Damn,' Dr Philo said again, and she pulled me by my elbow to the end of the block. The world seemed a blur of noises and smoke. Automobiles sped past, fearsome and purposeful. She held up an arm and one of the vehicles yanked to the edge of the sidewalk. 'Perfect,' she said, opening the door. 'Get in quickly, please.'

I obeyed despite my apprehensions, and she tumbled in after me. Breathless, she gave the driver an address and sat back.

'What was that?' I asked. 'Who are those people?'

Dr Philo began a reply but I confess to missing it, because the vehicle lurched into the traffic and I tumbled against her. My hands went somewhere indistinct, my face undeniably in her breasts. Then the car swerved the opposite way, which disentangled me from the embarrassing situation but tossed me against the opposite door.

'Ease up, will you?' Dr Philo called forward. The driver replied in a foreign tongue. I found handles on the door and clung to them.

We proceeded to careen through the city, my stomach pressed back when we accelerated and pulled forward when cars ahead required us to slow. I tried looking out the window, wondering if I would recognize anything, while attempting to attend to Dr Philo's explanation of that crowd. Candidly though, the ride was like a toboggan run down an icy hill. I concentrated primarily on holding down my breakfast, thin lab gruel that it had been.

Eventually we reached a quiet area of the city, and the driver halted as abruptly as he apparently did everything else. He announced the price for our ride and it was a staggering sum. My Joan could have fed dinner to an army for that cost. Yet Dr Philo paid without hesitation, without even haggling. I held my tongue.

'Here we go,' Dr Philo said. She held the door as I climbed out. We stood in a place the size of a small corn field, but it was paved just like the roads. She held her arms out as though framing the building. 'Your basic American grocery store. Taa-daa.'

Outside the market stood racks of wheeled

metal cages parked one into the other. Dr Philo pulled on the end of a chain of them, at which one unfolded with a great clatter. I glanced around but no one remarked upon our hubbub. She piloted the cart toward the supermarket's doors, which opened at our approach though there was no doorman in sight. I jumped back of course, as she strolled through the door without me.

Then Dr Philo noticed my absence, turned, and held a hand in my direction 'It's all right,' she said. 'Come on in.'

Inside the place was lit as brightly as a surgical theater, and seemed the size of a city block. She led me down row after row of commodities, so many sizes and varieties I wondered how anyone could know enough to purchase the right thing. Three sizes of eggs, available in white or brown shells. Possibly forty forms of bread, lined up on their shelves and wrapped in a material like soft glass, a window but somehow flexible. I imagined all the commerce of century-ago Lynn collected in one giant room, and still this store outrivaled it. Eventually we came to flour, which incidentally I know a little about. A baker of breads and pies, Joan often asked me to purchase flour on my way home from court. There were nine kinds in this market, available in three different sizes.

'This will not do,' I told Dr Philo, holding a five-pound bag in each hand.

'No? Why not?'

'How am I to choose which to buy when I cannot see whether it's wormy or spoiled?'

'Wormy?' She was smiling at me.

'I am quite serious. Moreover, how do I know that these containers are a legitimate measure? Do you believe this is five pounds? I've known many a grocer with a thumb on the back of his scale.'

She laughed. It was a fine melody, no tone of mockery but rather of delight. Then Dr Philo embarked upon an explanation about the government enforcing food quality standards, as well as uniform weights and measures. It reminded me of my professor in law school who taught contracts, his bow-tied confidence in written documents as the reliable basis for trust in transactions. Dr Philo similarly believed what she was saying, and evidenced no foolhardiness about it. In the end I surmised that people here and now simply trust the sellers. The weight on the package will be accurate, and flour moths are a thing of the past.

That means my skepticism as a customer must also be a thing of the past. Hm. What an odd way to conduct commerce.

Dr Philo saved the market's most stunning revelation for last: the produce. I remember Christmas when I was six, and in addition to mittens my grandmother had knitted from thick lamb's wool, and calf-high boots my father had purchased all the way down on Hanover Street, my mother gave me the unprecedented joy of an orange, an entire orange all my own.

Here there were oranges singly and by the bag, bright and unblemished, as well as lemons, limes, and more. I saw strawberries perfect and huge, though outside it was the budding of springtime, ripe berries ordinarily months away. There were bananas piled in jaundiced bunches, potatoes by the dusty sack, carrots long and orange, peppers and cucumbers, tomatoes in May, one marvel upon another. I realized too that I craved these foods, and wondered when the flavors of the world might be returned to me, when I would taste more than lab porridge and the memory of throat-scouring salt.

Here stood pyramids of apples, I counted seven different varieties, glossy under the lights. The horn of plenty had arrived on this earth and it was displayed like a shrine.

Yet inexplicably the people moved their carts dully amid all of this abundance, picking and choosing as though it were as ordinary as firewood.

Seized by boldness, I grabbed an orange. 'May I?'

'I suppose we can risk upsetting Dr Borden's caloric experiments without the world coming to an end,' Dr Philo said. 'Would you like a bag of them?'

I read the price. It was breathtaking. 'Thank you, no. One is plenty.'

She placed my orange in the cart beside oatmeal, raisins, and soap she'd chosen earlier. I followed her to a line of people standing behind carts like ours. Most contained many more objects, with nearly all of the goods wrapped in that soft glass material. As we advanced, racks displaying small, bright packages formed us into rows like so many cattle on our way to branding. I saw money change hands, and realized: this is where we pay. Whilst we waited I scanned the people thumbing through magazines, poking away at miniature versions of the computer device Dr Gerber had demonstrated for me, playing with their infants, or staring blankly into the air.

Soon though, my attention was riveted on the young woman in charge of our line. She operated a device like a cash register, though instead of ringing and showing the cost, it beeped and produced a slender sheet of printed paper. Despite a face that made no effort to conceal its thorough boredom, she worked with the speed of a dervish. A stocky fellow stood behind her, packing purchases into sacks, and he could not keep up. More than her competence, though, I was fascinated by the ring she wore in her nose as though she were some kind of pygmy. There was another hooked through the bone of her right eyebrow. Hm. I could not imagine anything more painful, but she evidenced no discomfort. Once our turn at her machine arrived, I saw that she had three more rings on each ear as well. When she opened her mouth to announce the total cost to Dr Philo, I could not decide which was more flabbergasting: the price of our little sack of groceries, or the fact that our cashier had somehow impaled a bar of steel into the center of her tongue. I cannot remember the last time I witnessed something so simultaneously disgusting and fascinating. When the transaction concluded and she said to us, 'Have a nice day,' I heard the metal clack against her front teeth.

'You too,' Dr Philo said, strolling away.

'Have a nice day,' I echoed, lingering for another look. She turned forward, bored as ever, and began tallying the next customer.

It was all I could do to restrain myself until we were outside. Again the doors swept open ahead of us, but I was too intent to recoil. As soon as they had closed I blurted, 'What nation was that woman from?'

Dr Philo scanned the roadway for another car to hail. 'What do you mean?'

'She had more piercings than a pirate.'

Again she gave that laugh, bright teeth and not an ounce of scorn. 'That's just a thing that kids do now. You'll see them with tattoos too.'

'Has America become a tribal place?'

'Now there's a question.' She tucked the grocery bag under one arm, waved the other, and a car across the boulevard honked, weaving through other motor carriages toward us. 'It's complicated, Judge Rice. If we are, it's not in the way that you mean.'

She opened the door and motioned for me to precede her. I shook my head no, bowing, not this time, and she clambered ahead. Once we settled in and she gave the driver the address of the lab,

I gripped the handles fiercely. Gradually I realized that this driver would not be tossing us hither and yon. As I released my grip, Dr Philo smiled. 'We must seem incredibly strange to you.'

'Not strange, especially. Wealthy.'

She turned in her seat. 'Do you think so? That market was nothing fancy.'

'Seven kinds of apples.'

'True.' She nodded. 'I am going to have to figure out how to explain all of this for you. So much has changed.'

I contemplated that idea as we sped through town. Everything was new, of course, but everything old remained immediate in my memory too. I would have loved to show Joan that market. The apple trees in our side yard in Lynn had produced such modest yields; she would have found the fruit of here and now to be miraculous.

Outside the car window, buildings blurred by. Lights flashed, people hurried along the sidewalks with phones to their heads. As we turned a corner a woman tugged her dog's leash, and the animal sat obediently at her heel. It was the smallest dog I had ever seen. Something about that image, about seeing the pitiful creature held on a tether, gave me a moment's courage. 'Could you possibly accomplish something else for me first, Dr Philo? At the lab?'

'I can certainly try. What is it?'

'I hesitate to ask, given what your project has already done for me. But I am a grown man, thirty-eight years old if you don't count the decades I was gone.'

'What is it you need, Judge Rice?'

'A proper bed. In a proper room, with a bit of privacy. Hm. I don't expect anything approaching the home I once had. But perhaps a window? A chair, a lamp? Possibly some books? Just a few: Shakespeare, Tolstoy, Dickens perhaps. I have no friends left on this earth, but still I might enjoy some modest comforts.'

Dr Philo did not reply. Had I erred? She kept her gaze steadfast out the window. I could see the muscles in her jaw working, but still she did not speak.

'Never mind,' I said at last. 'Forgive me, excuse my mistake. Please. It's just that in this new world, I do not properly know my place.'

She turned then, and shocked me: her eyes brimmed with tears. 'Not the littlest bit did you make a mistake. It just shows . . .'

I waited. She wiped a knuckle across her cheekbone but did not speak.

'It shows . . .' I prompted.

'It shows that Carthage has no idea what you are living through. It shows that this Project has its head completely up its ass.'

She had never spoken to me with such heat before. 'I beg your—'

'It also shows what a wimp I have been about getting you taken care of. But the answer isn't Carthage. That guy won't let go of a nickel till he's squeezed six cents out of it. The answer is the world.' She nodded to herself. 'Oh yes, everybody wants to be Judge Rice's friend.'

'I'm not certain I understand.'

'You want a few creature comforts? They're on their way. You want some friends? I will get you thousands.'

When we returned to the Project, the protestors were ready. They had shaped themselves in a triangle, their captain at the apex. Like a preacher he would call and they responded in kind. To my ears the sounds collided chaotically, but Dr Philo made sense of them.

'Crazier every day,' she said. 'This way, Judge Rice.'

She led me unnoticed along the building's flank, to the rear. There the feeling was less of laboratory or office and more of industry, with a place for unloading and storing goods, parking for cars, and no crowds. Dr Philo swept a card through a device on the wall and I could hear the doors unlock.

We had barely stepped inside when a wave of exhaustion swept over me. I slumped against the wall but Dr Philo supported me instantly. She straightened under my arm till I stood upright, then guided me forward. Despite the grocery bag in her free hand, I felt her strength firmly against me. She whispered reassurances, to keep walking, we were almost there and the like. I barely heard her words, instead discerning the more important element, the tone of concern and affection. As we hobbled past the guard, it dawned upon me that she was a person I could genuinely trust. And so my hand, which had hung in the air past her arm, came down to rest upon her shoulder, and drew her near.

Dr Philo's only reaction was to stop speaking. The silence was not awkward, however. Instead, as we waited for the elevator, it felt as comfortable as the manner in which we held each other.

The doors opened and there stood Dr Gerber. His face lit at the sight of us, though Dr Philo pulled away from me. I steadied my legs as though at sea.

'Oh ho. Welcome back, intrepid travelers,' he cried. 'But I must give you a warning. Carthage is on the warpath. Something Billings did or didn't do, and the boss was shouting about it while I was trying to work. Anyway that was my cue to go for an evening stroll, and I encourage you two to keep a low profile too.'

'Thanks.'

We moved past him, Dr Philo pressing the button to send us upward. Before the doors touched, Dr Gerber caught one with his hand. 'Remember kids: don't do anything I wouldn't do.'

'Give it a rest, Gerber,' Dr Philo said. Then the doors came together.

'I don't understand,' I said.

'He's teasing me,' she replied. 'It's complicated.'

Upstairs I found the energy to reach the chamber

on my own powers. On the way in I noticed a counter of some kind, numbers in bright red: 21:07:41. There was one by the chamber, one in the control room, and now that I recollected, one in the glass foyer downstairs.

'What is that device counting?'

'That's the number of days since you were reanimated,' she said.

'Is it significant in some way?'

Dr Philo pressed a combination of buttons to open the chamber door. 'Not that anyone has told me.'

I went straight to the bed, but remembered my manners and leaned on it rather than lying prone immediately, as I was inclined. First I thanked Dr Philo for the supermarket trip, which I said felt like a trial expedition to the here and now. 'Also I am grateful for your speed at catching me each time that my energy collapses. I appreciate the trusting manner in which we walk together.'

She pursed her lips at that, not speaking, and again I wondered if I had erred in some way. Dr Philo shook her head as though a fly were buzzing near, then dug into the grocery bag and placed my orange on the table.

'I'll check back after hurricane Carthage has passed,' she said, punching the security numbers again. 'Have a good rest.'

And she was gone. The room immediately felt mechanical and gray. There was aught else for me to do but hoist my weary bones upright, cross the room, and pick up that singular orange. It was brighter colored than any I'd seen in my prior time. The smell was wonderfully familiar, calling forth associations that ranged from that childhood Christmas gift to Joan's recipe for fruited ham. The peel was thicker, so my thumb could dig it open and away easily. The fruit within was unmarred. I spread the wedges – and mystery of mysteries, there were no seeds. How could that be possible? How could a fruit persist in this world without reproduction?

I pulled one section free. My mouth watered at the prospect; this was a perfect orange, the Platonic ideal. I paused, aware of how desire can be its own reward, and recalled what eating one felt like, how refreshing, watery, and tart. I brought that wedge up to my nose. The scent was fine, milder than I recalled but my desire not one whit reduced.

Oh, I felt foolish for cultivating such sensuality about a fruit, however fine a specimen, and bit the wedge neatly in half.

There was almost no flavor. It was watery, yes, and there was a slight tang. But the rich wash of sensation I remembered was somehow missing. I took another bite, and the taste was the same. Bland, to be honest. Dull. I ate more, each section thumbing away effortlessly as one would hope, but the meat of the fruit tasted far less, well, less *orange*.

Half of the way through, I stopped. Were my memories that much stronger than the truth? Or did oranges in the here and now somehow contain less flavor than their imperfect ancestors? I found that notion hard to fathom. The farming expertise that cultivated this fruit to its visual ideal could not have forgotten the most important element, could it? Not possible, not in a race so competent and advanced. The explanation I settled on was far simpler: somehow in its century of being inanimate, my tongue had lost sensitivity.

I set the fruit aside, concluding that the fault lay not in the orange but in myself. It must have been me.

CHAPTER 19

LOVELY EVENING

(DANIEL DIXON)

The deadline is my friend. Sure, there's pressure, and compromises when you're running out of time. But take it from yours truly, if it wasn't for deadlines nothing important would ever get done.

That particular night my editor had been bearing down on me to write an update for *Intrepid's* website. I'd stalled him as long as I could. Normally I can bang out a piece like that half asleep: anecdotal lead, hooking quote, news peg by sentence four, stakes in the fifth paragraph, three sources, inverted pyramid structure and a nice kicker, easy as drinking a beer.

But with all the back and forth with Carthage that day, including his tantrum about Billings, I'd been as distracted as a teenage waterboy at cheerleading practice. Not to mention tracking down all those people who'd claimed to be the good judge's descendants, a first-rate goose chase that scored a colossal zilch. What kind of desperate fool pretends to be related to someone just for the possible fame? Plus I'd been interviewing bigwigs for my book:

pray tell, sir and ma'am, what the Lazarus Project means to our disintegrating society and all that hot air. So the day job was coming in at something like fourth place – but what magazine would fire a reporter hooked into a story as rich and rare as this one?

There were also the cosmic questions. That's what I called them. Such as what is life now that it persists outside of the rules we've understood for all human time? Nothing would ever bring my parents back, of course. But if Carthage had outsmarted freezing to death, what other tricks might he accomplish in the years ahead? If he beat ice, could he someday beat fire?

By habit I checked the digital counter of old Frank's reawakened days. Fourteen hours and forty-one minutes into Day 21. Ho hum. The guy snored in his glass cabin like a millionaire on vacation. The real squeeze was 9 a.m., when my story had to be filed.

On the plus side, the regular clock read 1:15 a.m., which meant the imminent arrival of the delectable Dr Kate. Life was about to improve. Maybe she could be the lead. I'd interviewed her just the other day about introducing the judge to the modern world. She described their trip to a supermarket, how our everyday life can be overwhelming compared with a century ago.

I dug in my satchel for that notebook and flipped to her comments, but new distractions always arrive just in time, and right then Gerber came bopping in.

'The mad scientist returns,' I called. 'What misdeeds have you been up to now?'

Gerber barely registered me. 'I've been strolling in the lovely evening,' he said, then bee-lined for his desk. He sat, sniffed around for a moment, then clapped the headphones into place. 'Lovely, lovely, lovely.' He nudged the mouse on his desk. His computer screen refreshed instantly, to a page filled with Chinese characters.

CHAPTER 20

DAY 22

(KATE PHILO)

No one told me anything. If I had known what the reanimation clocks meant, what they were counting, I doubt I would have wasted Judge Rice's time wandering through the fruit section of a Safeway. Months later, when people re-read Dixon's article about the supermarket trip, when our outing appeared to squander the judge's precious limited time, they would say it showed one of two things. Either the whole project was a hoax, or I had no feelings whatsoever. Either way, I was evil.

The truth is, I was not one hundred percent awake. I'd worked my usual shift, 1:30 a.m. till midmorning, by which time the rest of the control room chairs were occupied. Only then would I fold my arms on my desk to nap. By noon I'd be refreshed enough for a productive workday, home for dinner, back after midnight. It sounds worse than it was; since moving to Boston after we found the judge, I hadn't had time to make one friend. There was nowhere else I wanted to be.

Judge Rice began fidgeting at about 4 a.m. though, waking fully before 5. Dixon had gone home by then, to my relief. So I opened the chamber door. Judge Rice followed me to the control room, pulling up a chair for another session at the computer. This time Gerber was intent upon his screen, so without a contradictory voice I showed the judge great buildings from around the world, hilarious jugglers, clips from Olympic games. Also, because he insisted, video after video about man walking on the moon. Judge Rice had a way of taking things in, making this little noise – 'hm' – as though he were in court, hearing evidence. It may have been a protection too, I think, to keep him from being overwhelmed. However bizarre our world might seem to him, each new discovery brought the same 'hm.' Duly noted. Proceed.

Still, it was clear his brain worked everything over. He'd slide the chair back for a pause. He'd walk a lap or two around the control room, scratching his puffy whiskers, then ask me please to continue.

I began to feel like his teacher. Oh, it wasn't the rich experience of a classroom, so many minds, such different energies from day to day. But the opportunity to instruct this unique man in the ways of today was the highest privilege.

When the early tech crew began to arrive, Judge Rice stood, bowed his thanks, returned to bed. I found myself watching him, a slow shuffle as the security door hissed closed. His weariness reminded me of my sister Chloe's toddler daughters, who play all day, then run out of gas in seconds, often needing to be carried up to bed.

When he began unbuttoning his shirt, at once I returned to my desk. I still had charts to complete, systems to back up. It was a long morning, but I wrapped up by 10:30. I was just settling down when Carthage wandered into the control room, Borden on his heels.

Or should I say, appeared to wander. Because their casualness was so visibly false, all the technicians made sure to look busy. My all-nighter meant I slumped unapologetically at my desk, but otherwise even Gerber sat up straight, adjusting his headphones as an executive might straighten his tie.

Borden sidled around the room's perimeter, pausing to scan the latest *Perv Du Jour* before continuing behind the desks. His mannerisms – tugging at the point of his beard, darting a tongue over his lips – made him look a bit like a wind-up toy. Carthage bent to an unused computer to check his email, as if it had changed since he'd left his office minutes before. After an interval whose duration I'm certain he'd calculated, he swaggered over to tap Gerber on the shoulder.

Gerber lifted one ear of the headphones. 'Yeeeessss?'

'All vitals good this morning?'

Gerber tilted his head from side to side. 'Everything's normal, other than odd sleeping hours last night. Spent a good three hours in the bullpen here, learning about the world online. But the good judge is out cold now.'

'Did anyone reattach monitors when Subject One returned to bed?'

'Not that I recall.'

'Which means,' Carthage snuffed, 'for all you know he could be dead.'

'If he is,' Gerber said, wearing a penitent expression, 'I think that would be bad.' He cackled, covering the exposed ear again.

By then Borden had reached the reanimation clock. I watched him. The next few seconds turned the minutes, then hours, then Judge Rice began Day 22.

'Dr Philo?' Carthage called.

I sat upright.

'Go awaken Subject One.'

'Excuse me?'

'Wake him up,' Borden said. 'Chop chop.'

'Your instructions have always been to let him—'

'Wake him now, doctor,' Carthage said. 'Right now.'

'Fine.' I slid my feet back into their clogs, rose, made for the security door.

'If something is amiss, do not touch Subject One or alter anything,' Borden said.

I paused while punching in the key code. 'Why would anything be amiss?'

Of course they didn't answer. I expected that. What I hadn't counted on, though, was the feeling of intrusion when I entered the chamber. The walls and floors were still institutional gray, cool lighting spilling in from the control room. But the chamber also contained Judge Rice's smell, the earthy leather scent I'd noticed before. His clothes were draped on a desk chair wheeled up to the bedside. This was a man's space, and I an uninvited woman. When had I last stood beside a bed containing a sleeping man?

The body was still, blankets rumpled enough that it was impossible to tell if Judge Rice were breathing. I inched forward, pausing to check the long control room window. Carthage and Borden stood close, staring in. I felt as though the judge and I were in a fishbowl. Or a jail. I noticed Billings had arrived too, hovering between my desk and Gerber's. Only then did my suspicions rise. What were they all up to out there?

Carthage motioned with his hands, urging me along. I reached Judge Rice's bed. He slept on his stomach and wore no shirt, the sheets low, revealing his bare shoulders. I checked the window again. Carthage put his hands on his hips in impatience.

I placed my palm on Jeremiah's back, below the left shoulder blade, just above his heart. The skin was smooth, warm.

'Judge Rice?' I shook him a little, my hand involuntarily turning the gesture into a caress. Could anyone see? I pulled back to shake him again. 'Judge Rice?'

He squinted one eye while opening the other. 'Yes? Good morning. What is it?'

'Dr Philo?' Carthage boomed through the audio feed. 'That's all for now.'

Outside the glass Carthage was beaming. Borden jumped up and down as though someone had scored a touchdown. Billings had a hand over his mouth, while Gerber took his headphones off with a puzzled expression.

'Is everything all right?' Judge Rice asked.

I realized my hand was still on his skin. 'Everything's fine,' I said, standing straight. 'Perfectly fine. Excuse me a moment, would you please?'

'Of course. Should I rise and dress?'

'Pardon the interruption.' I tucked a sheet in. 'You go on back to sleep.'

By the time I reached the control room Gerber had his hands on his hips, standing two feet from Carthage. 'I am saying explain yourself, right now.'

'We did it,' Borden said, hopping from foot to foot. 'We actually did it.'

'Did what?'

'It's not in your field,' Carthage said, putting down the phone he'd used for the chamber audio. He was trying to make it appear like he wasn't backing down from Gerber. 'Dr Borden and I completed an experiment today. It succeeded. That's all.'

Gerber sniffed. 'You two have tests going on that you haven't shared with me?'

'Or me?' I said.

'It's on a need-to-know basis,' Carthage said.

'And you didn't need,' Borden added.

Gerber scratched his head, which I took as my opening. 'If I didn't need to know, why did you need me to go in there?'

Carthage spoke down his nose. 'None of your business.'

'You were necessary in case Subject One was near death,' Billings said. 'He would respond to you before anyone else.'

Gerber froze, fingers in his curls. 'What are you talking about?'

Carthage glared at Billings, who continued anyway. 'Twenty-one days, Kate. That is how long we expected our esteemed barrister to live, post reanimation.'

Billings went on to describe the body-mass calculations, Borden's salt strategy, the odds that Judge Rice would not have woken at my touch. 'In truth, my dear Kate,' he said to me, 'we half-expected you to find him cold.'

'So wait.' Gerber pressed downward with his hands, as though he were a traffic cop telling someone to slow down. 'You had a life or death situation going on, but you didn't bother to share it with your senior research staff?' He laughed. 'That's hilarious.'

Carthage folded his arms. I stood there steaming.

'At least *I* told you,' Billings said, facing me. 'They didn't want to explain even now. Perhaps that brings me a smidge back into your good graces?'

'This place is incredible,' I said. 'Billings, you feel like a hero for telling me after the fact, when Gerber and I might have helped solve this problem. And you two.' I turned to Borden and Carthage. 'You may know science, but you know nothing about what the life of the man in there is worth. This place is not a zoo.'

Carthage just made his weird lopsided smirk. 'There you are wrong,' he said. 'That is precisely what this place is. A zoo. What you fail to recognize is that Dr Borden and I are the zoo-keepers.'

CHAPTER 21

DRESSED TO MEET THE WORLD

My name is Jeremiah Rice and I begin to awaken.

It began in earnest on the twenty-second day when Dr Philo came for me, stirring me from sleep so deep I felt thawed once again out of the ice. Twice now she has placed her hand on me directly. Though my mind has no awareness of the century I spent insensate, my skin knows every second that it has gone without human touch. When her hand lifted away that morning, I felt immediately parched.

With a deep breath, I sat upright. Some debate was underway out in the control room. I observed how Dr Philo remonstrated and Dr Gerber laughed, Drs Carthage and Borden remained as impassive as gargoyles and Dr Billings volleyed from one duo to the other like a diplomat. I wondered if I were the agent of this dispute, if my request for privacy and other amenities had created a conflict. At last the two in charge swept from the room like general and lieutenant, king and minion, Billings at their heels, whilst my friends went to their desks, continuing to speak animatedly across the room.

I rose to don yet again the attire of prior days, and noted that the fabrics were tiring. The surgical clothes given me early on were inappropriate for public wear. My trouser cuffs, frayed before I went overboard, now were beyond mending. The shirt button at my throat remained clasped by a last thin thread. Hardly would I ask for a change of clothes, however, until I knew that my last request's dispute was resolved.

I placed some of Dr Borden's porridge in the windowed box that heats food faster than any stove imaginable, pressed buttons to initiate its humming and turning of the platter inside, and in minutes was swallowing down my ration of gruel. Thin pleasure, to be sure. I thought the spoon had more flavor than the food. Setting the empty bowl aside, I heard the restraining door hiss. In charged Dr Philo, her sleeves rolled up.

'Big day today, Judge Rice. Big day.'

'What new pleasures and adventures have you planned, Dr Philo?'

'What I promised yesterday – to find you a thousand friends.' She picked up my half-eaten orange. 'You all set with this?'

'I apologize. I simply—'

'No problem, your honor.' She tossed the remainder in the waste bin without comment. 'I'm glad you're dressed. We have a lot of ground to cover.'

I stood, rubbing my hands together as if to warm myself. 'Lead on, doctor.'

Outside the protestors were barking like dogs, led by one at the front with a hand-held device that magnified his voice such that it echoed off the buildings. Between cheers he taught them a drill of some kind: one of their number would volunteer to stand a bit aside, and at a signal from the leader the rest would rush to form a circle around that one. Then another would volunteer and the group would rush to surround him. They hurried from spot to spot, reminding me of a barn cat that lets its mouse escape a dozen times before making the kill. I heard their leader call the exercise 'swarming,' though to me it suggested coercion, entrapment. To my relief, this time we skirted the green without attracting his notice. Whatever their game, I did not want to play.

Dr Philo took me, as if she had read my thoughts that morning, to a haberdasher. She called it something else, and the store's name was 'Garb.' But the moment we stepped inside, I recognized the form of establishment.

A salesman descended on us. 'You are that reawakened man, aren't you?' he said, scurrying across the carpet.

'This is Jeremiah Rice,' Dr Philo said.

'Honored to meet you sir.' The salesman shook my hand vigorously. 'My name is Franklin. And today we would be looking for . . .?'

‘I don’t know,’ I said, turning to her as well. ‘A gray suit?’

‘Everything,’ she told Franklin. ‘Time to bring the man up to date.’

‘Excellent. Marvelous. I just knew today was going to be a special day. Marcy? Oh Marcy?’

A freckled waif came from the back room, a silver ring through one nostril – the oddities of here and now were apparently limitless – and folding a shirt as she entered. Franklin told her where to find his phone, which he explained to me also contained a camera. My experience with photography consisted of long held poses with the captain and crew prior to the expedition’s departure. The camera was larger than a breadbox, stood on three legs, and had a cloth draped over the back. When she returned with a device smaller than a pack of cards, I was perplexed. But Marcy dutifully pointed it at me in my worn clothes, displaying the photograph a moment later, my whiskered face, my surprised eyes.

Franklin bustled back. ‘This is going to be so much fun.’

I cannot say the subsequent hour fit that description, exactly, but there was a certain amusing giddiness in trying on so many garments. The store boasted a wealth of options. Dr Philo left to buy herself a coffee, while I tried on each of a stack of shirts. When she returned, she pulled Franklin aside and they chatted a moment. He nodded, looking at me meaningfully.

'What conspiracy are you two concocting?' I asked.

Franklin only hurried over. 'Let's see about some shoes.'

So passed the morning: shirts, socks, pants, jackets. Marcy photographed everything. When I pulled on a pair of navy pleated trousers, Franklin assessed my appearance, then called to Dr Philo. 'This is going to be better than winning the lottery.'

Lastly came undergarments, which I tried alone in a dressing room. The fabric was soft like a cat, and snug. Finally Franklin had me dress in a complete wardrobe and pointed me at a mirror. A man of here and now peered out at me: thin lapels, no waistcoat, a softer shirt with its collar already attached.

'Marvelous,' Franklin said. 'Now there's only one last thing.'

I turned to him. 'Yes?'

He wiggled a finger to instruct me to face the mirror again, then brought one hand up on either side of my face, palms over my sideburns. 'These.'

'But I've had them since—'

'Not an option. They simply must go.'

'They must?'

'We're not providing all of this merchandise for free if you're going to walk out of here looking like that.'

'I beg your pardon? You mean to say you are giving me these clothes?'

'In exchange for photos of you for ads, yes. That's what your friend negotiated. Now, wait right here.'

In a moment Franklin returned with a corded device which had one end shaped like shears. Plugged in and switched on, it buzzed like a bee against a window. 'Hold still,' Franklin said, pressing me into a forward lean, while Marcy held a waste basket beneath. In two sweeps he had taken most of my whiskers. Another half minute of close work lifted the stubble away to give me clean cheeks. Just like that.

Marcy took more photos whilst Franklin stepped back to survey his handiwork. 'Marvelous. Believe me sir, you will thank me. Now go show your friend the new you.'

I ran a hand over my smooth face, as unknown to me as a stranger's skin, then tugged my sleeves down snug and marched into the sales area. Dr Philo was standing by the window, sipping her coffee. I cleared my throat. She turned, and brought one hand to her mouth. 'Oh my God,' she said. 'You, you look . . .'

'Franklin insisted on my sideburns. What do you think?'

'What do I think?' She lowered herself into the nearest chair, clearly unaware that she was staring. Then all at once her face went blank, as calm as a pond. 'You look fine, Judge Rice. Just fine.'

'He looks fantastic,' Franklin announced. 'Now, last thing, we find you a tie.'

I followed him to the racks and he selected

several with bright colors. Marcy photographed away while I stood before another mirror, holding them to my neck: blue, green, a patterned purple one you would never have seen the likes of in the gentlemen's stores of Lynn.

Then I felt Dr Philo's hand again, in the middle of my back again. I held perfectly still. She looped a yellow tie around my throat.

'That's an excellent shade,' Franklin said. 'Nice and bright.'

Bringing her hands under my arms, she proceeded to tuck the fabric through my collar, then tie it with surprising skill. 'I used to do this all the time for my father,' she said, finishing a neat knot, then sliding it snug to my throat.

'There we go,' Franklin declared.

'Thank you very much, sir.'

'Oh no,' he said. 'It is I who thank you. And now you are gorgeous.' Franklin turned to Dr Philo. 'Isn't he gorgeous?'

She made final adjustments to my tie, smoothed it down my chest, and said not a word. Only stepped aside and directed me toward the door. I opened it on to a clear spring day.

CHAPTER 22

THE BANDIT

(KATE PHILO)

Years ago when my father died, instead of flying back to Ohio I decided to drive. My mother passed away when I was twelve, so there was no need to rush to give or receive comfort. Chloe was on the scene anyway. Instead of jetting disconnectedly overhead, I wanted to feel the distance. It gave me time to remember, time to cry. He'd been declining for almost two years, my beloved round daddy, but that does not mean I was prepared for the fact of it, the finality when his death arrived.

I drove north from New Haven, across central New York, into Pennsylvania then down toward home. I kept the cell phone off, only checking for messages when I stopped for gas or a snack. Each time, Chloe's updates showed that she had things in order: the casket selected, funeral songs chosen, relatives notified. She was an insurance litigator, skilled in detail, handling these tasks with her accustomed efficiency.

When I arrived, it was to discover efficiency times

ten. I climbed out of the car before an open garage door. Inside lay boxes, chairs, kitchen gadgets, paintings, a disassembled bed. *What the hell?* I entered the kitchen. A stranger was packing up the everyday silverware. He glanced up, said hi, returned to his work.

I found Chloe upstairs in our bedroom, our childhood bedroom, separating books into two big boxes. I stood in the doorway, stupefied. 'Hello?'

'Hi Katie-bug,' she said, giving me a hug so quick and weightless you would have thought she was part hummingbird. Chloe had a look on her face though, almost as if caught at something. Then she returned to her task. 'I hope you don't mind the disruption, but since we're both in town I figured we'd get a head start on all this nasty dividing stuff.'

'Really? If you think so.'

I had no interest in participating. The one thing I wanted was a cable-knit cardigan my father had bought long ago on a trip to Ireland. He'd worn it constantly the winter I was 17. I found it in his closet, thin at the elbows, missing buttons, but it smelled like him. Except for the funeral, I wore it the whole time I was home: drinking wine with a high-school chum on the rusty backyard swing set, standing in the kitchen in the morning waiting for water to boil, on quiet walks through my childhood neighborhood, the houses looking smaller but the trees become giants. Meanwhile my sister slaved away upstairs or in the basement, re-enacting her half of the ancient roles of predator and prey.

After the blur of the funeral, riding home in a limousine I thought was unneeded but Chloe insisted showed proper decorum, she coughed, removed her masking sunglasses, seized my elbow. 'I can't be silent one more second, Katie-bug. I have to say right now that I am worried about you. Extremely worried about your future.'

'Don't be,' I said. 'I have my dissertation defense in three weeks, a great post-doc job lined up at Hopkins starting in July. I'm on my way, Chloe.'

She shook her head. 'You don't have him to puff you up anymore. It's reality time.'

'Puff me up? What are you talking about?'

'We both know what I mean. Just try Katie-bug, please. From now on? Try your best not to be insignificant.'

While I gulped in disbelief, my sister put her shades back on, her job done.

I should have been furious, I suppose. Instead I felt sorry for her. So I did not correct her. I did not explain that my father was not puffing, but loving. Nor did I pierce Chloe's view of herself as the responsible executor of his estate, when her behavior was more like a thief.

Is that the younger child's job? To bite her tongue out of pity? Possibly. Meanwhile I was the one acting like a criminal, sneaking that sweater out to my car on the night before driving back to Connecticut only when I knew Chloe was asleep.

I defended my dissertation, landed the next job, then the next, then the Lazarus Project. Each advancement served in my mind as a rebuke to my sister's putdown. In my nerdy world, not for one second have I been insignificant.

Enough years pass, I forget these things. Chloe has her husband, her two girls. But she is all the family I have left. That circumstance apparently enables me to excuse scorn, insults, even her decision not to divide my father's estate evenly. 'I knew you needed the money more,' she announced, when I found out five years after the fact.

True. Still I fumed, I stomped, then I let it go. Yet it did not quite let me go.

I was strolling through Cambridge with Judge Rice. June, a windless evening, streetlights dappled through the trees. By that point we walked arm in arm, whenever we had privacy. I delighted in being his teacher. He was amazed by everything: this traffic light was brilliant, that parking meter a revelation. I prompted him to tell me about days in his court. Judge Rice's memory was spotty in that area, but on rare occasions a case would come back to him in detail. His favorites were the ones in which both sides were partly in the right. He called it 'competing legitimate interests.'

There was a banging from a stand of trash bins a few feet away, a metal top clanged to the sidewalk. It scared me, I hooted, jumped aside. The barrel tipped over, more noise, garbage spilling into the alley.

Who should poke his head up from the cans then, but a fat old raccoon, his face masked like a bandit? He made no effort to run or hide, but rather growled at us.

Judge Rice laughed. 'Bold creature, isn't he?'

'He startled me, though.'

The raccoon returned his attention to the empty soup can between his little black paws, glancing up at us while he licked his lips.

Judge Rice offered his me arm again. 'Seems this fellow knows what he wants.'

'He sure does,' I said. 'Good thing for him that I already ate.'

We moved away slowly, calm regained. But two things stayed in my mind. The first, say what you will about human traits in animals, was that the raccoon's face echoed Chloe's expression when I caught her dividing the books. I recognized it. The spoils.

The second thing was that in the moment I leapt back in alarm, Judge Rice had jumped forward to protect me.

CHAPTER 23

'FOR MY NEXT TRICK'

My name is Jeremiah Rice and I begin to receive a welcoming.

Each day Dr Philo brought me from place to place in Boston, one corner of the city to its opposite. Newspaper interviews, business meetings, long marches down one street after another. Everywhere people greeted me, shook my hand, and provided me with whatever merchandise my heart desired or they felt to be beneficial to my needs. At no place would anyone accept payment.

Restaurateurs held their doors open to us, and when we demurred because of Dr Borden's diet for me, they extracted promises that we would return. I met teachers, lawyers, clergymen, clergy*women* by glory, plus women lawyers, doctors, and more. The city's people came from all nations, Japanese and Russian and Brazilian and African-American, and all manner of mixtures thereof.

Everyone knew my name. They hailed me on the avenue, called from passing cars, saluted on passing transit vehicles. As I walked a side street, an upper window opened and an enormous woman stuck out her head and waved a meaty arm.

'Hey theah, Jerrr-oo-mmiieee-uhh.'

'Hello and good morning,' I called in reply.

She laughed. 'Good mawning ta you too, ya crazy fuckah.'

'Hm,' I said, recoiling.

'Actually,' Kate leaned near, 'it's kind of a compliment.'

'Thank you.' I waved the woman goodbye, then muttered to my companion. 'Your world is mad.'

But oh the voices, to hear so many voices once again. In my time I had disapproved of the long-voweled accent of Boston, which I equated with brawling, ignorance, and drink. In the here and now that same drawl sounded melodic, expressive, sincere in the best and earthiest way. Ha. It was akin to entering a house and smelling a favorite food on the stove.

And the crowds, the throngs outsized even those from the weeks before our expedition set sail. I met police officers who stood straight and puffed their chests. I held babies, thrilling to their animal aliveness even as my heart clenched with the memory of little Agnes. I played checkers in a park with old men who defeated me without mercy, for which I thanked them.

The city opened its arms to me. I saw a film, so bright, frenzied, and loud it caused me to perspire. I visited the control tower of Logan International Airport, giant aircraft going and coming in a pandemonium as frightening as it was sublime. I visited the Old North Church, symbol in the story of early American freedom. I rode on a bus that became a boat that became a bus again, as we toured the harbor and commons. I strolled the lawns of Harvard University, I stood to applause in the Statehouse chamber, I rode an elevator to the Skywalk of Prudential Center, the city at my feet and off to one side the infinite Atlantic.

I must say a word about touch. In my time, reserve was lauded. Men shook hands only, women touched arms only, couples of any standing contacted in public only with their eyes. Here and now seemed the opposite, with displays of intimacy in every direction. Couples swooned in one another's arms in broad daylight. Men hugged, I saw it repeatedly. Women strolled arm in arm. Travelers crowded onto trolleys and trains, like so many sheep in a fold.

This contact, I hasten to add, extended to me. I was hugged, touched, patted, squeezed like some fruit perpetually being gauged for ripeness. Hm. At first it demanded accommodation on my part, a resistance to the impulse of withdrawing, but by degrees I came to like it. It seemed almost to treat bodies as friends. It felt warmer.

One day Dr Philo broke a shoe on the sidewalk, and we stopped at a shop to have it repaired. The woman at the counter was wizened, with three hairs bristling from her chin. Her husband labored in back. She brought the shoe to him, then returned to the counter. Lacking other customers for the moment, she eyed me, and I wondered if perhaps she recognized me. After the cobbler returned from behind his curtain, she rang up the cost and made change for Dr Philo. As we made for the door the woman rushed around the counter and pulled me down into an embrace so fierce it surprised me. What's more, she planted a buss on my neck and thanked me for showing the world that Boston is a smart city. *Smaaht* was how she said it.

Out on the sidewalk again, Dr Philo elbowed me. 'All the women fall for Judge Rice,' she teased.

'I will never wash my neck again,' I replied.

Not everyone delighted in my presence. Dr Philo took me to the Cathedral of the Holy Cross, which I had visited long ago on the day between my father's death and his funeral. I had sat there all the silent afternoon. The loss of my last parent was a finality without mercy. Moreover, a barrier no longer stood between me and mortality. My generation would be next. Thus in the here and now when I stepped beside Dr Philo to open the heavy doors, their weight was burdened by personal history. Whilst we stood in the foyer, an old woman crept toward me with her rosary raised.

'Get thee behind me, Satan,' she hissed.

'I beg your pardon?'

'Remember man that thou art dust, and unto dust you shall return.'

'Why are you accosting me?'

'We are given only one life on this earth,' she said. Her manner of speaking bared yellow teeth. 'Then there is life everlasting.' She crooked a bony finger at me. 'You are a walking blasphemy. Your existence is a sin.'

'While you,' Dr Philo called over her shoulder, drawing me away, 'are a nasty old crone.'

'Get thee behind me,' the woman said, louder.

Dr Philo led me into the central nave, where the echoing stones compelled us to silence. At once I had fresh eyes for beauty. The stained-glass windows shed multicolored light on the pews. The aspiring arches drew our eyes toward God.

The woman's anger remained in my mind, naturally, but not topmost. There was too much competition. I was a student of the present and every day brought a deluge of novelty: a web of colored lines on a map corresponded to routes in the city's transportation system; streetlights shone when the sun went down, with no one needed to spark them; signs beside the roads directed a ceaseless stream of vehicles like so many bees in a hive; refrigeration; lawn mowing machines; timepieces worn on the wrist.

Often I reminded myself that our species had not become smarter over the years, nor any more moral than is its nature, and what I witnessed merely represented the culmination of a century's exertions.

Possibly the rate of change and discovery had been higher when I was a youth, and the combination of steam power and coal had multiplied a thousand-fold the force a man could exert with a lift of his hand – provided that hand were guiding a mechanical lever. Possibly neither of these eras came near in courage and adventure to the decades in which people cast monarchy from their backs and shouldered the burdens of democracy. Perhaps those times shrank beside the days when men sailed toward the edge of the globe, and discovered a new world. And those days possibly were eclipsed by the dawn of the scientific method. Which in turn must bow to the invention of the plow. And so on backward to the commencement of human time.

Yet then I would encounter another tool or toy of the present, and surrender my judicial prudence all over again. For example there was the device through which images from one time and place are sent to another, countless options, a torrent of information, a lifetime's worth of narratives happening at once – the television. Soon I found it predictable, however, and dulling of the senses. There were only two subjects, death and money, both taken to violent excess. The one exception was my old amusement, baseball. The game was unpredictable, at least, with moments of alertness and speed. Dr Gerber's computer held more appeal, until I inadvertently spied that journalist Dixon savoring a screen filled with pendulous breasts.

He hardly held supremacy for lewdness, however;

I heard obscenities everywhere, as though the world were populated entirely by longshoremen. Drivers, pedestrians, shop keepers, professionals, all exercised the lower end of their vocabulary without reserve or apology. Had no one told them that coarseness lacks dignity?

One afternoon Dr Philo and I sat on a trolley about to depart, and two school girls hurried on at the last moment: pigtails, plaid skirts, as fresh as apples. They flounced into their seats, met eyes, and simultaneously pronounced a single syllable of filth that no lady of my era would have uttered at any time.

I startled easily: when an engine backfired, a police car passed shrilly or someone yelled. The violent images from television had made me suggestible. A door slammed and I wheeled expecting to see a gun. A jet bellowed overhead and I resisted the urge to cower against the nearest building. A car honked its horn and I jumped.

Another disconcerting observation: memory was worth less than a fig. You could have brought me before a black-robed justice, and with my hand upon the holy book I would have sworn before him, God, and all, that I knew every building on Newbury Street, the names of each crossing avenue, the nearest place horses could be watered. Yet when Dr Philo and I strolled that boulevard one sunny afternoon, peering into shops and pausing to enjoy some flowering azaleas, I found the order of the cross streets had changed. In my memory they fell, from east to west, in reversed alphabetical order:

Fairfield, Exeter, Dartmouth, Clarendon. That day however, when we passed Dartmouth and Dr Philo detoured into a shop to buy a coffee, I meandered ahead expecting to see Clarendon at the next corner. The sign read Exeter.

'One moment,' I said to her. 'Hurry on with me, would you?'

She held the coffee at arm's length whilst keeping up, and I was certain the next block assuredly would be Clarendon. Yet the sign read Fairfield. I stopped in complete perplexity.

'Something wrong?' Dr Philo asked.

'I presume that no one in the past century changed the order of boulevards.'

'I imagine not.'

'Fascinating,' I said. The rather, though, it felt a bit frightening. In what other realms have I misinformed myself? I could be wrong about the street where I lived. I might be misremembering the law. My literary references seem right, but no one around me is well-read enough to correct any errors. My grasp of the past feels thin.

Thank goodness one region remains sure, as certain in my person as my bones, and it contains a population of two: my Joan, firm in mind, quick in temper, generous in tenderness, and my Agnes, a barefoot laughing sprite of joy. Much is disconcerting in this land of unknowns. So long as that one region is secure, none other matters. The heart knows truths that cannot be altered by the sequence of the streets.

* * *

Everywhere we went, there were cameras. Sometimes it was a news person. Sometimes it was Daniel Dixon, who on odd days would follow Dr Philo and myself at a distance but whom I could not persuade to join us. Often the camera was borne simply by some person who recognized me, and had a telephone in his pocket or her purse. I posed with the checkers players. I posed with the babies. I smiled with a pilot. I stood beside a surgeon after watching with astonished eyes as he removed a diseased man's tumor, dropping it in a pan like so much rancid meat. I posed for a photo with my arm, as requested, around the shoulders of a lovely shop girl, no more than sixteen, who had wires all through her mouth for a therapeutic purpose I was too intimidated by the sight to ask, and my discomfort in the moment was outdone by her delight in it.

One evening in Harvard Square we encountered jugglers of surpassing skill, including a fellow who tossed flaming batons to his partner whilst both of them rode unicycles up and down ramps. Meanwhile the city sped by uninterrupted all around.

'For my next trick,' said the cyclist in a top hat, 'I need to borrow a 20 dollar bill. Who has a 20?'

A man raised his hand, the rider wheeled over, thanked the man for volunteering, snatched the money and tucked it his back pocket. 'Presto, it disappeared.' Then he zoomed away while the crowd laughed.

Later he returned the cash, and at the end of the show he ambled through the crowd with the top hat outstretched. People put in dollar after dollar. I was astonished – and felt like I'd been to an impromptu circus.

One night Dr Gerber took us, over Dr Philo's objections and then begrudging agreement, to what he called a nightclub. I had no money, and thus felt somewhat like the second rider on a horse: no stirrups, no reins. At the entrance a muscular man dressed entirely in black scanned me with his eyes and sneered, then waved us in.

The music was deafening, the lights bright and spinning. The songs were less melodic than those in Dr Gerber's headphones, with an emphasis heavily upon the drums. Men and women mingled in close quarters. I witnessed a kind of public animalism, flirting gestures and suggestive clothing unimaginable in my former time.

Dr Philo drank water but Dr Gerber bought two alcohol combinations which were as clear as water and came with an olive. He handed me one, then poured half of the other into his gullet. I took one sip and thought of the fluid my father had used as fuel for our old kitchen lamp.

Dr Gerber went by himself to the dance floor, swaying his hips, jerking his shoulders, tilting his head side to side. His hair followed, but lagging a little, and with no offense meant I thought it appeared comical. The music's beat was so loud and low it made my chest feel like a drum. A wave of nausea passed through me, but I fought it. I did not want to upset the evening.

It was thrilling to see people of every shape and color socializing together. I watched them moving, dancing, or working their way to and around the bar.

'The crowd is from all the human races,' I shouted to Dr Philo.

'What?' she answered. 'I can't hear you.'

I leaned down to repeat myself, and found my mouth poised over the curl of her ear. Her hair brushed my face. The words would not come and I straightened again. She simply smiled and turned to watch the dancers.

A different kind of light began flashing in the next song, blindingly bright but shining for the merest fraction of a second. It made the dancers look like machines, moving in the jerky gears of a clockwork. My stomach clenched and I closed my eyes till the song ended.

Gradually I downed perhaps half of my drink. It seemed stronger than the port I was familiar with, but it had other properties, an aggressiveness perhaps, a vigor. By mutual invitation my companions both danced for one song, though it would be a stretch to say they did so together. They barely acknowledged one another, turning and bending to their own impulses.

My experience with dancing was limited to a few youthful jigs and the occasional waltz with Joan, who carried herself at those times like a glass of water filled to the brim, all elegance and elevation. Here and now the lights whirled, people orbited one another, and no one touched. It was the opposite of the easy body contact I'd seen on the streets, and I wondered which was sham.

As the song finished, a smiling Dr Philo returned to the counter and took a long draw from her water. I intended to ask if we might return to the lab. I'd grown tired, and the music's unceasing throb had troubled my stomach. How could people endure it for an entire evening?

Suddenly a man stood between us, calling an order to the fellow behind the bar. Next he bent and shouted something to Dr Philo, who made a quizzical expression I construed to mean she had not understood him. The man was broad shouldered, and smelled strongly of cinnamon and lime. He pulled out a pen and began drawing on a napkin: one triangle below, one triangle above, a line connecting them, and as he was darkening the upper area I saw it was identical to the drink with the olive Dr Gerber had bought me. Lastly the man drew a question mark and looked at her.

Dr Philo blinked, realized his meaning, and mouthed 'no thank you.' Then she stepped around him to stand beside me, took my arm in both her hands, and rested her head on my chest. I held my breath. Let it last, let it last.

The stranger pulled up in a manner that attempted to make him look taller. His drink arriving, he paid and swaggered away. Dr Philo released my arm and drained her water. She tilted the glass and jiggled loose the last chips of ice. I turned to the space between myself and the bar, and disgorged my dinner.

Thus my first visitor the following morning was Dr Borden. He stood on a little stool beside the examination table, squeezing a pump that tightened a cuff on my upper arm. 'I'm thinking it was a bunch of external factors,' he said.

'Quite possibly. The music was deafening, and the drink—'

He raised a finger to silence me. He listened through his stethoscope, whilst releasing the squeeze of the cuff. I wondered what he was hearing. Sometime I ought to wear that listening device.

Dr Borden pulled the earpieces down and wrote something on his clipboard. 'You really are in fine shape, considering.'

'I am glad to hear it,' I said, giving him a hearty voice. 'But it puts me in mind of a question I'd like to ask of you.'

He stepped down from the stool and folded his arms. 'Fire away.'

'Doctor, I submit that you and your medical team need not be measuring my health any longer.'

He tucked the stethoscope's listening part in his pocket, hooking the other ends around his neck. 'What do you mean?'

'My heart has shown no indication of stopping, nor my blood pressure of vanishing. Yet you persist with these assessments, and others which are invasive of my privacy. I am well. More so every day, and here we are—' I checked the numerical clock in the control room – 'on Day 69.'

Dr Borden produced from his kit a metal cylinder with a conical black tip, and I turned so he could insert it in my right ear. 'Please continue.'

'It cannot have escaped your notice, despite last night's incident, that my appetite has returned.'

'I am aware of that, yes.' He moved to the other ear. 'Go on.'

'My sleep habits are consistent. Daily activity levels. Levity of mood. Speed of reading and conversation.'

He put the device away and produced another one, similar but with an arm that had a light at the tip. He raised it to my right eye. 'Come to your point.'

Hm. I had hoped for dialogue. I might have known better, having encountered his type among attorneys often enough. He moved the light to my left eye, then alternated between them.

'My point, doctor, is that I am fully restored, and as you say, in fine condition. Might it not be time for me to regain some freedom from examination? Must my voiding continue to be weighed? Could we hazard giving this room a curtain, and me a modicum of privacy? Might we stop waking this man for blood pressure tests during the night?'

Dr Borden sighed and stepped away. He leaned against the near wall and contemplated the floor. He tugged on the point of his beard. Finally he adjudged our conversation more important than his shoes, and lifted his face. 'Do you remember when I spoke during the news conference?'

'I was not present for your remarks.'

'That's right.' He snapped his fingers. 'I'd forgotten. Well, that day I referred to the people who opposed our work as "ignorant". The word escaped in an unguarded moment, and revealed the height of our arrogance. Now there is a subgroup among the protestors that calls itself "The Ignorants". Their signs say things like "I Don't Matter" and "I Know Nothing".'

'You had expected the dissidents to lose interest.'

'Instead they gave grown in size and rage every day.' He waved the eye tool at me. 'Your meeting with the vice president sparked his political opponents, and I fed the flames. Now every news story, and every sign, and every shout I hear on the way in or out of work confirms that they are not the ignorant ones.'

'I fail to see how responsibility for the protestors falls upon you. We are a free society, free to assemble and speak. Further, I do not understand how this relates to your medical scrutiny of me.'

'There is one explanation for both things,' he said.

I held my tongue, waiting. Dr Borden shifted his weight from leg to leg. He flicked the eye device on and off, light projecting on his other hand. I kept my face in the cool posture of one hearing unreliable evidence.

'What is your reluctance?' I asked finally.

He pointed with the eye device at the ceiling, where a microphone hung.

I nodded. 'In Greenland, Second Officer Milliken injured his wrist, after a barrel fell on it. A week later he did not want to remove his bandage. Yet we could smell the wound, we knew what was happening. Finally the captain ordered us. We held him down and unwrapped the linen. The stench was unbearable. We knew, all of us, that he would have to lose the arm. We drew away, but he could not even weep in solitude. There is no privacy on a ship. Here, likewise.'

Dr Borden stood. 'Hey tech folks?' he called at the ceiling. 'Hey Andrew?'

A control room technician, a handsome black man, raised his eyes from his desk.

'Would you pause audio output for a minute?' Dr Borden pointed at me. 'Physician-patient confidentiality.'

'Got it,' the technician said, pressing some buttons. 'All dead on this end, doctor. Just signal me to restart, OK?'

Dr Borden put his tool away, then closed his bag. 'You know, Carthage is truly brilliant when it comes to cells. His discovery of their latent life potential? That's genius, the real thing. And then proving his outlandish theory of hard-ice, something completely outside his discipline, by finding naturally occurring examples? Uncanny. Beyond comprehension. A cell, however, is nowhere near as complex as a human being.' He motioned at my chest. 'I need to check your breathing.'

I unbuttoned my shirt, letting it fall from my shoulders. He stepped onto the footstool and pressed the cold stethoscope to my skin. 'Deep breath.' He checked high and low on my left side, then my right, then moved to my back. 'Deep again please. Now cough.'

I did as I was told, until he stepped down, indicating for me to rebutton. 'It is amazing, how fully you've healed. You'd never know those lungs were filled with salt water, and iced for a century.'

'You were explaining the strengths and weaknesses of Dr Carthage.'

'Yes.' He folded the stethoscope away, and gave a wan smile. 'The truth is, you surpassed any expectation we had for your survival. My ignorance, and believe me I am the ignorant one here, was in assuming you would die within days at most.'

He went to the window, surveying the control room. 'Then there's you, the personality. We never knew if you would even open your eyes. That's pretty far from you gallivanting around town, being smart, being popular.'

The doctor faced me again, and removed his glasses. His eyes looked sunken and small. He rubbed the bridge of his nose. 'Carthage has grown too excited by controversy and attention. He insists on gathering data and on keeping you here because he cannot admit that we are out of our depth.' He placed the spectacles back on his face. 'He has no idea what else to do.'

'Doctor.' It was my turn to speak plainly. 'I am not a cell. I am a sentient being. You could have asked me.'

'Well now.' Dr Borden's face brightened, as if the idea had never occurred to him. 'Tell me, your honor. What can I do to make you more comfortable here, until we can figure all of this crap out?'

It was not a question I'd prepared for, despite my rhetoric. I scanned the room, every corner of it confirming the constraints on my freedoms. 'I would like a curtain. The end of monitoring, of being filmed. I would like a chair, reading lamp, and some books.'

'I can do those things.'

'I would like variety in my foodstuffs.'

Dr Borden tugged his beard again. 'Let's put that one aside for a while, OK? That porridge must be pretty boring by now. But there are scientific reasons we keep your diet so simple.'

'I would like the liberty to come and go as I please.'

He chuckled. 'I think Carthage is the only one here with that privilege.'

'It is hardly a laughing matter.'

'True. But it is also not within my power to give you that freedom. I don't have the authority.'

Hm. There was more to be unearthed. 'Let us stipulate to treat this matter as we are my diet. Which is to say, as tabled items which we will reconsider.'

Dr Borden nodded. 'Fair enough.'

'Lastly, I would like to be of use. There is much to enjoy and learn about here and now, but I am accustomed to a less ornamental existence.'

'What do you mean by that?'

'I would like to be more than a curiosity. This second life contains the opportunity, and perhaps an imperative, to serve a larger purpose.'

He stared at me then, holding perfectly still, before nodding quite a bit. 'You're correct, of course. There is a role for you to play besides celebrity. Let me take it up with Carthage. Very good.'

He placed the clipboard beside his kit, lining things up so they were tidy. At the doorway he turned halfway back to me. 'I'll see about the curtains, and your greater purpose, if you'll stay out of the nightclubs.'

'A fair bargain.'

Even as I watched his clipped walk through the control room, I heard the security door open again. I felt so certain about who it would be, I did not immediately turn from the window.

'Good morning, Dr Philo.'

She laughed a little melody. 'Good morning, Judge Rice.'

CHAPTER 24

IN THE FRONT ROW

(DANIEL DIXON)

I found him. It wasn't that hard, when he's so handsome his face belonged on a coin. He might spend his days wrangling shouters and marchers and public praying types, our organizer of protestors, but the guy's mug was like a cross between a surfer dude and a Canadian mountie. Yours truly just linked up with the wire services' photos from major religious protests across the country. Sure enough, he started popping up like one of those hide-and-seek characters in children's books.

There is a little thrill that never goes away, when I dig something up that's hard to find. One time I convinced a city coroner to tell me what type of blood was found under a murder victim's fingernails, and it matched the dead woman's own son. Gruesome, but to me it was a little jewel.

So the first thing was hunting down this protest leader's name. That took digging, and the better part of an afternoon. Finally I found a photo in *The Washington Post*, taken on the steps of the

Supreme Court: four lawyers all wearing their best credibility, and beside them in a Stetson ten gallons deep, stood our boy: Wade, T. J. Wade.

This rabble-rouser had given me the creeps right from the start. And once I read his background, I knew why. Wade was an evangelical hell-raiser about two inches shy of the Klan. He specialized in nasty tactics. For example using a hidden camera to trap liberal politicians into saying something breathtakingly stupid – a job, I have to say, they seem to make awfully easy for him. But worse, too: making noise outside a soldier's funeral to protest federal spending policies. Holding a news conference to blame a hurricane on the queers.

Twice Wade had come before the Supreme Court to test the limits of free speech, and neither time did he stand anywhere near the side of reasonableness. Somebody with a fat wallet liked keeping him in the noise-making game, I suppose. Lawyers who argue in front of the supremes don't come cheap.

Wade had management skills, I grant him that. He'd pulled the motley sign-wavers together, increased their numbers a little every day, worked up schedules so they could still hold jobs, and through it all, raised their rage about four notches higher. But it was the box lunches that impressed me most: all these people sitting on the lawn munching quietly between their regularly scheduled outbursts. Wade started timing the demonstrations to suit the news cycle, just like we did with video releases.

He had one trick I hadn't seen before: each morning he'd hold a news conference to review the coverage from the day before. Was this headline fair? Did supporters of the Project get more column inches than his group? One day Wade read quotes from reports about the prior day's press conference and compared them with what he'd said, which he verified right then with a tape recorder. Of course most reporters had errors, here and there. It's tough to catch every word when you're taking notes at top speed. But Wade wasn't much on excuses. Who, he demanded – grimacing as though wounded, while facing the TV cameras that could not get enough of his pretty mug – who in that shoddy press corps would have the courage to print corrections and retractions? Who among them would have the integrity to tell the story about how his innocent group of life-loving protestor-citizens was being hammered by the godless and unfair media?

Well, a gold star to you, Mister T. J. Wade, because making a spectacle over tiny details had exactly the desired effect. Which was that every reporter – and probably every damn editor back in every damn newsroom – became super-cautious with quoting, and headlines, and making sure stories were balanced right down to the word. It was a masterpiece: the man was all but looking over people's shoulders while they wrote.

For some reason he left me out of it. I knew better than to think it was because my stories were fair. Look, if someone hits an old lady on the head with a baseball bat, do I have to go out and get a balancing quote from the president of the Society for Hitting Old Ladies with Bats? Hell, no. Fair is for sissies. I had no intention of giving this flake a break, handsome pro or not, which made it a pretty puzzle why he left me out of the press attack. Did he think I wasn't important enough? Well, fine by me. But he might regret it.

Besides, it wasn't his politics that made me dislike Wade. I've seen all kinds. It was his calculation. Each morning he'd harangue the protestors about bringing someone new with them tomorrow. At noon while he handed out those lunches, he'd tell the crowd they were being ignored, they were making no difference, what were they doing about it?

'Remember the impact of Martin Luther King,' he said, 'and what he said about "the fierce urgency of now".'

Wade was invoking a civil rights leader on behalf of his anti-Lazarus Project agenda. Each afternoon before the protest for the 6 p.m. news, he'd count heads, frowning with disappointment. During the taping, he'd stand to one side chewing on the inside of his cheek. Like he was thinking and gnawing at the same time.

I had a bad feeling that Wade was just biding time, keeping the crowd frustrated while he dreamed up some new maneuver to win headlines.

The man was a mess on wheels, just waiting for the opportunity to inflict itself.

And when it all came down, I aimed to be sitting in the front row.

CHAPTER 25

INDEPENDENCE DAY

My name is Jeremiah Rice and the world begins giving itself to me.

Moving stairways lifted me into the innards of buildings without my taking one step. Music played in elevators, waiting rooms, even the bathroom of one hotel though the melody was appallingly drab. People were fat, gelatinous flesh spilling out of their clothes, or fit as a draft horse, or so slender I wanted to sit them down somewhere for a good hot meal. In the aquarium I saw a turtle the size of a tabletop, sharks with expressions a mixture of malice and stupidity. I fed penguins, who stank. At the science museum I stood mesmerized by a motorized sculpture.

And motion? Everywhere people jogged, they strolled, they rolled in mechanical chairs with motors on the back. Dr Philo and I stood on a bridge over the Charles and watched the sleek rowing crews dragonfly up the river, while cars honked and trucks bellowed and jets roared overhead.

One afternoon we visited a zoo with crowds of children. One toddler girl lost hold of her balloon, and while she wailed in despair it rose like a red beacon, dwindling irretrievably every second. That night in the privacy of the laboratory's shower, I thought about Agnes, what a balloon of a father I had proved to be, and I wept.

Mercifully, the world offered an endless supply of distractions. The next morning we entered a shop for Dr Philo to buy coffee. A line of people waited their turn, and their requests took fully 20 seconds to declare, there were so many options, so many preferences I was astonished. I wondered how much time they had spent trying the various flavors and sizes before finding the one they liked. Dr Philo ordered a tall double-espresso mocha latte with skim. She laughed when I made her repeat it, as though I were learning to say hello in a foreign tongue. It was no compensation for Agnes, no such thing existed, but that laugh leavened my heart nonetheless.

I received gifts. Security people at the Lazarus Project opened most of them, for safety's sake, and stored the better portion in the basement. Carthage forbade me to write thank you notes, saying it would only worsen the cult of me.

'What does he mean by that?' I asked Dr Philo.

'That he is narrow-minded,' she replied. 'Ignore him.'

There were clothes, books, trinkets, dolls, hand-thrown bowls, sunglasses, a woven blanket, on and on. One day I opened a box to find a long tapered cone of hard material. It was bright yellow, with a space in the underside in the shape of a skull.

'Go ahead,' Dr Philo said, 'try it on.'

I did so, the odd hat fitting awkwardly, the cone projecting in front of my face. 'At least it matches my tie.'

'Oh my God that is spectacular,' Dr Gerber said, rising from his desk and approaching.

'I feel like a duck,' I said. 'What is this object, anyway?'

Dr Gerber's eyes were wide. 'It's a bicycle helmet, and it is a beauty.'

'Are you kidding?' Dr Philo laughed. 'It's grotesque. Gaudy, too.'

He shook his head. 'I love it.'

'Then you may have it,' I said, removing the hat.

'No way,' he said. 'Nobody gives Gerber anything.'

'That may be so. But I am giving this to you.'

Dr Gerber took the helmet reverentially, it seemed to me. He turned it halfway round and nestled it down on his head. The cone was at the back, I now saw how it gave the helmet a tapered stern. 'Thank you, Judge Rice. Thank you.'

That hefty reporter smirked at his keyboard. 'You look like an alien.'

'You know, Dixon,' Dr Gerber declared, 'I am not a clown.' Then, with consummate dignity, he and his crown marched back to the desk.

Often a gift came with a request: would I please take a photo of myself with the object and mail it? I knew where that would lead. I had seen what Franklin did in newspapers with the pictures of me trying clothes on in his store.

Not all gifts came from strangers. One afternoon Dr Gerber repaid the helmet by presenting me with a metal object the size of a packet of matches. A cord in its side ran to two tiny buds, which he instructed me to place in my ears. Then he thumbed a button and music began, sounding almost inside my head, as clear as if the players were in the room with us.

'It only holds two hundred songs, so I picked the essentials.' He counted off on his fingertips. '"Jack Straw" from *Europe '72,* "Friend of the Devil" from *American Beauty,* "Wharf Rat" from *Skull and Roses.* The basics.'

The other personal gift came on Independence Day. Promising a special evening, Dr Philo brought me to a hotel beside Rowe's Wharf. By that time the salt smell did not burn my throat as before. It seemed a fine, fancy place. We rode an elevator to the rooftop, where tables were arrayed as in a plaza. Dr Philo spoke with a man at a podium by the door, and he led us to a table near the edge. There was a warm breeze, the sun was setting, and the city quarreled below. A waiter presented us with lists of the offerings.

Until that moment I had remained under Dr Borden's dietetic dictates, lab gruel that nourished the body but not the palate. Yet my frequent indigestion had persuaded me that his approach was nonetheless prudent.

'I am not sure I can eat any of this.'

Dr Philo nodded. 'That's why I chose this

restaurant. These are raw foods, pure basics, all organics. This is as natural a meal as I could find with this view in the whole city. And you can have anything on the menu you want.'

'Anything?'

'Absolutely anything.'

I ordered a slice of bread. Also a plate of tomatoes. Some bits of cheese. Dr Philo smirked, encouraging me to be more adventuresome. But I demurred. After the first plates came, I took one bite and had to close my eyes a moment, the experience was so sublime: the pierce of sunshine, the malt of earth. When a man has gone a century without flavor, I explained to her, a simple slice of tomato, seasoned with salt, is a masterpiece.

She gave me a wistful look. 'Our time and culture takes an awful lot for granted.'

By way of reply, I tore into the bread, a huge bite. She laughed. I had wanted her to laugh.

As night fell, the only light was a candle on the table. With popping sounds down in the street, I imagined school boys playing with firecrackers. But at our table, there was quiet. For the first time, the very first since my reawakening, we lacked things to say. Forks clinked, the ice in our glasses jingled, but conversation stalled. There had never before been a lull.

I fooled with the candle. She gazed out over the water. Grand sailing ships stood at anchor in the harbor, tall masts and crews high in the rigging.

Suddenly there was a report like a cannon. I

jumped but Dr Philo placed her hand over mine. 'It's all right. You're in for a treat.'

Credit her with understatement. I had seen fireworks in my former times, little red poppers we called lady fingers, or a pinwheel of gunpowder atop a pole. In Lynn, too, we seized upon any excuse for a neighborhood bonfire. Agnes would ride upon my shoulders, while Joan held my arm and wished upon the rising embers. Here and now, that night, were marvels of a different order: great chrysanthemums of color, whistlers, drippers, bombs whose fragments exploded anew to spread more lights, orbs of one hue with rings of another like Saturns over the harbor, and my favorite, the white flash followed a moment later by a deep loud boom. At the end there was a chaos of rockets and noises, dozens of detonations in a matter of seconds. We cheered and clapped.

Afterward on the street there were carts hawking balloons, flags, and little cloth animals. We had strolled past one cart loaded with trinkets when Dr Philo veered back. I ambled up and she had purchased something, the vendor was just giving her the change.

'This is for you,' she said. 'A reminder of our many walks through this city.'

She handed me a raccoon. The same masked face as our trash-can friend, but made of plush cloth and with eyes of glass. I stood it in the palm of my hand.

'Thank you, doctor. I don't know what else to say. Thank you.'

Suddenly Dr Philo snatched it back, holding it against her belly.

'What's the matter?' I said. 'Have I done something wrong?'

She shook her head. 'I am so silly. Here you are, a district court judge, and I give you a stuffed animal. What was I thinking?'

'I am touched by it, though.'

'It's totally stupid. I apologize.'

'It is not stupid,' I said. To prove my point, I took the raccoon back, and held it to my cheek. I put its head to my temple. 'See? He looks like me.'

She brightened. 'You look ridiculous. Both of you.'

The next day I felt an unfamiliar agitation. Partly it was indigestion, but this was also a galvanizing of the spirit. My nature is not a restless one, as a rule, but all that morning I could not content myself to wait in the chamber till Dr Philo came to fetch me.

The only person working in the control room was Dr Gerber. He sat as ever, immersed in the world of his computer, with headphones on to shut out the world, and that bicycle helmet to protect him from whatever his imagination thought might strike him unawares. I rapped on the glass, but it had as much effect as if I'd been knocking on the front door of my old home in Lynn. He did not so much as turn his head.

I put in the ear buds Dr Gerber had given me, and listened to the first song that played. It was a sweet thing, quiet, almost a lullaby.

There is a road, no simple highway
Between the dawn and the dark of night.
And if you go, no one may follow.
That path is for your steps alone.

Suddenly I missed Joan with all my heart. Her impatience with me, her humor, her strong hands. What was this infatuation with the here and now, compared with her loyalty and deep friendship?

And what sort of man was I, to be awakened all this time and to have thought so lightly on her? My wife was forty-four when I sailed, and I left her neither reserves nor fine estate. How had she fared? Could she afford to remain in our home? If Agnes had married, one fine day, who escorted her down the aisle? Which friend of mine had performed that lonely office? How had I been so foolish, to leave them for even one minute? What had become of my conscience? How had I dared to risk so much?

During the Arctic expedition I missed Joan and Agnes constantly, wishing to share the adventure's every detail with my wife, yearning to feel my daughter's fierce animal strength. But those desires had been eased by the knowledge that I would see them in a few months' time. Now, I lacked any such comfort. Now, I ached. I considered asking Dr Philo to take me to Lynn, to visit my former home. Yet I also feared that the sight would rend my heart.

Oh my loves. I ceased the music, fighting tears of shame and regret and loss. I sat on my bed in that chamber, and experienced pangs as though I were being stabbed.

Banal as it is, nature's call aided me, for it caused Dr Gerber to stand and make for the washroom. From the edge of my vision I noticed, the silly helmet still on his head. I waited at the window, wiping my face dry with my sleeve. As he returned I pounded the glass with both hands. He looked at me with surprise, then came to the window.

'Please,' I said, pointing toward the security door. 'I beg you.'

He marched over and poked the combination numbers. I expected him to enter, like everyone else. Instead, Dr Gerber stepped backward and held out his hands. 'Well? Are you coming?'

For the first time, I strode through the security door unescorted. 'Thank you, doctor.'

'Took you long enough.' He moved toward his desk. 'I've been wondering when you would wise up about that whole secure-chamber thing.'

'What is the combination, then?'

That pulled on his reins. He stopped, digging a finger under the helmet to scratch his hair. 'Now there is a question to get a man in hot water.'

'I have been patient,' I answered.

'Too patient. Rules were meant to be broken.'

'That's not a maxim a judge would normally endorse.'

Dr Gerber smiled. '2667. You press the button that looks like an empty tic-tac-toe game, then 2667. And you promise never to reveal who told you.'

'You are an angel, sir.'

'Not 1 percent. Remember though: you didn't learn it from me.'

'Learn what?'

He laughed, wiggling the fingers of both hands. Only then did I notice the sound, a chanting, almost like a distant threshing machine. 'What is that noise?'

'That?' Dr Gerber motioned me to follow. 'Our biggest fans. And now there are more of them than ever.' We reached the elevators, he ran a card through some sort of device on the wall, and the doors opened. 'Just press L, and go see for yourself.'

'Our fans?' I moved alone into the little room, saw the L he described and pushed it. The doors whooshed closed. As I descended, the chanting grew louder.

There must have been four hundred of them, all wearing red shirts, all angry. The handsome man with the hand held loudspeaker stood to one side, leading them, raising their pitch. I stood in the atrium, just yards away, stunned.

So far they had not spotted me; this rage was generated for themselves. Through the glass, the leader's plaints contained a certain musicality. There was a rhythm to his words, and he concluded each successive phrase on a slightly higher note. When he paused, they cheered. When he asked a question, they shouted answers. When he lowered his head in prayer, they raised their hands in holy fervor. There was a heat to their devotion, a zeal, and it frightened me.

By contrast the security guards, three across at the front door, wore faces as blank as stones. Likewise police cars blocked the road to the left, the officers standing with crossed arms. Television cameras clustered on the other side, watching like crows with unblinking eyes. Trucks behind them pointed giant dishes at the sky. I made a mental note to ask Dr Gerber to explain those trucks later.

Suddenly someone noticed me, a woman in the front. She shouted and pointed, and the entire company followed the direction of her finger. They surged forward in one mass. The handsome man called to them to stay back, but he was like a goat before a locomotive. The guards drew nightsticks, the police came closer, and I felt a hand on the small of my back.

I recognized the touch immediately. 'Dr Philo.'

'You should not be here. You are baiting them.'

'I merely came to observe.'

Now the police and guards stood shoulder to shoulder. The leader jumped up and down in front of the mob, waving them back with his arms. A photographer dashed into the space between the crowd and the building, snapping in both directions as he ran.

'You are not invisible, Judge Rice. Come with me right now.' Dr Philo pulled on my arm, and I followed her lead. She ran a card through a device as Dr Gerber had, the elevator doors swept open, and she rushed me inside.

'You have no idea the danger you were in,' she said as the tiny room rose toward our floor. 'What were you doing down there?'

'I could not bear to sit another minute in that chamber, waiting for my life to recommence. I heard them, and needed to see. Why do they hate me?'

'It's not hate. It's more like fear, of what you represent. Your existence challenges their faith.' The doors opened and we stepped into the laboratory corridor. 'I actually feel sorry for a lot of those folks,' she continued, 'because reality is messing with their beliefs. It must be painful.'

'I have a larger significance to them.'

'The world is changing in ways they don't like. You are a living example of that.'

I nodded. 'This is precisely what I have been pondering.'

'You have?'

'In my discussions with Dr Borden, yes. Thus far everyone has treated my reanimation as a scientific feat, without assigning any task for me beyond absorbing this world and being polite. If I have larger significance, I must become the equal of that role. I must make better use of this second life.'

We had reached the control room door. Dr Philo stayed me there with a hand on my arm. To me, her touch was most articulate. 'Do you know what you will do?'

'Not yet. I have been fascinated by learning about this world. But I know with certitude that I cannot let this opportunity go to waste.'

'Maybe a good first step—'

'Hell on a hockey stick,' bellowed Dixon as he charged off the other elevator. 'There's damn near a riot down there!' He lumbered past us waving his notebook and yanked back the control room door. 'I've got to file some kind of story about that gang out there. Out of control.'

We stood a moment in the hallway, after which I turned to Dr Philo. 'What should I do now?'

'Now?' She smiled. 'How about visiting patients at the children's hospital?'

That was her way, unflappable, and this habit of mind earned both my admiration and my curiosity. Should any matter go awry, from a meal in the lab misprepared to a museum closed, an unduly aggressive stranger or an unexpected downpour, any other person would reveal annoyance, a dollop of upset. Dr Philo was the opposite. At a bump she would go smooth, toward a wrinkle she showed calm, in calamity she would become as still as a pond. The judge in me, trained by temperament and experience to mask opinion, respected her powers of restraint. The husband and father in me, educated by affection, wondered where her emotions went. To what interior location did they burrow?

One night I saw her self-mastery overcome, the remembering of which makes me grin. We were meandering in the North End, where Italian restaurants stand cheek-by-jowl. My digestion had complained for days after the rooftop restaurant, convincing me to return to the staple of laboratory oatmeal. But my senses remained revived, my appetite for scent and flavor undiminished. Thus, in time and with minuscule doses, did I begin supplementing Dr Borden's gruel. Had his original monitoring continued, my overseers surely would have noticed diminished porridge consumption. Instead I enjoyed a measure of dietary freedom, which I indulged modestly and with a sensuality of enjoyment that would have shamed me in my former life. That night in particular, Dr Philo had introduced me to several foreign delights: the rich flavors of prosciutto, the salty tang of Tuscan pecorino cheese. Afterward we were ambling, with her hand snug in the crook of my arm.

All at once a huge-bellied man stood before us: an unshaven shadow on his jaw, a black bow tie at his throat, and a red-stained apron around his waist. '*Amores*,' he said, holding his hands together over his heart. '*Va bene.*'

'No,' Dr Philo said, 'we are not lovers.'

'*Si, si,*' said the man. He opened his hands and waved them around our bodies, indicating their closeness.

'Dr Philo is my friend,' I explained.

'Guide,' she interjected with a smile.

'Chaperone,' I added, also smiling.

'Bodyguard,' Dr Philo said, raising her free hand in a small clenched fist.

The man in the apron smiled widest. '*Lei pretende,*' he stage-whispered. 'You pretend.' Then he pushed us closer, and seemed somehow to summon himself to order.

'I don't understand,' I said.

Dr Philo leaned closer. 'Shhh.'

The man in the apron began to sing. But sing is a woefully insufficient word to describe what he did, what he gave to us. Ha. I confess I am unschooled in the operatic arts. They struck me as too ritualized, too formal. But there on the sidewalk of Boston's North End, we encountered a tenor of surpassing skill and instrument. He began in lower registers, the words slow and notes long with vibrato. But the recitation gathered momentum, accelerated, rose in volume and pitch. In less than two minutes he was in full voice, high, clear, and passionate. The music was strong yet he did not strain. I felt myself warming but his face betrayed no embarrassment, only that he closed his eyes in concentration and surrender. On the final phrase he brought his full breath, great volume, one hand held open with the palm upward as if supplicant to the sky. At last he finished, opened his eyes, grinned, whilst people all along the street applauded, whistled and called 'Bravo.' He gave a modest bow.

Then he leaned to whisper. '*Amore, signori. Amore.*'

I turned to Dr Philo, allowing her the first opportunity to protest. But my bodyguard had been disarmed. One hand flattened on her bosom, she was crimson. She was radiant. I found myself stammering.

A camera flashed. Dr Philo winced, thanked the aproned man, and hurried me away down the street. I had the sensation that we were in flight. Yet I had no reason to flee.

That night when I saw Dr Philo standing by the security door, I waved her inside. I was already abed. She came halfway into the room. 'Are you enjoying all of this?'

'It is a kind and wonderful world you live in.'

'You live in it, too.'

'Ha. So I do. And what an adventure. I like it here and now. I feel a need to hurry, to experience everything.'

'We have all the time in the world.' She tugged on a corner of my blanket, remaining at the foot of the bed. 'By the way, tomorrow's a big day.'

'Don't spoil the surprise,' I said. 'But please

remember that I wish to do more than be entertained.'

'I promise your contribution tomorrow will be extremely important to the Lazarus Project. In the meantime, try to get some sleep.'

'I certainly will.' Just then I yawned, like a child after bedtime prayers. Silly as it may sound, I remained yet unaccustomed to existence; that yawn brought impeccable pleasure. What an astonishing thing, this reflex sucking of air and the resulting relaxation, this having a body. So numerous are the gestures and sensations we take for granted, whilst this creature, this living machine, is the only friend we have with us our entire lives, fellow traveler on the first step and the last, witness from first breath after the womb to last gasp before the hereafter. I flopped my feet side to side under the covers, and gave thanks for the loyal companionship of my animal self.

She meanwhile had tiptoed to the door and paused, leaning against the wall like a tired child herself. I called out: 'Dr Philo?'

'Judge Rice?'

'The feeling grows upon me that you are an attorney pleading a case in my court. Thus your appellation for me seems less apt with each day. Would you kindly consider henceforth addressing me as Jeremiah?'

She laughed, a song in three notes. 'If you'll stop calling me Dr Philo.'

'I cannot do that, though. My manners—'

'What's good for the goose, Judge Rice.'

'I don't know what that means.'

'It means we're equals. If I'm going to address you as a friend would, then you must do the same with me.'

'I see.' I lay back. The ceiling was blank. 'Hm.'

'Informality means as much today as formality did in your time.'

I rose on one elbow. 'Well then. We've struck a bargain, haven't we? Kate.'

She smiled. I'd seen that expression once before, yes, whilst Kate held a surgical mask down with her finger. 'Good night, Jeremiah,' she replied. 'Sweet dreams.'

Kate turned the lights the rest of the way down. I stretched to the near table, grabbing the raccoon and tucking it beneath my pillow. The security door hissed closed and I was alone with my thoughts. They flickered and rose as flame does from a candle.

PART IV

PLATEAU

CHAPTER 26

SWARMING

(ERASTUS CARTHAGE)

Thomas raps twice and leans his head into your office. 'She's waited 20 minutes, sir.'

'Excellent. Show her in.'

'May I share one line first, from today's story?'

'By all means.'

'"This is the work of Erastus Carthage, the conquistador of cell mysteries".'

'Dixon wrote that? "The conquistador"?'

'He did, sir.'

'I'll be damned. If he helped the Project any more, people would suspect us.'

'I thought you'd be pleased, sir.'

Thomas scurries off, your mood prepared perfectly. This conversation may be delicate, but the goal is clear. Rare is the day that you fail to accomplish your objectives.

Dr Philo enters with shoulders high, a boxer climbing into the ring.

'Please,' you gesture at a chair, 'make yourself comfortable.'

'Thank you.' She sits on the chair's front edge.

‘Coffee? Tea?’

‘I’ve had breakfast, thanks.’

‘Yes. Well Dr Philo, I have been following the public life of Subject One with considerable interest. I wanted us to meet so that I could commend you.’

‘Excuse me?’

‘There have been no untoward incidents. Publicity has been uniformly positive. He remains healthy. In sum, we have cause for long-term optimism.’ You make the slightest possible bow, perhaps more of a nod. ‘Congratulations.’

‘Oh.’ She half turns her head, eyes narrowed. ‘Well. Thank you.’

‘What, for example, do you have scheduled for Subject One today?’

At last she inches back in the chair. ‘Actually, it should be interesting. In an hour he has his first television spot.’

‘Local or national?’

‘Local production, but national broadcast.’

‘Taped or live?’

‘Live. Why?’

You adjust the task list on your desk. ‘I want you in the booth. Should he inadvertently bring any trouble on himself or the Project, you shut it down.’

‘What’s your concern?’

‘The gotcha risk feels high. Even seasoned media people can be sandbagged.’

‘I’ll be on guard. But I’m sensing something larger behind your questions.’

At that you push back from the desk, cross to the credenza and squeeze sanitizer on your hands. 'Are you aware that Subject One has expressed an interest in using his reanimation toward a larger purpose?'

She nods. 'He said he wants to be more than merely a time-tourist.'

'Precisely.' You stand behind your desk chair. 'Coincidentally, there are now entities who have expressed an interested in enlarging the work of the Lazarus Project.'

'Meaning what?'

'That's unclear, for the moment. Our technology could have many applications. The point is that there could be no greater visual aid, for these ongoing discussions, than the living, constructive presence of Subject One. Thus it's my hope, and here is what I wish to impart to you today, that his conduct will continue to reflect well on our organization and its greater potential.'

'I see. But of course we both know he is not your employee.'

'Of course.' You feel your blood rise, but manage a smile. 'I mean only that we might align his interests with ours.'

'I see,' she says again. She folds her hands as if in prayer.

'I remind you that I have repeatedly asked you for a complete dossier on his history, to ascertain if there are any liabilities we ought to be aware of.'

'You might notice that I've been occupied with showing Judge Rice the world.'

'Your deadline is Friday morning when I arrive at my desk. Not one minute later.' When she frowns, you add, 'Have I not been patient?'

Dr Philo cools one degree. 'You have. Sorry.'

'Friday morning, then. First thing.'

To lighten the moment, you stroll to your favored spot by the window. The demonstrators, now four hundred strong and all wearing red, are usually inactive at this hour of the morning. But today they have formed a cluster around a limousine that pulled up to the front entry. They surround it four deep.

'Come see this,' you call to her. 'They have the most ingenious domination technique. It's as though they form a human corral.'

She reaches you just as the driver steps out of the car. In seconds a swarm forms, circling him and pulling him away. He attempts to move to the entry, but they thwart him with a mash of bodies. Surrounded, he goes still while they chant at him from all sides.

'I love these people.'

'Damn it,' she says. 'The studio was sending a car for Jeremiah. I bet that's it.'

'Wait.' You raise your hand. 'Thomas?'

He's at the door instantly. 'Sir?'

'Please call a town car immediately for Dr Philo and Subject One.'

'Yes sir.'

'Instruct the driver to use the rear entrance.'

'Will do, sir.'

There is the littlest thrill, right then, the pleasure of a tiny token of indebtedness entering your account with this woman. She now owes you. And your objective, of seeking her allegiance as the Project grows into what it ought to be, has been fulfilled thanks to the rabble below.

'Dr Philo.' You fold your hands together like a minister who has just finished preaching. 'Is there anything else that I might do for you?'

CHAPTER 27

THE PRINCE

(KATE PHILO)

I could have predicted he would be wearing the yellow tie. I had made sure he bought at least one red, one blue, one green, but yellow it always was.

'I'm afraid we have to hurry, Jeremiah.' I pulled his curtains closed, not wanting the control room staring in at his empty chamber. 'Issues with the car.'

'I'm perfectly ready.' He marched ahead to the security door, raising his hand toward the keypad. Then he stopped, stepping aside. 'Lead on,' he said.

I punched in the pass code, wondering what game the judge was playing. But I was too stressed to bring it up just then. Carthage's odd behavior had rattled me, an unexpected warmth that aroused all my suspicions. In the corridor Dixon wanted to stop us for some questions but I pushed past, explaining that we were running late. I pressed the elevator call button, feeling his eyes on me while we waited.

When we reached the security desk, Gerber was standing there slumped like a sad clown. 'I forgot my badge,' he said to me. 'Please tell this brave protector of our safety that I do work here.'

'He works here,' I said, writing my name and Jeremiah's into the register.

'Hey Judge Rice, quick question,' Gerber said. 'I know we're cool on not monitoring you any more, and giving you privacy. But I was wondering if you would mind if I attached just one diode, just one little electronic thing, when you're asleep at night?' He held his thumb and forefinger an inch apart. 'You'd barely notice. And we'd learn a ton. It would be a contribution to society.'

'Is that right?' Jeremiah asked. 'Then the answer is yes.'

'Could we talk about this later?' I said. 'We're late.'

'One moment,' the guard said. 'If this gentleman does work here, I'll need you to sign a voucher.'

'Please go ahead,' I waved Jeremiah on. 'I'd rather our friends in the red shirts don't see you again. The car should be waiting in back.' He ambled off across the atrium, while I bent over the page. 'I'll sign, but is this really necessary?'

'We're just following Dr Carthage's rules.'

Gerber chuckled. 'Apparently I am just the sort of person that I need to be protected from.'

When Jeremiah was out of earshot, I turned to Gerber. 'What's this night monitoring all about?'

He shrugged. 'Nothing. Maybe nothing.'

'Maybe?'

'I'll tell you later. Go. Thank you for letting me work today.'

I hustled across the atrium. 'Send me an email about what you're doing.'

Gerber wiggled his fingers in my direction. 'Go go go.'

Jeremiah stood by the car but he had not climbed in yet. Instead he was talking to a slender woman in a white beret. She stood between him and the open door, and instantly I felt my hackles rise.

'Excuse me,' I called, breaking into a run. 'Excuse me, is there something I can do for you?'

The woman turned to me with complete calm. Still my usual self-possession was eluding me. 'No thank you.' Then she faced Jeremiah again. She was holding his hand, their eyes locked on one another.

He stood like a statue. 'Do I know you?'

'No,' she said, 'but we are a part of one another.'

'How can that be?'

She shook her head. 'It doesn't matter. Everyone wants something from you, but I thought it was important for you to know that I don't. Want anything, I mean.'

'Who are you?' I said. Closer, I saw that she was beautiful: high forehead, brilliant blue eyes. 'What do you want?'

'I'm Hilary,' she answered, keeping her eyes on Jeremiah. Then she stepped back, releasing her hold. 'And all I wanted was this. Just this.'

The tenderness of her voice kept us all still for a moment. Then I broke the mood. 'I'm sorry, but we have an interview to get to.'

'Of course.' She backed away. 'Sorry if I delayed you.'

'Thank you Hilary,' Jeremiah said, almost whispering.

'You're welcome,' she said, stopping at the curb. We climbed into the car, quieted, I told the driver the address. She was still standing there, melancholy, dignified, as we pulled into traffic and away.

I settled back in the seat. 'Who was that woman?' I asked Jeremiah. 'Have we seen her before?'

'Hilary someone.'

'What was that all about?'

'I don't know.' Jeremiah directed his gaze out the window. 'I'm not sure.'

The drive gave me time to wonder why I had reacted so protectively. Clearly she wasn't one of the protestors, so it wasn't that kind of danger. Plus we had met thousands of strangers in recent weeks, without my defenses being so triggered.

Was it jealousy? There was a definite intimacy to the moment I'd interrupted. So what? Who was I to barge in like that? Of course I'd felt drawn to Jeremiah. How could anyone spend that much time in the presence of an intelligent man, a handsome man, without experiencing occasional stirrings? But I had no delusions. I knew he belonged to me in no way whatsoever.

Still, I wondered once again about sexual differences across the century. After the snarky men of recent years, promise-today-disappear-tomorrow guys, it might be nice to be with someone less sexually sophisticated. Jeremiah's reactions to billboards, the covers of women's magazines promising '22 Ways To Make Him Scream Tonight,' the provocative clothing people wore at Gerber's disco, all revealed to me his reserve. By contrast, I had a hard drive full of memories of men pawing at me, urging me to manifest a fantasy they'd had, trying to talk me into some scenario I suspected came from the most recent porn they'd seen online. Probably every woman wonders at some point: what portion of the love professed in my ears was base desire, and what part genuinely for me? Maybe with a man from a simpler sexual time, answering that question would be easier.

Jeremiah stared out the window, watching the city with bright eyes. I felt an odd reversal. In the stratospherically unlikely event that we were ever lovers, would I seem a callous sophisticate to him? In relative terms, I might be worse than the most caddish of the oafs who'd made moves on me.

Or was Hilary a different kind of danger altogether? Their connection had been visible the moment I stepped outside. But it was not quite sexual. It seemed possibly a bit spiritual. Maybe I'd felt threatened needlessly. There was nobody I could ask, no person I could discuss these things with.

'I am remiss,' Jeremiah said, turning abruptly. 'I have neglected to ask what the purpose of today's interview might be.'

I shook my head to clear it. 'Funny thing, I was just speaking with Carthage about your interest in serving a larger purpose.'

'Is today an opportunity to end the lark, and consider the greater good?'

'Well, he certainly thought so. Carthage has people interested in building the Project into something bigger. He wants you to help, with raising money I suppose.'

'That is not what I meant at all.' Jeremiah pounded a fist on his thigh. 'That Carthage. He annoys me like a wasp.'

I shifted in my seat. 'I didn't know you had formed a judgment of him.'

'That man would not bother to breathe if it did not contribute to his self-aggrandizement.' He smoothed his hand over where he had pounded. 'I have observed his conduct toward others.' His voice fell. 'I have noted his treatment of you.'

'But we all see that. We just tolerate it because it enables the Project to exist. If not for Carthage, I would not have a job, much less a . . . well, a you.'

'Kate.' Jeremiah turned sideways in his seat, taking both of my hands. 'I cannot imagine why I, out of all humanity, received the gift of a second life. Nor do I much understand why the people of here and now exhibit such fascination with me.

But I do not need to fathom these things to know that they present me with an opportunity many, many times greater than what we had hoped with our modest expedition to the north. If I were to spend that chance on something as small as Carthage's money wishes, it would be akin to wasting this second life.'

'Then the time to seize that opportunity is now,' I said. 'Right now.'

'Here we are,' the driver said, pulling over. He hopped out, clambering around to open the curb-side door.

Jeremiah looked down at our hands, smiling. 'We seem to have arrived.'

'I'd say so.'

'Hoist anchor, Kate. Here we go.' He scrambled up out of the seat. I hurried along after him.

'You're late,' the ponytailed woman said. 'Follow me.'

She spun on her running shoe and we did as we were told. She was young, barely thirty, carried a clipboard, wore a headset around her neck which she raised to bring the mouthpiece near. 'They're here, we're going straight to make up.' She called back over her shoulder, 'You do know this is live TV, don't you? Time matters.'

'Excuse me, miss?' Jeremiah said.

'Yes?' She did not break stride.

'What is your name?'

'Oh.' She slowed. 'I'm Alex.'

'Hello Alex.' He held out his hand. 'I'm Jeremiah Rice.'

'Hi, then.' She shook his hand. 'Right.' Again Alex strode ahead.

Of course Jeremiah was the featured attraction, I merely the protective caretaker. So I followed mutely while they rushed him to make up, where they sprayed his hair in place, then to wardrobe, where a man with a tiny whisk broom brushed Jeremiah's jacket, picking at invisible pieces of lint. Each department had a name for him: 'talent' in one, 'our guest' in another. Everywhere Alex led us, a TV hung near the ceiling, showing the program Jeremiah would appear on momentarily. It was the 'Tom and Molly Show,' half news, half talk, two hosts: a tall blonde woman with a chest that I would have bet cash was doctored, who seemed to have the role of the serious one, the asker of tough questions, beside a shorter man with a perfect tan, jaw square like a backhoe, a yuk-yuk laugh like a cartoon character.

Finally they led us onto the set. The floor was filthy cement, sticky from coffee spills, cables running underfoot, with a little raised island of carpet and chairs that sat in the bright lights. I noticed a poster on a side wall, a giant enlargement of Jeremiah shaking hands with the vice president. Over Gerald T. Walker's head someone had pasted a thought balloon: 'I am using you.' Over Jeremiah, there was a reply: 'Your zipper's down.'

Jeremiah tapped my arm, pointing to the opposite offstage side. There were action shots of baseball players all along that wall: hurling a pitch, diving for a grounder, swinging for the seats. 'I love that,' he whispered.

'I wonder if the station has a box at Fenway.'

'What is Fenway?'

'Shhh,' said Alex, silent in her sneakers, rushing past.

Up in the lights, a woman in an apron was teaching Tom and Molly how to whip cream properly. A staffer approached Jeremiah with a mike, threading the wire up his sleeve. Another man stood at Jeremiah's elbow, pointing at a camera. 'When the red light is on, that one is shooting you. Look right at it for the intro and exit. Otherwise just face Molly and Tom when they speak to you, OK?

'It's just like a conversation,' the sound man said.

'Only fake,' the cameraman added.

'Thank you gentlemen. Would you please tell me your names?' Jeremiah held out his hand.

They told him, shaking hands in turn.

'Time-wasting assholes,' Alex said, breezing up. 'We're about to cut away, then you're on. Stay here. You,' she pointed at me. 'Follow me.'

'Good luck,' I called to Jeremiah.

'I'll do my part,' he answered.

The booth was a bank of controls and mixers, back behind the cameras. Two men in headsets worked computers, while a screen to the side showed what was being broadcast. Just beyond stood a man I imagined to be the director, because he spoke into his mouthpiece to control which cameras shot next. When he said, 'Cut to Four and zoom,' a different angle appeared on screen.

'And that,' the current guest was saying, handing out servings as the camera neared her face, 'is how you make the perfect strawberry shortcake.'

'Cut to one, closing shot.'

'Thanks so much Elise,' Molly said, smiling. The show's theme music came up, stirring strings above a marching band of horns. 'We'll take a quick break now, and be right back with the national weather. Stay tuned.'

'Let's see if I can clean my plate before the break is up,' said Tom, yuk-yukking until the moment the lights blinked out.

The onstage smiles vanished just as quickly. Tom hurried off, handing his plate to an underling just offstage. Molly trotted to a table where she picked up her cell phone to poke at its screen. The woman in the apron sat a moment alone, then stood.

'This way please,' someone called, and she wandered forward in the dark. Then the house lights came up, bright as day. I stood still, blinking. The dirt showed even worse.

All at once a slice of my past returned to me, from interviews in those weeks after we first returned from the Arctic. All the news outlets wanted us. I remembered the smell I found on my clothes, somewhere between excitement and fear. Everything was speculation then, or hope. Meanwhile back in the chamber a body lay encased in ice, which became the man now standing 15 feet away, wearing a yellow tie I was the first to knot around his neck.

Alex led Jeremiah to a seat, then came to stand beside me. 'He'll be fine,' she said, scanning the set as if hunting for something amiss.

A dowdy older man waddled to a side area, wearing tweedy clothes like someone's bad idea of Sherlock Holmes. He scanned his notes, tucked them in his jacket pocket, folded away his glasses. He took out a curved pipe, biting the mouthpiece, then stared into space.

'Places,' called a voice overhead. The house lights dropped. 'Three, two—'

'Lights up,' said the director, 'give me Three zooming to Waldo.'

Spot lights flooded the side area, where the man in tweed took an imaginary draw on his pipe and blew out clear air. 'Waldo's Weather welcomes you back with windy good morning wishes,' he said, 'and today's question of the day: how do weather forecasters know the future? And why are their predictions often incorrect? Elementary, my good Watson.'

He continued with his patter, explaining barometric pressure, the prevailing wind direction for different kinds of fronts. Screens behind him displayed a series of simple graphics, puffs of white for clouds, blue arrows to represent wind. His segment lasted about three minutes. Jeremiah sat on the dimmed main stage. I felt his solitude. When Waldo started the forecast, a national map with various storms or calms, Tom ambled up while Molly put down her phone. They took their seats, adjusted their clothes. Tom angled his head side to side, stretching his neck muscles. The lights came up.

At first it was a game of softballs: what had Lynn been like? Were the people of nineteenth-century Boston friendly? Then Molly began homing in.

'What do you make of our society today? What are our shortcomings?'

Jeremiah answered instantly. 'You're vulgar.'

Tom laughed loudly. 'Ya think? Ya think?'

'I hear obscenities everywhere. Also I find a needlessly heightened sexuality in all manner of transactions, from advertising to news to how people dress in public.'

'Wow. Any other criticisms?'

'Your culture today is violent. I have seen bloody entertainments, vicious computer games. It is no surprise that violent crimes are an everyday occurrence.'

'Isn't solving those problems the responsibility of the political world?' Molly asked. 'And if so, what about your great friendship with the vice president?'

'I would hardly describe a single meeting at his request as a friendship. If that were so, I could claim a closer bond with a president.'

'Wait a second,' Tom said, pretending to scratch his pate like a hayseed. 'You met the president too?'

'Not the current one, no sir. But in 1902 President Roosevelt conducted a Progressive Tour of New England, with a dinner stop in Lynn. As a judge and civic leader, I spent three hours in his company, far more than with Vice President Walker.' He leaned toward Molly with a pinched grin. 'You might say we were great friends.'

She smiled too, but coldly. Some kind of game was on. 'Would you say you have led a charmed life, Judge Rice? I mean, Harvard Law School, the youngest judge in the state at the time of your appointment, grand adventures exploring the northern seas—'

'Do you mean aside from the fact that I died? And lost everything, friends and home and family?'

To me, Jeremiah was beginning to sound like a scold. But I understood his intent, his interest in using this moment in the lights.

'Well,' Molly persisted, 'your life has been one great spectacle since reanimation, wouldn't you say? One crowd after another?'

'People have been incredibly generous and kind, for which I am grateful. Honestly, though, I encountered larger crowds in my past life. The energy people spend today on gossip about celebrities was, in my time, directed toward exploration and learning. Once our group announced that we were sailing above the Arctic Circle, people waited in line to see us. We drew thousands, filling churches and opera halls. I never drank more champagne.'

'Now you're talking,' Tom guffawed. 'Good times.' Molly narrowed her eyes but he pressed on, oblivious.

'Hold on Three,' the director said. I noticed that the cameras did not cut to her face, so the audience would have no notion that she was annoyed.

'So tell me,' Tom said, 'what sort of fun do you like to have now? Is there anything good on TV?'

'Little,' Jeremiah said. 'It is mostly shallow, false, and predictable.'

'Ya like any of it?'

'Oh yes. Twice I have seen the Red Sox play on the small screen. Those games struck me as entertaining and full of surprises. A fine ball club.'

'You can say that again,' Tom yukked. 'Did you know this station is part-owner of the Sox? Hey, we could catch a game, ya know.'

'Honestly? In the stadium?' He sat up straight. 'That would be splendid.'

I brought one hand to my mouth. How was it that Jeremiah struck an antagonistic tone with the smart one, but was fast becoming friends with the frat boy? They laughed, making plans to talk later about going to a game. Finally Molly saw her chance, charging back into the interview.

'What do you say to people who insist that you are a fake?'

'Pardon me?'

'A hoax, a sham. There are many, many skeptics out there.'

'Hm.' Jeremiah looked off for a moment, thinking, the silent airtime weighing tons. 'I suppose there would be, yes.'

'What do you say to these people, who think you are little more than an elaborate publicity stunt?'

Jeremiah turned so that his knees were nearly touching hers. 'There have always been people for whom cynicism is a reflex. Perhaps disbelieving feels safer. Either way, there is little to be gained by insisting to them that something is so, when they do not wish to believe it. Therefore, we must let our deeds be our ambassadors. Our challenge is to live with all the sincerity that is in our hearts, and hope that those who doubt will come to see the truth.'

'Right,' Tom said, chortling. 'Good luck with that, fella.'

In that moment I felt the secret thrill of a teacher who sees her student surpass her. Jeremiah no longer needed me to navigate this world. He was ready to shape it to his will.

'That's all we have time for,' Molly said. 'Thanks for joining us, Judge Rice, Boston's own time traveler. Headline news is next, plus the results of a new survey: how often does the average married couple have sex? The answer may surprise you.'

'Uh-oh,' Tom said. 'Is my wife going to want to know this?'

Molly made an open-mouthed smile. 'We'll be right back.'

The theme music began playing again. 'Camera Two,' the director said, 'snug on his mug till we cut away.'

Jeremiah's face filled the screen. The sound man on my right removed his headset. 'Looky looky, what a prince.'

Alex stood on my other side. 'Prince of what?' she said.

'Prince of the world that is going to eat you alive.'

CHAPTER 28

PLAY BALL

(DANIEL DIXON)

No question, my first mistake is wearing shorts. All those months inside the four walls of the Project, without a break to report on a single desert expedition or tour the Everglades in an airboat, my legs have become pasty white. But I don't know where our seats will be. If we're parked out in the bleachers somewhere, full sun for the whole afternoon, I have no intention of roasting in long pants.

I still can't believe I am going. Our old Frank had scored three seats for a Saturday afternoon home-stand against the Yanks, by agreeing with a TV show to be filmed during the game and interviewed after, but I didn't pay attention to details. The chance to watch the Bronx Bombers spank the Sox at home was too good to pass up. I have loved the Yankees about since I could walk, and couldn't care less who they beat on any particular day.

The only disappointment is that Dr Kate had some research thing to finish for Carthage that day. Then, out of the whole remaining lab staff, only Gerber wanted to see the game, which left seat number three available for yours truly.

As a result I'm not carrying a camera, or a notebook, or much besides a wallet and phone, when I hit the Project offices that day. As any reporter with ten minutes' experience will tell you, this is always when the biggest news happens.

After muscling my way through the shouters and oddballs outside the lab's front door, I come bopping off of the elevator just as a line of guys in suits begins strolling out of the private conference room. I pull back for a second. Carthage shakes each one's hand, thanking them for coming in on a weekend. He's smiling but these guys are as dour as undertakers. Each one has a green binder tucked under his arm. Thomas swipes his security badge and presses the elevator call button for them.

I duck behind a door and whip out my phone. Only a cheapo camera but it will do. The suits are not talking, not a word. There are enough of them that some have to wait after the elevator fills up. Hey fellas, I think as I snap, *smile*.

After the second elevator loads, the doors whispering closed, Carthage turns to Thomas. 'What's your take?'

'Six interested, three eager. Too bad Bronsky didn't show.'

'Maybe four. How many will break the confidentiality contract?'

'You saw how readily they signed, sir. I think we're secure in that department.'

'Let's do a full review and debrief.'

'Yes sir.'

They march off toward Carthage's office. Funny, I have never seen Carthage consult anyone before, much less his lackey. Anyway I can't help snooping in the conference room, and yes, they've left two goodies behind. One is a list of names, which I photograph in a heartbeat. The other is one of those green binders.

Of course I don't have a briefcase or anywhere to hide the damn thing. I hustle out to the hallway and swipe my badge to enter the control room.

'Dixon.'

It's Thomas. I turn, holding the binder behind my back. 'What's up?'

'What brings you in on a Saturday?'

'The ball game, remember?'

'Right.' He thinks for a second. 'When did you get here?'

'Dunno.' I shrug. 'How long does it take to walk down this hallway?'

Thomas makes some kind of internal calculation, then makes for the conference room. 'Have fun at the game.'

I open the control room door. 'You bet.'

But he's already gone. In the control room, I snoop through the glass as he hustles out with that list of names. He must have forgotten that Mr Bronsky had a binder coming too.

Gerber is rocking out at his desk, headphones clomped on his ears, a grin of bliss on his face. I look around for some place to stash the binder, but everything seems too obvious. Then I see the out-box type basket where Gerber puts old *Perv Du Jours* after posting a new one. Not much chance of discovery there. I stuff the binder underneath the pile, scrambling the papers over it to look naturally messy.

Gerber is in shorts too. And if my hams look strange, his are downright comical. He's wearing plaid Bermudas like something out of 1949, legs as bald as plucked chicken, with the palest skin this side of a salamander. We are such lab rats in here, I swear. The Lazarus Project menagerie.

I goose him with my thumb. 'Our hero awake yet?'

'Yes indeed,' Gerber says, removing the headphones and straightening in his chair. 'Already up when I got here at 6.'

I scan the closed chamber curtains. 'He's that stoked to see the game?'

'Or something,' Gerber answers. He points at the clock. 'We ought to get rolling, since they want us there so early.'

'On the case,' I say, starting around the corner. 'What's the pass code again?'

'2667,' he calls, without a thought. But I'm thinking: bingo. Finally got it.

I've never liked the lock-down part of this place, as if somebody must be doing something illegal.

Or old Frank is somehow a prisoner. Punching in 2667, I notice the letters above each number like on a phone. Maybe the pass code is actually a word. The door slides back and the judge is sitting reading. He's wearing a suit and a bright yellow tie. You'd have thought we were going to a debutante ball.

'What's with the get-up?' I ask him.

'I'll need to purchase a hat somewhere,' he says. 'A tall one that befits the grandstand. Do you know of a good place we might stop along the way?'

The fact is, he's going to roast in that outfit, not to mention how popular a tall hat would be in the snug of Fenway Park. He'll be pissing people off four rows back. Which amuses me to consider, until a better idea comes along, and whistling a happy tune.

'I know just the lid for you,' I say. 'And a perfect spot we can get one.'

'Excellent,' he says, setting his book on the bed as carefully as if it was the Bible. I snoop and it's *Great Expectations.* I remember ninth grade agony wading through that doorstop, dull as a raining Sunday.

Our Frank jumps to his feet, tugging his vest sharp. 'Shall we be off?'

I notice that lately he has more spark to him, and it's not just about a baseball game. He's faster to learn things, quicker to answer questions, less likely to need a nap. It's as if he's finally all the way awake.

'Yeah, let's grab Gerber and get moving. You know you're throwing the opening pitch?'

'What? I did not know that, no. My goodness, what an honor.'

'Well, just make sure the ball makes it all the way to the plate, OK? Don't embarrass us all.'

'No, of course not.'

'Come on.' I hook a thumb toward the door. 'Let's head out.'

He follows like a pup on a leash.

Carthage had Thomas hire a town car, but there was no way I was going to a ballgame by limo. Germs be damned. If the sneezes, coughing and handshakes of half of Boston haven't killed the guy already, riding the T to Fenway Park won't do any worse. We sneak out the back door while the town car idles out front.

For the entire T ride the judge babbles about ball games in the days of old. Apparently there were these local characters who would carouse beforehand at a bar called Third Base, then pour themselves into the bleachers under a banner that said 'The Royal Rooters.' They were so rowdy, sports writers gave them as much ink as the games.

'Those crazy madcap palookas,' Gerber says, winking at me.

The judge doesn't notice. He's just getting warmed up. 'There were other fans, equally devoted but with behavior more appropriate to my station. I joined them whenever the press of cases abated and

I could hurry away to the Walpole Street grounds. Oh, and now I remember, later they played at Huntington Avenue. Lucy Swift of New Bedford, for example. She never missed a game, always wore a black dress, and kept tallies on batters and pitchers in her own little black score book. Michael Regan too, he ran a prominent Boston furniture company. A hard worker, but somehow he always found time to watch the Pilgrims play.'

That one gets my attention. 'The Pilgrims? Who the hell were they?'

'One of the parent teams for the Red Sox, along with the Cincinnati Red Stockings. This was always a premium baseball town, I'd say. Fifty-cent tickets when the other teams charged twenty-five.'

'What?' Gerber yelps. 'Fifty cents? Do you have any idea what today's tickets cost?'

People up and down the car look at us, then studiously turn away. It's one of my favorite things about mass transit, how people fake like they aren't listening. It's the same in New York subways, BART in San Francisco, the D.C. Metro, everywhere experts in eavesdropping.

'I can't imagine. Four dollars? Six?'

I just laugh, I can't help it. 'Not quite.'

Gerber cackles too. 'Try nine hundred.'

'I beg your pardon? That's impossible. Why, in my time the players only earned perhaps three thousand a season.'

'Well bub, now they get a thousand times that much,' I say. 'Or more.'

That sets him off again, this time about all the special players in the great season of 1903. 'That year was the first World Series, you see, to settle the feud between the American and National leagues. Pittsburgh went ahead of the Red Sox by three games to one. The pitching was amazing, blistering speed, even though the leagues had moved the mound back a few years before because no one could get a hit off Amos Rusie. Oh, it is all coming back to me now.'

'I can tell,' I snore at him. 'How wonderful for you.'

There are plenty of buffs out there who dote on dusty baseball lore, but not me. Sure, when yours truly covered the legislature I knew every committee chairman and which lobbyists bought him the most drinks. When it comes to sports, though, just tell me who's in first place, and if it isn't the Yanks then how many games back are they, and how long till the playoffs. When people carry on about early baseball, I can feel myself growing cobwebs.

By the time we reach the Fenway stop and move with the crowd toward the stairs, the judge's mouth is running like a lawnmower.

'Buck Freeman, he was first baseman. Jimmy Collins, oh he was a quick one. He played third, and was also team manager. But the real strength was Bill Dinneen, the pitcher. Of course we had Cy Young too, the greatest hurler ever, but he was older by then. Also Iron Joe McGinty, who pitched three double-headers all by himself that August. At any rate, the Red Sox came back from that three to one deficit to win four games straight and take the first World Series.'

At that an old man turns from climbing the stairs next to us. 'And it was Big Bill Dinneen pitched three of those four comeback games,' he wheezes. He's wearing an ancient Sox cap that fits his noggin like a second skin.

'That's correct,' the judge says, like they're instant brothers. 'Exactly correct.'

One more second of this gung-ho nonsense and I'm going to slap somebody. I bend away toward Yawkey Way, the alley beside the park. I know what will cork him.

Sure enough the vendors are out with their carts, hawking T-shirts and hats. I dicker with one for half a minute, and come back a few bucks poorer but with a nice fresh cap, blue with a red B on the front, and pop it on old Frank's head.

'Now you're a legitimate fan,' I say.

Gerber points at him. 'Why, look. Isn't that man a Royal Rooter?'

The judge stops right where he's standing, takes in all the people wearing ordinary clothes for a game, ball caps and T-shirts and not a top hat in sight. Then he adjusts the lid, and puffs his chest out like an old time bodybuilder. 'I smell victory.'

'Nah,' I say, leading him in. 'They're just boiling the hot dogs.'

* * *

The TV crew is waiting, along with a guide from the stadium. We get a complete tour of the downstairs. We meet the team owner, a white-haired guy with a tan so perfect it would make a movie star give up sunblock. The judge shakes hands with everyone, a big sincere hello-there, I don't care if it's a janitor with his mop and bucket. The camera guy leans in constantly to get his angle. Frank and the owner both seem oblivious. I just try to stay out of the lights.

Finally one of the handlers leads us through a maze of halls toward the field, pausing in the last bit of shadowed doorway as if to build suspense. Grass and light beckon from beyond. I'm thinking it's corny to hesitate there, until a second later when we march into the reality of the park. Now I don't care which team you like, or what century you were born in, coming out of the door onto that giant lawn and the summer sun and the rows of seats rising all around you, I tell you that is really something.

'What do you think of that, old Frank?'

He rotates in a slow circle. 'Why do you call me that?'

'No reason,' I say. 'It's an old joke.'

'My name is Jeremiah Rice,' he replies absently, taking in the whole scene. 'We might see ten thousand people attending a game, in my time. Today must be three or four times that sum.' He kept turning. 'So much humanity.'

The stands are nearly filled, bat boys and old

timers hanging around the dugouts, out-of-towners posing for snapshots, the general excitement before a ball game. There's a good half hour of folderol, what with baseball being all about a long windup before the pitch if you know what I mean. Then the announcer calls forward an *a capella* group from Tufts University to sing the national anthem.

'I know that college,' the judge says. 'I went there.'

The kids have decent voices. A tall guy, skinny as an oar, sings incredibly low. One soprano with big red hair has a terrific set of knockers.

When they reach the land of the free, and hold that note, damn if the judge doesn't knuckle at one of his eyes. As they finish and the crowd cheers, Gerber leans over. 'You all right?'

He nods. 'I had forgotten.'

What an odd duck, I swear. Then they announce that a special guest will throw today's first pitch. At the name Jeremiah Rice, a big cheer goes up. He marches to the mound, an umpire and the team owner at his side. Before he arrives, though, a chorus of boos comes from somewhere, too. There it is, one moment capturing the world's regard for the judge: fair to partly cloudy.

The ump hands a ball to the judge. He weighs it, feeling the laces. He does the damnedest thing then, shucks off his coat to give his arms more freedom. But he needs somewhere to hang it, and while he's looking around the whole stadium is waiting. It's only the opening pitch, pal.

That's the moment the team owner gives a go-get-'em swing of his fist and says, 'Let 'er rip, Jeremiah.' The judge turns, sees the guy's outstretched arm, and hangs his jacket on it. Half the stadium breaks out laughing. The owner keeps a good friendly smile on. Maybe he's not oblivious to the camera after all.

Our Frank's face is as serious as if the whole pennant race hangs on this pitch. He stares down the catcher, who holds his glove fat and forward like a ten-year-old couldn't miss. The judge cranks his arm back, lifts a leg high, snaps down like a whip, and hurls that pill like nothing I would have expected: a hot line for the plate, zooming high and left, only to slice down in the last few feet, drop like a rock and hit the catcher's unmoved mitt with a satisfying smack.

The place goes nuts. Frank takes his jacket back, thanks the owner, and shakes everybody's hand all over again. The fans eat it up. He tips his brand new cap. This is one adaptable freak, I give him that: from I-need-a-top-hat to curve-into-the-strike-zone in less than 90 minutes.

The seats were ridiculous. Fourth row, just off the plate so we looked down the third base line. I convinced the judge to take off his jacket, but when I reached for the tie he jerked back.

'Oh no,' he said. 'Certain standards must be maintained.'

The camera man set up below us, and we forgot

he was there in about two beers' time. Gerber told the kid working the stands with cold ones to stay close and keep them coming. The first one went down like air. The second had all the coolness to make a sunny day lie down like a dog baring its belly. Our Frank took a beer like a good lad, but after one sip he made a face.

'What's the matter now?' I wiped foam from my lip.

'No flavor,' he said. 'It is perhaps the only sense my body hasn't regained. Things don't have as strong a taste.'

'Maybe it's not you,' Gerber said.

'Whatever do you mean by that?'

'Maybe the stuff we're drinking today is really just overpriced piss.' He smiled and took a big gulp. Frank considered his cup sideways, then set it down beneath his seat.

It was a pitchers' game, strike outs and brush backs and no one on base. In other words a typically dull baseball game, one of the finest things on earth. I bought the judge a program so he could handicap the batters. He had this theory that doubles were the indicator, that ever since Honus Wagner, the guys with the most doubles also had the best averages. I said that was B.S., till he shoved the program in my face and proved it, player after player right down the roster.

'Whaddaya know?' I said, and raised an arm to signal the kid selling hot dogs. He worked his way over and I ordered four. 'Frank, you have got to chow on one of these babies. You'll think you died and came back to life.'

Gerber burst out laughing. 'Dixon, you have really have a gift for tact, you know that?'

'Relax,' I said, passing dogs along. 'He knows what I mean.'

'I do,' the judge said. 'And I believe I will try one of those.'

'You will?'

'I've had quite enough of Dr Borden's fortified oatmeal.'

'Rebellion,' Gerber said, one hand cupped at his mouth like a mock yell. 'Insurrection.'

'Here,' I said, 'try it this way.' I squeezed some ketchup and a big dollop of mustard down the length of his dog, then did the same on one of mine.

Frank sniffed the result. 'When in Rome . . .' And he took a good fat bite.

'Now isn't that the best thing you ever tasted in your life?'

'Oh my heavens,' he said with his mouth full. 'It's all *salt.*' He looked around for something to wash it down, then reached between his feet to hoist that beer and slugged a good bit back.

'Now we're talking,' I said.

'How can you eat these things?' He took another gulp.

'Diligence,' Gerber said. 'Practice, practice, practice.'

The judge was quiet for the next few minutes,

serious as a chess game. He worked his way through that hot dog though, an inch at a time, easing the job with plenty of beer.

For a moment I entertained the idea that we might get the guy boozed that day. I can't say why that appealed to me so much, but it definitely did. Gerber must have had the same notion, because the second the judge's cup was empty he signaled the beer kid for another round. When the frosties arrived, our Frank did the old beneath-the-seat again. Oh well, more for us I guess.

The innings passed, the Yanks went up by one, the Sox took the lead, back and forth, all short shots and tight play. The judge fixed so hard on the game he sometimes sat with his mouth open. But the pace was totally easy, the afternoon stretched out like a cat sunning on a sofa. At one point he turned to me. 'Would you explain something please?'

'Sure.'

'Why do you wear those?' He gestured at my shades.

'To protect our eyes from the sun,' Gerber said.

'Ha. That is why neither of you is squinting. We could certainly have used some of those spectacles in the Arctic seas.'

'He's lying,' I said. 'That's not it at all.'

Gerber chuckled. 'Why do you wear them, then?'

'So I can ogle women without getting caught.'

'Of course.' Gerber nodded. 'The other major reason.'

'Like right there.' I nudged Frank. 'See that blonde down there?' A hot little miss was just then standing to straighten her shorts: extremely, wonderfully brief cutoff jeans which had ridden oh so sweetly up her nice backside. Peaches, peaches, peaches.

'Oh my heaven,' the judge said. 'Is that attire allowed?'

'It's a matter of taste,' Gerber answered. 'Some of us prefer a different kind.'

He pointed with his chin at a rolling thunder thighs honey, squeezed into black tights about nine sizes too small, her arms jiggling, legs rubbing against one another as she waddled down the aisle.

'Oh my heaven,' Frank said again.

'The prosecution offers exhibit B,' I said, pointing to the absolute babe coming along the row, long hair pulled high, T-shirt cut from below to show her yummy tummy, with the sparkle of a piercing at her navel.

'Oh my heaven,' the judge said, shaking his head. 'My wife wore more as undergarments.'

'Yeah.' I wolfed down the last of my hot dog. 'Isn't it great?'

'The defense humbly requests that you all check out exhibit C,' Gerber said, grinning like a man with the winning lottery ticket. He gestured toward a woman across the way, her belly as round as a barrel, her chest so huge it provided a platform for carrying many sodas and hot dogs. 'I'm in love.'

'Oh my heaven,' Frank said again. He had one hand over his mouth.

'Let us now give thanks for exhibit D,' I said, 'over there in the white shirt.' In fact this young lady's chemise left absolutely zilch to the imagination. The lettering on her front read 'Love me Ortiz me.'

'Oh my heaven,' the judge said once more. 'What do the words mean?'

'It's a joke about a player's name,' Gerber said. 'And I give. I surrender to your argument, and throw myself on the mercy of the court. What is my sentence?'

'For the rest of the day,' I said, 'Frank gets to wear your shades. And we'll just see which he stares at more, your evidence or mine.'

'Fair enough,' Gerber said, handing them over.

'Instead of concealing my leering,' the judge said, hovering them over his face, 'the rather, let these protect me from both kinds of immodesty.'

Which is how, in the papers the next day, any photo that was not of the frozen man's monster of a pitch instead showed him hoisting a beer or laughing behind dark glasses.

One thing I forgot about Fenway fans was their annoying tradition at the seventh inning stretch. With any other self-respecting team, the crowd knows that TV stations are airing a bunch of commercials for beer and trucks. The fans stand a minute, jaw with people around them, or buy another pop.

Not at Sox games, oh no. Instead the PA blasts

that Neil Diamond tune 'Sweet Caroline,' and people howl along at top volume. It sounds as awful as you would expect from a choir of drunks. The judge looked left and right, trying to follow the words. I all but covered my ears.

When we got to the line 'Hands . . . touching hands,' every Fred Fatso and Joe Six Pack in the place raised whichever hand wasn't holding a beer high overhead. The judge did too.

'Whoa,' Gerber cried out. 'That is trippy.'

I leaned toward him. 'What is?'

'I've seen that before.' He pointed at Frank's outstretched paw. 'But it was frozen.'

Weird and true. There was the image from the Arctic video, the same hand making the same gesture. It struck me what a distance we'd come. What a long way from the man encased in ice. I wanted to ponder that a minute, but the damn song was too distracting.

Look, I'm all for camp, irony and all the trimmings. But after the tune said 'good times never felt so good,' everyone in the crowd grinned and hollered 'so good, so good, so good.'

Enough. I elbowed the judge. 'Come on. I need to hit the head.'

He gave me that oddball look he often does when I use figures of speech. Still, he always puzzles out what I mean, and he followed me right up the aisle. 'Remember Section 37,' I pointed at the sign, 'in case we get separated.'

When we first hit the john he was on my heels.

One look at the long row of piss pots, though, all with lines of guys waiting, and he drew back, putting one hand on the wall.

'Don't touch that,' I advised him. 'They may not have cleaned it since 1922.'

The judge jumped away like the wall was electrified, then looked down at his paw as if it was swarming with bugs.

'Just do your business quick. You can give your hands a good wash around the corner.' I headed to a different line. 'I'll meet you outside.'

He shuffled off, not saying a word. Poor bastard, imagine being scared of something as ordinary as a public washroom.

I had to wait for him, but our old Frank came out at last, looking like he'd spent a week at sea. He was halfway to me when a woman intercepted, a short-legged jellyfish in a red track suit, carrying a pink purse big enough to hold a bowling ball. I ducked behind the pillar, cursing myself for not bringing a notebook.

'I knew I would meet you eventually,' she was saying, her arm tangled in his like she was part octopus. 'I just knew it.'

The judge stopped walking and tried to work his arm free. I decided to let the scene play out.

'How may I help you, madam?'

'You already have.' She was grinning like a shark. 'You gave me hope.'

'I'm delighted,' he said, pushing one of her hands down his sleeve.

'It's my husband. He died of pancreatic cancer nine years ago.'

'My condolences—'

'No, it's fine. Because we had him cryogenically frozen, you see?'

Her voice was over-modulated, like the soprano loudmouth of a church choir. She pulled the judge's elbow in a death grip until he bent down.

'It cost fifty thousand dollars,' she said in a stage whisper. 'I never put much faith in it, but he insisted. Nine years later,' she poked his chest, 'along comes you. Oh, I have plenty of faith now.'

The judge took off Gerber's shades. 'Thank you for sharing your story with me.'

'You won't get away that easily,' she wagged a finger. 'I want to ask you for something.'

His eyes scanned the crowd for me, but didn't look by the pillar. 'Of course.'

'I knew it,' she said, as loudly as if she were telling the other people exiting the john. 'I knew you would be generous.'

The judge took a dignified stance, courtly even. 'How may I be of service?'

'Isn't it obvious? I want you to get them to wake him up.'

'Oh, I see,' he said. 'I'd be delighted to help, but I'm afraid that is beyond my—'

'Don't you go being humble on me,' she said. The woman tilted her head coquettishly, which maybe, I say *maybe* she could have gotten away with twenty years ago. Now it made my insides turn. 'I'm sure you have all kinds of influence with the scientists.'

'I wish I did,' Frank said. 'Regardless, they are far short of trying their experiment on me with other people.'

The woman stepped back, hands on her hips. 'Are you saying no to me?'

'My dear, I am saying that I have neither the influence nor the ability—'

'I just cannot believe this.' She looked around as if for witnesses. 'But you said.'

'Pardon me?'

'You said you would help us. All of us who have watched you, brought you into our living rooms, given you our attention.'

'Wherever did you get such an idea?'

'We must let our deeds be our ambassadors. What about all that?'

'Hey Judge, Judge Rice.' A skinny guy had come up on his other side. He was dressed entirely in Red Sox clothing, from his hat to his socks. 'How about it, fella? Would you sign my program for me here?'

The judge took the guy's pen and scribbled, still talking to the woman on his arm. 'Indeed I meant what I said, ma'am. But it did not concern your husband's circumstances. It was intended for the people who maintain that I am not real.'

'Me too?' said a girl who'd been pushed forward by a trio of her teen friends. 'Can I get an autograph too?'

Judge Rice, still holding the guy's pen, looked her up and down. 'My dear, you don't have anything for me to sign.'

'Sure I do,' she said, lifting up her shirt to reveal a belly so cute and young I'm not even allowed to think about it. The friends giggled behind their hands.

Old Frank hesitated. 'I don't feel quite comfortable—'

'It's OK,' she said. 'Go for it.'

A passing guy wolf whistled, and the girl gave him a smile that would melt an ice cap. Which was when the biddy decided to give the judge a bop on the arm with her purse.

'I believe you're real,' she said. 'Real selfish.' She nodded at the crowd that was beginning to gather, bringing them in on it. 'How hard would it be to get the Lazarus people and the cryogenic people in the same room? Huh? How tough is that?'

Oh lady, I thought, you just gave me an idea of what was going on when I stopped by the lab today. A guess at who those men were, and what's in that green binder.

Just then three truly hammered guys staggered up, arms over each other's shoulders, still singing Neil Diamond. 'Hey whoa!' the one on the right shouted, though he was only a few feet away. 'Holy shit – it's Judge Rice.'

'Hey man, my buddy here is getting married next weekend,' said the guy on the left. 'Any chance you could do the wedding? Like, are you allowed to do that stuff anymore?'

By this time the expression on old Frank's face was verging on panic. It was hilarious, people pulling him in four directions at once. The crowd had grown, and the camera crew inched up the ramp too. But I still held back. It wouldn't hurt the guy to be humbled a notch, get a taste of the world without Dr Kate playing goalie all the time. Besides, this was too good a show.

Then the middle drunk guy, wearing a fast food crown, hauled his head upright like it weighed 200 pounds, and managed to get out two slurry words: 'bachelor party.'

The other two immediately leapt into some kind of crazy frat boy dance. 'Bachelor party, bachelor party.'

'I'm not finished speaking,' said tracksuit lady, trying to climb the judge's arm again.

'Hey mac, could I have my pen back?'

'Could you sign my friend's tummy too please?'

'Bachelor party, bachelor party.'

I started over, ready to rescue, but a security guard got there first. He was not the mellow Boston-Irish-been-around-forever type. He was muscle-bound and swaggering, wearing enough gear for a tank. 'Everything all right here?'

Oh the frat boys vanished like smoke. It was funny to see how fast they sobered, hoisting their buddy in the middle straight toward the men's room. The teeny-boppers were nearly as quick, bellies covered and flowing into the crowd. But Miss Pink Purse stayed, fastened to the judge like a barnacle, He turned in his usual stiff way.

'Hello officer. I was just explaining to this kind woman—'

'You are not a nice man,' she said. 'We have given you food, attention, clothes. How can you refuse to help?'

He turned back to her. 'I will attempt to speak with Dr Carthage—'

'No you won't. You're just saying that to shut me up.'

The goon puffed up. 'Lady, why don't you give this guy a little room, OK?'

She balled her hands into little fists. 'Maybe you are a phony after all. Just a big fake.'

'Yes that's what I am,' the judge said, his dander up at long last. 'A fake. You figured it out. Now will you leave me alone?'

'Let's go ma'am,' the guard said, stepping between them, almost bumping the lady with his chest. 'Move it along here or we'll have to send you home.'

Frank leaned toward the guard. 'That won't be necessary—'

'Come on,' I said, pulling the judge's arm. 'Let's get out of here.'

The guard spoke over his shoulder. 'You go ahead sir, we'll take care of this.'

‘Selfish phony,’ the woman yelled. ‘Complete faker.’

‘Besides,’ the goon added. ‘Wait’ll I tell my wife I helped the frozen man.’

I dragged old Frank, who craned his neck backward. The crowd fell away as soon as there was nothing more to see.

‘Hey wow,’ I jostled him. ‘Aren’t you the Elvis of reanimation?’

He shook my hands off and got right in my face. ‘We both know that you abandoned me completely.’ And off he marched, straight for section 37. Dixon ditched and deserted.

Well excuse the shit out of me, your fucking royal fucking highness.

I wouldn’t have guessed the judge for a sulker, but he popped Gerber’s shades back on and shut the door behind. No cheers for the home team, no smile for the camera. The TV crew was going to love that post-game interview.

‘What happened back there?’ Gerber asked.

‘Tell you later,’ I said.

‘The twentieth century met the twenty-first,’ the judge said, crawling back into his mope.

No skin off me. The Yanks went into the ninth up 3-2, with two down. I was one out away from celebrating. But the Sox rallied. One guy hit to shallow right and got on base, then the next batter bunted and hustled, and bingo, there were two men on. The place was raging, and our Frank couldn't help but stand and join the noise. Gerber stood beside him and whistled.

Now in the old days, when all was right in baseball, you could count on the Red Sox to choke like a snake eating a car. Instead this ham-handed galoot from the Dominican stepped to the plate, swung at the first pitch, and hit that ball so hard I imagine it is still up there somewhere, not quite ready to come down.

So, pandemonium. Sox win, 5-3. The galoot ran the bases, his pals slapping him high and low as he crossed the plate, while the fans hollered themselves hoarse.

'Nuff said,' the judge shouted, shaking his cap in the air. 'Nuff said.'

Folks nearby stared at us. Gerber gave me a look that said what the hell? I shrugged. He laughed, shaking his wooly head, and yelled 'nuff said' too.

Well, fine. The seats were free, I'd put away a half dozen dogs, and Gerber bought the beers, so who cares who won? Aside from the crazy lady episode, the judge had shown himself to be a generally good time, too.

The loudspeaker started up this tune 'Tessie,' which I hadn't heard before, and which brought the weirdest moment of the whole day. It was some kind of victory song. I just sat back while everyone else bellowed the lyrics. Then I happened to notice that the judge was moving his lips with the words. Not singing, but mouthing right along.

Now you tell me: when in hell would he have heard those lyrics, much less learned them by heart? And I realized I was asking myself the same question for the ninety-seventh time: who in hell is this guy?

CHAPTER 29

JUST LIKE AVIATION

My name is Jeremiah Rice and I begin to accelerate.

I first noticed in the mornings, because I woke earlier. Next I realized what was occurring with books; I was reading faster, finishing sooner, yet enjoying them no less. *Madame Bovary* fell in a single afternoon. It felt as vivid as inhaling with a perfumed kerchief over my face.

Subsequently I grew aware that my mind, which had shaken off the seaweed of lethargy, regained its prior keenness, then seemed to attain more. I understood quickly, I replied promptly, I adapted readily. Still I dismissed these changes as the false allure of pride, the mind always overeager to praise itself.

However, the final and persuasive indicator was my appetite, hunger that no volume of Dr Borden's fortified gruel could assuage. I snacked, I nibbled anything in reach, I dined outside of his dictates. It was neither a matter of disobedience nor discretion. At the baseball game I devoured some of the foulest foods of my life's experience, yet sought more. The next morning, expecting indigestion, I instead discovered myself standing at the chamber window, curtains parted to spy on that reporter chomping through doughnuts as a work horse does oats, whilst I leered like a dog begging at table.

I heard the door slide back. 'Good morning, Kate. I've missed you.'

'Sorry, it's just Andrew.' The technician, a black man, hesitated in the doorway.

'Ah Andrew. May I ask you a question? I've been meaning to for some time.'

'Of course.'

'What is your training?'

'Well, I was a Princeton undergrad. Now I'm at Harvard in cell biology, ABD.'

'ABD?'

'All but dissertation, sir. I'm writing my doctoral paper on you.'

'How odd that is to hear. Please let me know if I can be of any help.'

'You already are, sir. I'm studying your mitochondria, based on blood we've been drawing from you.'

'I am relieved to know all those needle stickings have a purpose. But may I ask one more question, a somewhat delicate thing?'

'Anything at all, sir.'

'Your credentials, your standing here. Is this unusual for a Negroid man today?'

'A little.' He gave a radiant smile. 'But that's due to the competitiveness of the schools I've attended, not my race. Plenty of black people go to college now, and a growing number have advanced degrees.'

'I am glad of it.'

'If I may, though, Judge Rice?'

'Yes, what is it?'

'We're not called Negroid any more. Just black. Or best, African-American.'

'Yes, I forgot that Dr Gerber had mentioned as much. My apologies. And thank you for speaking with me today.'

'It's an honor, sir.'

Andrew started for the door, then caught himself. 'I nearly forgot. The reason I came in is that your first appointment of the day is here. In the private conference room.'

'Thank you. Do you know where Dr Philo is this morning?'

He set a chair in the doorway, enabling me to exit later. 'Sorry sir, but I don't.'

Alone again, I removed Dr Gerber's electrodes, setting the tangle of wires on a side table. In the control room, Dixon was passing as I entered.

'Pardon me, do you know where Dr Philo is today?'

'You know, it's been a while since she improved the scenery around here,' he said. 'I think she had some deadline to meet for Carthage. 'Scuse me.'

He hurried on, evidently for the washroom, leaving his box of doughnuts unattended.

* * *

'Oh,' the interviewer said, 'I didn't realize you hadn't finished breakfast.'

'One moment please,' I replied, completing my purloined snack. 'The person who manages my schedule has an obligation today, so I was unaware you would be coming. My apologies.'

'No need to butter me up, Judge,' the reporter said, pulling papers from a briefcase. 'It won't influence what I write.'

I marked the man for the first time. He was tall, well dressed, large hands but elegant. He gave his name, Steele, and named the publication for which he worked. Another newspaper, but his manner of declaration was off-putting. 'Nor have I any reason to flatter or utter falsehoods,' I said.

He nodded, not speaking, organizing his papers instead. He switched on a small box, placing it between us on the table.

'What is that device?'

'You honestly don't know?'

Long ago I developed a dislike for people who answer a question with a question. I decided to use Steele's rhetoric back at him. 'Why else would I ask?'

He pursed his lips as though patronizing me. 'It records our conversation so I have an accurate transcript later. It protects you from being misquoted, and it protects me if you claim I misquoted you.'

'Apparently accuracy is a concern for you.'

If Steele was discomfited by my remark, he gave no sign. Nor did he embark on a line of questioning based on prior news coverage or simple assumptions, as other reporters had. The rather, he began by producing a copy of my senior thesis at Tufts. I scanned it with a kind of vertigo, feeling the chasm of time that had passed since its composition. The document compared Iago's powers of persuasion in *Othello* to those of Satan in *Paradise Lost*. Once upon a time I concerned myself earnestly with such things.

'Any important memories about that project today?' Steele asked. 'Anything significant come to mind?'

'Only that humanity's capacity for deception, and self-deception, remains undiminished.'

'Anything about the project itself? What you read? The scholars you quoted?'

I smiled, flipping through the pages. 'I was twenty years of age. Though I will say that your questions do spark a desire to reread Milton.'

The reporter next showed me an article I had published in law school, in the Review. It concerned interstate commerce and a dispute between rail companies in adjoining states.

'Anything of note about that case you'd care to share?'

'Strange, how little I remember from that time. A law review paper would be a major endeavor. Yet I would not have said I had published anything.'

Next the man produced a *Globe* clipping from the day I was sworn in as a judge. How he had moved that article onto a fresh sheet of paper baffled me.

'Is there anything about your swearing-in that was remarkable? Anything you particularly remember?'

I fell silent. Seeing that article reminded me of Joan, my confidante, my ballast. On the wintry morning it was published, she used her good sewing scissors to cut the clipping from the newspaper, then pressed it into her scrapbook using one dab of brown glue whose piquant scent reached me across the room. Other women seemingly had more time for such things. The items that merited inclusion in Joan's book therefore ranked with her of the highest order: an invitation to our wedding, the announcement of Agnes's birth, her parents' obituaries. Not the deed to our home, nor articles about cases I'd heard however controversial or celebrated. Not one clipping, I now realized, from the dozens of news stories prior to our expedition. How had I dared to leave her? How had I trifled with what was most precious?

'Judge Rice? Any comment?'

'Forgive my reverie,' I said. 'I was remembering not the event, but my wife's response the following day.'

'How do you explain having no recall of significant events and writings?'

I failed to hear, for the moment remaining adrift. What good was life, without those most dear? The desire I felt to hear Joan's voice, sharp and intelligent, was like wanting enough air to breathe. My craving for Agnes's fierce hugs, those slender little arms, eclipsed entirely any interest in the here and now.

I collected my wits. A judge must always pay close attention to what people before him are saying, yet I confess I needed to ask the reporter to repeat himself.

'We'll come back to it.' He eyed his notes. 'What were your favorite cases, among those tried in your court?'

'You are expecting a level of recollection quite beyond me, sir. The press of cases was so great, I might strain to recall a trial two weeks after its conclusion. Yet you inquire about events that occurred more than one hundred years ago. Moreover, a trial's result would be of paramount interest to the parties, but my concern consisted primarily in providing a fair process.'

'You don't remember any particular crimes or suits before your court?'

'None in sufficient detail to discuss them without risking egregious error.'

'How convenient.'

I wondered at that reply. What could he be implying? The reporter nodded at his notepad, a habit he apparently followed to avoid making eye contact. 'Let's shift a bit. Do you remember anything about your reputation as a judge?'

'I would be the least fit person imaginable to comment. I did my best.'

'You do recall being controversial?'

'Every case has a winner and a loser, at least one of whom may be inclined to find fault with the jurisprudence.'

'But you experienced something more than that, didn't you, Judge Rice?'

'Did I?'

Finally Steele raised his face. Indeed he glared at me. 'Weren't you famously lenient? Or should I say, infamously? Didn't you release a drunkard on his own recognizance, only for him to torch a shoe factory, killing four people?'

'How can you suggest such things?' I cried. 'Are you manufacturing this information?'

'It's all in the public record. Wasn't your expedition actually a form of escape, to avoid a movement to have you recalled from office?'

Hm. Now I realized. There would be no baseball offers at the end of this conversation. This man's interrogation had a forward lean, an intent to do me harm. Why had Kate not apprised me in advance? Indeed, where was she?

'Let me explain as I am able,' I said. 'May I stand?'

'Suit yourself.'

Yes, my energy was surging. Despite all those years studiously motionless on the bench, now I paced like an animal caged. 'Foremost, no. I was not lenient, I was judicious. My responsibilities were to uphold the law, safeguard justice, and respect precedent. If I erred in a ruling with a dire result, any ruling, you may be sure that my conscience paid close heed, if only for the sake of future cases. I am certain history will prove that I did err on occasion, in fact, because I am a human being and courts are human systems and we all err. If there were any movement to recall me, I remain blissfully unaware. I remember a number of significant fires in Lynn, some with tragic consequences, but none linked to a case of mine.

'Your preparation for this meeting, moreover, cannot have failed to find the many ways I contributed far beyond my proscribed role to the city's well-being, which modesty prevents me from enumerating. Thus your questions indicate a predisposition on your part, against me. We are a free people and thus you may publish what you please, but with your ink comes a grave responsibility.'

I stopped before him, but my blood was high such that I could not hold still. 'Lastly, sir, you are woefully mistaken if you perceive my motives for joining the expedition as anything other than scientific inquiry. I was excited, yes, of course. It was a thrilling time on this earth, discoveries all around us. Learning seemed to be sitting there, simply waiting for someone to come along who was curious enough. In many ways I was reluctant to go, loath to leave my family, and that was so even when I felt certain of returning. The fact that I never did—'

My voice betrayed me, catching in my throat, and I felt myself unmanned by the tears that spilled from my eyes. I turned away.

My interviewer gave a respectful minute before his next question: 'Do you know how much money they have spent to find you and bring you back to life?'

'I have made that very inquiry. No one will tell me.'

'Carthage says this project has spent over twenty-five million dollars.'

'I have learned that money is different now than in my time. Regardless, I find this to be an inconceivable sum. Breathtaking.'

'Yes. It would feed every hungry child in Massachusetts for a year. It would provide shelter to every homeless person in Boston.'

I assessed him. 'If I understand your implication, my reply is that I did not choose to die, nor seek to be reawakened. Your quarrel is not with me.'

That answer seemed to satisfy him. He chewed on the end of his pen, as if deciding which path next to take. 'Not a quarrel, more of an observation.'

I made no reply.

Steele sighed, then turned to a fresh page. 'Judge Rice, what do you know about the circumstances of your reanimation?'

'I don't understand your meaning.'

'Do you know how they did it?'

I turned to him. He seemed utterly at ease, hands folded on the table, pen beside his notebook. He presented a bland affect, as if he were bored.

'Do you know,' I said to him, 'I have no notion at all.'

'You aren't curious? You haven't even asked?'

They were brilliant questions. How could I have overlooked such a basic investigation on my own behalf? 'No. Though you certainly inspire me.'

Steele paused, then looked at his watch. If he intended to convey disrespect, he succeeded brilliantly. I felt it in the roots of my hairs.

'Judge Rice,' he continued, 'forgive me, but you have said repeatedly that you are a person motivated by a desire for learning. Yet you have made no effort to understand your own experience. Do you expect me to believe you?'

I scoffed. 'What you believe, sir, is a matter of indifference to me.'

'Well, that gets to my real question, then. Which is, why didn't you choose someone better?'

'I don't follow you.'

'If you're going to stage a phony reanimation, why choose a flawed judge for your character? Why not a better one? Or some other profession altogether, one that doesn't leave a career-long paper trail?' He gestured at his stack of documents. 'All these rulings and decisions you could be quizzed on. Why not build your hoax on something simpler?'

Now I understood who the TV interviewer had meant when she described skeptics. But in his unvarnished animosity, Steele had brought to mind an old witticism of the court: *If a man calls you 'friend,' he isn't. If he declares 'trust me,' don't. If he says 'I'm telling the truth,' hide your wallet.*

Thus I knew better than to attempt to convince this reporter; each word defending my legitimacy would only confirm his disbelief. My college papers were a feint. He could have written his article before entering the conference room.

But he miscalculated. By challenging my credibility directly, this man awakened my dignity, which was not the result of being a judge but rather the reason the governor had appointed me one, not the outcome of years on the bench but the credential that qualified me to sit there.

'Good sir,' I said, sitting at the head of the table. 'This conversation is at an end.' It felt good to behave like a judge again, a man in possession of his own powers. I gestured two fingers toward the door. 'I bid you good day.'

If there is any person on earth more confounded by time than Jeremiah Rice, I would like to shake his hand and offer my sympathies. After all, how old am I? How many years of my existence do not count? Time, always elusive, has become unknowable. Moreover, my chamber had no timepiece. The only means of knowing the hour was to rise, stand at the far end of my window, and read the clock on the control room wall. That day, chagrined by the audacious reporter, I nonetheless resisted the impulse to demand immediate explanations of anyone. With Kate absent, only one other person at the Project enjoyed my trust. An opportunity to speak alone with him would require patience. Oh, the hunger of curiosity is a powerful force. It had led me to sea, I remained mindful, with the ultimate consequence. I would do better to master it now.

Dawn was approaching by the time the last technician began gathering his things. I hastened to the door. The technician sat again, remembering some incomplete duty. At last he darkened his computer and departed. I pressed 2667, the air hissed and the door slid wide. For the first time, I marched through on my own volition. My quarry's face bore the sickly color of computer glow.

'Dr Gerber?'

'Whoa.' He jumped in his seat. 'Whoa, whoa.' He pulled the headphones down and panted, one hand on his chest. 'You almost gave me a heart attack.'

'I apologize,' I said, 'I didn't intend to startle you.'

'It's OK, man, it's OK.' He laughed. 'Just give me one second to bolt my brain back on.' Music came thinly from the headphones in his lap.

'Do you mind terribly if I interrupt your work for a few minutes?'

'You don't sleep much anymore, do you?'

'My mind has other functions to perform, it seems. Things it seeks to understand.' I hesitated. 'Important things.'

Dr Gerber made a face, inscrutable at first, then

wistful. He touched a key and the music stopped. 'We are about to have a strange conversation, aren't we?'

'Quite frankly, I'm trusting you to tell me the truth about some things. I felt I could rely upon you to do so in a manner no else can.'

'Not even Kate?'

'Possibly.'

He sighed. 'I knew this day was going to come. Better me than some of the others, right? And hey, you happened to catch me on a night when I'm not . . . well, let's just say I am feeling unusually clear-headed.' He set the headphones aside and placed a hand on each of his knees. 'Fire away.'

I'd had all day to ready my question. 'How did you people wake me up?'

'Instead of telling you, why don't I show you?'

'You can do that?'

He tapped various keys and a video began playing on his screen. There was the control room. People were working at every desk, I recognized many of them. Carthage was listening while everyone offered opinions about something. The words were not clear but the mood was dour.

Then the Dr Gerber on the screen spoke: *Well, there is such a thing as desecration of the dead.* Kate nodded agreement. *We're guilty of that already.*

Superstition, Carthage scoffed, and he delivered a long speech. *Aren't you curious?* he concluded.

In the end, that is the only question that matters: don't you want to know?

Then Dr Borden did something with his equipment, people reacted with gasps, and the lights went out. There was a general noise of complaint. Next the computer displayed an image of me, my body in contortions, arching and flailing. Smoke, actual smoke, rose from my skin. I could watch for only a moment and then, despite the depth of my interest, I was compelled to close my eyes.

'OK, so how are we doing in there so far?'

I blinked back to the present. Dr Gerber had pulled his chair close, his brow creased with worry.

'I know it's not pretty,' he said, 'but it worked. Here, hang on a sec.' He spun away, returning with a glass of water. I took a goodly gulp.

'How are you doing there, Judge?' he said.

'There was smoke.'

'Sublimation is my guess. Ice from your body going directly into vapor.'

'Was I the first one?'

He nodded. 'They've been looking all over the world. You're the only person they've found. But I mean, a human would have to be flash-frozen, then preserved for all this time, and then found somehow among all the ice on the planet. Imagine the odds.'

'Were there other species?'

'Tons. Mostly little things, tiny.'

'Might you show me some of them?'

'Sure.' He went to his keyboard and began tapping. 'This all started three years ago, before I came on board, so you'd need someone else to fill in the details. Carthage didn't snare me till they went looking for you. Ah, here we go.'

The image was blurred, but it showed a creature of some kind, tiny and with a tail, lying perfectly still. A counter in the lower corner of the screen was moving with breathtaking speed. 'What are those numbers?' I asked.

'Time. It's measuring in, um, thousandths of a second.' The creature began moving, slowly, just its tail.

'A clock like mine?'

'Only much shorter.' The little animal increased its vigor, then abruptly stopped. 'That was the first one,' Dr Gerber said. 'It lasted 9 seconds.'

'Would you be so kind as to show me others?'

'Well, Judge Rice, let me be straight with you.' He rested his forearm atop the screen. 'It wasn't a nice thing for you to see how we woke you up. There may be other things that also aren't so nice. You might ask yourself how much you really want to know. What's important, and what's only curiosity.'

'I appreciate your concern. But this information is important. Extremely.'

'You're the boss.' He cackled and tapped more keys.

The next image was a krill. Its reanimation followed

the same motion as the first, slow then fast, for 22 seconds. 'Continue please,' I said. 'Perhaps a history, as you provided me with for aviation?'

He did exactly that, one specimen after another for more than an hour. Dr Gerber explained each refinement – raising the immersion solution's salt content, strengthening the magnetic field – and the resulting addition to the awakened creature's lifespan. He showed me a species I recognized, a sardine. The little fish lasted a full minute, again with frenzy in the final seconds. Next came a shrimp, which thrashed wildly but lived for 2 minutes and 20 seconds. After that video, Dr Gerber did not play another. He only stared at his screen.

'Yes?' I said to him.

'Do you get it yet? Do you see?'

In that instant I entirely understood. The increased appetite, the reduced sleep, the inability to sit still. I was the sardine, I was the krill. 'Has anyone determined yet how to stop the frenzy?'

He shook his head without looking at me.

'Aside from myself, is any other reanimated creature alive today?'

Dr Gerber did not move.

There it was. An ocean of information beyond what I'd expected. Hm. I ambled away through the maze of desks, carrying dread like a weight. This energy in my blood was a trick. It signaled not a return to vibrancy but the beginning of completion. My road was clear: acceleration, then death.

'In every case?' I asked him.

Dr Gerber nodded. 'So far. Look at these.' He brought a chart onto his computer: parallel lines, rising and falling, but over time climbing steadily.

'Those are me?'

'Yup.' He touched different lines with his finger. 'That's heart, respiration, blood pressure, sleep duration, calories consumed, everything.'

I turned away again. The lines confirmed what I felt within my skin.

It was different the first time, in the sea. There was a moment when I knew all was ended. There would be no returning to Lynn, no seeing Joan or Agnes again. That knowledge was infinitely more painful than the cold of the water, but I lived with it only for a few seconds. This time I would have the same knowledge, but a duration of loss. Time would mean pain. Starting now, I discovered as I scanned the room, four walls in the bowels of a building where the majority of my second life had passed. Was this all? Was this everything?

It felt unfair. I was still new, growing accustomed to having a body again, to having a life. I found myself staring in the window to my chamber. There were piles of books, a few clothes, my neatly made bed. I had never seen it from this vantage. It looked rather humble. In truth, how small a man is.

I read the clock: 6:08 a.m. 'How long have the other creatures lived?'

'Depends on their size. Bigger goes slower. It's about body mass.'

'Can you predict how long my body mass will continue?'

'That's the weird part. You should have burned out after 21 days.'

'I defy the pattern?'

'So far.'

I placed my hand on the cool glass. 'I wish I were tired. I would love to be tired.'

At first he did not reply. Then his voice was soft. 'Hey Judge, I'm really sorry.'

'Why would you be sorry, Doctor? As John Adams observed, "Facts are stubborn things".' I crossed to the nearest desk and touched a pencil someone had left there. It rolled until it reached the bookshelf and stopped. I began to think beyond myself. 'Many people are expecting a great deal of me. Vice President Walker, Carthage, even the unfortunate woman at the baseball game. Oh, but won't the protestors be happy, when I go the way of those shrimp?'

'Yes they will. Which is exactly why those people piss me off. I don't care what they stand for, anyone who finds pleasure in a stranger's suffering is a twisted biscuit.'

I scrutinized him from across the room. He was hunched forward, hair in a tangle around his face. 'Dr Gerber?'

He tucked his wild locks back. 'Judge Rice?'

'I'd best make ideal use of the time left to me.'

'That's something maybe everyone ought to think,' Dr Gerber said.

I looked around the control room, an empty chair at every desk, and felt a kind of nakedness. 'Have you told anyone?'

He snorted. 'I tried to get Carthage's attention, but he is not one who listens very well. Besides,' Dr Gerber chuckled, 'he's in the fame and money business now. Thomas makes it worse, goading him. Carthage has succumbed completely to the hunger. Which means, of course, that he is about to get eaten.'

'Are other people aware of this?'

He sat back. 'They might suspect. Billings would, if he ever looked up from his microsamples. But you've seen how Carthage keeps everyone else heeling like dogs. I'm pretty much the only one he lets loose to find things like this.'

'Kate does not know?'

'I can't imagine how she would. I only figured it out a couple of weeks ago. Besides, she's been busy enjoying life with you.'

I felt the weight of my infatuation with her, the affection that had grown between us, another brick upon the load. Kate was a lovely person, trustworthy, attractive to a degree that my private thoughts sometimes shamed me. Yet my conduct had already marooned one woman. Conscience would not allow another. 'She must not be informed.'

'You think?'

'There's aught to be gained by worrying people.'

'You're protective,' he said. 'It's admirable. But

what if we can find a way to stop the process? That's what I've been working on.'

'At the risk of absurd understatement, I am inexpressibly grateful for your efforts. Even now,' I strode back and placed a hand on his shoulder. 'I thank you for telling the truth. It equips me for what may lie ahead.'

'That's what freaks like me live for, friend. Even if the truths are ugly.'

'Friend. Yes. This one will take some time to digest.' I started toward my chamber, and one more question occurred to me, a tangent, but a thing that had annoyed me. 'Doctor, why does that news reporter call me "Frank"?'

He snorted. 'Forget that leech.'

'It is willful disrespect. He knows my name perfectly well.'

'Remember what I said before about what's worth knowing. Does Dixon deserve one minute of your remaining time? Or is he completely unimportant?'

Before I replied the hallway door banged open and Kate barged in. She looked a mess, face worn and hair a-tangle. Yet her fatigue was fetching, too, softening her features. I felt at once the looming limits of our time together, it brought a swell of fondness. She dropped in a chair like a rag doll, lowering her head onto crossed arms. 'One of these days I am going to wring Carthage's neck.'

'What has Dr Charming done today?' Dr Gerber asked. 'And so early, too.'

She lifted her head. 'Just made me pull an all-nighter to get him a report he won't even read till next week. I feel like some college student who blew off the whole semester and now is trying to save her ass in the final exam.'

'Well,' he said, 'did you save it?'

She dropped to her arms again. 'I'm too exhausted to care.'

Dr Gerber turned to me, his eyebrows raised. 'Still need to know?'

'Completely unimportant,' I said. He nodded, clamped the headphones back onto his wild hair, and returned to his computer. And I went to her.

CHAPTER 30

GOING HOME

(KATE PHILO)

He touched me. It was as simple as that. He placed a consoling hand on my shoulder. We had touched many times before, of course, from helping him out of the wheelchair to strolling arm in arm, but at none of those times was I coming off three days of missing him. *Life without Jeremiah Rice tasted vanilla.*

Imagine walking down a street past something so ordinary you barely register it, a fire hydrant. He asks you what it is, as you explain he listens so intently you find yourself speaking with greater care, less certainty, more humility about what you don't know: hoses, pressure, ladders, fires, children in the spray on the summer's hottest days. He is grateful, says so. Four days later on a tour of a firehouse Jeremiah spies the old man in a chair to one side to whom no one is speaking, engages the man in a spirited discussion of these strange devices called hydrants. Now imagine every moment like that, every day. With this man's curiosity at my side, the world possessed a newness, a richness. Jeremiah Rice gave me back the world.

What I felt at our reunion that morning, I resisted thinking about, much less naming. But I knew it was not scientific. 'I need to get out of here,' I said.

'Wait one moment,' he answered. 'Please.'

I watched, exhausted, as he went to the security door, punched in the numeric code, vanished inside. Well, well, well; someone was figuring things out.

'What's been going on around here?' I called toward Gerber.

He pulled his headphones back, I could hear guitar noodling all the way across the room. 'Say what, oh princess fair?'

'Never mind,' I said. Usually I got a kick out of his kookiness, but right then I did not have the patience.

Jeremiah came trotting out of his chamber, pulling on a Red Sox cap. He also wore that signature yellow tie.

'Look at you,' I said. 'When did the judge get so cute?'

'I'm ready,' he said, tugging his jacket sleeves down tight. 'Let's go.'

'I'm sorry Jeremiah, but I'm too tired for one of our epic jaunts today.'

'I was thinking of a place where you might rest a while.' His face brightened. 'If you're willing to drive a little.'

'Where would that be?'
'High Rock. In Lynn.'
How much did this man know? 'Do you have any idea what my all-nighter for Carthage was about?'
'None, nor do I care. He is not worth my consideration.'
This too was something new. Jeremiah without the deference. I sat up. 'Would you like to see that place again?'
'With you, I would.' Even his voice was different.
I glanced over, Gerber was reading his computer screen, nose inches from the glass. If he was eavesdropping, he hid it perfectly. I stood. 'We're out of here.'

We used the loading dock, to avoid the gauntlet. Already protestors were gathering in the little park, joining the few dozen who had kept the all-night vigil. As we pulled away I glimpsed what I thought was the woman in a white beret, Hilary, leaning in a doorway. But then she was gone. 'Did you see that?'
'I'm sorry, Kate.' Jeremiah turned backward in his seat. 'Did I see what?'
'Nothing, never mind.'
We wound through the quiet streets. Jeremiah's leg jiggled up and down. 'What's on your mind?' I asked.
His leg stopped at once. 'Many things. Many.'
'OK Sherlock, spill. How did you learn those numbers?'

'I promised not to reveal the person who taught me,' he replied. 'Apparently there are people who would prefer to see Subject One liberated.'

I turned left to put us on 93 North. 'They can stand in line behind me.'

Once we were moving my weariness seemed to dissolve. It was a stunning summer morning, the city leafy and subdued. I bought a schooner of coffee, which may have helped too. We were both occupied with our thoughts. Mine were about the feeling that something was stretched as far as it could go, on the very verge of breaking. *If Jeremiah were free, I could resign from the Project.*

The road north of Boston was not pretty when I'd come researching for Carthage, while the judge had been at a baseball game. It looked the same when I drove it again with Jeremiah. Fast food, gas stations, fenced lots, oil depots' giant holding tanks, the classic American exurban underbelly. Riding with Jeremiah always sharpened my awareness of such things. As we turned off Route 1 into Lynn proper, I made my offer.

'Let's say we have the whole day here. Would you like to see your home first?'

'No,' Jeremiah said instantly. 'Not yet.'

'Really? I'm surprised.'

'Do you remember how Dr Borden restarted my stomach? By giving me small bits of food, in tiny meals, until my powers of digestion restarted?'

'Of course I remember.'

'That is what I prefer to do with my family as well. To you they never existed, expect perhaps as abstractions from history. To me they are newly dead, newly gone. I cannot simply stroll up my former front walk. I cannot be blithe.'

I pondered that one for a minute. What did I know about this man? How could I imagine life inside his head, life within his heart? If I could manage it, I did not want to add to his hurts.

'Tell me then,' I said, 'what small bite of Lynn would you like to take first?'

'High Rock,' Jeremiah replied. 'From the height of land we can survey the city's general condition. Also the prospect surely will raise our spirits.'

'I need to warn you. I was just here, and some of that view may not be pleasant.'

'Lynn has never sought to duplicate the hereafter on earth. Besides, this seems to be a day for that sort of experience.'

'What do you mean?'

He didn't answer. I didn't push.

The Lynn Historical Society had given me a map on the first visit, so I fished it out of the back seat, handing it to Jeremiah. His head was a periscope, peering down lanes as we passed them. 'This city experienced explosive growth in my time,' he said. 'When we were building the public library, we learned that the number of named streets had gone from ninety just before I was born to more than seven hundred by the turn of the century. So many buildings went up, it was common entertainment for people to collect the scrap wood and hold a bonfire. Word would go around beforehand, and people would come from across the city to enjoy the festivities. We would all line up for photographs. Then the heat of the blaze would force us all out into a large circle.'

'It sounds nice. Kind of innocent.'

'Lynn was never innocent.' He traced one finger across the map. 'This was always a city of boozers and brawlers, not quiet like Marblehead or Beverly. That is why Lynners made fine soldiers. They had fighting experience, if only the bare-knuckle kind.'

As if to prove the point, we passed a long brick wall topped with razor wire, trash at its foot. The wall was covered with graffiti: obscenities, a fifteen-foot penis, all sorts of symbols expressing something beyond translation.

Still Jeremiah smiled, alternating between poring over the map and scanning the roads. I let him ramble on, content to be away from the Project. The bounce in his voice was exactly why I'd thought this outing was a good idea. 'Everything is much less cluttered,' Jeremiah announced.

'Really? I thought you would find things built up.'

'In my time, between the wires for trolleys and for electricity, there were whole webs over the streets. Someone finally made sense of all that.'

'I didn't know there was electricity out here in the 1900s.'

'More than in Boston. With General Electric

here, and Edison's genius creating so many opportunities, Lynn was a bright little city for its day.'

We drove past a car wash. Black men in hoodies stood sullenly with drying rags. As one lifted his eyes to watch us pass, I felt a flush of intimidation. Then another man said something, the first one snapped his towel in response, all the men laughed, bright faces, bright teeth.

'What do you make of those guys?'

Jeremiah remained sideways in his seat, staring back at them. 'I find it fascinating that there is a business cleaning automobiles. Such an enterprise had not occurred to me, though it seems obvious. Is it extremely lucrative?'

'The opposite. Those men probably get the lowest wage allowed by law.'

'Yet they seemed good humored in their work. I haven't seen such levity at the Lazarus Project. Wait please, slow down please.'

I eased to the roadside. 'What is it?'

'Here, right here. This was where the Lennox Building stood. I know this place. Over there, a knife sharpener used to set his stone wheel. You came on Tuesdays, and while the sparks flew, for a nickel he would put a fine edge on every knife and scissors in the house. And over there, right there by that large cardboard box, that was where the hurdy-gurdy player parked his wagon. Oh, the children loved that. Why, one time I brought Agnes here—'

I waited, but he had stopped. 'Agnes?'

He held up a hand. I could see the muscles in his jaw working. I felt like a shallow fool. How had I allowed all this time to go by, yet never raised the topic? Remembering his first news conference, how he choked up about his family, I felt as insensitive as a brick. Jeremiah's hand was still up. I twined our fingers, bringing it into my lap.

'It's all right,' I said. 'You don't have to say a thing.'

'Can we commence moving again please?'

I lay the map in my lap while keeping his hand, followed the circuitous streets till we reached the lane up to High Rock. From historical photos I'd seen, I expected a larger place. Instead there was just a narrow road up a hill, duplexes with their faces crossed by fire escapes, *Beware of Dog* signs, a dead end.

We parked behind a rusted minivan, an 'East Lynn Bulldogs' sticker in its rear window. I climbed out slowly, not wanting to crowd him.

'Here we are,' Jeremiah said, striding ahead up a set of concrete steps. His mood seemed to have improved, or so I hoped. Agnes I would ask about later.

I clambered after him. At the top, a few acres of lawn surrounded a stone tower maybe 90 feet tall. Beer cans cluttered its base. The tower was boarded up, graffiti on the plywood. But scotch pines grew out of the rocks nearby. I always marvel at that, how trees can live in places where there seems to be nothing to sustain them. I circled the tower and found Jeremiah by the eastern fence. The view was sweeping. Lynn sprawled below, streets and houses, ocean glimmering in the distance, a jet booming overhead toward Logan.

'So many church spires,' I said. 'This must be a devout city.'

'Or sinful, and needing salvation. What are all of those spindles?' he asked, pointing. Antennae rose all through the view. Somehow I had looked beyond them.

'Cell phone towers, I guess.'

Jeremiah nodded, looked down, saw the litter of cigarette butts at his feet.

'Ugh,' I said. 'I hate that.'

He took off his Red Sox cap, punched the crown, tugged it back on. 'Well Kate, we see how time has shaped this place. Might we go elsewhere please?'

He strode back down the steps. Again I found myself following him, wondering if this trip might turn out to be not such a great idea.

'Your courthouse burned down years ago,' I told him as we drove down the hill, 'but they built a new one on the same spot. Would you like to see it?'

He nodded. 'Very, very much.'

Even with the map, it was difficult to reach. We ran into a maze of one-way streets that somehow kept us circling the area without getting closer.

'I hate to think that this might be a metaphor,'

Jeremiah said, 'and receiving justice is as circuitous as reaching the courthouse proper.'

When I turned onto a cross-town road for the third time, I pulled over. Two men stood on the sidewalk, one of them resting his sneaker on a fire hydrant. I lowered Jeremiah's window. 'Why don't you ask these guys for directions?'

He leaned forward in his seat. 'Excuse me? Excuse me gentlemen?'

As soon as the men stopped talking, I realized I'd made a mistake. One had tattoos across his forehead and throat, the other piercings in his eyebrow, nose and lip. Both wore the narrowed eyes of the perpetually angry.

'I beg pardon for interrupting your conversation, but I'm wondering if I could trouble you for some directions please.'

The one on the left, Mr Tattoo, raised his chin. 'What?'

'These roads are Byzantine. Might you direct us to the courthouse?'

Mr Tattoo took one step closer, dropped a hand from his hip. 'What?'

'Never mind,' I said to Jeremiah, but he craned further out the window.

'The courthouse. The Essex County Judicial District of Lynn Courthouse. Would you be so kind as to tell us how we might drive there from here?'

Mr Tattoo exchanged looks with his friend, who spat on the sidewalk. Then he turned back to us. 'Fuck you, asshole.'

I gunned the car, we were away. Jeremiah fell back in his seat, an astonished look on his face. Then I couldn't help it, I just burst out laughing. He tilted his head at me, starting to laugh himself.

'Fuck you, asshole,' he mimicked, which made me laugh harder. The weight was lifted, we were back to being us again, ourselves. I left Jeremiah's window wide, opened mine, let the summer day pour in.

I also gave up on the courthouse, turning in the opposite direction. In a few minutes we passed a building that made Jeremiah cry out.

'There it is, the public library. Eight years' work for me and many others.'

We parked by a central lawn. The library was stately, tall with pillars. Lower windows were decorated with flowers on construction paper, the work of preschoolers. We climbed two steps, looking back. Lush maples shaded the lawn.

'This area is quite close to how I remember it. But why is no one using the benches? Why is no one walking here?'

'I don't know. Want to go inside?'

'This is enough.' He crossed his arms on his chest. 'This is plenty.'

We stood there, absorbing the summer day, a dignified place he had helped to make, a patch of green. I resisted an impulse, then surrendered to it: I took his arm.

Jeremiah placed his hand over mine. 'Thank you for bringing me here.'

'I wish we'd come sooner.'

'I wish everything had come sooner.'

'What does that mean?'

He patted my hand. 'Let's go to the beach.'

Along the way he was full of exposition. 'All along here,' he waved his hand as we drove one avenue, 'once was crowded with ten-footers, row upon row.'

'Ten-footers?'

'Square shoe-making sheds, ten feet on a side. But factories spelled their doom. The Vamp building was the largest one in the world. It was under construction while we prepared for the exploration.'

'Vamp?'

'That's the curved upper of a shoe. The building was shaped like one. Wait, here it is. I didn't recognize it.'

I had stopped at a light. We were beside one of the city's restored buildings, trim and well painted. It had a Chinese restaurant and dry cleaners downstairs, signs for a yoga studio above. Neighboring store fronts were empty, but the place had a feel of recovery rather than decay. 'You know this place?'

'My friend Ebenezer Cronin had an enterprise here.'

'Cronin Fine Boots.'

'You've heard of it?'

'You were wearing a pair when we found you.'

'Was I indeed? Those boots were magnificent. Calf high, and oiled to withstand the salt and wet.

He was an underwriter of our voyage, as well. What became of that pair, do you know?'

'Somewhere back at the project, probably. I could look.'

'Would you please?'

'No harm in trying.'

The beach was surprisingly pretty, but deserted. We walked past the concrete sea wall, to a lawn where giant anchors painted glossy black lay at odd angles. The Boston skyline rose to our right, closer than I would have imagined. Meanwhile tankers squatted on the horizon, tiny at that distance yet somehow conveying their immense size nonetheless. I'd bought sandwiches; we sat on a bench in the blaze of the sun. Humidity pressed down on us, but I felt so removed from my routines that I didn't mind. While we ate, Jeremiah reminisced.

'That island to our east is Egg Rock. In my time a lighthouse stood there. The beacon swept the sky on stormy nights, it was a lovely and lonesome thing. Gone now.'

I shaded my brow. 'Looks that way, hard to tell.'

'That arm of land is Nahant. Where Boston Brahmins brought their families in summer.'

I rolled up my pant legs, swigged from a bottle of iced tea, felt the fatigue of my all-nighter like a blanket. Under the steady sun, Jeremiah carried on about Lynn history, his voice falling into a murmur. I did my best to listen, but it worked like a bedtime story, lulling: the floating bridge on Glenmere Pond.

War with Cuba and how Lynn answered the call. A soap company with a product so strong not only did it scour your skin, it also worked well on floors. The fire of 1889 that claimed nearly four hundred buildings. Streets with Algonquin names.

Wabaquin, Paquanum, Tontoquon. Wabaquin, Paquanum, Tontoquon. I drifted off to sleep.

Waking is one of my favorite things. I know that makes me unusual, most people struggle each morning. For me, returning to consciousness is a pleasure, if there's time to do it well. My favorite is Saturdays. I wake whenever my body wants, but don't get out of bed for half an hour. I might read or make a phone call, but often I simply lie there to let my mind wander.

On that bench by the water, I kept my eyes closed so Jeremiah would not know I was awake. I'd slid down during my nap, head now on his lap. It was an intimacy I would never have dared while awake. The sun had dried my mouth but I held there, unmoving, enjoying. When he shifted, his thigh muscles flexed under my neck, strong like a horse, thoroughly male.

At last I opened my eyes, to see that Jeremiah was playing a game with his fingers. It was boyish, not something I would have expected of him. He held his hand in front of his face, quite close, while wiggling his fingers one at a time, incredibly fast. I'd never seen a person move fingers that quickly.

'How do you do that?' I asked.

He jumped, jamming his hand under his leg. 'Whatever do you mean?'

'That game. How do you make them move so fast?'

'Hm. It's an old parlor trick.'

'Fun. You'll have to teach me sometime.' Feeling sticky from the humidity, I sipped my iced tea. It was warm, but I took a good gulp. 'How long was I out?'

'I'm sorry, I don't have a time piece. It's late afternoon. Do you feel better?'

'You just sat here all that time?'

'Where would I rather be?'

I ignored what that question implied. 'This is your town. There must be a million things you want to see.'

'Kate, I imagine that very few people reach the end of their lives and regret having spent too many hours relaxing beside the ocean.'

We sat in silence for a minute or more. Little wavelets flopped themselves against the sand. 'Kate,' he said, 'if a physician told you that you had an illness, and would only live for a year, or six months perhaps, what would you do with that information?'

'Let me think,' I said. The question did not strike me as odd, because the man had lost his life once already. What would I do? I snuggled tighter against his leg.

'When I was getting my doctorate,' I began, 'I paid my way by teaching one hundred level classes to undergraduates.'

'One hundred level?'

'The basics. That's how most PhD candidates can afford all those years of school, they teach introductory courses – at the university's slave wages, by the way. Anyway all my peers hated it, grading papers, preparing labs. Not me. I loved it. None of the drive to publish, no impatience with the pace of experiments, zero concern with career.'

I sat up, lifting hair off my overheated neck. 'It's thrilling to work at the cutting edge of science, no question. This project with Carthage will launch my work in any number of high altitude directions. But if I had only six months to live, I think I would spend them teaching youngsters how beautiful and interesting the universe is.'

Jeremiah nodded slowly. 'A fine answer, Kate. But why don't you do this now?'

'It's complicated. I guess you could say I want to do something *significant*.'

'Hm,' he said. 'My intention, upon retiring from the bench, had been to become a law professor. I consider few things more significant than engaging young minds.'

'Maybe you could still do that,' I offered. He was silent. I wiped my face with my hands, stretched my legs lazily. 'I'm sorry I snoozed so long. What else would you like to see while we're here?'

He gazed out at Egg Rock. 'One more thing.'

'Your home, right?' I had driven by the place of course, doing my homework for Carthage. It was a lovely brick house, set on a rise, in a part of town that had experienced a wave of renovation. Antique gaslights hung on either side of the ornate front door.

Jeremiah heaved a deep sigh. 'No thank you.'

'Really? I've been wondering for a long time when you would want to go there.'

'My disposition at this moment is not to dwell on the past, but to contemplate the future mortality that abides within me.'

I turned on the bench to face him. 'I don't understand.'

'I feel the pull of my home, yes, but also the tremendous weight of what I have lost. What time I have left must not be spent entirely on grieving. Not if I am to be of use.'

'But your house, where your family—'

'I could not withstand it.' He stood abruptly. 'There are things about me, Kate, important forces in my present condition, that you do not know.'

I wanted to ask what he meant. But I did not dare. 'Sorry. I'm sorry I pushed.'

He smoothed his pants. 'That is not where I want to go. Not today.'

'Tell me then, Jeremiah.' I spoke softly. 'What do you want to see?'

'The cemetery.' He lifted his chin, as if there were something on his face in danger of spilling. He closed his eyes hard, opened them slowly like an owl. 'I want to visit my grave.'

* * *

The first time I came to Pine Grove Cemetery, researching for Carthage, I drove through, a graveyard map from City Hall riding in the passenger seat. With Jeremiah, he asked me to park at the entrance so we could march ourselves in.

'Let us approach this by degrees,' he said. 'Please.'

The entry featured a gothic stone building with a paint-peeling sign that said 'Office.' We peered in the windows. Papers on the floor, tipped over chairs, it looked as if the place had been abandoned in a hurry. All that remained of officialdom was a sign detailing the cemetery's rules.

'No climbing on graves?' Jeremiah said. 'What sort of person does that?'

'Don't ask me.'

We strode up the entry hill, a shady lane between gorgeous pines. I imagined them as two-foot saplings in his first lifetime. Jeremiah paused, picking a cluster of needles off the blacktop. I watched him spread the needles from their base, testing the tips' sharpness against his thumb.

'Everything OK?' I asked.

He looked at me as if returning from a distance. 'There are so many things that I have been too distracted to see, properly see. I believe I have my eyes back now. And do you know?' He held up the cluster of needles. 'Everything is miraculous.'

'You are an incredible human being, Jeremiah Rice.'

He waved the compliment away. 'A man with tangled thoughts. Please, lead on.'

I was in no hurry. I knew what lay ahead. I shuffled, I ambled, but I was unable to think of a single thing I could do to protect him. So we went the long way.

Following a curve of road, we came to a clearing with a cannon at the crest. The hillside had rows and rows of low gray stones, each with a metal holder on its side for flowers or flags. Jeremiah squatted before one of them.

'Private, 23rd infantry, second division. What is this place?'

'Didn't you have military graveyards in your past life?'

'Not remotely approaching this.' He cast his eye down the long arc of memorials. 'At the battlefields of the War Between the States, perhaps. But not in the boneyard of one little city. What incredible conflagration is this from?'

'World War II,' I said. 'Gerber told you about that one.'

'All these died in that one war? All these boys, just from Lynn?'

'There was a huge evil in the world, Jeremiah, one of the worst and strongest in human history. It was extremely difficult to defeat. I can't explain it any better than that.'

He took off his cap, inching ahead, stopping every few stones. Delaying made me anxious about what was next. Jeremiah read the soldiers' ranks aloud, one grave after another. 'I'm looking for familiar names.'

I set my jaw. 'You'll find plenty of those further on.'

That caused him to straighten. 'I'm being morbid. Let's continue.'

We hiked past an idling backhoe, two men behind it having a smoke, nodding wordlessly in greeting, into the older sections. Jeremiah began to exclaim. 'Kitchin, Newhall, Mudge, these are families I recognize. John and Hannah Alley, I knew them. Older folks.' He put his hands on his hips. 'Kate, where is our destination?'

Not fifty yards away, a small plot held a pillar bearing the name RICE. I pointed. 'There.'

'God in heaven,' Jeremiah whispered, creeping forward.

I hung by his elbow, as if to catch him. The memory came to me of that night on the roof, when he leaned on me so heavily. I had wished for him then, that this world not overwhelm or harm him, little realizing that the greatest places of pain are found within.

Jeremiah stood before the graves of his parents with a hunch to his chest as if someone had punched him. An oak tree had grown to maturity within the family square, he leaned on it for support.

'*Remember man that you are dust.*'

'What's that?'

'Scripture.' He moved forward, touched his mother's stone. 'Truth.'

'Are you all right?'

He faced me. 'I barely remember them, Kate. But I remember what it is like to miss them.'

'Did you see your parents, you know, in the time between? All those years you were frozen? Or experience them in any way?'

'If I did, I had to leave the memory behind when I revived.' He dug with a fingernail at the lichen on his father's marker. 'My recall goes directly from falling into the frigid water to opening my eyes with you sitting beside me. I remember your smile.'

We both stood there, staring at the gravestones. 'Well anyway,' I said, 'this over here is what I think you wanted to see.'

The tree had crowded the next stone, but I guided him. 'There. Who gets the last laugh now?'

'Jeremiah Rice' was carved across the top, above his birth date and a day in early 1907 that I assumed was when the expedition returned without him. There was a gavel etched on the stone, and a ship. Below, the carving read, 'Devoted family man, respected judge, friend to all.'

'I love that,' I said. 'Friend to all. You were the same outgoing man then as you are now. The frozen time didn't change you.'

Jeremiah made no reply for half a minute. 'Mark it down in ink,' he said finally. 'This is my strangest moment in the here and now.'

My mouth went dry, but I managed to speak. 'Are you ready for the hardest?'

His answer was to take my hand in his. Even in the anguish of that moment, I felt the privilege of being with this man, of guarding his heart when

I could, of providing comfort when I could not. Here was a moment beyond my capacity, I knew that well. I squeezed his hand, and led him forward.

The stone on the tree's other side matched his in height and lettering. 'Joan Rice, Aug. 15, 1934.' A bouquet of flowers was carved under her name. 'Devoted wife and mother.'

'I am so sorry, Jeremiah.'

'She outlived me by twenty-seven years.'

'I can't imagine how this must—'

'I wish she had remarried. I wish my Joan had not been alone all of that time.'

I searched for the right thing to say. But he moved on to the next one, his body looking like it had gone hollow. 'Agnes Rice Halsey, Oct. 17, 1926. Loving daughter. Died in childbirth.' Her carving was an angel with rays of light streaming from the head.

'Joan suffered the loss of Agnes too,' he said. 'She had eight years alone.'

'But in childbirth, Jeremiah, she went in childbirth. You may have descendants after all. I tell you what. When we get back, I'll find that list, I'll dig through every person who came forward, better than Dixon did. Her Mr Halsey wasn't buried here and that's a great clue. We'll find your family, I promise.'

Jeremiah stood rigid, his face as blank as sheet metal. 'Hm,' he said.

'I am terribly, totally, sorry,' I said. 'This is the worst.'

'Hm.'

'Look, Jeremiah,' I said. 'In the world of today, it is OK for men to show their feelings. Especially grief. Totally allowed. Especially grief this stupefyingly huge.'

'Hm.'

I reached up and laid my hand along his upper arm. Jeremiah gasped, buried his face in my shoulder, exploded against me in sobs. One of his hands fluttered in the air like an injured bird. I brought it in against my chest. My other arm I wrapped around him as far as I could go, holding tight, while his back heaved like some kind of animal that was flailing against its cage.

CHAPTER 31

THE HUNGER

(DANIEL DIXON)

When my cell phone told me the caller was the Lazarus Project offices, I assumed it was Carthage wanting his daily bout of scheming on how to play the press. The last person I expected to find on the line was Gerber.

'You might want to get back here pretty soon,' he said.

'What's cooking?'

'Our fans in the park have outdone themselves.'

He wouldn't give me anything more, which all but guaranteed that I would hustle straight back to Boston. It was a shame though, because I was having one of those days where instead of getting paid, I should have been paying someone. Like when I worked for that paper in Florida, and every spring break they would send a photographer out to the beaches to find the latest bathing-suit style. He would come back saying it had been crowded, hot, drunken kids and a real annoyance. Then we would see his roll after roll of bikinis and thongs, and the newsroom would razz the photographer for the rest of the week.

That's about how much fun tailing people was for me, like snapping pics of beach babes. Only I was staying in the shadows, driving half a block behind, opening a newspaper wide when my sidewalk bench needed to become an instant hiding-place. One time years back, the mayor of the city where I worked had a reputation as a boozer. I tailed him three nights before catching him at an uptown bar. It was an easy mark while the guy sucked down five martinis, but then he marched out the door as steady as a surgeon. I hustled outside just in time to see him get behind the wheel and drive off. Now there's a fine dilemma, because a reporter is not supposed to become part of the story, but if I sat mum and he plowed into somebody, it would be on my conscience. Before I could decide what to do, a squad car zipped by, lights on. Later it came out that the mayor's wife had hired a private eye to shadow him, hoping to get him caught and scared sober. The whole thing cracked me up: this pathetic drunk just wants to get a load on, and meanwhile he's being tailed by two people.

Well, my marks that day had given me plenty already. I had ideas about where I could catch them later, too, if necessary. I high-tailed it back into town, working side streets to dodge the traffic.

I could have kissed Gerber for calling me in.

When I pulled up the place looked like a murder scene. Four or five black-and-whites blocked the street, there were lights and camera crews and people shouting back and forth. I squeezed behind a TV dish truck and approached the first cop I saw. 'What kind of circus do we have here?'

'Lotta noise, mostly,' he said. 'Losers didn't feel they were getting enough attention, so they made a human barricade across the boulevard. We've popped like sixty of 'em for blocking traffic, assembly without license and whatnot. And now they won't give their frickin names.'

'What do you mean?'

He pointed at men clustered behind yellow crime tape, all wearing red shirts. They sat on the curb, looking like sheep. 'They all say their name's Adam, no last name.'

I chuckled. 'Guess it beats John Doe.'

'Them,' he pointed at a group of women, all in red, behind tape on the other side, 'they're all named Eve.'

'I get it.'

'Subtle as a hammer, right? Meanwhile we got real crimes to deal with tonight, once their little party is over.'

'What are you going to with all of them?'

'Adam and Eve? I dunno. Fetch a snake? Feed 'em apples?' He laughed. 'Naw, they got a downtown overnight coming. Once transport gets here.'

His boss started over, a lieutenant, and I rolled

out of there. I heard him tell the cop to keep the area clear of gawkers, meaning me. I'd planned to use the rear door, but T. J. Wade was holding forth to reporters on the sidewalk. I couldn't resist.

'I told them not to do it,' he told the cluster of microphones. 'I told them this was not the time for civil disobedience.'

He was about as convincing as a dog owner ordering his pitbull to let go of a burglar's leg. I dug out my trusty notebook.

'We have been patient,' Wade continued. 'We argued against this project in court. We begged the Commonwealth of Massachusetts to investigate the diabolical doings of this nefarious group.'

I chuckled, trying to imagine who inside the lab's walls fitted that description. Gerber, spacing out to the latest Dead bootleg? Thomas, licking Carthage's shoes?

'All to no avail,' Wade said. 'And so these good people took matters into their own hands. You see them now, being arrested for doing what they believe is right. They are going to jail as a matter of conscience. Perhaps they remember the teachings of Gandhi: "First they ignore you, then they laugh at you, then they crack down, then you win." So here is the crack down, my friends.'

Earlier it was King he quoted, and now Gandhi. This guy was shameless.

'We're not the ones redefining mortality. We're not the ones using unethical science. But we are the ones willing to suffer, because our consciences cannot stand by.'

I wrote it all down, but there was no denying the nasty taste in my mouth. If this movement was like Gandhi's and King's, then I was like Princess Diana. The paddy wagon arrived, cops started loading all the Adams and Eves, and just when I thought the show couldn't get any more carnival, some of them started singing 'We Shall Overcome.'

That one stung. I mean, quote anyone you like, no hair off me. But I worked five years at a paper in Baltimore, and the last time I heard that song was at the funeral of a twelve-year-old. Stray bullets don't care where they land. There was nothing civil rights about these protestors, just a calculating dude with a knack for keeping the tape rolling.

'Our responsibility is to keep the roads clear,' the police spokesman meanwhile told one reporter, off to the side. 'These people are endangering drivers through here, and they are endangering themselves. Simple as that.'

The wagon loading was dull, no one resisting, so I badged myself into the building. I could email alert my editor, and file copy on this in minutes. The lab bullpen reminded me of a newsroom in the morning, before reporters arrive. Few lights on, no phones ringing. Billings was bent over his computer like some underpaid bean-counter in an 1800s sweatshop. Gerber, feet on his desk, eyes closed, was blissing to whatever stoner reveries jammed in his headphones.

I paused by the *Perv Du Jour* basket, thinking now might be a good time to sneak out that green binder. But I checked the board first and sure enough Gerber had a new offering.

That night's entry was different, because it had a highly identifiable origin: walkerforpresident.com. Here was Gerald T. Walker's trademark toothy grin, hand outstretched as he's introduced to Jeremiah Rice. A caption ran beneath: 'Tuned In, In Touch, and Ready to Restore America's Global Leadership in Science and Technology.' At the photo's edge, you can see Dr Kate's slender ankle and foot.

Gerber had also posted a screen-capture of Frank speaking and the veep leaning to catch every word. The caption: 'Listening to America, Proud of Our Nation.'

Finally there was a picture with Walker's arm thrown around the judge's shoulders. The judge wore a pained expression, but Walker was smiling like he just beat two weeks of constipation. I swear, his teeth are pulled so far back he looks like a horse about to sneeze. The caption: 'Reanimate America. Walker for President.'

'Makes you want to gag, doesn't it?' Gerber had sidled over.

'What?' I chuckled, taking my hand off the basket with the binder. 'I was feeling choked-up and patriotic.'

He sniffed. 'Worst case of the hunger I've seen yet.'

'What are you talking about?'

'You know what I mean.' He waddled back to his desk; pressed a button to blank the screen. 'All these people, all the same hunger. Gimme a piece, gimme gimme.'

'What's so terrible about folks using old Frank? Nothing new about that.'

'True. And I'm sure the judge can handle it.' Gerber picked up his headphones. 'But look at all the signs. The sites, the bloggers. Media frenzy like he was a movie star. That army of freaks saying they were his offspring. This bit from Walker. Sheesh.'

'Human nature, Gerber.' I tapped the *Perv* sheets. 'The usual. Hell, a century ago it was a dozen women claiming to be the long lost daughter of the last Russian czar.'

'If this is the same old thing, then it's getting worse. It's like *everybody* is pretending to be long-lost Russian daughters, the whole country.' Gerber held his hands wide. 'When you add in the crazy scene in this place, no wonder everybody is perving all over our judge.' He rubbed his scalp with the headphones. 'I don't like it.'

I thought about pulling out my notebook. Was this a conversation I'd want to quote some day? Or was it just late-night Gerber? 'In my opinion,' I said, 'you ought to stick to science. This is a clear case of same-shit, different-day. No harm in any of it.'

'I'm not sure about those protestors. They irritate the crap out of me.'

'They've definitely grown more annoying.' I dug the notebook out after all, flipping to find a clean sheet. Shadowing the judge and Kate all day had given me hours to kill. I'd whiled away the hours fooling with letter combinations from the chamber's security pass code: BOMS, CMNR. Maybe they added up to nothing, but often people choose passwords that signify something to them. BNOQ. Would the letters reveal a secret about Carthage? Then I found AMOS and knew I'd struck gold. Whatever it meant, one day I would find out. 'You should have heard them out there tonight.'

'There's this want, want, want everyone seems to have,' Gerber continued. 'And with the folks outside our doors, you have the added danger of piety. Whenever anybody gets too righteous, it makes me nervous.'

I wrote down what he said, but on the page it only looked like basic doper paranoia. 'Why is that?' I asked.

Gerber ignored the question. 'The worst was that reporter who came through here yesterday. God what a smug son of a bitch.'

'What are you talking about? I'm the only reporter allowed in here.'

'I didn't catch his name, you'd have to check the sign-in at security. I just know he had an OK from Carthage. He came in for an interview, but he was full of accusations about what a lousy judge Jeremiah apparently had been. He gave the reporter a heave-ho, but not before he'd been rattled. Who does that guy think he is? Challenging somebody about something he did or didn't do a hundred years ago? What's he trying to prove?'

'Carthage promised me exclusive access to Subject One. And no one else.'

Gerber rolled his eyes. 'Don't tell me you've got the hunger too.'

'Hell no,' I said. 'Just another story to me, another byline. But Carthage and I had a deal. And I can just guess who that fucking reporter was.'

'You're completely missing my point.'

I jammed the notebook in my pocket. 'Right this second, with all due respect, I do not give a rat's ass about your point. I have been bullshitted again.'

Gerber laughed and turned his back. 'Well aren't you suddenly Prince Charming?' He pressed a key on his computer, and the screen brightened. A bunch of graphs all pointed uphill.

I paced for half a minute. I deserved an explanation. With Carthage gone home, the only people with any answers were the good judge and Dr Kate. And I knew right where I could find them.

CHAPTER 32

ON TIPTOES

(KATE PHILO)

Whatever calm we attained over the course of that evening in Lynn, as soon as we turned onto the street of the Lazarus Project offices, it was shattered. Jeremiah had pulled himself together, taking a long, melancholy walk around the cemetery while I waited by the entrance. My cell phone rang several times, Gerber's extension at the Project offices, but I had no stomach for his weird ways right then. When Jeremiah returned, I took his hand for the meander back to the car. We drove out the causeway to Nahant, along the shore up to Beverly, not speaking the whole time, finally easing back toward Boston.

We drove directly into a spectacle. Police vehicles blocked the entire street. Bright banks of lights beamed from fire and rescue trucks. I rolled down my window and people were singing as police carried them into what looked like giant armored cars.

A man in uniform waved his flashlight. 'Move it along here, please.'

'I need to drop my passenger off at the loading dock in back.'

'Street's closed, ma'am.'

'But he lives in this building. How's he supposed to get home?'

'What can I tell you sweetheart? We got upwards of a hundred people blocking the road and creating a hazard. Gonna take a good two hours to get 'em all processed.'

I was at a loss. Jeremiah slumped against his window, shaking his head as though he was saying no to everything, no to the whole world. 'What should I do?'

''Go get a large pizza, eat it slow, come back at around 11:30.'

'It's *him*. Oh my God it's him.' A photographer behind the cop had spotted us, leaped forward with his camera.

'Hey buddy,' the cop pulled on his arm. But there were others right behind, and in seconds we were surrounded by flashing lights.

I closed my window, put the car in reverse, and backed away fast. At the intersection I cut hard to the left and zoomed off. Within a block I could see a TV truck following us, but I cut through an alley toward the Commons and he fell from the rear view. 'Lost him.'

Jeremiah was somnolent no longer. 'What in great glory was that?'

'Some demonstration against the Project, I guess.'

'I mean that wave of camera people. And that man who chased us.'

'Well, we call them paparazzi. I don't know what the word means, it's Italian. They're people who get paid for photos they take of rich or famous people.'

'Why would you run from someone who wants to take your picture?'

'Because their appetite is endless. In fact they can be dangerous, because they don't believe in limits or privacy. People have died trying to escape them.'

'But we're not rich or famous.'

'Not rich anyway. But you are getting pretty well known, Mister.'

'If that is the result, I would expect everyone to strive to be anonymous.'

'That makes sense, if you come from another century.'

Jeremiah fiddled with the glove compartment latch, then quickly sat on his hand. 'What happens now? We wait till nearly midnight?'

'No,' I said, taking Storrow Drive toward Cambridge. 'We go to my place.'

He didn't answer. I took it for affirmation. I drove faster. In retrospect, I could not have been more foolhardy than if I'd been racing toward a car accident.

Miracle, I found a parking spot just up the block from my apartment. We climbed out, I took his offered arm. It felt different in that moment, more muscled, more of a pleasure to grasp. I used both hands.

'This is where you live,' Jeremiah said, studying the arching trees.

'The Project is where I live. This is where I sleep, and do laundry.'

'Do you have laundry tonight?'

He sounded so guileless I looked at him sideways, but his face gave nothing away. Was this really happening? We inched along that sidewalk together. Inevitably, we arrived at my front step.

'Jeremiah, I feel just terrible about the cemetery—'

He placed a finger over my lips. There we were, facing one another, silent, streetlight through the trees streaking his face, this incredible man. I put one hand behind his neck, summoned my courage, kissed him.

I believe, I want to believe, I hope I remember truthfully, that he kissed me back.

Then the strangest thing, I thought I saw a flash. I peered into the dark. Could someone be hiding there? Hadn't I lost him? 'Hello?' I called. 'Who's there?'

There was no answer. 'Let's go inside,' I said. Jeremiah followed close behind.

Between a man and a woman, everything can be changed by one kiss. Touch, intimate information, the admission that each person yearns for the other. Some would say intercourse is the alteration, and that's true, but there is no denying the barriers that fall after one heartfelt kiss.

Sure as night follows day, the questions came next. What does he want? What are the rules? How do the sexual mores of his time compare with today's? What do I want?

No lights on, for starters. They would be too bright for what had just happened. 'Wait here,' I told Jeremiah in the front hall. Then I tossed my bag on a chair, hurried into the kitchen where I thought there might be a candle.

Also I needed a minute alone. I hadn't been intimate since Wyatt, the law professor. Yet I had just kissed Jeremiah Rice on my front stoop. That was real. I willed myself calm, then dug in the chaos drawer: batteries, spare keys, half a red candle. Grabbing an unfinished wine bottle on the counter, I poured the remnants in the sink and wondered if it was some kind of metaphor. Old wine, old history, old loves, goodbye.

Except that I had no notion of what Jeremiah was thinking. On that fine summer night with him standing in my front hall, I felt a simple truth. My life's experiences had no more equipped me for the present situation than they had prepared me for parachuting.

I corked the candle in the bottle, using a burner on the stove to light it. The flame was gentle, silent. I cupped a hand around it with a sweet feeling, like I was protecting something fragile on my way back to Jeremiah.

He had taken a few steps into the living room. 'This place smells like you.'

'Coffee and stress?'

'Lavender,' he said.

'My shampoo?' I laughed, putting the candle on a table. 'I've used this overly floral stuff ever since college. Now it's my signature scent.'

'I like it.'

'Thank you,' I said. It came out barely a whisper.

'Kate.'

It was just my name, but in a tone I'd not heard before. 'I'm listening.'

He brought his arms around me, I lay my head on his chest. Jeremiah caressed my shoulder, but the touch wavered on my arm.

'You're trembling,' I said.

'Not at all.'

I pulled his hand against me, his wrist between my breasts, held it till it went still. So did I, so did I. Any second now, I imagined, he might ask me to make love. How he would say it, I didn't know. How I would answer, I didn't know. I rested against him, savoring. He took a deep breath.

'It is impossible to enumerate the ways in which you have helped me in this inexplicable time.'

Such vocabulary, at such a moment. I smiled at the formality. 'My pleasure.'

'Nor can I list all the experiences I have relished which were improved by your company. My second life feels as though it has been lit by you.'

'I feel the same, Jeremiah.'

'Shhh.' He rested his chin on the top of my head. 'Shhh.'

I nestled in him, patient. The candle flame wavered, then held.

'Please remember that I have said these things to you. Promise me Kate, months and years from now, that when you think of this time, you will remember how grateful I am to you. Can you promise me that?'

I nodded.

He began whispering. 'One thing only has maintained my sanity through the maelstrom of here and now. It is so dear to me, I nearly choke to say it.' He paused, swallowing before continuing. 'When my mind has struggled to understand, when my memories have proven inaccurate, when I have felt the loneliness of a century's time standing between me and what I knew and loved, one thing has sustained me. It has been fixed, like north on a compass.'

I waited, closing two fingers around his yellow tie.

'My family,' he said. 'My anchor, Joan, my firefly Agnes, and the ironclad love I feel for them yet. In all the confusion of here and now, my devotion to them, regret at leaving them, desire however futile to experience them again, has been the one thing I have known, truly and undeniably known. It is rock.'

I felt so small then, small-minded. I hadn't done

anything, yet I felt selfish somehow. I whispered too. 'What is it that you want me understand?'

'I am speaking with great presumption, Kate, for which I beg your leave. But I am as yet unready for the fruits that might come between us as man and woman, delicious though I know they would be. My bond with the past remains too strong.'

'It is not adultery,' I whispered. 'You are a widower.'

'Further, I worry about the effect upon you when time has . . . when my time . . .'

'When what? What time?'

'Moreover, the only woman I have ever known, I mean *known*, is Joan. That is my life's entire intimate world: her. I am not yet beyond that.' Jeremiah fell silent, tightening his hold on me. Then he relaxed, stood apart and upright, cleared his throat. 'Also you are exhausted, while my energy is fresh. My suggestion would be for you to retire, after giving me a good book, and a blanket perhaps for when fatigue does find me, and we will speak in the morning.'

I drew back, searching his face. 'Really?'

He nodded. 'Honestly. And I thank you for this unforgettable day.'

'What about that kiss? What did that mean?'

'Hm.' He touched his forehead to mine. 'Wonderful.'

'I didn't dream it, then.'

'*We are such stuff as dreams are made on.*'

'Hah. *And our little lives are rounded with a sleep.*'

'Listen to yourself.' He made a thin smile. 'Well done.'

'You're not the only one who ever read *The Tempest*, you know.'

So we parted, hands releasing last. But only temporarily. 'As yet unready' is a hundred miles from no. I blew out the candle, turned on the lamp, blinked in the bright light of disappointment. Meanwhile the want had been revealed by both of us. *Fruits delicious as I know they would be.* No, there was no taking that back.

CHAPTER 33

THE RAGE OF AN ANT

(ERASTUS CARTHAGE)

The man arrives in your office all but with his hat in his hand. Actually he has nothing in his hands at all, but that is as articulate as any words he might say: no documents, no abstracts of publishable ideas. No letter of resignation either. Thus you decide to have a little fun.

'Doctor Billings, at last.'

'Carthage.' He tips an imaginary cap.

Apparently he is game as well. Heaven bless those British, as skilled at minor diplomacies as any species on earth. And why would he not be? The radiance of the summer morning pours through your office windows. The chant of protestors below lends the hour a certain musicality. And this wretch, having failed in his research, has come to plead. You meet eyes with Thomas, who stands at ease by your diploma wall, then place both palms flat on your desk. 'To what do I owe the pleasure of your company?'

That appears to baffle him. He stammers, then reclaims his even keel. 'You instructed me, I doubt you've forgotten, to return today with the results of my work on the smaller specimens.'

'Of course, yes. But we parted unpleasantly, did we not?'

Again your feint, again he draws back, collecting himself. 'Doctor, I submit that all of our partings have been characterized by their dearth of warmth and collegiality.'

A fair riposte, that. And that word, 'dearth,' is rather choice. You nod, ready to let the preliminaries end. 'Indeed that may be so.'

'Erastus Carthage is famous for many things, but charm is not one of them.'

'I take both halves of that sentence as compliments.'

'As you would.'

'Well.' You clap your hands together once. 'Enlighten us. What has the great and wise Graham Billings unearthed?'

'Carthage, how many years have you conducted biological research?'

'I couldn't begin to guess. I published my first paper at sixteen, perhaps you knew that, so it has been decades.'

'And in that vast span of trial and error, seeking and sometimes finding, has there ever been a ten-week period in which you could design assays, perform them, and draw meaningful conclusions? In five fortnights?'

'Are you implying that I set you up for failure? Or that the deadline was too close? Do you honestly think ten more weeks would prove revelatory?'

'I'd be delighted to answer your questions, following your answers of mine.'

You give Thomas a look, and he is smiling. Good. He understands that this banter is not a sign that you're weakening, diminished by public opposition and tight finances. There are reasons to prefer Billings resigning to you firing him: maintaining friendly relations with Oxford, avoiding potential insult to a Brit who is one of the Project's potential investors, even respecting Billings's reputation. Any indignity he suffers should occur not on the professional level, but on the personal. Thomas's grin confirms his comprehension of these nuances. He is coming along nicely.

'No,' you concede. 'Not once in my career. Ten weeks is often insufficient time to acquire proper equipment, much less perform something useful with it.'

'Then why did you grant me these weeks anyway?'

'To teach you, Doctor. You were asking for more time, when you knew the outcome already. You were denying persuasive data. That is sloppy science, and you needed to learn.'

Billings opens his mouth, but restrains himself.

'But I am presuming,' you say, holding your arms wide. 'I could be mistaken. Bestow upon me, please, the fruits of your labor.'

'There is nothing to bestow, and you bloody well know it.'

'Nothing whatsoever?'

'Not of use to you. There are trend lines in the metabolic data—'

'Trending how?' This could be interesting.

'Erratically. I suspected there was an indicator, a mark at which we might intervene and prolong the specimens' lifespan. But the marks occurred inconsistently.'

'You wanted to keep them alive.'

Billings sighs. 'In the work interval given, that proved unattainable.'

You rise from your chair. Billings was chasing the very thing you need, the thing your potential investors have repeatedly requested: prolonged survival. If a businessman has a warehouse of frozen bodies, he won't give a nickel to someone who can wake them up. For someone who keeps them awake, he will go to the vaults of Fort Knox. And if Billings has found the crucial answer, and is holding back . . .

'Need I remind you, Dr Billings, that your work here is contractually the property of the Project? And that the life of Subject One is at stake.'

'I can provide a copy of that contract,' Thomas interjects.

You wave this suggestion away. 'That shouldn't be necessary.'

'It's not.' Billings rises to the bait. 'I know perfectly well that every jot and tittle in my notebooks belongs to you.'

'Not to me,' you say, 'but to this grand enterprise.'

'Fine, then.' His jaw clenches. 'It's oxygen. The accelerating metabolism creates more ammonia than the liver can process without aid. The number of cases was too small to confirm the method. But I rescued several acceleration-stage sardines by applying super-saturations of oxygen.'

'Damn,' you say. All that manipulation, wasted. 'You are mistaken.'

He sniffs in disdain. 'I beg your pardon?'

'It's not oxygen.'

'But if you read my papers, you'd know that—'

'Anyone can hyper-oxygenate a fish tank and a sardine will remain alive. But the human body contains only so much hemoglobin. No matter what you do externally, Subject One's blood can transport a finite amount of oxygen.'

Billings pulls his chin back as though you'd poked him. 'Blast. That's a beast of a hole in my theory, isn't it now?'

'The answer is not oxygen.' You enjoy the pleasure of informing him. 'It's salt.'

'Salt? How so?'

You consider. There is no harm in sharing Borden's discovery. 'Zero salt intake, Dr Billings, prevents the ammonia problem from beginning.'

'Indubitably. But that diet's utility will diminish over time, because the body innately contains salt in its tissues. It's a prerequisite of muscle contraction.'

You sigh, facing the bookcases, the top-shelf titles all your own. 'Billings, you are no fool in the lab, but we have been ahead of you on this question forever. Borden solved the lifespan problem with salt nearly two months ago.'

You turn, expecting to see him bent, dejected. Instead Billings sits, chin held high. What a strange man.

'With salt alone, you say? Brilliant.'

You turn away again. 'Doctor, need we say anything further to one another?'

'I'd like one more day, if you please. You needn't pay me. But my haste with the oxygen studies has left materials in disarray. I'd like to place the data in a coherent format, should this avenue prove useful someday to someone down the road. Also I'd prefer a proper goodbye with the technicians who've assisted me.'

'You may have your extra day, Billings,' you say, one hand raised as if swearing to tell the truth, the whole truth. 'Without pay as you said and as is appropriate. Surrender your security badge to Thomas by noon tomorrow. He will have severance documents ready.'

Billings nods, but not only to himself. 'All my career, I've advanced from one lab to the next only by answering inquiries. I've never lost a job before.'

'You'll live.' You return to your desk and sit.

Billings stands. His walk possesses a stiff, dignified, air and he moves with the speed of a snail. He stops in the doorway; must there be a valedictory? 'I must say, Carthage, working with you has been—'

'Goddam it, where is he?'

Billings jumps back in surprise, as Dixon comes barging through the doorway. He bumps Billings on the way but it does not so much as break his stride. Dixon barrels up to your desk and puts his hands on his hips. 'You and I have to talk,' he says. 'I demand an explanation. Now.'

It would be easier to respect this man if his hands were not so fleshy, the fists of a piglet. 'You demand? You demand something from me?'

'As I was saying,' Billings began, trying to regain his moment.

'You're goddam right I do,' Dixon blusters on. 'I have carried your water all these months now, in article after article, and then you go and break your word.'

'Calm yourself Mr Dixon, be seated, and in a moment I will hear you out.'

'I will not be seated. And I will not wait.'

The audacity. The ingratitude. You lean to see past him. 'Dr Billings, you were saying?'

'He just expressed it better than I ever could. Good luck to the filthy lot of you.' And Billings leaves the room smiling.

It's a bit unsettling, that crooked grin, and you pause to ponder how he could have, despite your intentions, wrested good humor from your exchange. Dixon puts his hands on his hips again, all righteousness and ignorance. A weariness possesses you. 'What is it, Mr Dixon?'

'You and I had a deal that there would be no

exclusives. But you let Wilson Steele interview the judge without me present.'

Something about your dissatisfaction with the conclusion of the Billings conversation abbreviates your patience for this one. 'Yes I did.'

'That was a direct contradiction of your agreement with me.'

'Yes it was.'

'Well, Jesus.' He pounds a fist against his thigh. 'What the hell were you thinking?'

'Mr Dixon, do you honestly want to know the answer to that question?'

'Why do you think I asked it?'

'Very well.' You turn your seat halfway from Dixon, giving him your profile. Essentially, you are addressing Thomas. 'I reneged on our agreement because Wilson Steele, in his sleep, is one hundred times the reporter and writer that you are on your finest day. He has a national platform for his work, a massive audience, and a history of writing best sellers. You are a small-time science magazine hack, who's quick with a simile but otherwise struggles to put three intelligent sentences together.'

Dixon takes the seat you had offered a moment before, slumps into the chair like a defeated boxer who doesn't know well enough to lower his chin. Since the damage is already done, you continue telling him the truth.

'You were useful for the initial propaganda about our work, but your limited reach and rudimentary skills are insufficient for the range and audience that we now need.' You rotate back and squirt a dollop of sanitizer on your hands. 'I gave Wilson Steele that interview because you are no longer of any value to me. There. Now are you pleased with the answer?'

'You,' he growls, shaking his head. 'You are one smug motherfucker.'

'Thomas,' you exclaim. 'Listen to him. A Shakespeare in our midst.'

Dixon rubs his face with one hand. You can all but hear him thinking, little wheels turning, his wobbly cogs of cognition. You are nearly out of patience, but at least he is showing the spirit Billings failed to provide. You will indulge him one last minute.

'What is in your mind, Mr Dixon?'

'Just working something out here. Something I've wondered, didn't make sense. And now that I'm getting close, you back door me.' He chews on a fingernail. 'Yeah. I suspect this project, and you cut me out. Huh. Kinda confirms my suspicions.'

'Whatever are you foaming at the mouth about?'

'You.' He sits forward in the chair, a strange grin on his face. 'You think your ego can keep you out of trouble. But you're dead wrong. You are going to regret treating me this way.'

You cannot help it; you laugh. 'Are you threatening me, Mr Dixon? Thomas, please relieve our puppet of his security badge. His work here is finished.'

Thomas strides over and unclips the lapel card, the reporter's sole means of access to Project offices and labs. You allow yourself a minor gloat. 'Do you honestly believe the world would accept your version of events over mine?' You scrub your hands together thoroughly. 'I had no idea you were so deluded.'

'I am really going to enjoy it, you know that?'

You switch hands. 'What are you going to enjoy?'

'The crashing sound you make when I bring you down.'

'Mr Dixon, would you please stop being so tedious?'

'You think I can't do it?'

You tend to your cuticles. 'No more than an ant can fell an oak.'

'But I know about you, Mister, and you are no oak. I know you are a fraud, and this project is a fake. You just confirmed it, right now. The only thing keeping me from writing about it is figuring out how many people here are in on the scam. You may have the world fooled, Carthage, but I have been paying attention all this time and I know the truth, and I have proof. You pompous fuck.'

You do not deign to reply. What is obscenity, really, but a person's way of showing he lacks distinction? Dixon heaves himself up from the chair and starts for the door. But he pauses on the sill. Is this now where the defeated make their vain last stands?

'One last question for you, Dr Carthage. On the record.'

You throw up your hands. 'Do your worst.'

'Who is Amos?'

You gulp in surprise. 'I beg your pardon?'

'Got you there, didn't I?' He sidles back. 'Why don't you just spill the whole beans on it?'

'Ho ho. So you found out about Amos Cartwright. Congratulations. I would never have thought you clever enough for that.'

'You will stop underestimating me sooner or later, pal.'

'Probably later.' You stroll behind your desk, stalling, wheeling your seat forward till your stomach presses against the drawers. 'What do you know about Amos?'

'Everything.' He digs a notebook from his rear pocket. 'I just need you to confirm the details.'

He's bluffing. He knows zero. Crumbs at best. You adjust your papers. There is the envelope for Billings, atop a pile of greater urgencies. This day's necessities are requiring more time than they deserve. You roll the chair back, again deciding to make this conversation travel the shortest possible distance. 'Then find the details for yourself, Daniel. All I can tell you is what exists in the plain public record.'

He does not answer. You fold your hands on the desk, fingers woven. 'Very well. Amos Cartwright was an international grand master in chess who lost all standing and medals when a tattletale revealed him to be a cheat. After which he hanged himself.'

Dixon has a pen out now, and he pauses in note-taking. 'How is it possible to cheat at chess?'

'Don't be a fool. There is no deception in the game of kings. But cheating the World Chess Federation is simple, if you use the power of reason. Imagine for example that you colluded with the person who compiles the draw sheets for tournaments, to assure that you would always be competing on an easy side, with all of the difficult challengers placed on the other half. They would exhaust themselves eliminating each other, while you played easy match upon easy match. Eventually one of their number would attain the finals, fatigued, and intimidated because you had breezed through the other side. That last one might still defeat you, but you'd place second at least. And often your advantage would prove insurmountable. Thus would you amass international standing, either by beating weaklings or by placing runner-up dozens of times.'

'Amazing.'

'Or so a certain federation official confessed, long after retiring, due to a deathbed discovery of morals he apparently had lacked during his professional career. Which revelation led the discredited Amos Cartwright to tie a noose. It made a minor noise in the media.'

'What does a chess cheater have to do with the Project?'

You look down at your hands as if they held aces. 'The answer would require a person with one hundred times your reporting capacity to determine.'

Dixon snaps his notebook shut. 'One sign of a stupid man is when he's too free with his insults.'

'You are saying Erastus Carthage is stupid?'

'The easiest kind: overconfident. But it's like I said before.'

'Yes?'

'I'm going to enjoy the crashing sound.'

He turns on his heel and is gone.

It takes several minutes to collect yourself. Amos Cartwright is not a name you expected to hear from that buffoon. Nonetheless, there is no way he can connect Amos to you, none. You have covered every potential avenue. It has been the work of decades, subject to more thought and care than cells or reanimation or your own breathing. He might write damaging things about the project, but not based on that.

Thomas stands at your elbow. 'Sir, what is our link to Amos Cartwright?'

'I used his name for our security password, that is all.'

'Why would you choose such a person?'

'Because, Thomas, we are as different from him as it is possible to be. He was a cheater and we have integrity, he squandered his intellect and we exercise ours diligently, he lied for most of his life and we will never lie, never.'

Thomas bowed. 'I see my question irritated you and I apologize. Besides, how much damage can Dixon do to us?'

'Far less than the good he has already done.'

'What about the investors, though? These cryogenics people always seem so close, but then turn reluctant. Isn't Dixon a danger?'

'Thomas, let us apply reason to the situation. There is zero we can do to control Mr Dixon at this point. Therefore I decline to expend a moment's further thought on him. As for our potential investors, even a novice fisherman knows that trout are not intelligent, just skeptical.'

'I'm not following you sir. Our potential investors are like trout?'

You push back your chair. 'What we need is something to stir them from their suspicious place on the bottom. Then we need a good lure, to hook them.'

You cross to the windows and peer downward. The protestors have finished their daily demonstration for the benefit of the noon news. They'll rest until it's time for the six o'clock performance. The previous night's arrests brought reinforcements. There must be nearly a thousand of them down there now, all in their absurd red shirts. Since that firebrand from Kansas arrived, the one with the superhero good looks, these people have shown far greater organization and media savvy. Sometime it might be interesting to meet him. For now, most of the group is gathered on the lawn across the way, eating box lunches. Devout members are kneeling on the sidewalk outside the front doors. It occurs to you that these people are very likely praying for you, or about you at least. And there is your answer.

'Thomas, we need additional incitement of our fans.'

'Those protestors are our fans, sir?'

'See how they lavish us with devotion. Like Mr Dixon, they've brought us valuable attention, too. The question is how we use them next.'

'To stir the bottom of the stream?'

'Yes, and I know just the thing. I'd like to extend them an invitation tomorrow. Simple, elegant, certain to stir. I'll need your help.'

'Of course sir. And galvanizing them against us will help the project how?'

'The more fervently your enemies hate you, the more they confirm your importance. But first, please fetch me Subject One. Our most convincing salesman needs to start work. It's time we prepared him to meet our future investors.'

PART V

FRENZY

CHAPTER 34

ENTIRELY TOO LATE

(KATE PHILO)

The note waiting on my desk was penned in handwriting so impeccable it had to be from Thomas, but the true author was equally unmistakable. 'In my office – NOW.'

Oddly enough, I felt no fear. Not even apprehension. At that moment Jeremiah Rice was in my kitchen, reading a weathered paperback of *Treasure Island* I hadn't even known I owned. I last saw him comfortably at the table, in the chair that gets morning sun, with the odd but endearing habit of sitting on his hand whenever it was not turning pages like a speed reader. By contrast, Erastus Carthage seemed in every way smaller. Thomas hadn't just underlined the word *now*, he'd capitalized it. Was I supposed to be intimidated by handwriting? Honestly.

All morning I'd run through the possibilities. Online I'd found a promising lab in upstate New York. It specialized in blood projects but they'd just landed a massive cell chemistry grant that would need administering. Also there were university post-doc positions, in Missouri and Iowa, that would do for a transition job. I could have emailed a resume before leaving the apartment, the cover letter copied to Tolliver, my former mentor at the Academy, so he could begin the background influencing.

Yet I hadn't. Instead I filled my coffee mug, caressed Jeremiah's shoulder, enjoyed my usual walk to work. It was a stunning morning, the previous day's humidity burned off into clear skies. The Charles River winked and glimmered as I crossed the M.I.T. Bridge. I wore a summer dress, green with small white flowers. I felt eighteen.

By the time I reached the loading dock entry, I'd convinced myself to follow the Lazarus Project thread all the way, to whatever conclusion it reached. Carthage's note only simplified matters. If he fired me, it would end in an hour. I'd be home for lunch, resumes mailed with time left to drive Jeremiah to Cape Cod for dinner. If Carthage didn't fire me, back to my desk I'd go, to see what needed doing. I stopped, there in the hallway, realizing that for once I did not have a list of urgent tasks waiting. I'd already grown that disconnected from the Project, that connected to Jeremiah.

Thomas was not in his usual place, manning the desk outside, but I could hear him laughing inside. I knocked, striding in to a complete surprise. Thomas sat in Carthage's throne, holding a remote control, while the boss stood across the room.

They were laughing at a giant television screen. It was the most private moment I'd seen with either man, and I began backing out of the room.

'A bishop,' Carthage cried. 'We've just been denounced by a bishop.'

Thomas laughed. '*Only God is the author of life,*' he said in a false basso voice.

'I'll come back later,' I said.

'No no, your timing is perfect,' Carthage said. He wiped a sleeve under an eye. 'Watch, Dr Philo.' Sobering, he pointed at the screen. 'Watch, and learn something.'

Thomas pressed the remote, images of a newscast played backward in fast motion. He was still chuckling to himself. 'Here,' he said. 'Here's the best part.'

The video began, a huge crowd wearing red shirts, gathered around a man in black with a Roman collar. People behind him waved signs or their hands.

'This person would be . . .?'

'The Bishop of Massachusetts,' Thomas said. 'His predecessor was a cardinal.'

'Just listen,' Carthage said.

'. . . conflicts throughout history between science and religion, clashes between reason and faith. So we must revert to basic principles, to the fundamental teaching from the Garden of Eden forward, which is simply this: only God is the author of life, and only the Almighty decides when life shall begin or end.' The bishop licked a fingertip, turned a page. 'We have prayed for the people engaged in this project because we reverence learning. Our faith includes belief in humanity's power to raise itself to greater heights of knowledge and understanding. But we have worried, too, about the aims of this project. Now, with this scurrilous invitation . . .' he held up a sheet of paper, 'we see these people as they truly are: sinners as we all happen to be, but unlike us they are intent on diminishing human life, on reducing it to chemical equations, rather than upholding it as the sacred gift of a Lord who with generosity and love created us in His divine image.'

The crowd cheered, but the bishop raised a hand to interrupt them.

'We have been patient. We have welcomed the man who embodies their accomplishments into our city and businesses and homes. I'm told he has even visited our cathedral. And we will continue to greet penitents with open arms.'

'I love that,' Thomas says. 'As if he wouldn't rather—'

'But we cannot conscience sacrilege. We cannot condone the trivialization of life, especially under the guise of false immortality. We cannot allow this . . .' he shook the paper again, 'this invitation to murder to go unremarked. We are left with one recourse.' He raised one hand high, as if proclaiming a benediction.

'This is the best part,' Thomas said.

'I hereby call upon the mayor of this city, the

city council, the governor of this state and even the vice president of the United States, who was unduly hasty with his endorsement of this enterprise, I call upon each of these individuals and the solemn responsibility they hold in the public trust, to shut this project down.'

The crowd began chanting. 'Shut it down, shut it down.' The handsome protest leader came forward, waving his arms like conducting a choir. 'Shut it down. Shut it—'

Thomas muted the sound. '*I call upon each of these individuals,*' he said, rising from the chair. 'Dr Carthage, that invitation was a master stroke.'

'Now remember Thomas, that one was your idea.'

'Hardly, sir. I'm here if you need me,' he said, strolling out of the office.

Carthage cleared his throat, pressed a button, the TV went blank. A panel of wood slid out to conceal it. 'Enough levity for one day,' he said.

'What have you done to get people so angry? What was on that paper?'

'A bluff.' He sidled over to his desk. 'An extremely successful bluff.'

'Where was that crowd? When did all of that happen?'

'Not 90 minutes ago,' Carthage said. 'Right outside our front door. You would have strolled directly into it, had you come to work on time.'

'I didn't have anything pressing, first thing today.'

Carthage sat with a sigh. 'Dr Philo, I hardly

know where to begin. So many things are occurring at higher intensity now, so much has changed. You seem unaware.'

I took one of the chairs angled toward his desk. 'Enlighten me.'

He raised one eyebrow, but checked himself, pushing a few papers aside. 'Well. Our friend Mr Dixon is a friend no longer, and seeks to do us harm.'

'From the looks of that coverage, we're doing that just fine by ourselves.'

'Also we are nearly out of funds. Many investors have come forward, eager to apply our technology to people they are maintaining in a cryogenic state. I had intended to provide them with conclusive evidence, by enlisting the aid of our undeniable success story, by introducing them to Subject One—'

'There is no such person.'

'—only to discover, abracadabra: he is not here any longer.'

I'd expected this much, so I tried my own bluff. 'Is that right, Doctor?'

'Let's not play games, shall we? Four different security cameras recorded that you and he snuck out of this building—'

'We did not sneak anywhere, because we were not doing anything wrong.'

'—yesterday morning, sometime after eight.'

'It was 8:21,' came the call from outside Carthage's office.

'Thank you Thomas.' Carthage picked up a pencil, brand new, not even sharpened, pointing the eraser at me. 'I am thoroughly disinterested in your justifications for your irresponsible conduct, your possible romantic conquests—'

'There is no such—'

'Please stop talking, Dr Philo. You are swimming in waters far out of your depth. A bishop is the least of it. While you've been off having adventures in hand holding, the world moved on. The more defensively you speak, the worse you make it for yourself.'

'Please spare me the brimstone. What are you going to do, fire me?'

'Is that what you fear?'

'Not even slightly.'

'Because being fired is the minimum that will happen, if Subject One is not in my office by four o'clock. Do you understand? Without dietary oversight, the consequences for him are catastrophic. The stakes for this project are likewise monumental. If things go any further awry, unemployment will be the least of your worries.'

'My sister Chloe is a litigator. She says there are two kinds of people: those who threaten to sue you, and those who do it. Which kind are you, Dr Carthage?'

He looked amused by the question. He tapped the pencil eraser on his desk. 'Have I not behaved, in the 14 months I have employed you, in a consistent manner?'

'You have, actually.'

'And how would you describe that behavior?'

'Honestly? Machiavellian. Manipulative. Grandiose.'

'Insincere, ever? Hesitant? Afraid of giving offense, even once?'

'You have always been exactly who you are.'

'Is that, by your sister's lexicon, one who threatens, or one who sues?'

I looked down at my lap. I was still holding Thomas's folded note. My summery dress felt frivolous, naïve. 'Sues.'

'Have you any theories to convince you that I would behave differently today?'

I raised my head again. 'On those other days, you held all the cards.'

'Is that not the case now?'

'No. The whole deck left here with me yesterday morning at 8:21.'

'Dr Philo.' He gripped the pencil with both hands, lowering them slowly. I realized from his white knuckles that he was livid, suppressing a massive rage with difficulty. 'I will not attempt to beguile you out of your righteousness, however misguided. Nor persist in appeals to reason you seem unable to hear. Nor succumb to the temptation to toy with your foolhardy feminism. Persuading one novice scientist to abandon her ignorance is not my goal. The survival of this project is. Therefore I simply repeat, so there is no ambiguity: if by 4 p.m. today Subject One is not in my office—'

'I know, I know, you'll fire me.'

'Hardly,' he laughed then, turning till his chair was sideways, his face in profile. 'Little Miss Muffet, firing is nothing. I've canned multitudes over the years. I fired Billings not an hour ago. Firing merely forces one to update a pitiful exaggerated resume, whine to some old professors, and find some cob-webby lab to call home for the rest of one's tenured, worthless days. Firing is so insignificant, it should come wrapped in a bow.'

He sat forward. 'You have leverage with him, I admit, and I repent myself of allowing that to occur. But my patience with your influence is ended. Thus let me be plain. Jeremiah Rice will be standing in this office by four o'clock, or I will ruin you.'

'Ruin me? What the hell does that mean?'

'You do not want to learn. Certainly no career and no reputation. But it will be much worse, I will do it with every power I have, and I will not relent until you are broken and destitute.' He tossed the pencil on his desk. 'And I will do it for sport.'

Carthage pumped the sanitizer on his desk, a white glop oozing onto his hand. I did not stay to watch the washing. No amount of scrubbing would make that man clean.

In the office supply room I found two large moving boxes. I carried them through the control room, where Gerber backed his chair out of my way.

'Whoa there, pilgrim,' he said. 'You look like the wrath of God.'

I put the boxes on a desk. 'Sometimes I would like to tear Carthage right in half.'

'The man is indeed a work of art,' Gerber bobbled his head in agreement. 'So, is he hassling you because you're bonking the good judge now?'

'Jesus, Gerber. You sound as bad as Dixon.' I picked the boxes back up, starting for Jeremiah's chamber. 'And no, for your information, I am not "bonking" anyone.'

'Oh.' He shrugged, wheeling back to his desk. 'My condolences.'

What a place. I could not wait to be rid of it. Meanwhile I punched the numbers to enter Jeremiah's chamber. Quickly it was clear that one moving box was all I'd need. His toiletries, a handful of books, the few of the clothes people had given him that he chose to wear, it amounted to less than one box. Between Carthage's ego and all of the media attention, I'd come to see our project as a big deal, the rebirth of Jeremiah a world-changing thing. To find it reduced to so few possessions was humbling.

I was on my way out, giving the room a final scan, when I felt the impulse to neaten it. The books formed a tidy stack on a shelf, earbuds on top. Making the bed, I felt something under his pillow. I reached beneath: the stuffed raccoon. First I felt sadness, a pang of loss. Some kind of innocence was gone now, would not be coming back. Then I felt anger, a flare of stubbornness. He had jumped to protect me. Now it was my turn.

I tossed the extra box in the middle of the room, a clue for anyone who might be interested. But then, video tapes would show everything anyway. Presuming the monitors were still running, that is. There's not much to document if your subject is gone.

I would have liked to say a few goodbyes, but there was no point in wasting my head start. Also I wasn't quite finished. There was one more thing I wanted, for Jeremiah.

The basement was bright, fluorescent tubes hung in pairs from the ceiling. Pipes angled here and there overhead. I'd been to the Project's storeroom several times, to deposit gifts Jeremiah had received on our walks through the city.

A new sign hung on the door: 'Lazarus Project Property. No unauthorized access. No removal of contents without written E. C. approval.'

Although I wondered how gifts to Jeremiah had become Project property, I felt sure E. C. would not approve my removal plans. I swept my badge through the reader, but the door did not unlock. I tried again, no luck. Had Carthage already blocked my access? This was a problem. If I went back upstairs, who would lend me their badge, knowing that the Project's mainframe keeps track of where and when each badge is used?

'Oh come on,' I said, jerking on the doorknob fruitlessly.

'Allow me get that, would you, lovely?'

I turned to be greeted by a crooked-toothed grin. 'Graham Billings, you savior. Would you mind?'

'Shown you the door too, has he?'

'Not quite yet. So Carthage has just fired you?'

'Approximately.' Billings swept his card through the slot, we both could hear the electronic bolt slide back. 'I'm half-fired, half-resigned.'

I laughed. 'We're in the same club. You're just a few hours ahead of me.'

'Although apparently my card still works.' He bowed. 'After you.'

'Always the gentleman.' I went ahead with the cardboard box.

Someone had organized the room since my last visit. Shelves lined the walls, as well as rows up the middle, with gray plastic bins on them. The bin labels bore unmistakable, perfect handwriting. 'So, why did you and Carthage part ways?'

'Hard to say, Kate. For his part, lack of glamour, I'd wager. For my part, I discovered things in the small species samples I didn't want a pig like him to possess. Then it was merely a matter of annoying him, and feigning intimidation.' Billings strolled to the far wall, pulled down a bin, poked through the papers inside. 'Here it is, lucky first grab.' He snatched a file, shoved the bin back. 'I'll still receive my contractual severance check, with which I intend to treat myself to three decadent weeks in Maui.'

I stalked the aisles, scanning labels for materials associated with Jeremiah, working from the most recent backward. 'Sounds like you have a good plan.'

'If I borrow a few documents for my next project, yes. Metabolic studies of reanimated species before we found the judge. A professional parachute, you could say.'

I stopped at the end of the row. The label read: Subject One Arrival Attire. I slid the bin outward as it tipped heavily.

'Let me help you there.' Billings set down his papers, took the bin, lowered it to the floor. 'What are we hunting for, might one ask?'

The bin was sealed with tape, on which Thomas had written the date we reached Boston with Jeremiah's frozen body. I broke the seal, yanked the lid, saw the topmost items: a well-worn pair of heavily oiled, high brown boots. I picked one up, tracing my finger over the ornate C on the sole. 'These.'

Billings crossed his arms. 'I have the strangest sense right now, as if I'd gone to the loo during intermission of a play, and returned having missed rather critical scenes.'

'They're his boots. He wants them back.'

'You'll hear no argument from me, Kate. I'm a thief here myself.'

With the boots in hand, I felt less distracted. 'Yes, I'm sorry. You said you'd found things in the small species, things you didn't want to share.'

'Indeed I did. Just between us girls?'

'Of course.'

'Well, it has to do with metabolics.' He grinned. It was the nerd's smile, I'd seen it all my professional life, whenever someone seeking something difficult or arcane had actually found it. Probably I'd worn that look a time or two myself.

Billings rubbed his palms together. 'What did Borden call it, "hibernating bear"? An apt phrase, that. You see, regardless of what species you've animated, they always recommence at an astonishingly low metabolic rate, processing food and oxygen almost in slow motion. Very nice, a gentle start on their tummies and the like. The pickle is that whatever mechanisms regulate metabolic rate, well, apparently they quite break down during the frozen time, don't they? Nor does the tempo stabilize once it reaches normal. No, it grows faster and faster, the creature moves ever more quickly, it consumes fuel at an exponentially accelerating rate, and the poor thing just burns right out.'

'I've seen this, of course, with shrimp and so on. What are you saying?'

'Our man Carthage may be a genius when it comes to reanimating, but he's built a sloppy record of *keeping* things animated, hasn't he?'

His meaning hit home. I stepped back, bumping against the shelves. 'Oh no.'

'And yet,' Billings continued, 'no one has done much study on why the poor creatures perished, much less on what might keep them alive longer.'

I could barely look at him. 'Except you.'

'We see where that got me. In a basement, stealing files. A shame too, for the little darlings die off no matter what, sure as the sunrise, and quickly, too.'

I dropped the boots. I felt as if I might drop too, so I lowered myself to the store room floor. 'How quickly?'

'It is an accelerating logarithm, Kate. Oh, I could show you some pretty graphs.' Billings was lost in the findings, his hands swooping in the air. 'Once the curve trends upward, it does so elegantly, at a uniformly increasing pace.'

'How do you know when it has begun?'

'Extrapolation is risky, my dear. All my data are from minuscule—'

'How will I know, damn it?'

Billings gave me a look of surprise, which melted into one of fondness. I felt the fullness of our history together. Nights in the lab finessing samples that refused to cooperate, frigid dives in polar waters, bourbon on the train while we escorted Jeremiah home. Not to mention endlessly commiserating on what hell it was to work for Carthage.

'Well, well. I may be slow, but hit me with a hammer enough times and it might sink in. Here I am prattling on about graphs, while you . . .' He cleared his throat. 'Right. You and I have made a proper muck of things, haven't we Kate?'

'Do you think so?'

'I'm straight out of a job. And you're in a far worse predicament, aren't you?'

'I don't know. Maybe. Probably.'

'I'm terribly sorry.' He sighed. 'I suppose it is entirely too late for me to suggest maintaining scientific perspective or upholding professional distance.'

'Entirely.' I fiddled with one of the boots. 'Who else knows about this? Has anyone told Jeremiah?'

'Not a chance. Carthage didn't even tell me, until I'd confirmed it myself. I thought I'd discovered a solution, but it turned out to be bollocks. Carthage thinks he has a better answer, but in the lab I've already found how his way fails.'

'So how will I know, Billings?'

'Indeed.' He coughed into his fist. 'Very well. Palsy. If he begins to shake like an old woman with Parkinson's, or some Bowery drunk fighting DTs, then you'll know he has taken his place somewhere on that miserable curve.'

I nodded. My throat felt clogged, but I had to ask. 'What if he's already shaking?'

'It's begun already? Well then. I'd say, well, monitor other metabolic signs. You know the lot. Increased appetite, diminished need for sleep.'

I began quietly, to weep. 'Then what?'

'I hate to see you this way, lovely. After all we've been through. Can't bear it.'

'Tell me. Please.'

'Ah Kate. There's no predicting the rate, only the bloody outcome.'

I cried for a minute or so, letting the tears spot my dress a darker green. *Jeremiah. Watching your fingers jiggle on the bench at Lynn. Reading in my house and sitting on your hands. Hugging at the cemetery and your hand flapping.*

Gradually I collected myself. One of the boots had fallen upright. I hugged it into my lap, looking into the opening like into a leather mouth. 'Is there anything I can do?'

He didn't answer. When I raised my eyes, I saw that Graham Billings was gone.

CHAPTER 35

WINNING LOTTERY TICKET

(DANIEL DIXON)

That was the day everything turned in my favor. If I had anyone to thank, it would have to be the bishop. I mean, at daybreak I'd been without a plan of any kind. Just a raging frustration like I was strapped in a straitjacket.

Fact is, that bastard Carthage had stumped me in about ten seconds. He knew right where to hit. No security badge, no going inside. That green binder might as well be on the moon. I'd spoken to my editor that night. He said he'd be damned if he would take on the likes of Erastus Carthage without hard evidence. He was right. The word of Daniel Dixon against that of Dr Nobel? The fact that I was telling the truth wouldn't matter a tinker's tit.

But the bishop changed the game. Or maybe he just made the game visible to me. I'd been watching it take shape for months now, always thinking it was about Carthage, or Jeremiah Rice, or window-shopping Dr Kate's personal merchandise. Not until the bishop spoke about the author of life and the crowd cheered him like crazy did I realize that this saga was actually all about me.

Because when fourteen-year-old Daniel Dixon pulled his parents from that fire, dead of smoke inhalation before a single flame had touched them, his relationship with mortality was permanently forged. That terrible night showed me right up close how the body endures after death, as if all it needs is one good clean breath to sit back up again and tell me to finish my homework. Not to mention schooling me that no matter how desperately we want to believe otherwise, death is the most solid, final, unarguable thing that exists.

While I coughed so hard I thought my lungs would come out my nose, with each gasp I was becoming the perfect dupe for Carthage. Who better than a sucker who spent the rest of his life wishing there was a way to cheat death?

All those years as a reporter, though, also taught me to see things as they are. A situation may be foggy at the start, but reality burns it off to amazing clarity. That's why I eventually was able to discover that the Project was bogus from top to bottom, stem to stern, start to finish.

The one thing I hadn't figured out was why. What motivated Carthage to concoct the whole business? He was never short of cash, and already had professional prestige, so why? I flopped onto a bench outside the Project entry that morning, to chew on that question a while.

Of course I sat alone. I always sat alone. Not

self-pity, just a fact. When you're not supposed to get close to the people you're writing about because it will wreck your objectivity, and when you're prickly by nature because you see the world's flaws too clearly, and hell, when you're forty-five and fat since childhood, you get to be a goddam expert at sitting alone.

At least the entertainment was first rate. I watched Wade work the noisy red-shirts into a good lather, waving that stupid invitation of Carthage's like a cape before a bull, and bringing the gang to peak decibels just as the bishop's limo wheeled up.

But the control was not complete. When His Excellency wanted to speak, it took Wade quite a few minutes to settle them down. Even then, they kept interrupting with shouts, chants, a manic energy that made me nervous. It felt edgy, like the pot was close to boiling over. I moved to another bench, to watch from across the street.

After the bishop left, they'd done one more bit of yelling for the cameras. Shut it down, shut it down, neither brilliant nor catchy but it made the point. As the news teams packed up, I thought of that old tree-in-the-forest question: if there's no media to publicize a protest, is it really taking place? Captain Handsome went somewhere on a break, but the shouters did not dissolve like usual. They were too het up, bustling around in their red shirts like a bunch of salmon trying to find the way upstream.

Who should flop beside me on the bench just then but Gerber, looking as rough as if someone stopped his reanimation halfway through. 'What the hell happened to you?'

'What do you mean?'

I laughed. 'You look like you climbed inside a vat of whiskey three days ago and crawled out ten minutes ago.'

'What day is it today?'

'Friday. Must have been quite a bender.'

Gerber dropped his face into his hands and gave it a long groaning rub. A few of the shouters noticed us, and turned to make some noise in our direction. They kept to their side of the street though. The bit about blocking traffic had come and gone. Besides, Boston's finest had arrested more than a hundred of their pals, who sat rusting in cells because the judge refused to set bail till they provided their actual identities. On a sunny summer morning, the sidewalk looked much more inviting.

'No,' Gerber spoke through his fingers. 'Not a bender. Just four straight days trying to figure something out.'

'Hey,' I said, 'you don't have to worry about my opinion. I figure you're probably not even in on it.'

He cocked his head, taking me in with one eye. 'What are you talking about?'

'That beautiful fraud known as the Lazarus Project.'

'You're crazy,' he said. He arched against the bench's back, letting his neck tilt till his face was pointed at the sky. 'What are the idiots yelling about today?'

'The usual. The Project, Jeremiah, God.'

Gerber brought his head back to level. 'Their signs are getting better.'

He was right. Wade had brought them from magic-markered cardboard to painted boards with good square lettering, held high on wooden dowels. The slogans were sharper too: *Smart ≠ Moral*, *Jesus Loved the Real Lazarus* and *God Is Not Ignorant*. My favorite was *I'm With Stupid*, only the T was a crucifix.

Gerber let out a long sigh. 'Am I wrong or are they louder than usual?'

'It might be your hangover.'

'You're not listening, Dixon. It's not partying. I have been working around the clock since Tuesday morning.'

'I thought you saved that kind of effort for NASA. What's cooking?'

'Only the toughest thing since we restarted the good judge's heart.'

'Come on. The guy's out gallivanting all over town with Dr Kate.'

'I thought we had a huge mess, but I may have found an answer. I always had a feeling the salt method was off.'

'What are you talking about?'

He kept on like I wasn't there. 'Then Billings

left these findings on my desk, before he bugged out, about oxygen saturation. Which was pure genius, except that he didn't have a delivery mechanism because of the hemoglobin ceiling.'

I chuckled. 'You are now officially speaking Greek.'

Gerber laughed too, but I had a feeling we were not amused by the same thing. 'This morning one of the techs was joking about being so tired he wanted an I.V. bag of coffee, and it hit me: transfusion.' He turned to me, goggle-eyed. 'Transfusion.'

'Yeah?' I said.

'Yeah, yeah. Just give the guy a bit more blood volume, not a ton, a pint or so would do it. There's the extra hemoglobin you need, which means more oxygen, which means less ammonia, which means no kaput. Done.'

I burst out laughing. I didn't care if it was lack of sleep or too much weed, the guy made no sense. 'Gerber, how you reached the top of your field, I will never know.'

'Haven't you been paying attention? Haven't you seen what's happening?'

'I like to I think I have.'

'Well, let me clue you—' Gerber caught himself then, and sat up. 'Sometimes I forget you're a reporter, you know? You've been around the lab for so long.'

'Don't worry. Whatever you say is peanuts compared to what I'm writing next.'

Somehow that took the wind out of his sails. He

went back to his slouch. 'Let's talk about that, then. Who knows if my idea will work anyway?'

'Well, I suppose I can tell you. It's not like you're tight with Carthage.'

'Who?'

I chuckled again. 'Right. Well, I've decided the time has come to blow the whole thing open.'

'What whole thing?'

'The hoax, the complete charade.'

Gerber rubbed his facial scruff. 'And you say I'm the one speaking Greek.'

'This Project, Gerber. I've been watching all along, and I finally figured out that it is a complete fake.'

'What are you saying to me?'

'There was no guy found in ice, no person brought back from the dead. It's all B.S. Don't worry, I figure only a few people were in on it, Carthage, Thomas, Dr Kate. The rest of you aren't acting, you really believe it. Otherwise why would a guy with your pedigree hook up with a bunch of phonies like them?'

'I'm beginning to think you're the one who's been boozing.'

'I have a whole collection of proofs, rock solid. Just wait, you'll see it in print.'

Gerber rubbed his face again, then squinted at me. 'Are you trying to tell me that Carthage gave you all this unrestricted access, for all these months, and the result is that you're going to reveal yourself as the stupidest man alive?'

'Or the savviest, I think.'

He stood. 'You know, Dixon, there are genuine problems with Jeremiah, things going wrong that no one knows how to stop. That's the real world. Your conspiracy fantasy, it's crazy. You're as twisted as those *goddam zealot protestors.*'

The last three words he shouted across the street. They definitely heard. They knotted tighter, they aimed their chant at him.

'What is it anyway?' Gerber continued. 'Why are they so pissed off today?'

'Probably this,' I said, and I handed him one of Carthage's invitations. Thomas had passed them out the night before. They were all over the street like litter.

WANTED: VOLUNTEERS.

> The Lazarus Project is enlarging its efforts to revive and strengthen human life, and is therefore seeking volunteers. We seek people to offer themselves for cryogenic stabilization for six months, after which the project will reanimate volunteers free of charge. Here is your opportunity to advance scientific knowledge and participate in the greatest achievement of our time.

Gerber read with eyes wide. 'What the fuck? What is this?'

'You see it for yourself, man. Let us kill you, then we'll bring you back. Who wants to sign up?'

'"Cryogenic stabilization?" Is this complete bullshit?'

'Is your reawakened Jeremiah complete bullshit?'

He frowned at me. 'But it's ridiculous. Why would Carthage taunt them like that? He barely knows how to find hard-ice, much less how to make it. And why would we freeze people if we—' Gerber shook his head. 'Why even start down that thought path? What the hell is Carthage trying to do?'

'Who knows? Maybe fire up some of that.' I pointed at the protestors, now all facing our way, hollering the old shut-it-down again. 'The man does love a headline.'

Gerber crumpled the paper into a ball. 'Am I living in a world of idiots?'

'If you allowed Carthage to fool you into giving your credibility to this bogus escapade, maybe you are the idiot.'

'Shut up,' he said, and threw the paper in my lap. Then he started across the street, yelling the same thing at the protestors. 'Shut up. *Shut up*.'

As soon as Gerber left the sidewalk, they took it as permission to do the same, and it was like watching a dog charge at a stampede. Only this dog was an exhausted, crazy-haired, skinny old geek, and the stampede was a pack of furious and frustrated people who'd spent months fighting for a cause only to see their prayers and passions not change a thing. They spilled into the street like a tide.

'Shut the fuck up,' Gerber said, gathering momentum.

'Shut it down, shut it down,' the crowd chanted. They fell into that swarm formation we'd seen them practicing, a circle of bodies in red shirts all trapping Gerber and closing in.

Wade came around the corner just then, his cocky smiling vanishing as he took in the scene. He broke into a run, yelling at everyone to hold back, clear away. But it was too late. Gerber bumped one protestor, who shoved him harder in reply. Then Gerber grabbed another man's sign, and the guy yanked back so violently it came free and hit him hard, diagonally across his forehead, drawing a stripe of blood. There was a pause, then a roar. And they descended on him.

I started toward the fight, but stopped with one foot on the street and one foot on the curb. I was not part of the Project. Also, if I tried to save Gerber I would get the same treatment. Wade pulled people off the back of the pack, but the ones at the front of the swarm pounded Gerber to the ground, then hoisted him upright again so they could batter him with their signs some more.

Something came flying end-over-end out of the melee. It lay in the street less than a second before I recognized what it was. The winning lottery ticket for Daniel Dixon, and anyone who wants to know the truth: Gerber's security badge.

⋆ ⋆ ⋆

'It's pandemonium out there,' I told the front desk guard, pointing. 'They're pounding hell out of Dr Gerber. You'd better get him some help.'

The guard took one look out the big front window and jumped from his chair. 'Henry we've got a fight out front,' he called into his walkie-talkie. 'Get me an ambulance and two black and whites, then hurry your ass down here.'

The guard rushed past me, pulling a nightstick from a holster on his hip. I waited till he'd pushed through the revolving door into the mayhem, then hustled past the security desk to the elevators, and swiped Gerber's badge through the electronic reader. I kept looking back till I heard the arrival bell, and the swish of elevators doors opening.

The bullpen of desks in the control room was practically empty, just two technicians murmuring over some problem in the corner. To stall for a minute, I ambled over to the latest *Perv Du Jour*. The site of the day was killfrozenman.com. People had definitely grown more inventive. There were the usual altered photos, this time with a drawing of a knife in the judge's throat, and a stick of dynamite crayoned into his mouth. But there also was a soccer ball wearing a Red Sox cap, with pruning shears jammed in one side. The top of Gerber's display, cream of the day, was a guy with a lippy grin toting an assault rifle. He stood outside someplace beside a watermelon with its top half blown off, red sprayed everywhere. The lower half wore a bright yellow tie.

One technician left the room, the other sat with his back to me. I reached into the *Perv* inbox, slid out the green binder as cool as a gambler collecting his winnings, then went straight to Gerber's desk.

It was just as I'd hoped. His computer was still on, files open. His headphones lay beside the keyboard, whining away. I pushed them aside and began slapping keys.

Everything was in impeccable order. I would never have guessed Gerber for the fastidious type, but there it all was, names, dates, file types. I created a new folder and loaded it with copies: photos going back a year, spreadsheets of daily vital signs, videos from the ship and control room and press conferences and even the judge's chamber.

I glanced in its direction, and saw the deserted room. No sign of the occupant, not even a shirt hung over a chair. Just an empty cardboard box, lying on its side. Wasn't that a perfect metaphor for this colossal con? A box full of nothing. And then a perfectly wonderful, nasty idea occurred to me, and I picked up the phone. Toby Shea at the *Globe* had done good work on the Project, writing sidebars that added color to my stories. It was decent stuff, given that he lacked my inside access. He deserved the first call.

'This is Shea.'

'Toby this is Daniel Dixon, the guy covering the Lazarus Project.'

'Really? What brings Daniel Dixon to be calling me?'

'Well, there's a lot breaking around the Project today.'

'Yeah, I saw the bishop on the noon news.'

'There's more, and I'll be writing a bunch of it. But there are some things I won't have time to get to. You've done good work, I thought I'd throw you a bone.'

'Thanks, I think.'

I looked around the room. 'Oh, you'll definitely thank me, Toby. For starters, Jeremiah Rice is gone. Vamoosed.'

'No shit?'

'There's more. If you give me your email address, first thing tomorrow I'll send you the location where he's hiding.'

He told me the address letter by letter. 'What's your angle on this?'

'Can't say, Toby. But it's real. Just call the Project, ask to speak to Jeremiah, and listen to the stalling and stammering.'

'All right, I'm on it. Thanks.'

'No charge.' I put the phone down gently. It felt damn good, to spin this place back in the direction of truth at last. To start the world dancing to my tune for once.

I decided to make two more calls, one to the *Herald* and one to the TV station that got us into the Red Sox game. Then the reporters' email addresses went into my pocket for use the next morning, and out came my trusty old thumb drive. I plugged it into the side of Gerber's machine, and with three clicks started the process of downloading that new folder into my permanent possession.

The computer told me the process would take approximately two minutes. What the hell, I figured. I reached over for the headphones and clamped them snug on my noggin. A song was just ending, in an ever-quieter fade. I just sat back, put my feet up, and waited with the silence to hear what was coming next.

CHAPTER 36

THE LAST EGG

(KATE PHILO)

When I emerged from the bedroom that morning, he was sitting on the couch right where I'd left him the night before. Only the book in his hands had changed, *A Tale of Two Cities* now, with *Jane Eyre* on the coffee table.

'Good morning Jeremiah,' I said in a sunny voice. 'How did you sleep?'

'Just fine, thank you,' he said, standing, a finger holding his place in the book.

We were such liars. I could see the blanket folded exactly as I'd left it. The pillow at the end of the couch bore no imprint from his head. But then, his free hand looked steady, calmer than the night before. A good sign? No way of knowing.

'Don't let me interrupt you,' I said. 'I'm just going to make a pot of coffee.'

'Can I be of any help?'

I pressed my palm to his chest. 'Just read, friend. I'll be right back.'

'Your hair . . .'

'What about it?' I said, pulling it back.

'No no, leave it down,' he waved a hand.

'Really?'

'Please. It is a vision of femininity.'

A what? I stood there mute, an awkwardness until he sat again. Finally I started for the kitchen in the back of the apartment. From that day forward, I never put my hair up again. Say what you may about his influence on me in those waning days, I make no apology. The scientist, the credible adult, as a result of his compliment I abandoned those appearances forever.

After a moment, I snooped from the hall. Both of his feet were jiggling like he'd had twenty cups of coffee. So much for steady hands.

So far, I believe I'd done fairly well with concealing what Billings told me. Jeremiah was pleased enough with his boots not to notice my mood when I returned to the apartment. I'd cried good and hard when I went to bed, but don't think he heard me. I resolved, while brushing my teeth, to use to the utmost my ability to hide my emotions behind calm. So I went about filling the coffee maker with water, grinding beans, humming to myself as if it was only my friend Meg from Baltimore in the other room, and we were planning a leisurely day at the museums.

What were we going to do with this day? How should we use the time we had left? Should I tell Jeremiah what was happening? Oh, he would know soon enough. What matters most, when time is running out?

The physical sensation, there in the kitchen, was that I had no feet. Gravity might be tethering me to the ground, but somehow no actual contact was occurring. Then the coffee was ready, I poured myself a hot mug, I opened the fridge for milk. What I saw brought my full weight right back to earth.

One egg. The yogurt was gone, lettuce, all the fruit, cheese, leftover Chinese. Everything else was gone, except one egg in a bowl. I took it out, weighed it in my hand.

'I apologize Kate.'

I started at Jeremiah's voice. He stood in the doorway with a melancholy face.

'I was famished last night. All night. It's hard to explain. Embarrassing too, that I ate nearly everything. I'm sorry.'

'It's fine,' I said, wrapping my fingers around that egg. 'I told you already, you're welcome to anything in here.'

'But I finished all sorts of things, Kate. Your cereals, bread, crackers.'

'We'll just go to the supermarket. It'll be fun.'

'I'm hungry all the time now.'

'You don't have to explain anything to me.' I could have told him then, perhaps I should have. But I turned away, splashed the last of the milk into my coffee, took a hot gulp. *I do not want to lose you.* 'I'll tell you what, Jeremiah. Why don't I fry this last egg for you right now?'

'No Kate. I appreciate your offer, but you see I

deliberately held back on that. In view of me eating so much already. I saved that egg for you.'

'That's just silly,' I said.

'It's not. I want you to have it.'

'Jeremiah, we can go buy three dozen eggs as soon as I finish this coffee.'

'That's fine, and very generous of you, provided you eat that one first.'

I stared down into my coffee mug. He was trying to be generous, with no idea what his appetite signified. It was all as Billings had said. My heart felt like a black scribble. 'Why don't we compromise?' I said. 'I'll cook the egg, and we'll share it.'

'Kate, when have I been in a position to give you something? I honestly would prefer if you had it, the whole thing. Please.'

I laughed in spite of myself. 'Now you listen here, Jeremiah Rice—'

There was a loud banging on my front door.

'Hold on,' I called, setting the egg on the counter. I hurried to the entry. I'd rented that place for almost a year, while spending nearly every waking hour at the Project. This was the first time anyone had knocked on my door. 'Who is it please?'

'Toby Shea, *Boston Globe*. I'd like to speak with Jeremiah Rice.'

Panic seized me. I had imagined our accelerating misery as a private matter, something the two of us would experience quietly together. At once I felt all sense of security turn into vapor. 'I need a minute,' I said. 'I'm not dressed.'

I hurried into the bedroom, peered through the curtains. I couldn't see the front door from there, but a TV truck was pulling into a space across the street. Meanwhile a woman with a notepad was marching down the sidewalk from the other direction. A photographer juggled his equipment while trying to catch up with her.

Back in the kitchen. Jeremiah stood where I'd left him. 'You look frightened. What is the matter?'

'We have to get out of here. Grab what you need right now. We'll come back later for the rest.' I threw a few things into a backpack, jammed my feet into sneakers, jogged back to the hall.

'Dr Philo?' There was more knocking. 'Can I come in now, please?'

'Just one more second,' I called.

Jeremiah had pulled on his high brown boots. I took his arm, pulling him to the low window of the kitchen. 'Be right there,' I yelled.

He gave me a puzzled look. 'Why are you not answering the door?'

'You remember those paparazzi I described to you?'

'Is it them?' Jeremiah stood so openly, listening, trusting. It was all I could do not to throw my arms around him.

'Not quite. But there are other people who could intrude in our lives too.'

'I don't understand. I'll do another interview. We've not done anything wrong.'

'That doesn't matter. They will stop at nothing.

They chased a princess until her car crashed and she died. Now they are after us. Please trust me, and come on.'

Easing the window open, I stepped out onto the fire escape. The alley behind my apartment was narrow: trash bins, locked up bicycles, the backs of houses on the next street. It was another sunstruck day, no clouds in any direction. There were no reporters in sight, either. Jeremiah climbed out next to me.

'Not a word,' I whispered. 'No speaking till we reach my car.'

He nodded. I tiptoed down the metal stairs, feeling his weight descend behind me. Now began the chase, the time of we two apart from the world.

Not until we'd gone two blocks did I realize. We had left that last egg behind.

CHAPTER 37

EVERYTHING ELSE

(DANIEL DIXON)

Imagine a surgeon lying on the operating table. A teacher curled in a too-small student desk. A chauffeur sitting in the back seat. A chef at a table, waiting for his food.

That was me, on the sunny morning when my days as a magazine writer came to an end. Instead of covering the news, I was making it. Instead of being a spectator, I was the spectacle. The first reporters trickled in to the hotel conference room, and I decided not to watch Carthage-style, from offstage. I came down among the chairs.

'What's this all about, Dixon?' one of them asked.

'You are not going to believe it,' I said. 'You are just not going to believe it.'

I had witnessed the scene thousands of times, how reporters settle themselves, TV people acting like they own the goddam place, print photographers ignoring the rows of chairs while they clamber for an interesting angle. An editor I recognized from the *Herald* gave me a wave. He'd brought a couple of interns, as young as spring chicks, though one brunette among them was leggy enough that I would have been happy to take her into a back room and treat her like a grown-up. Peaches, peaches, peaches. So I'm a pig; sue me. Even the *Phoenix* sent someone, butch-haired and wearing a peasant dress, as you might expect from an arts weekly.

The crowd was maybe not as large as I'd hoped, but plenty enough. I was relieved to see no one flying the flag for the Lazarus Project. That meant none of the contradiction I'd worried about. I'd rather tell my whole story, let them do the denying and explaining.

The early signals were good. Toby Shea was not there, nor the others I'd emailed that morning. I could just imagine what they were interrupting, at the little love nest across town. Better yet, if the sweethearts bolted, a phony reincarnated man running off with an attractive woman, the tabloids would go crazy. It would give the lunatic media the thing it likes most of all: a chase.

At six minutes after the hour, Carthage's preferred lateness for starting these things, I went to the front and called hello. The reporters murmured their way down like a crowd in a theater. I picked up my projector remote. Damn if I wasn't nervous. I felt like a high diver, peering over the edge at the water way down below. Then I jumped.

'Thanks for coming, ladies and gentlemen. I know you're here because it's your job, but I think you are also going to enjoy yourselves. First, though, I have to apologize. We all pride ourselves, in the news biz, on being skeptical, right? Suspicious, hard to fool, independent in our ideas? Even so, sometimes we get duped. I asked you all here because I was duped. And I think I have some responsibility for you being duped too.

'In the last eleven months I have filed more than two hundred bylines on the Lazarus Project. You've picked up those stories, localized them, adapted them for your readers and audiences, printed the photos, played the videos. And along the way, we have collectively tricked the public into believing in something that does not exist.'

A hand shot up at the back. 'What does not exist? Can you clarify, please?'

'Relax, you'll get the full story. Or as close to the truth as I can come at this point. I've prepared four proofs and I'm going to lay them right out for you.'

The hand rose again. 'Proofs of what, though?'

'Damn buddy, did you forget to pee on the way in here?' Everyone laughed at that, and I could feel my guts untying. 'Easy, OK? I'm going to give you proof that the Lazarus Project is a fake. A phony. The whole shebang.'

I felt the in-breath. I saw their eyes widen, their backs straightening in the chairs.

'Now your skepticism is in full gear. You're not going to believe me, because you already believe them. And what I wrote before. That's fine. Just let me start, and you judge for yourselves.'

I nodded at the hotel guy in the back of the room, who lowered the lights. When I pressed a button on the remote, the first photo went up on the screen. It felt like a lifetime since I'd snapped it, on the bridge of that ice-crusted research vessel: Captain Kulak and Dr Kate standing at the front window, looking out at a spot-lit wall of white.

'This is the night we found the iceberg that allegedly contained Jeremiah Rice. When I snapped it we had been near the berg for about twenty minutes. What do you notice about Dr Kate Philo in this photo?'

I remembered the first time I looked at this pic. I enjoyed seeing her sweet backside in that tight diving suit, dead center. But now all I saw was the diving suit.

'What you have here is a researcher, supposedly just awakened in the middle of the night. Now, this is one of the coldest places on earth. No one wants to dive unless it's totally, absolutely necessary. You can die in an instant.

'So let me ask: how often do you all get out of bed and put on specialized clothes? Anybody here this morning slap off the alarm and then dress in football pads? Anyone here wear a flak jacket while brushing your teeth? Then why would a scientist start her day in diving gear, unless she already knew that she'd be going in the water?'

'What are you saying here, Dixon?'

'I'm saying that they made mistakes, that they left a trail.'

'Yes but a trail of what?'

'Decide for yourselves. And let me clarify, right up front, that I don't think all of them are in on it.' I shuffled a little while talking to calm my nervous energy. 'Some people at the Lazarus Project are doing an honest job based on what they've been tricked into believing. But the central crew is just a pack of actors.'

'You realize how defamatory that accusation is?' that same reporter persisted.

'Easy.' I wagged my fingers at him. 'Four proofs. Hold on to your hats.'

The first proof was interruptions in documentation. I showed them the video of the digging at the ice, which ends when Jeremiah's hand is revealed. They'd seen it before, but not in slow motion. Now everyone could see how it blips, how in the instant the hand ought to be visible, instead there is a rush of divers, the screen fills with bubbles, there's a minuscule skip in the tape, and only then is there the hand.

'Let me show that again.' I froze one second before the skip, Dr Kate's glove at the lower right, then one second after, and her hand was higher. 'Now sure, the diver could have accidentally shut off his camera for one second, because of the jostling, then right back on. It's possible. But it looks to me like the video has been doctored.'

I heard them rustle in their seats, so I hurried to the day of reanimation, and the moment Dr Borden gave Jeremiah the full blast from his electric panel. The lights went out. Billings yelled. The lights came back and there was Jeremiah, breathing. Again the editing was plain to see. And the blackout was so basic a stunt it seemed amateurish.

'How we doing?' I said, because the crowd had gone quiet. No one answered.

'OK, proof two. A man from 1906 should not know things from today. But what if he does? I'm showing little things here, I admit. But these are brilliant people, and a well-oiled deception. Still, even geniuses make mistakes. The little things add up. Let's watch some baseball.'

I showed them Jeremiah's pitch, the ball smacking the catcher's mitt. 'You get it? The mistake is that he was way too good. In theory at this point the guy has been unfrozen for two months. Come on. He must have played college ball. Otherwise aren't we seeing unreal heat for a guy who hasn't thrown in a hundred and ten years?'

A few people chuckled at that. I was rolling. 'Now check this out.'

I pressed play, and there was the TV station's footage of Fenway Park, everyone on their feet, giddy from beating the Yankees. They're singing 'Tessie' with gusto. Then the camera zooms in on Jeremiah, and he is mouthing right along with the words.

'Pretty neat trick, right? How does a guy born in 1868 know the words to a song the fans started singing in 2006?'

'Jesus H.,' said the hippie from the *Phoenix*.

'I know, right?' I replied. 'Now let's hear it from Jeremiah Rice himself, or whatever his real name is.' Then I showed a bit the good folks at Fenway had allowed me to copy from their security cam. It showed that lady accosting Jeremiah. He holds up his hands like he's being robbed and declares, 'Yes, that's what I am. A fake.' Out of context, sure, but I felt clever enough about that clip that I played it again anyway. 'Yes, that's what I am. A fake.'

The reporters were all busy writing, heads down. A few tapped rapid-fire on their laptops. Now I was hitting my stride. 'Proof number three. The loot.'

These were snapshots and I flipped through them rapid-fire: Jeremiah trying on running shoes. A tailor holding a jacket while Jeremiah slips an arm into a sleeve. Jeremiah grinning at a jeweler, while holding a gold watch up to his ear.

'Are we going to get copies of this material?'

'Absolutely yes,' I said. 'I'll tell you this, too. Jeremiah has received so many goodies there is now a big locked storeroom of them at the Lazarus Project offices. I can't guess what it's all worth. But don't let that loot take your eyes off the big prize.'

I showed my photo of those men from the

meeting room, waiting by the elevator. Carthage is speaking while Thomas stands at attention.

'These guys are money,' I explained. 'Potential investors. Most of them run cryogenics companies, a few are biotech. Maybe you recognize some faces. Their folders contain a prospectus for commercializing the Lazarus Project's discoveries. Basically Carthage was looking to sell out, which is acceptable capitalism but unusual science, wouldn't you say? Oh, and the minimum entry point was one million dollars.'

I enjoyed the silence that greeted this news. 'Not all loot comes in the form of money,' I added. 'Sometimes access is almost better than cash.' On the screen I flashed a photo of Vice President Gerald T. Walker and his toothy trademark grin, with his arm tightly around Jeremiah's shoulders. There was a guffaw from somewhere in the room.

'Finally, proof number four, the romance.'

Oh, I had a quiver full of those arrows. Between my camera and the video files, I'd been stung by them a hundred times over the weeks: Dr Kate hugging Jeremiah before releasing his straps and wheeling him to the roof. The two of them squeezing hands at the first news conference. Jeremiah and Dr Kate strolling Back Bay arm in arm. Jeremiah and Dr Kate snuggled against each other in front of the moving sculpture at the Museum of Science. Dr Kate on a bench by a beach, her head in Jeremiah's lap. 'Not exactly the professional scientist-research subject relationship, am I right?'

I kept going. The two of them on a sidewalk at night in the North End, some fat guy singing melodramatically to them while Dr Kate leans against Jeremiah and moons like a teenager. A telephoto shot, the knockout of the series, in a cemetery north of Boston, the two of them so glued together it looks like they're having sex standing up.

'Get a room,' someone called, and people laughed.

The last one in that sequence was the night-time kiss outside her apartment, backlit by a convenient streetlight, as clear as if they'd done it on stage. I left that photo up a little longer, then switched off the projector like Perry Mason saying the defense rests. 'I'd guess that leaves not too great a margin for doubt, does it?'

The lights came back up. People took a minute to collect themselves. I thought about a snake digesting a fat frog it has just swallowed. That was them. Me, I just felt relieved.

'So let me understand this,' said a reporter in front. 'You're saying the Lazarus Project is fake, and they concocted this scheme for money and political influence?'

I held my hands out wide. 'If the people at the Lazarus Project have a better explanation, I'd like to hear it.'

'Why aren't you just writing this story yourself?'

'Believe me, I'd love to. But I've become part

of the story. They played me, and like a good Boy Scout I passed the garbage right along. That's why I'm handing it over to all of you. And, frankly, crossing my fingers that you get it right.'

'This coverage has been all yours, the whole way,' said a familiar voice from over by the wall. 'Why did you get it so wrong?'

I craned my neck, and damn if it wasn't Wilson Steele, looking like someone had pissed in his cornflakes. Which would be yours truly. How had he snuck in here without me noticing?

'Great question,' I said, stalling. I stared at my loafers, as if they had the answer. But they just looked as beat and unpolished as a reporter's shoe-leather existence. And then I experienced the great what-the-hell of my life. At that point, what did I have left to lose?

'Look, Wilson,' I said. 'All of you. We each have our blind spots, you know? If we're honest with ourselves. Weaknesses we may not even know we have, but the spinmeisters and professional deceivers can spot from a mile off. There are certain events in my past that made me an excellent tool for Carthage's fantasy, even with all my experience, a reporter perfectly susceptible.

'What events?'

'None of your goddam business,' I bristled. 'Besides, I'm not the only one he duped. You guys right here, you let this stay a press pool story, with everyone writing from my filings, for way too long and you know it. As far as I know only one newspaper got past the walls. The rest of you went right along with the game.

'But here's the main point I want to make, on the record and for the record. I am not Carthage's manipulated mouthpiece any more. And as far as I'm concerned, all embargoes and exclusives and deals of any kind, well . . .' I laughed, I had to laugh. 'Hell, they're dead.'

The reporters sat as still as statues, not even taking notes. It was like we were throwing a year's work out the window, running the correction to beat all corrections, and they knew it.

'Excuse me,' someone at the back called out. Now I have been to maybe two zillion news conferences in my career, and I cannot remember a single time that a reporter said, 'Excuse me.' No, you bark your questions, you interrupt, manners are for sissies. The rest of the room must have felt the same way, because everyone turned, a path cleared, and I saw that the speaker was Tucker Babcock, senior political columnist at the *Globe* practically since the days of my first byline. If Boston had an elder statesman of the news, Tucker Babcock was it – from his white beard to his bushy, intimidating eyebrows.

'Walk us through it, Dixon,' he said. 'Can you give us more detail on how you developed this information, and reached this conclusion?'

Well, I have been around long enough to know what a softball like that means. The days of being some unrecognized hack were at a definite end.

I took a chair from the front row, turned it backward, and flopped into it. 'So far you've heard the highlights. Now I'll tell you everything else.'

CHAPTER 38

THAT KIND OF MAN

My name is Jeremiah Rice and I begin to tremble.

Nor can I stop it, either. I awakened that day to the unusual sensation of ropes coiling up and down my legs, beneath the skin. Or was it snakes? My acquaintance with those creatures was limited to the harmless slitherers basking on our garden wall of a summer's day. Now these snakes were within me, strong, uncontrolled spasms. Over the minutes my muscles calmed, lowered to a tremor, and at last drooped as loose as sails without wind. I placed a palm on my chest and my heart had resumed its regular thrumming pace. A breeze raised the curtains into the room as though lifted by a ghost.

It was July, the miracle of July. When we set sail in August all those years ago, I did not know that my final July had just ended. This time, I knew. This time I lay back in bed, tasting the air and it was delicious, the sour tang of ocean a few hundred feet away, and three months after my awakening, the scent of salt no longer painful.

I had slept. After losing count, so many nights of wakefulness I longed for the peace of mindlessness, I had stretched myself beside Kate in the white iron bed of this inn, the lull of her breathing as steady and serene as the surf. Once during the night I was aware of our entangling, body to body with bedclothes between. Otherwise I had dozed into the depths, swimming deep waters, surfacing only now in midmorning.

Beside me the bed was empty. Through the warped opening in the bathroom door I could hear the shower running.

My view of life had changed in recent days. I found myself noticing, with breathtaking acuity, and . . . what was the word? Language came and went too quickly now, as if my mind lacked some glue to keep it long enough to say. *Appreciating*. Yes, I found myself appreciating everything. I could never pretend to be an artist or spiritualist, just a man of law, a servant of precedent and procedures. Yet now I was heightened, aware of each thing however humble. At dinner the innkeeper lowered a match to a candle, and the wick seemed to pull the fire into itself. The bread had a thick crust I had to bear down hard upon to bite, and foolish or no, I felt a fondness for my strong teeth. A lump of ice chimed in my water glass when I raised it. Life was filled to bursting, rich as a kingdom. The shortness of time was teaching me to notice.

When a man is dying, the world is loud, insistent, and vivid. Each thing however modest becomes exaggerated, because it is the last of its kind: the glint of a wave, the cry of a gull, the weight of clothes on my bones. More than once I wished that I had infinite pockets, so I could tuck aside one thing after another, keeping them somehow before everything vanishes. Yesterday a bee veered near to inspect me, then hummed off on its tireless errands, and I nearly wept as the sound fell away.

That first time, in the icy sea, I experienced the loss of everything in seconds. The pain was so unspeakable, vast and sudden, that fading consciousness brought relief. This time, losing the world by degrees, in full consciousness, is proving harder.

Once I thought I would become an excellent judge upon aging. Experience would give me wisdom. Now I know that I will never grow old. Yet I feel ancient already: less the master of my body, swept by tides of emotion, mindful that each thing I perceive is already on its journey away from me, and the wisest act I can perform is to *appreciate*.

Even now, the angling of the light into this room. The curl of the curtain as it falls from a slackening breeze. To call these things symphonies would be untrue. They are but two of the hundred thousand simultaneous extravagances known as existence.

Of course my keenest appreciation has been of Kate. She laughs and it is music. She takes my arm when we are strolling and it is serenity. She becomes pensive, increasingly of late, and I wait with affection for the shadow to leave her face.

A spasm gripped my foot, then passed. Hm. How much longer could I conceal my body's paroxysms from her? I wanted to shield Kate from worry for as long as possible. Perhaps today I would tell her. At least there was no pain.

Through the window I heard children playing. My mind leapt to Agnes, my cherub, and to Joan. Was I wrong to keep myself from Kate in their name? Was it honorable to remain steadfast in my vows regardless of how time had distorted them? The world of here and now made little sense. Joan was my foundation and firmament. When all else was unknown, her fidelity and generosity were certain and enduring.

Yet if I said that waking that dawn to find myself entwined with Kate was anything shy of comfort, anything less than delight, it would be falsehood.

Once upon a time, so long ago it feels like it happened to a different Jeremiah Rice, a woman loved me with devotion beyond my deserving. She bestowed the singular gift of a daughter, my heart's joy. Yet I left them blithely, arrogantly, certain I would return in a few months' time. On that voyage I lost everything of myself, yes, but worse, I inflicted who knows what hardships upon them, what undeserved suffering.

Now a woman of a new era offers me her kindness, her intimacy, whilst I know it is a matter of hours or days before I depart from her too. Am I to deny what happened the first time? Am I to join her in tenderness, give in to the desire like a fire in my blood, and inflict another generation of harm? I have already left behind one woman, one child. How can I conscience hurting another? Do I want to be that kind of man?

I sat upright, throwing back the sheet to see my diminished body. My time was escaping. Was the man ever-grateful for Joan's willingness incapable of being willing himself? Did I truly believe that withholding would spare either Kate or myself any grief?

Of course not. The bond existed already, consummated or not. The sweet entanglement of our sleep proved it. Our loss would occur, then, regardless of the happiness beforehand. My leg shuddered from ankle to hip, as if an instruction to me: it is better to live generously than to regret having lived with restraint. I would surrender to Kate that very night, I vowed it, and give her my fullest remaining self, grateful and entire. I was willing, yes, because sorrow is the price we pay for joy.

With that I roused myself, rising to dress. My clothes had begun to hang loosely, despite all the foodstuffs I gorged. My shirt slouched, my trousers drooped. At least my boot, my trusty old seaboot, slid on snugly and held me like the handshake of a friend.

I heard the shower stopping, and hurried with the other boot. Kate deserved private time to dress and settle in herself. She was generous, taking time from work and driving me up and down the coast. Rockport had galleries, Hyannis hotels. Everywhere change, everywhere cars and crowds and haste. Then we reached the National Shore. The relentless waves at Nauset pounded with their drumming and rush, a rhythm unchanged since I'd last seen them in my twenties, two turns of the century ago.

Eventually we landed in Marblehead, settling in this little inn among old houses near the docks. It chafed my masculinity, but as I had no cash, Kate paid for everything. One day she handed me some bills, so I might explore whilst she rested. Kate needed naps, of course, because I could persist without breaks both day and night. I returned with bread, grapes, and cheese, waited hours until she woke, and we made a light meal on a dock deserted but for we two. A wood drake swam by to lecture us. I felt as though I had never beheld a duck, its iridescent feathers, its comical nagging. A thing of beauty.

Kate nibbled and chatted whilst I showed restraint as well as I could. Then her face took a melancholy cast. 'Go ahead, Jeremiah,' she said, pushing the wedge of cheddar toward me. 'It's all right.'

I devoured that cheese as a dog would. The remaining grapes lasted seconds more. Kate ambled to the end of the dock. I followed and stood near. She leaned against me without a word. Even her silence was a pleasure. I promised myself to remember. If I was learning to appreciate, I must also honor experience by remembering.

That morning in our room I reached into the closet for my jacket, and tremors ran through my fingers. I wagged my wrist to shake them away, but that trick was becoming less effective. I hurried to make the bed, as I had done every morning with Joan. What are habits but a steady way of either honoring or diminishing ourselves?

The shower curtain slid back with a scrape of rings on rod, and I hastened to the hallway door. My instinct, call it perhaps my base animal self, could not resist, and it glimpsed through the cracked open bathroom door before my conscience had a change to intervene. I was the plaything of my own eyes.

There stood Kate amid the steam, hair wet and clinging to pink skin, stunning lovely brightness, the long, lean flank of her. She brought her nearer leg up on the toilet seat and rubbed downward with her towel.

I burst from the room and down the stairs, my body roaring and ravenous.

CHAPTER 39

WHERE ARE THEY?

(KATE PHILO)

He slept. After four days that I know of, four long nights without his eyes closing, at last he rested. He lay himself beside me, he curled his body into mine, he slept.

Sometimes when I see someone lose his temper, I imagine a place elsewhere in which a person is praying, or gardening, or performing some meditative action the opposite of the anger in front of me. That place is what it is like to sleep with Jeremiah Rice. The world may rush and rage, but you are in a realm of deepest calm.

Drying myself after a shower that morning, I considered another aspect too. When a man is revving so high he practically hums, a night of sleep is like hearing that a cancer patient's chemotherapy has worked. There may be a reprieve. Forty winks for Jeremiah made me hopeful again. I slept better too, relieved of worry for those tender hours.

Maybe it was the power of touch. Over those celibate months I had forgotten the effect of body on body, the warm weight, the way my arms wrapped him by instinct. So what if we hadn't had sex? I didn't expect it. There are many ways of taking a man inside yourself and filling both of you with pleasure. There are many ways of making love.

Oh, who was I kidding? What I felt for this man was want, in every meaning of the word: in my heart, in my sex, in the memories I hoped to hold for the rest of my life. Ultimately, I now understand, my yearning for Jeremiah might best be described as curiosity. After all, what is love but the desire to know another person as thoroughly and deeply as possible? Every quirk and passion, each response to the changes of time, every possible inch of skin? Also perhaps to be ourselves known, with all our flaws, yet somehow miraculously still be desired? In days past they spoke of lovemaking as a man and woman knowing one another. That is precisely how I wanted Jeremiah Rice. At long last, completely, to know him.

Also to save him from dying alone.

I left the bathroom wrapped in a towel, to see that he'd gone out. But not before making the bed first, which amused me. Jeremiah had done it in the motels on the Cape too, no matter how clearly I explained how the hospitality industry works. He'd listened, nodded, said he understood, made the bed the next morning anyway.

I was glad for the minutes alone. Not that I felt burdened by him, no. I craved every second that I could get. But matching his tirelessness was exhausting.

Also I needed to catch up online. I wanted to see what the world was saying, what Carthage was up to, without leading Jeremiah to think I was doing anything more than taking a vacation. While the computer booted up, I pulled on underwear and my last clean shirt. It was as yellow as a sunflower.

I sat at the dressing table that served as the room's desk, tucking my knees to one side. We were staying in a B&B, so the place was better equipped for downtime than for surfing. I had ninety-four new emails. None from Carthage. Half a dozen from Chloe with subject lines whose use of capital letters increased with each unanswered one. Plus interview requests, the usual attacks on my conduct and character. Ironically, those people were helping me grow a thick skin. If you're going to vilify someone anonymously and with lots of obscenities, at least check your spelling.

At the Project's site my account was disabled, password invalid. The public home page announced that Carthage was holding a news conference that day to refute the slanderous allegations against the Project.

Allegations? A quick search found this headline: 'Former Insider Claims Fraud at Lab.' One more search produced a video of Dixon's news conference, unedited.

I watched all fifty minutes, my emotions covering

miles along the way: surprise that Dixon had the nerve to challenge Carthage, dismay that he sincerely believed he had revealed us, concern about harm he might cause to the reputation of good people. I even felt badly for Dixon, figuring no one would be more damaged by this error than him.

When he reached his fourth proof, my sympathies evaporated. The vulture had been spying on us the whole time. It didn't matter that my relationship with Jeremiah was chaste. In Dixon's lens, we looked sordid. I felt rage at the invasion of privacy. Yet I kept viewing the photos, tugs of nostalgia at the waiter who sang to us, until the one where I held grieving Jeremiah in the graveyard. With his coarse sexual hinting, Dixon had managed to diminish even that.

My first impulse was protective. I could take this onslaught, ugly as it was. I could explain everything. Jeremiah, for all of his intelligence, was unequipped.

My search found one more story, media writing about the media, which was most chilling of all. Yes the paparazzi were seeking us, they staked out the Project offices, they chased every tip and rumor about our hiding place. The scary part was that some of the protestors were following them. Wade tepidly disavowed the conduct of his followers, one of whom was quoted: 'It doesn't matter whether these people demean the sanctity of life through science or through lies. They are evil and must be stopped.'

I closed the laptop. Now I felt especially glad

Jeremiah had gone for a walk. I needed to think. I pulled on jeans and jogged downstairs for the breakfast on which the Harborview Inn prided itself, a big coffee before anything else.

'There she is,' sang Carolyn, the proprietor of the inn whose white hair belied her energy and poise. 'And you have the place all to yourself.'

I had learned Carolyn's past over three prior breakfasts. A former travel agent, she bought the inn when she retired. That first winter she discovered yoga. Seven years later she not only attended class daily, she also fell into poses during conversation. Carolyn seasoned breakfast with her chatty history of Marblehead, banter about Massachusetts politics, jokes about her knees' ability to forecast storms – all while standing on one foot, or turning her head frighteningly far to the back, like an owl.

The first day she noted my coffee consumption. The next morning, she swapped the dainty teacup at my place for a tall red mug. I was, therefore, a fan.

She brought a thermos, filling my mug while stretching at the waist. 'Your friend had breakfast earlier and went out. Ate like a teenager, to tell you the truth.'

'I'm sorry about that. He has an endocrine problem.'

She arched her upper back, chest high. 'You don't need to tell me. The guy has thyroid written all over him. Scrambled eggs for you again?'

I blew on the coffee to cool it. 'Please.'

'Here's the day's blues,' she said, bringing newspapers from the counter. 'I'll be in the kitchen. Holler if you need anything, OK?'

'Thank you.'

'I mean anything,' she said, holding out the stack. 'Any thing.'

'Thanks very much,' I said, puzzling at her meaning as she stretched and bent her way out of the room. Then I turned the papers over and saw the *Herald*'s front page.

'WHERE ARE THEY?' read the headline, above a photo of our kiss outside my apartment. I flipped to the *Globe*. 'Couple Missing in Alleged Fraud.' It was incredible, complete with pictures of our faces cropped to look like mug shots.

I gulped coffee. It was clear the reporters believed Dixon. Carthage issued one written statement: 'We do not stoop to refuting nonsense.' Now there were questions about who was bankrolling the Project's work. Through it all, every reference to Jeremiah included me, our disappearance likened to the escape of Bonnie and Clyde.

Meanwhile Jeremiah was dying. There was nothing I could do. I had felt his body jump and twitch. I saw him eat enough for four people. In Falmouth a tremor struck just as he was raising a spoonful of chowder, spilling it on his front, and I ran for the restroom rather than have Jeremiah suffer the indignity of cleaning himself up in front of me. After that I'd managed to arrange most meals to be outdoors, at hamburger stands or lobster roll shacks.

I often wondered how much he knew. When we sat on the beach at Nauset, I watched him pour sand from hand to hand for a solid hour, studying the falling granules as intently as if they held the secret to everything unknown. I didn't dare interrupt.

Neither, however, did I find the courage to tell him. It was all another drive, another beach, anything but the truth. I felt like a scuba diver, swimming along with my tank full of oxygen, while the person beside me unknowingly runs out.

I threw the papers across the table. Right then, Carolyn returned with my toast and eggs. We made eye contact and she did not flinch.

'None of it is true, you know,' I said.

She set the plate beside my coffee. 'It's not important to me.'

'It is extremely important to me,' I said. 'And to Jeremiah. It's all lies.'

'I want you to know something.' She held a chair and arched her back. 'All kinds of people come through here, not all of them saints. I can keep a secret.'

'We have nothing to hide. There are predators, though, who would love to—'

'I don't blame you, anyway. A guy that unique? I'd want him for myself too.'

'That's not at all what I'm doing. Not the littlest bit.'

Carolyn smiled, not saying a word. She topped my coffee and left for the kitchen.

Is that what I was doing? Keeping him to myself? Or protecting him? Giving peace to him? Or to myself? I heard the inn's front door swing wide, Jeremiah's boots ringing on the wood floors. Passing the dining room he peered in, veered back to me.

'I had to obtain more food,' he said, 'and get some air. I love this old town, all the well-preserved houses. I hope you weren't worrying about me.'

'Not a bit.' I stroked his hand, then saw the papers spread on the table. I flipped them face-down. 'Did you chat with anyone while you were walking?'

He considered. 'Some children by the docks. I confused myself in the streets, and needed directions back. They were playing stickball. I showed one boy how to hold the . . . the . . .' He raised his hands, pantomiming while he searched for the word.

'Bat?'

'Exactly. *Bat*, yes. The lad had never heard of choking up.'

'Jeremiah.' I stared at my plate. 'Did any of those children recognize you?'

He smiled. 'I'd say so. The boy with the bat asked if I was "him".'

'Damn it all.'

'Are we in trouble?'

'Some people are after us again. Bad people.'

‘Hm.’ One of his hands fluttered up. He stuffed it in his pocket. ‘We need to go.’

‘Yes.’ I stood, my chair trumpeting on the floor as it slid back. ‘I’ll have to square things away with Carolyn.’

He led the way into the hall. ‘Let’s pack our things first.’

‘OK. But we don’t have much time.’

Jeremiah stopped short then, so quickly I bumped him. He took both of my hands in both of his own. He spoke in a solemn voice. ‘I know.’

So there it was. Unsaid, but somehow said. I raised one hand to touch his cheek. ‘I know too.’

CHAPTER 40

THOSE WHO STILL BELIEVE

(DANIEL DIXON)

Last time I was in a hospital, it was the night my parents died. The doctors admitted me for observation due to smoke inhalation. But I understood it was actually so they could help me handle a diagnosis of permanent orphanhood. Really, though, what help can there be? They gave me sedatives, so I did my crying quietly. The drugs lasted till the next day when my aunt and uncle picked me up and brought me to their house, where I lived four more years till college. It was never home; it was never supposed to be home.

I'm not singing any blues here, we all get our share. Only trying to explain why, when I hopped off the T that morning and made my way to the main entrance of Massachusetts General, I found myself hesitating on the threshold. The white stone exterior held so much glass I could see the giant paintings inside. I just stood there a minute.

There was no question of whether to go in, of course. While the regular media were busy chasing the missing couple, no one had thought to pay a visit to the person who already paid a physical price for their lies. Only me.

Was it creepy, doorstepping him in the hospital? Was it overboard to bring a camera? The answer is that it would make a great story. Anything is permissible if it makes a great story.

The woman wearing a 'volunteer' tag at the welcome desk could have been four hundred years old, but she looked up the room number and pointed me toward the elevators with cool competence. The young thing at the fifth floor nursing station was too skinny for my taste, but her directions had a little surprise at the end.

'Four doors down sir, but please keep it brief. He already has someone with him.'

Scooped after all. As I drew up to the half-closed door, though, I recognized the British accent chatting inside.

'Transfusion?' Billings coughed. 'Of course. Brilliant.'

'Hello, gents,' I said, swinging the door back.

It was like entering a walk-in freezer. Gerber took one look at me and rolled onto his side, staring at the opposite wall. Billings crossed his arms and scowled.

'Hey guys, I just came by to see how the patient is doing.'

Billings pointed. 'With a camera?'

'I take one everywhere, you ought to know that by now.'

'Parasite.'

Enough of him. He wasn't the one I came to see anyway. But Gerber, on inspection, looked like a prize fighter who should have retired three bouts ago. His eyes were blackened, he had a strip of stitches across his cheekbone, and one wrist was in some kind of splint.

'Whoa,' I said. 'You look like hell.'

'So says Mister Sunshine,' Gerber replied, still studying the wall.

'You have some nerve, coming here,' Billings said.

'Give it a rest,' I answered.

Billings started to speak, then shut his mouth without a word.

'Tell him about the song,' Gerber croaked. 'Start there.'

I resisted the urge to pull out a notebook. 'What are you talking about?'

Billings sniffed. 'That "Tessie" song you wrote about. You only did enough homework to find out they started singing it at Red Sox games a few years ago. But they sang it in Judge Rice's time as well. It was from a Broadway show.'

'You can't possibly still believe? Even now?'

'Don't be daft,' Billings said. 'The facts are plain. Your ideas are speculation.'

I crossed my arms. 'So now I'm supposed to believe he remembered the words for over a hundred years?'

'And while we're on the topic of shoddy reporting,' he continued, 'I'll have you know that I was wearing diving under-gear that night at the iceberg too. You didn't notice, because mine wasn't the backside you were ogling.'

'Look.' I gave a monumental sigh. 'There is no way at this point that you or anyone is going to change my mind about all of this.'

'Nor would I waste my breath trying.' Billings pivoted his head back to Gerber like a tank turret fixing on a target. 'You were speaking of hemoglobin.'

'For oxygen saturation,' Gerber said. He sounded spectacularly tired. 'Transfusing two units ought to be enough. The frenzy should pass, we'll break the cycle, and Judge Rice can live to inspire the tabloids for another day.'

'If you can find him,' I scoffed. 'That guy is as vanished as Amelia Earhart.'

'I'll follow the paparazzi,' Billings said. 'I have a trusty old motorbike. Also a certain debt that needs repayment. And now,' he approached Gerber's bed, 'you rest. You've done your part.' He turned for the door. 'Two units. I'll find him.'

'Thanks,' Gerber said, almost in a whisper, but Billings was gone. I tried to picture him on a motorcycle, helmet and leathers, and it did not compute.

We had an awkward silence then, Gerber and I. The nurses' call button rang a few rooms away. Someone hurried down the corridor, rubber heels squeaking on the linoleum. Gerber picked at his blanket.

Finally I was the one to break. 'I want you to know I believe you had no part in the fraud. They duped you, just like they duped me. I think you are actually legit.'

Gerber laid his hand flat. 'You know nothing.'

'I don't know why you're so pissed at me,' I said. 'I was the one who ran for help, when they all went berserk on you.'

Gerber blinked a couple of times, and I thought his eyes might be brimming. I couldn't imagine why. A sore wrist? A couple of stitches? What was there to cry about?

'Remember that bike helmet Judge Rice gave me, the one you teased me about?'

I put my hands on my hips. 'What about it?'

Finally he faced me head-on, and his look was solid ice. 'If I'd been wearing it that day, I wouldn't have gotten hurt.'

CHAPTER 41

KINDS OF POLITENESS

(ERASTUS CARTHAGE)

'I'm sorry sir,' Thomas says, standing in the doorway and wringing his hands. 'The printer is broken. A problem with the ink.'

You are facing the mirror, retying your necktie. 'For God's sake Thomas, use your brain. Does this place only have one working printer?'

'Of course not sir. But you insisted on keeping your computer separate from the network. You're not linked into anything else.'

'What time is it?'

'Quarter to eleven, sir.'

'Plenty of time. We have till six minutes after.'

'What would you like me to do, sir?'

You finish knotting, it's perfect, good enough for a banker. You lift the remote. 'I would like you to deal with it.'

'Yes sir. Of course.'

So he departs, and you command the television on. It remains tuned to the news channel that has found delight in your misfortune, the one which presented that fool's nonsense allegations as certain facts, and the one that you have not been able to tear your eyes from for the past five days. You wonder if they will have the temerity to attend your rebuttal speech that morning. If they do, would that be evidence of fairness, or gall?

As if in answer, the station breaks to the latest developments about you. Their position is evident even without sound, because of their symbol for this coverage, pasted electronically in the upper right of the screen: the Lazarus Project logo, standing on a house of cards, with one wall fallen inward. Subtlety is not this channel's strong suit.

But then, what developments could there be? Dixon has made no new allegations, despite repeating his initial claims for five days on every talk show and news program with a chair large enough for his hefty carcass. Meanwhile your press event hasn't even begun. How can there be developments without you?

The answer is a clip of Gerald T. Walker, vice president of the United States, standing at a podium in Wisconsin. Oh wonderful. A candidate, that most appetizing of human creatures, weighing in with his considered opinion based on the manufactured version of a fraction of the story. You do not bother to raise the volume, just wait for the ticker scrolling across the bottom of the screen.

And there it is: *Walker withdraws Lazarus Project endorsement, demands 'verification of reanimation claims,' calls for audit of all federally funded research.*

Tidy as a birthday present, and maligning not just you but every scientist in the country. He also conveniently forgot that this was a private lab, recipient of not one penny of federal coin. Here you thought reason had triumphed over emotion back in the Enlightenment. Apparently the vice president neglected to study history, a crime he would hardly be the first politician to commit.

'Thomas.'

'Sir?'

There is such a pleasure in how punctually that young man presents himself for duty. 'Do you have that printer working yet?'

'Almost, sir. Apparently it's a toner problem, and we're tracking down a replacement cartridge.'

'Fine. Please reopen my speech. We must add a reply to the vice president.'

'Yes sir. I'll be right in for your dictation.'

It only takes a moment, three sentences about Walker jumping to conclusions, how he will change his view once the facts become clear, and how the public would do well to follow that example. Thomas hurries off to update the document.

You stroll to the window, casting your gaze down on the street. Your fans are gone now, alas. Boston police finally took a dim view of their assembly, especially after what they did to Gerber. A nuisance, really, to have your best operations scientist still hospitalized a week later. You thrill a little to think of the protestors following the paparazzi now, chasing the chasers. Yet you liked having the crowd below, the motley opposition, a reminder of the world's cavernous ignorance.

Today is an opportunity to shine the light of reason into one corner of that grotto. This is going to be the lecture of a lifetime.

Your strategy is flawless. Instead of wasting precious time dismantling Dixon's flimsy fabrications, you are going to address the real issues, the scientific substance: discovering hard-ice, methods of reanimation, and above all, how Subject One was a predictable link in a long chain whose end remains nowhere in sight, beyond the horizon. Forget the allegations of a troll; let reality do the persuading. If these reporters have five brain cells between them, they will understand where rightness, factual rightness, lies.

You check the television again, and there is that house of cards once more. You capitulate, and turn up the volume.

'. . . Chinese laboratories saying they have duplicated reanimation of shrimp found in hard-ice. The officials added, however, that their findings proved conclusively that this process could not work on human beings.'

The program cuts to a man in a white lab coat, his face is familiar. He has an Australian accent and speaks with a frown, as if solemnity confirmed credibility. Yes, he worked here; you fired him for something or other. 'The wide range of tissue densities in a human body,' he declares, 'makes uniform melting a physical impossibility.'

'But we did it,' you tell the idiot box. 'We did it right here.'

'It is true for all primates,' the man continues. 'A person is not a Petri dish. A chimp is not a shrimp.'

You mute the television. A lie delivered in rhyme, science reduced to an advertising jingle.

Not for you. No, now is your moment to manifest the opposite. Today the media will receive a tutorial on cell biology, on glycogen stores and oxygen retention. A dash of physics, a brief explanation of magnetic fields, and they will be submissive playthings. It will take some time, granted. Two hours, perhaps, but they will learn something every minute. This is your moment to show the world the power of reason. How could they resist the muscularity of logic, the firmness of facts, the elegant strength of a proof?

'Thomas.'

'Sir?'

'The time, Thomas?'

'Ten fifty-five, sir.'

You wave him in. 'Again please. Events compel us to add a few more sentences.'

Twelve times you have addressed the media in a formal conference like this, twelve times since the discovery of Jeremiah Rice in the Arctic Ocean. On each occasion there was this moment, just beforehand, in which you stood slightly offstage and listened to the murmur and din. Their energy was like oxygen to you, their curiosity like food.

Yet this time the assemblage is silent. It's a puzzle. You stand at the edge of the atrium, one hundred chairs arranged in rows before the podium where you will put the allegations to rest, and ponder: why are there no conversations? No greetings from one scribbler to another? No calling from reporter to cameraman about the light or angle?

'What do you make of it, sir?' Thomas stands at your side.

'I'm assessing it myself.'

'Your speech is ready.' He offers you a manila folder. 'The printer was still a problem, so try not to touch the part of the pages where there is text. It could smear.'

You raise an eyebrow. 'Thomas.'

'I know sir, and I apologize.'

He remains, leaning forward, and you wonder if he is hoping for a compliment. He will have to wait. Instead, as you take the folder, he clears his throat. 'Do you think, sir, if you consider the present predicament, is it possible that we've made any mistakes along the way here?'

'Thomas, I'm surprised at you.'

'Not in the science, of course. No one else on earth could achieve what you have. I only mean, here we are, defending our work. I thought we were miles beyond all that.'

You flip open the folder, run pages under your

thumb as a dealer strums through a deck of cards. 'Absolutely not. You are about to witness our moment of triumph. And as for those times where *you* erred, Thomas . . . well, I want you to know that I forgive you.'

'What?' He flinched. 'You forgive me?'

'I do. After all, just look at them out there.' You point the folder at the reporters and photographers. 'See how courteously they are behaving?'

'Yes.' His throat is tight. 'Like guards politely escorting a man to his execution.'

'Nonsense.' You chuckle. 'Thomas the worrier. Just watch. This is the moment when the power of our desire for knowledge enlightens multitudes. It will be splendid.'

Thomas takes two steps back. 'Good luck, Carthage.'

What an odd tone. No matter. He'll be fine. You march into the briefing room, as confident in your power as on the day you first introduced Subject One to the world. This time, though, the source lies deeper. It resides in your long reverence for the scientific method, and in reason's unending capacity to improve the world. At the podium you open the folder, fill the water glass, arrange the papers. The room remains silent, then someone coughs and it sounds like a bark. You peer in that direction, but cannot tell who made the noise.

Only then do you realize. The atmosphere in this room is unlike anything you have encountered before. A whiff of coldness, a hint of hostility.

Some of the reporters are scowling. Others trouble you more by their inattention, checking cell phones or gazing out the atrium windows. You wonder if you should trim your lecture. If you should refute Dixon directly – though it would mean stooping, and you do not stoop.

You wish them all good morning. No one replies. Quickly you reorganize the morning's plan in your head. Half the science, then Dixon. But which do you omit, hard-ice or reanimation? Which of his charges should you ignore, and which address directly?

Buying seconds to make these decisions, you take a sip of water. As you set down the glass, however, you notice that the pages have indeed marked your hand. Letters, in reverse as though in a mirror, appear in dark black ink on your thumb and wrist.

Immediately you pull a tube of sanitizer from your jacket pocket. These news people will have to wait a moment. You could no more address a crowd with dirty hands than without trousers on. Thus you take the time to rub thoroughly, fingers and palms.

Half a minute passes, an eternity before a crowd. You glance toward the doorway. Thomas is gone. Likely the pressure was too much for him. Still, Borden is there. A heart desires to beat. The reporters fidget, but you will make it worth their while. Putting the lotion away, you collect the papers, tap them on edge into order, and clear your throat. You have your faults. Everyone does. But for reasons the world will never know, which are your deepest and oldest truths, you have never exaggerated, nor taken short cuts, nor misrepresented the least thing. It is humiliating at this hour to profess publicly what all your life you have vigorously lived. But there it is. And here they are.

Manners extend only so far, and they begin asking questions.

'Dr Carthage, did you alter in any way the underwater video of your team finding Jeremiah Rice?'

'Why did the lights go out during the reanimation?'

'How would you describe the relationship between Dr Philo and Judge Rice?'

'Doctor, how do you respond to the accusations that your work is a hoax?'

'Are you a fraud?'

'NO,' you shout with all your strength. 'No, no, no. Everything we have done is fully documented. The video cameras have never paused, the computers have monitored constantly and released the data simultaneously. Our staff is impeccably credentialed, and for every minute of this project's existence we have set the highest standards, the absolute highest, for precision and integrity.'

That stops them for a moment. It gives them pause, while you collect yourself.

One reporter cannot hold his tongue. 'Where do you get your money?'

That triggers another round of shouting. 'What is the source of your financing?'

'Why hasn't the Lazarus Project issued a Form 990 like normal non-profits?'

'Are you in this for the money?'

'NO,' you cry again. 'Who are you people? How dare you make such accusations? Spend ten seconds online! Acquaint yourself with my history, my achievements and publications. Meanwhile, please show the courtesy of allowing me to read my prepared remarks, which should allay your concerns. Then we'll see which, if any, interrogatories remain to be answered.'

They are silent. You have won the moment. Now is your time.

Ah, time. The clock on the atrium's far wall, bright red and hanging over the security desk, counts on relentlessly. It reaffirms your triumph: the minutes are winding down in Jeremiah Rice's ninetieth day.

'Good morning,' you declare once again, regaining your poise. 'Thank you for coming today. Last August, a Lazarus Project research vessel was plying the Arctic seas . . .'

You lift the first page of your speech and the words stick in your throat. The text is illegible, the letters smeared into one another. Worse, ink has remained on your hand despite the washing, there for all to see. You open your mouth, but the usual flow of words escapes you. In fact you struggle to speak at all. 'The Lazarus Project . . .'

Your hand is filthy. You cannot utter a word. A massive weight of expectancy burdens the air. The universe sits at your feet, awaiting instruction. Yet here you are, in your ultimate moment, marked by an indelible stain.

CHAPTER 42

EYE OF A WHALE

My name is Jeremiah Rice and I begin to be hunted.

I was sitting on the bed whilst Kate packed our last things, when the innkeeper knocked on the door.

'They're here,' Carolyn said. 'On my street. Two TV vans. And by the looks of it, a pack of those protestors on their heels.'

'Damn it.' Kate slid the computer into her shoulder bag.

'It's OK, you have time. They're going door to door, and they're still more than a block away.'

'Fine.' Kate went calm. It gave me confidence, to see her self-mastery as ever. 'Let me think.'

'We have a back stairs,' Carolyn said, turning to me. Her forehead wore a crease of concern. She and I had enjoyed lively conversations each morning, whilst she brought plate after plate of food until I felt shame. Now she looked me in the eye. 'I'd bet they don't really know which of you they want. If they get too close, you should split up.'

‘I don’t know,’ I said. I felt like a passenger, unequipped to participate in the decision.

‘No,’ Kate said. ‘Not a chance.’

‘I’m just suggesting—’

‘Do you have a storeroom? Somewhere we can leave our things?’

‘A cellar, sure.’

‘Perfect.’ Kate’s face was as serene as if we were discussing what to have for dinner. ‘Please tell them we checked out. Say we’ve left for, oh, Portland, Maine, to catch a ferry to Nova Scotia. We’ll be back later today, and I’ll settle our bill then.’

Carolyn waved it away. ‘My bill should be the least of your worries.’

In minutes we had secreted our things in the basement, cut through the kitchen to a small sewing room at the back of the house, and wrestled open an old warped door. A flight of whitewashed steps led to the alley. As we hurried down, I considered that this was the second set of back stairs Kate and I had used for an escape in five days. I was tiring of being anyone’s prey. Fleeing was not the right use of this time.

‘Hey, people?’ Carolyn said. We turned back. She stood on the top step with hands on her hips, a solidity to her stance like a general surveying his troops. ‘Jeremiah, be sure to eat enough. Kate, if it becomes necessary, do not be afraid to let go. And remember, both of you: this inn will always be a safe place.’

* * *

We hurried for the first few minutes only. The streets were labyrinthine, our pursuers easily shed. After an hour we were well across the town, miles from the inn. Kate took my arm and held it close. 'Let's be tourists,' she said. 'We'll blend in better.'

After our experiences on Cape Cod and in Boston, the performance came easily. We strolled. We peered into shops. Marblehead was a quaint town, full of eighteenth-century houses and narrow lanes. With my legs moving, the tremors eased.

There was something else too, a keenness. It was as if all my senses were ticklish; they felt everything however small. A building's shadow darkened the adjacent alley. The smell of bacon cooking somewhere tugged my appetite. On a sun-drenched window seat, a tabby examined the underside of her paw, gave it a slow cleansing lick, and I felt I might weep.

At that, I realized. I was taking stock, making an inventory of last experiences. Gerber had never said precisely how much time remained. I surmised from the severity of my spasms that the sand in the upper bowl of the hourglass was nearly gone. How astonishing this world was, though, as rich as it was fleeting. My heart could burst with gratitude. There was not just a glimpse of beauty in this world, like stars here and yon in the firmament, there was an orgy of it, an excess like vines swarming a building, an ocean of it in every direction. Yet also I felt a stabbing of loss, that even as I experienced the world in its wildest abundance it was all falling away from me, mercilessly, forever. Thus did my mind capture each thing, seizing on it to savor it. Kate pointed at a flower, saying its name, Snapdragon, and I felt a flood of appreciation: for the flower and its rosy optimistic hue, for how humanity feels compelled to name everything as if there can never be enough names, for her slender finger, for the simple human gesture of pointing, and yes, for what it is that happens to a man when he hears a certain woman speak even as common a word as Snapdragon.

The morning passed in such minutiae, yet I was staggered by them. In a bakery Kate bought herself a coffee around which to wrap her hands, and me a muffin, still warm, with raisins in its middle like secrets. We climbed a hill to an old churchyard where a bell rang the hour as if no centuries had passed. We sat on a bench in the shade, and for a goodly interval neither of us spoke. A breeze stirred the tree overhead, sounding like applause. She reached down and took my hand. The moment needed nothing.

Oh but inevitably my left foot began twitching, slightly at first then wagging side to side. I fiddled my right in a similar manner, feigning that it was extra energy, but Kate stiffened and sat upright. 'We're probably safe now,' she said, glancing at her watch. 'How about we start back to the inn?'

'Fine idea.' I stood too abruptly though, lacking

any other means of concealing my tremors. 'We should . . . we definitely should, what is the word I want?'

Kate stared at her coffee cup. Her lips made a thin line. 'Yes, let's walk again.'

We trod on the cobblestones, we angled through the town's web of streets. She held my arm as ever. We had little need for words. The thing I most needed to say would not form itself into language. Eventually we reached an intersection that I recognized. Two blocks southward lay the inn, the car, commencement of the next chapter. But my time was dwindling and I did not want to run anymore.

'Kate, I need to tell you something.'

'Actually you don't,' she said. 'You don't have to tell me anything.'

'I do, though. It's about my shaking—'

'There they are.' A young man with a notebook straightened from peering in the windows of Kate's car. 'Wait. Stop.'

We were running without a word exchanged. Kate ducked up a side street and I followed close behind. My boots skidded on the cobbles, but we dodged through the lanes and the reporter's calls fell further away.

Kate pulled me into a dress shop and we waited at the front window as a television van sped past, the station letters written large on its side. Two more cars followed close behind, I presumed it to be the protestors. A motorcycle buzzed after them, the red-helmeted rider leaning as he hugged the corner. Then we turned, and saw the shop clerk with a hand raised to her mouth. 'It's you, isn't it?'

'Please,' Kate said. 'We'll be on our way in one minute.'

'Hey Courtney,' the girl called over her shoulder toward the back room. 'Guess who just came in?' She raised a cell phone. 'I've got to text this to Ethan. Can I take your picture?'

Again we ran. Streets that had confused me suddenly became allies. All the odd angles and switchbacks gave us a maze of paths to follow. We tended downward, away from the inn and the main area of commerce, until a road spilled us out onto a long pier. We sprinted down it, till we reached a padlocked gate with a weathered sign: PRIVATE.

The place seemed oddly quiet after our panic, rows of sailboats floating in silence.

'They'll never look for us here,' Kate panted.

'It says "private."'

'I can read.' She pulled my arm. 'Come on.'

Trespassing, I was trespassing for the first time in my life. Kate handed me her shoulder bag, then clambered over the stile. Her summery yellow shirt came untucked, I saw a pink flash of skin. 'Hand me the bag, would you Jeremiah? And hurry.'

I followed her, though ceasing the running had commenced my trembles anew. It took hard concentration to close my hand around the bar at the top of the gate, and hold it firmly for the time it took to vault over.

Already Kate had dashed on, and I hobbled after with my stomach clenching like a boxer's fist. A wave of hunger swept over me, as intensely as if it were a lack of air. Could that short race have exhausted all the food I'd devoured that day?

'Over here,' Kate called from ahead. 'Hurry.'

Yet I paused. What had become of me, that I had allowed circumstances to decay this far? Where was my judicial prudence, my disciplined mind? I bent at the waist, gulping great breaths, and willed myself to think clearly.

There had been no demonstrations when the Lazarus Project was reawakening little sea creatures. The protests began with me. Although most people had been kind and generous, I had to give weight to the other side's arguments. I was the one they cursed in the cathedral. I was the one the woman had jabbed at the baseball game.

Carolyn was mistaken. They knew exactly who they wanted, these jackals. I was the one they hunted, I was their prey. Therefore to take responsibility for my existence, and to protect Kate, it was my duty to act.

I straightened, my body no less gripped, but my mind clarified and purposeful. I noticed my surroundings then, the air breathless, the water still, the sailboats all nosed into their slips. Excellent. The world sometimes made such orderly sense. And it was still morning, a whole day of possibility ahead.

Kate ran back to me. 'What's the matter? We have to hide.'

'I apologize. Lead on.'

As she went ahead, I could hear from behind the thud of a car door slamming. It came from well up the hill, but I knew: soon they would find us. Kate hid behind a sailboat made of some sleek white material, neither wood nor steel, looking as if it could glide through the roughest waters. I ran a finger along the hull and it felt like fine china.

'What were you doing back there?' she said, staring over my shoulder. 'You have no idea what these people will do if they catch you. They have no restraint.'

'Kate.' I took one of her hands. 'I need your attention now.'

She came back to me then, serene, her powerful calm returning. 'I'm listening.'

Here was my moment, my opportunity to prevent another Joan from happening. 'Kate, I have tried countless times to recall what I experienced in the time I was gone. Heaven? Hell? Some place of completion or rest? There was nothing, nothing I could . . . return. No, reverse. What is the word?'

'Remember?'

'Remember, yes, thank you. Wherever I was, it is totally forgotten.'

She stood there, holding my hand, waiting for

what I would say next. In her patience I felt a surpassing tenderness.

'That, my dearest friend in the here and now, is what I ask you to do for me.'

'I'm sorry?'

'Forget me, Kate. As though I were a century during which you were . . . you were frozen, yes, and you awakened with a clear heart.'

She chuckled, and gave my hand a squeeze. 'For such a smart guy, you can be quite dumb.'

I drew back. 'Whatever do you mean? I am trying merely to—'

'You are trying to be some kind of noble something or other, and you should just stop it. I am grown up, I do not need rescuing by anyone. If anything—'

'But if these people are as cruel as you say—'

'Jeremiah, hear me out a second, would you? My turn?'

My body wanted to run in a hundred directions. But I concentrated, I willed it to remain still. 'Please.'

'In grad school I spent a summer crewing on a research vessel in the North Atlantic. One morning a whale approached our ship, swam right alongside, black as coal. He floated there, looking at me just like a person would, only the whale's eye was larger than a dinner plate. After a minute he gave a sour exhale, plunged off into the rest of his day. Then I noticed the captain, standing down the rail. A tough old Scotsman. He leaned my way and said, "Fix it fast." I said, "Excuse me, sir?" He poked his thumb against his forehead. "Fix it fast in your mind, because you may not see the likes of that again".'

'I am sorry Kate, I can't . . . I don't understand—'

'You are my whale, beautiful man.' She thumbed her forehead. 'You are fixed in me.'

Ah, her parable. I closed my eyes, trying to collect thoughts that scattered like panicked mice. Was there any way to spare her? I could think of only one possibility. I opened my eyes and let all the world's colors rush in, beginning and ending with her face. 'I believe Carolyn was correct. We should split up. We'll be harder to chase.'

She gave me a look, then, an expression I could not interpret. Was it joy or anguish? 'Jeremiah.'

'Yes?'

'I just wanted to say your name again.' She pressed her forehead against my chest, then straightened, pointing out to where the pier forked. 'You take the dock over there, hide yourself in the boats till dark. I'll go the other direction. We'll meet at the inn, the back door, after the church bell rings nine.'

'Perfect,' I said, though I had no intention of obeying. I was their quarry, I would lure them away from her. 'Excellent.'

Then she drew near, as if she knew my mind, and curled into my embrace. Kate seemed so small then, warm and close. Yet I could feel my heart pounding against her, exhaustingly fast. Her ear was right there on my chest, she had to know.

'Kate, I hope I have not been a . . . some kind of a . . . what is the word?' Language flailed in my mind like fish netted and dropped on a ship's deck. 'A bad thing then. I hope I am not a bad thing that happened to you.' I pressed her hand, as if the force of my squeeze would express what words could not. 'I did not ask for this. I meant no one any trouble. You, Kate, of all people. I meant you no harm.'

She leaned back to look at me. Her eyes were glistening. 'Be assured, Jeremiah.' She reached up to caress my face. 'You have caused me no harm.'

What a moment we shared then, holding one another, silent and still. A few seconds only, yet they were as rich as the entire time since my awakening. But there was a twitch in my face, under her hand. Then a huge tremor climbed my frame, from my toes to the sky, like the deepest shudder.

I stepped away. She stood straight, regarding me with calm. What more could I say? How might I express everything I felt? My hands leapt and jerked like injured birds, and I slapped them against my chest to keep them still. But they continued, wandering over my person, trembling, until my fingers fastened on just the thing. Yes. Yes. They wrapped around it on my jacket like an organ-grinder's monkey grasps a coin.

At that moment I heard more doors slamming.

A child's voice cried out, 'Over there, I saw them go down there.'

Kate looked away, then back. 'You need to hide.'

'You mean we need to hide.'

'Yes, of course.' She took my face in both her hands, and she kissed me. It was her breath I experienced more than her lips, somehow, the awareness of her living self against me. Incomparable, and then it was over. 'Now go.'

It took only an instant. I yanked hard on my coat, I tore the object free, I pressed it into her palm. Peering over the hull I saw a reporter hastening down the pier.

'A button?' Kate said. 'I don't understand.'

'You will,' I answered, moving away down the dock.

The reporter reached the gate and rattled it against the lock. I knew it would not delay him long. I turned, and I ran.

My feet are like wings, they barely strike the dock, I hold my arms wide for balance. There, after the last sailboat, floats a dingy as if provided by God, eight feet of aluminum with two rough oars. Not until I have clambered aboard and unknotted the line does it occur to me that I am committing a crime. I vow to make restitution if I return, but an honest man knows a dishonest deed. The irony of it; Judge Rice perpetrating a theft.

In ten pulls of the oars I am among moored sailboats, hopefully a sight no paparazzi could fail to see. To those jackals I must be like knotted string to a cat, the tease they cannot help but follow. I know the open Atlantic, my escape, lies to the north. It would be that direction, wouldn't it? North yet again. I remove my coat and toss it in the bow, then check the sky for direction. At that I set my trusty boots against the other seat, draw hard on those oars, and begin working my way unconcealed across the harbor. I sight the rocks over my right shoulder, then face astern whilst concentrating on north, north.

Rowing calms my hands. One pull at a time I am leaving the harbor, leaving what a harbor is, leaving what harbor means. My mind navigates through harbors of all kinds that I have left, beautiful protections, quiet anchorages in the past and the here and now.

Settling into the exertion of it. Surely they've spotted me by now. And what is life but a little row in a small boat, every moment leaving what we know, every stroke unable to see where we are headed?

Wash of water under the hull, piercing light on the waves, briny stink of the air. I know the future, my future. Grim and inevitable, I have withstood it once I shall withstand it again. But there will be no embrace of crushing cold this time. The rather, I feel I could dissolve into a million particles, turn into dust turn into light. And I have spared her the sight of it. Spared her more than that; surely they must be pursuing me now. Dull drum of the oar hitting the boat's side at the finish of a stroke. Surf seething against the rocks. Precision of observation now, the exact shape of a wave, the creak of my boots as I straighten and bend, my mind accelerating along with everything else.

Escorted by a gull, his tiny pink eye. A gull, if one contemplates, is an astonishing thing. Aloft, balanced on the wind, appetite as ceaseless as curiosity. A bell buoy gongs somewhere behind, a mob of wild roses crowds the bluff, the warm stain of sun on my shoulders, lungs like a bellows brightening the forge inside me. Amazing, all of it, incredible. The gull concludes that I am not something to eat, and veers back toward land.

My eye follows. Kate is small now, a trim figure in a yellow shirt on that vivid dock. What has she done, why did she not hide? A pack has formed near her, holding a few paces off. They cannot harm her now. Why would they when it is Jeremiah Rice that they seek? One of the gang points in my direction; they have seen me; now they will chase me. She said she needed no rescue yet that is what I have done. This is how I this is how I save her.

Yard by yard the rowboat attains the point, then surpasses it. Rocks obscure the view, my last glimpse. Everything is so fast now, everything, it seems impossible to concentrate, even on the loss oh even on the loss of her. Calm water, little circles, tiny what are they, what is the word, why can I not recall the word it breaks my heart, ah yes *whirlpools*, little whirlpools chase the oars after each stroke. Exquisite, incomparable. A pool of whirl, was there ever anything lovelier. The land falls the harbor falls ever smaller away. Already I feel lighter, light. I bend my back to the task, a stroke a stroke a begin-to-sweat a stroke. A little farther north each time.

CHAPTER 43

THE HOUNDS

(KATE PHILO)

Where did he go? It was as if he vanished. I gave him a few seconds while I collected myself, and he was gone. My ploy had worked.

The first reporter vaulted the pier fence, sprinting up to me. I held out both hands. 'Wait!'

Miraculously, he did. Then I saw it was no miracle, he was out of breath. He bent at the waist, while the others one by one climbed over the gate. They took the time to hold each other's cameras and notebooks. Politeness among parasites. A gaggle of protestors came charging up behind, a big noise, but somehow the gate stopped them. They waited, not climbing over.

'Gave us a good chase,' the reporter said, panting. 'That was fun.'

'Fun?' I scanned the harbor, Jeremiah still not visible. Then I saw him, the little boat to which his enormous life was now confined. He was not even slightly concealed, just rowing right across the center of the harbor. *Go*, I said inside. *Get away and I will hold them here.*

The others came along, loud as horses on the boards of the pier. They began yelling my name, raising their hands like so many schoolchildren. I held my arms high again, and after a moment they fell into a murmur. One or two of them took pictures.

'Where is Jeremiah Rice?' the first one said.

He had held me, you see, as never before. I felt his life beating against mine. Then he drew back and tore something from his coat and thrust it in my hand.

In the edge of my vision, the very periphery, I could see the little boat making its steady way. I wanted to yell. *Come back. We'll make what we can of every second.*

The first reporter pointed out over the water. 'Who is that out there?'

I turned as if I had no idea, shielding my brow. 'Where?'

My heart was pounding. All was nearly lost. But always in the spectacular moment, my talent is self-possession. The powers of reserve would save him from this mob. Otherwise what would he be returning to, if he could somehow hear my pleas? What besides an angry crush of questions, plus my desperate affections for the few remaining hours? These carrion-eaters did not deserve to see Jeremiah die. *If I cannot be with you, I can at least protect you.*

'Is that him?' someone asked.

I knew that my moment had come. 'It's all true,' I said, which hushed them completely. But I stopped, not adding a word. They waited, with cameras and mikes and notebooks, jostling one another on the pier.

Just then one of the protestors overcame his reluctance, and clambered over the gate. The rest of the group poured after him, galloping down the dock. Someone yelled, 'Don't let her get away.'

But the TV crews did me an unintended favor, possibly because they didn't want to miss anything I might say or do: not one of them turned to film the gang of shouters running toward me.

Somehow, being ignored chastened them. Halfway down the pier they drew up, as though the leader had pulled on invisible reins. They had no weapons, they had no audience, they called no thunderbolts down from the sky. In fact they had nothing. Suddenly it was clear to me why they had always yelled so loudly: to conceal that they had nothing. Ignored, they were feckless. By the time they reached the scrum of reporters, the protestors were shuffling, almost shy. They arranged themselves in a semicircle on the dock, audience for a play's final scene.

I waited, wanting to run, staying put. Jeremiah needed time to escape their line of sight. I squeezed his button in my fist, but otherwise held still, buying precious seconds.

Eventually one man nudged the fellow beside him. 'What did she say, anyway?'

'We thought we had everyone fooled,' I said, a masterpiece of calm. 'But apparently not Daniel Dixon.'

I went silent again, stalling. A tendril of my being stretched across that harbor, burning like an inflamed nerve, toward Jeremiah, toward the idea of him at least, as the reality itself moved steadily beyond my grasp. *Come back. This is killing me.*

They fidgeted in place. I could feel their attention dividing. Why was he rowing so conspicuously? He should be hiding. Would they chase that little boat, or stay here? When I realized that they were waiting for me to tell them, to give the signal, I felt a surpassing power. I could save him, though it might destroy me. I could actually save him.

All it would take was a lie, one lie.

Just then a motorcycle buzzed down the footpath. The rider hopped off, dashing toward me, lifting his helmet as he ran. The look on his face was nearly as pleading as Jeremiah's had been only moments before.

Billings. It was all I had lacked, the final push, the last audience member to arrive. I folded my hands at my waist, as matronly as a schoolmarm welcoming third graders to the first day of school.

'It was a hoax,' I said. 'All of it.'

Their pause was like the passionate in-breath of a fallen toddler, silent seconds before crying full-voiced for mom. But when they exhaled the experience was entirely different: they howled and barked like I was some sly fox, full of dodges and feints, yet finally treed at last, as I deserved, while now down at the trunk circled the hounds, ignorant, inevitable, eager to feed.

The coverage was merciless. One tabloid ran a photo of my face beneath a giant headline: PANTS ON FIRE. I could hardly sue for defamation, when I knew it was true. My refusal to reveal Jeremiah's whereabouts and true identity only fanned the flames. Still, I devoured the papers every day, every inch, but there was no story about a rowboat being found, much less one with a person in it. I could only speculate about how Jeremiah's end arrived. Was it quiet, a lonely surrender to stillness? Or violent like krill in the lab, one last spasm bursting his heart? Did he lower himself over the side, trusting the ocean to finish the job? Or lie on his back in the roasting sun? My mind considered the possibilities, all of them horrible, until I developed a fantasy: he is not dead, he is still out there somewhere, still rowing.

I heard the late night TV shows made hay. 'The vice president declared his support for zombies and werewolves today,' one host joked with a picture of the candidate beside Jeremiah. 'I guess he's counting on the undead vote, which is strange since he's already way ahead in New Jersey.'

The Project's ships were called back into port, ending the global search for hard-ice with a whimper. When the ninth fraud suit was filed, the Lazarus Project closed its offices with no forwarding address. Some pompous graybeard columnist at the *Globe* called for the attorney general to investigate.

The media stayed with the story for weeks, probably because there was a considerable cast involved. Each player needed a turn in the spotlight of hate or revelation.

Thomas, for example. File him in the you-never-know department. It turned out that he was actually T. Beauregard Fillion, heir to a steel industrialist's trust. He had basically bankrolled Carthage from start to finish, nearly thirty million dollars over the years. When the project collapsed, so did the investors in reamination technology they'd hoped would turn his donations into an even larger fortune. Someone at the Project leaked memos Thomas and Carthage had created, based on polls they'd had done, on how much a person would pay to have a loved one reanimated. Sell the car? Mortgage the house? On the last page someone had written, 'There is no ceiling.' The press reported that the handwriting was impeccable.

'I am proud of what we accomplished,' Thomas said in a long Sunday profile in *The Washington Post*. 'It was worth every penny to work with one of the great minds of all time, and to be present when he made scientific history.'

Almost overnight Thomas landed a job with the copycat lab in China. Sanjit Prakore, who Carthage had fired for spilling his tea, now runs that lab. He too was quoted in the *Post* story:

‘We believe Mr Fillion will be a tremendous asset to our ongoing work. We expect him to be most helpful.’

Probably so, since he owns the rights to all of the Project’s intellectual property.

Gerber recovered after two weeks, there was a story about it in the *Globe*. On his way out of Massachusetts General Hospital he stopped to make a statement exactly one sentence long: ‘For nearly all of human history, religious zealots have committed unjustified violence in the name of God.’ In the news photo he was giving a goofy thumbs-up, leaning on the arm of his wife. Gerber had a wife, who knew?

A few months later he landed a job with NASA, managing the satellite program that measures climate change at the poles. I felt glad for him, the odd duck. I read about that in *The New York Times*.

Speaking of which, that was also where I learned about Amos Cartwright. A famous chess cheat, yes, discredited and stripped of international standing. But Amos also turned out to be the father of a son, one grandiose compensating narcissist by the name, changed in court when he was eighteen, of Erastus Carthage. And what resourceful investigator spilled those Freudian-flavored beans? Wilson Steele, of course.

Steele wrote a few more stories related to the Project, on how Borden couldn’t land a job, on the many unpaid debts. He was the one to reveal that

Dixon erred in using 'Tessie' to prove the judge was a fake. The song, originally about a woman singing to her parakeet, came from a Broadway hit in 1902. Steele went hunting to see if 'the authentic Judge Rice' had any living descendants, which caught my interest. But before he found anyone his new book came out, *Shudder*, about earthquakes, with press junkets, a book tour, the next hot topic.

By then, Carthage could not be hurt by any newspaper because he had already hanged himself. He left a letter that said, 'We are the opposite of Amos Cartwright.' As Jeremiah would say: hm. I can't decide which was worse, that he proved himself wrong by dying exactly as his father had, or that his suicide note contained an unintended self-parody by using the royal 'we.'

I had not seen Carthage again, after the last time in his office, but people said he never recovered from that debacle of a news conference, reporters shouting accusations while the scientist at the podium froze so pathetically, Borden had to lead him stammering from the room. You might have expected Carthage's tragic suicide to be front-page news, and it truly was tragic, because for all his flaws the man was a genuine genius. Instead I found the story buried deep in the B-section, a few inches of text under a blurry photo of his face. Apparently it didn't merit reporting on TV. All that brilliance, all that waste, but it was already old news.

The opposite was true of Gerald T. Walker, as the whole world knows. On the next Halloween, the most popular mask was his face with its trademark toothy grin. The following Tuesday, he swept thirty-one states to become the next president of the United States. While it was a minor matter in Walker's wide-ranging political platform, he championed greater accountability of scientific study, including an audit of every single federal research grant. Polls showed that a vast majority of the public approved of that policy. Hail to the chief.

Daniel Dixon, my own personal space-invader, went on to make a fortune. A seven-figure book deal, packed lectures for which he is paid handsomely, a movie coming out next year in which the star playing him is ten years younger and magazine-cover handsome. Oddly enough, Dixon also gave two hundred thousand dollars to a Pennsylvania burn hospital, refusing to explain his reasons, which brought another round of headlines feting him as a hero, truth-teller, philanthropist.

As for Hilary in the white beret, who loitered outside the project's offices, I have some entertaining suspicions. There's no finding her, of course. I searched on the Internet, the Boston area phone books. But if tombstones tell a truth that surpasses time, then I'd be willing to bet her last name is Halsey. That would make her daughter of the daughter of Jeremiah Rice. In which case I send a silent blessing to Hilary Halsey, wherever she may be.

* * *

And that leaves me. Carthage said he would ruin me, and I suppose at some level that is what happened: career, home, prospects, all gone. But it was not his doing; no, I did it to myself. Or the world did it, anyway. The first few times I went to my apartment, the tabloids had staked it out. But they weren't patient, because there's always a new scandal to point a camera at. Soon enough they were only around daytimes. I rented a truck one night, planning to haul out all I could carry. It went well enough, a long, sweaty effort, until I entered the kitchen to find a single egg sitting on the counter. Nearly three weeks it had sat there. I didn't cry, because I couldn't breathe. Eventually I washed it down the sink, running the water till it spiraled. Then I went back to work because there was nothing else to do: taking down bedding, packing kitchen appliances or winter clothes, sticking it all in a storage shed in Danvers, calling my landlord to say he could keep the rest. When he asked where to send the security deposit, I said he could hold on to that too. No sense revealing my location.

Which, of all places, is still Marblehead, still the Harborview Inn. I rented that room the whole first summer, for a small fortune, then paid a pittance for the winter because the place was practically closed. In March Carolyn said she needed help for the coming season. Hiring me for the wage of room and board, she said, would be cheaper than training a college girl with a teenager's appetite.

Also I wasn't likely to fall in love with some college-boy waiter in town, stay out all night, and sleep through the hearty breakfast I was supposed to serve the inn's guests.

A safe bet. It was a monastic dwelling she gave me at the back of the house, what a century ago had been the sewing room: a dresser, table, lamp, bed. But the window let in ocean breezes. No one in the inn had any reason to come through the kitchen to disturb me. The back stairway we'd used to escape gave me a private entrance too. Carolyn asked me nearly every day to join her for yoga class, saying it would do my heart good. Instead I spent those months in the healing habit of silence.

Mourning is a mysterious maze. Often I asked myself what should happen next, but there were no obvious avenues. I was infamous in Boston, reviled from the North End to South Station. I knew of no research openings anywhere. I was too ashamed to contact Tolliver at the Academy. I'd probably damaged his reputation enough already. In a trade publication I read that Billings might open a lab outside London, to study the Lazarus samples he'd kept. So I emailed him a timid greeting, just fishing. He wrote back to say that if the lab opened, if it won funding, if there were a need for someone with my skills, then he might offer me a job, but I would have to understand in advance that at no time could my name be listed on any report's authorship, 'for obvious reasons.' He signed his email, 'your devoted friend, GB.'

Such is devotion in the world of scientific research. Yet I can't say I was disappointed. Who would want to go back that way? Not when I'm already discredited. Then I learned that the lab in China had hired Billings. Not a month later they reanimated a sardine that remained alive for months. The article lacked detail, but apparently the breakthrough had something to do with oxygen saturation. To me it seemed as if everything that occurred, in China or elsewhere, was happening too late.

Chloe had two cents to add every day. Her emails were superior, scathing. Yet I could not resist reading every word, letting their poison in. The blame they assigned, the condescension, felt like penance. She urged me to 'learn something from this whole pathetic mess, Katie-bug. Learn something.'

Well, what have I learned? I mean besides the world's fickleness, how people turn vicious when they feel tricked, the difference between the wholesome appetite of scientific curiosity and the empty avarice of personal ambition? Something instructive happened, I am certain of it. Something educational took place in the months between that night in the Arctic and that morning on the pier. Yet the lessons remain unclear.

Maybe this, maybe at least this: when love comes into your life, it calls upon your whole being to be worthy. If you rise to that challenge, it will plant roots and you will blossom. I know. I lived such a love greatly, if briefly, with a fine and rare man.

That man taught me the power of noticing, of *appreciating*, which cannot be unlearned.

So, rather than follow Jeremiah's request that I forget him, instead I honor the night in my apartment, when he must have known he was dying, yet he made me promise never to forget his gratitude. What a gift. I have indeed fixed him fast: the most inconsequential gesture, the least word. I savor those memories. I regret nothing.

Into the crucible of my interior life, Carolyn found an opening. Summer flew past, I prepared to bundle against another fall. Already the morning wind off the harbor had a bite to it. Then one of her yoga friends, principal of the local high school, lamented after class one day that she was losing a biology teacher to maternity leave.

Without asking, Carolyn volunteered me as a long-term substitute. Then she returned to the inn, stood in my doorway. She did a tree pose, while declaring that she was firing me from the inn.

After all those years in a lab, so many men but so few women, I knew better than to reject this sisterly generosity.

On my first day they had a quiz scheduled, on the components of a plant cell. Their teacher had drawn one as a parting gift, arrows pointing to various features, with blanks for the students to fill.

A few bent diligently to the page, pencils moving, but many sat still, gazing out the window or staring into space. I studied the room, its lab sinks, periodic table, rows of desks. When I told the students to pass the papers forward, one girl immediately began chatting with her neighbor. She had strong features, straight blonde hair, very pretty.

I stood by her desk. 'What's your name, honey?'

'Honey?' She tossed her head so her hair swept back. 'It's Victoria.'

'May I please see your lab notebook, Victoria?'

She handed it over while looking away from me. Most pages were blank. A few had scribbled numbers I assumed were from in-class projects. The sheets with the most marking primarily contained drawings of field hockey sticks, quite colorful, plus equally artful renderings, repeatedly, of a boy's name: Chris.

'Class dismissed,' I told them, though twenty minutes remained. 'That's it for today.'

'Awesome,' one of the boys said. As they all hurried off, I shuffled to my desk. There sat my first stack of papers to be graded. Victoria was the last one out the door. I overheard her saying to her chatting companion a single word: 'Deadly.'

The quizzes went into a recycling bin. That afternoon I stayed long after school, digging out every microscope in the place. I cleaned them all: wiping the dusty bodies, replacing dead illuminator bulbs, polishing lenses. Early the next morning I borrowed a bucket from the inn, scooping it full from a brackish shallows in the harbor. It felt like someone was watching over my shoulder, a co-conspirator from across the centuries. The bucket grew heavy while I lugged it to school.

As the students filed in, they noticed the microscopes instantly, made skeptical expressions. Doubt is a fine place to begin. I dipped a slide into the bucket, then held it high. 'Do you see anything on this piece of glass?'

Of course they did not, mumbling as much in reply. But I knew how rich that seawater was, how vital with paramecia, flagella, algae. I smiled. 'Your assignment is to dip a slide for yourself, put it on your microscope, then draw the most interesting thing you see.'

At first the students moved like I was forcing them to eat poison, grumbling, not bothering to conceal their scorn. Gradually they formed a line.

'You too, Victoria.'

'Oh, right.'

She came last, gossiping with friends the whole time. She held her head away from the bucket as she dipped, as if the water would sting. But I waited. By then most of her classmates were quieted, working their slides into focus. Victoria slid the little glass plate under her microscope's stage clips, shared one more laugh with the girl at the next lab station, tossed her hair to one side. Once she'd exhausted her repertoire of delaying tactics, Victoria lowered her face to the eyepiece.

At first she squinted. Then she adjusted the focus. Then she stopped fidgeting. A boy across the room needed help, but when I checked back on her a moment later, Victoria was concentrating on what she saw. After a long stillness, without taking her eye from the lens, she picked up a pencil.

Then I heard her whisper one word to her friend: 'Cool.'

When an email arrived from Chloe that night, I deleted it without reading. I wasn't cutting her off forever, but right then I didn't need the criticism. Nor would it hurt her for a while to listen to the sound of her own voice.

A few months later Billings did send me a note about job openings. China desired scientific supremacy so zealously, he explained, they would not be particular about my history. Already they were modifying fishing boats to search for hard-ice at the poles. Someone would have to command those vessels.

Could I actually do that? Could I go that far back, and start over?

'Of course you'll need to come clean about everything,' Billings wrote, 'and explain that it was not a hoax but instead was exemplary science. They're very forgiving, if you have what they need, which you do. Besides, you were besotted with love.'

Besotted? I closed his email without replying. Then I went to my back stairs, my escape route, to examine what I felt. Not like I was throwing away a career, no. More like I had finally relaxed my grip on the reins of a horse I'd proven myself capable of riding, but had never loved. I felt no pangs as it galloped away out of sight.

So I go now from the inn, each day, across town to the school, walking to work as I did in another lifetime. I stand at the front of the room, all the bright faces angled up at me, even the sullen ones attending with the corners of their eyes just in case something interesting happens.

Quickly I became known as an easy A, because I don't care if my students memorize the facts. All I want is to cultivate their curiosity. Yes, my old friend remains undiminished even now: the simple yearning to know. If these students cannot tell a xylem from a phloem, it will not unduly handicap their college hopes or impede their careers. But their lives will depend entirely on whether they possess wonder, an eye for beauty. For many people, the unknown is something to fear. Instead I want to give my students the humility and courage to believe that anything they do not understand therefore contains an elegant magic.

I anticipate the day when someone brings up my past. Another teacher, a student who searches me online, a parent with some grievance. It's all but certain to happen; we live in a cynical time. Educated by a wise judge, I will not argue or defend. Thanks to repeatedly watching a video of him that remains online, I have a better reply prepared: *We must let our deeds be our ambassadors. Our challenge is to live with all the sincerity that is in our hearts, and hope that those who doubt will come to see the truth.*

At the end of the school year, when I collected everyone's lab notebooks, I flipped through Victoria's first. The pages were thick with use. I was amused to see that boy Chris still figured prominently in the margins, the back cover. But the rest was filled with notes, measurements, drawings done with accuracy and care.

'Hm,' I said, though if I am honest, it came out more like a laugh. Victoria might never become a scientist, or physician, or even take one more biology class in her life, but she will forever possess the power of inquiry the notebook manifests. I had reached her. Curiosity had reached her. Sorry Chloe, but Victoria's progress was plenty *significant* enough for me.

The teacher on leave has had her baby, yet remains undecided about whether to return next fall. So I begin to have a glimpse of the future, a place I might belong.

Meanwhile I find solace in knowing that I remained worthy. No, more than that. I feel pride. After all, I loved Jeremiah Rice enough to stand between him and the evil in this world. I loved him enough to let him go.

But not completely. I smile to think of what I held on to. Most nights I meander this town's narrow streets, seeing lights on inside the antique houses, envying the occupants their domesticity. Eventually I find myself down on the docks where

I held him, where I released him. Some nights it is cloudy there. On others, the moon shines a bright path across the black water. Regardless of weather I am glad to be there, glad to have kept one thing of Jeremiah's: small, brown, round.

It is no mighty totem, no sacred talisman. It is a nothing, really, meaningful only to the one person who knows what it signifies: that he existed, that he loved me in return. Truths as strong as these can be sustained by the humblest of objects. This one hangs on a simple chain, resting above my heart.

There on the dock I reach up and touch it, three fingers around the rim. What I have left of him. One button.